"Kass's remarkable stories are honest, observant, utterly believable but with the weight of fable. Poignant and funny, the stories pull the reader into their vortex, where the light is pleasingly bright and disorienting at the same time. *Knuckleheads* introduces an important writer, one whose work I didn't know I was so desperate to read."

- Laura Kasischke, *The Life Before Her Eyes, Be Mine*

"In their quiet, accumulating intensity and sly pockets of humor, beauty, and grace, Jeff Kass' stories recall Ron Carlson and Charles Baxter at their best. *Knuckleheads* is a knockout!"

- Davy Rothbart, *FOUND Magazine, This American Life*

"Howlingly funny, engrossing, and culturally observant, these stories unfold effortlessly with ambient ferocity and compassion. By the third paragraph of the first story I knew I'd go anywhere Jeff Kass wanted to take me—with a great sense of amazement."

- Lewis Robinson, *Waterdogs, Officer Friendly and Other Stories*

"With the vivid, lyrical qualities of Colson Whitehead's *Sag Harbor, Knuckleheads* is a high-octane protein shake, equal parts heartbreak and hilarity, a thing of both sweat-reeking adrenalin and nostalgic, time-stopping beauty. For those who know Jeff Kass' gorilla-hearted poetry, this story collection is both a surprise and no surprise at all. Here we see his swing-for-the-fences skill with the line, but now it's prose and jeez, what can't this man do? Kass achieves what all fiction writers want—he makes us believe and makes us care. Even those of us who stayed as far away from the jocks as possible will want to cheer."

- Steve Amick, *The Lake, the River & the Other Lake, Nothing But a Smile*

TAKEDOWN

JEFF KASS

Terry – enjoy!
Go Blue!
– Jeff

FIFTH AVENUE PRESS

Takedown

Editor: Alex Kourvo

Layout and Illustration: Ann Arbor District Library

This is a work of fiction.

Fifth Avenue Press is a locally focused and publicly owned publishing imprint of the Ann Arbor District Library. It is dedicated to supporting the local writing community by promoting the production of original fiction, non-fiction and poetry written for children, teens and adults.

Printed in the United States of America

First Printing, 2017

ISBN: 978-1-947989-13-9 (Paperback); 978-1-947989-14-6 (ebook)

Fifth Avenue Press

305 S Fifth Ave.

Ann Arbor, MI 48104

fifthavenue.press

For JR, Philosophy Teacher Extraordinaire
and Pioneer High School Legend

PROLOGUE

JANUARY: MOLOKINI CRATER, HAWAII

THE WORLD WAS NEW. And blue.

The world was a new blue globe.

The water around Jarrold felt amorphous, a warm vast embrace.

A new sex.

It was something he'd never felt before. He could see why rich people paid good, inherited money to do it.

Snorkeling.

With rented gear.

Schools of fish fluttered past in shocking pink and orange. The water above, and around, and below, felt as if someone with gentle fingers were massaging every square inch of his skin. He let his muscles go slack, and grew so engrossed following a moray eel with its big curious eye as it peeked out from the coral that he almost forgot about the job he had to do.

He didn't.

He never did.

He became the eel then, his own curious eye following the college kid, slithering through the warmth. When the student followed a reef shark, stalking the beast for the best underwater picture he could snap with his five-hundred-dollar camera, Jarrold stalked the student. There was a symmetry to it. A natural food chain.

He focused on the kid's expensive gear, his carbon-fiber wetsuit and pressure-resistant snorkel. Gifts from his father, he'd heard the kid brag on the boat, his mouth big and raucous, while he drank three beers more than he should have. The kind of twenty-year-old who tries to act like he's been drinking forever, not understanding it's only dumb-asses who do something like get drunk to go snorkeling.

The boy had a tattoo on his ankle. A blue block M. What a poseur. Probably had a bounce in his step when he strutted through his hippy city, entered a trendy shop and inked his allegiance to the football team into his leg. As if any of the brain-dead players gave a damn whether he rooted for them or not. As if they wouldn't have confiscated his girlfriend quicker than he could sing *Hail to the Victors,* banged her silly, then dumped her back at his dorm so he could help her plagiarize her midterms.

Well, at least the rest of the kid's life wouldn't be lengthy. The ankle skin would still be taut, the tattoo still vivid when his spirit vacated his body.

It didn't matter why the boy had to die. The assignment paid well. That's the way the world worked. The kid's dad knew it. Someone must have died for him to attain his deluxe snorkel money. That's why Jarrold didn't want to miss his opportunity to gaze at the exotic marine life. What luxury. What privilege. What aquatic miracles with their rainbow-colored outfits and shocking purple stripes. Some of them were four feet long. Look at their fat bulbous eyes!

The kid swam after the shark and around a bend in the reef until he was consumed by shadow. No one else in the tour group was anywhere close. Jarrold slithered behind. So silent. So sleek.

The rest was easy. Slap one palm around the boy's forehead and pull him backward. With the other hand, push the snorkel farther into the kid's mouth so water rushes in. Let the boy kick and squirm. He wasn't a weak boy. He could kick! But he wasn't Jarrold, all eel and steel and uncompromising muscle. All undersea grip and pull. Look at the bubbles. So full of air and desperate life! Look at the boy's eyes growing fat and round like fish eyes!

Shove the snorkel down his throat.

The moment it was over was Jarrold's favorite part. The way the boy slowly sank and how a school of fish circled and seemed to bear witness. The kid's oblong descent was something new. Something fresh and puzzling in their fish day. Look at the boy sink into the quiet.

Into the warmth.

Above, and below, and all around.

July: Grand Canyon National Park, Arizona

Jarrold bent to tie the lace of his hiking boot.

A hundred yards ahead, the group he was watching stopped for a water break, and one of the kids shrugged off his backpack and turned around to face him. With his head angled downward, Jarrold dug his fingers into the clay-dirt mix on the ground, squeezed the loam and felt its richness play along his fingers.

It was beautiful here.

Luminous.

He laughed out loud. Breathed in the fresh, unpolluted air. What a lucky person he was.

He could be in a gloomy office right now with a roomful of balding twenty-six-year-olds, all of them swooning over name-brand bowties and twelve-dollar coffees. He could be fake laughing instead of real laughing, braying with a horse mouth like he wanted to impress some chunky middle manager who resented him, then spending the rest of the day devising further shenanigans that would siphon money from the unconscious public.

Instead, he was here.

In the sun, the breeze, the glory of the natural planet and its panoramic views.

His only task was to become any inconspicuous tourist no one would notice, then to take care of business. He flexed his forearm and admired its tautness. Felt the strength in his calves as he stood to once again follow the group of fake-hipster hippies as they resumed the dawdling walk they called hiking.

He'd never been to the Grand Canyon before, had never had any kind of summer experience where he hadn't been working a bullshit minimum-wager, a loser buttering popcorn at a third-rate movie theater or pushing grocery carts through the rain.

Never again would he be irrelevant like that.

He was twenty-nine now but looked twenty-one, lithe and tan with cheekbones like axe blades and his sandy hair cut into the side-swept bangs so popular with the aspiring hipsters.

He wore a white baseball hat with a logo advertising Corona beer, a pale orange t-shirt with a picture of a pinkish amphibian native to Arizona, a pair of khaki shorts, and his sturdy discount hiking boots. He could have been any college kid.

He wasn't.

The target and his group had been plodding along the Canyon's south rim on the Bright Angel Trail. Layers of rock looked as if an armada of aliens had swooped down and swabbed them with a thousand paintbrushes dipped in different shades of red. A candy-blue sky shone where the rock leveled off and promontories, crags and shadows asserted themselves so that everything looked dramatic, the geological history of the planet showing off right in front of Jarrold, taking a bow.

He opened his senses, thrilled he could drink in the world's finery without hearing any cars, any belching trucks or beeping crosswalk signals.

When you're pushing grocery carts, you don't even know tranquility like this exists. Not really. You see it on TV but you're not physically present, not feeling the millions-years-old legacy humming beneath you, the rock and red, the swimming-pool sky above, around, and below.

What spectacular views.

What an aptly named trail.

If you really thought about it, Jarrold was a kind of bright angel too.

If you really thought about it, he was.

Nearing sundown on the South Rim.

The group of kids was resting from their leisurely non-hike. Eating granola from a plastic bag, passing a joint around. Two of the girls were cute, the kind who would never have looked at Jarrold in high school with his thrift-store clothes and same backpack since seventh grade.

Now he wanted to bang both of them. Simultaneously. Or if he could only get one, he'd go for the curly-haired blond in the maroon t-shirt. She wasn't the target's girlfriend but he'd been trying to match her pace all day, to speed up when she sped up, her muscular thighs pushing into uphill switchbacks. Jarrold wanted to peel her olive-green shorts off. To smell her sweat, taste the deepest parts of her.

He deserved that, and he could probably get away with

it. Eliminate the target, then comfort the girl in her grief. That would be an unnecessary risk, but he could be patient. Wait a year and road trip to her college and find her at a party. Pretend he was twenty and tell her he'd lost a friend once too, how hard it was to move on, but he knew he owed it to his friend to try. Then he'd give the girl the bang of her life. He felt himself getting aroused and relished the feeling, put his hand to his groin to hold his potency, breathed in, enjoyed how his excitement made him feel stronger. He was so much more consequential, so much more substantial than these rich kids who had no moral center. No character.

His lungs swelled with the evening's chill and he tried to soak in the history of the vista around him, absorb the aura of all the tourists thrilled by what river can do to rock. Closing his eyes, he waited for his groin to relax. Now was not a time for lust. It was a time to keep an eye on the kids as they got high, to be patient until an opportunity presented itself.

He didn't have to wait long.

After a half-hour of smoking and sharing granola, the target laid his hand on the cute girl's arm and Jarrold could read his lips as he told her, *be back in a minute.*

No, he wouldn't.

The kid headed toward the lip of the canyon, his hand already unzipping his fly. Before he extricated himself from his shorts, he looked back to check if any of his friends could see him, then scooted around a cluster of boulders to be absolutely sure he'd be out of sight.

Jarrold made himself a shadow against the wall of rock and inched closer. The target was taking his time urinating, leaning back, luxuriating in the long, full stream he was letting loose over the rim.

Then the kid whooped—*whoo-hoo!*—full of power, excited to be pissing amongst such splendor. With one hand holding his unbuttoned shorts, he raised the other in triumph. What an achievement! Pissing over the edge of the Grand Canyon! When he turned around with one arm still raised, he bumped into Jarrold, now inches from his face. It was like walking into a lamppost and the kid stumbled and opened his mouth—to do what? Scream for help? Apologize for desecrating a national park?

It didn't matter.

Jarrold's rock-hard hand, so quick—lizard-quick—covered the whole of the kid's mouth and chin. Before the kid could react or fight or do whatever might have saved him had he not been stoned out of his gourd, Jarrold swept his ankles from under him with a kick and the boy fell backward. With one final shove against his face, Jarrold released the kid's chin and watched him tumble over the edge. It was then the boy shouted, a surprised, half-swallowed wail, plaintive and lost in the swirl of his fall, an uprush of barely audible sound that grew even fainter the farther he fell. After only a second or two, the boy was almost invisible, a tiny black bird, a speck in the dance between the sky's shimmering blue and the purple and salmon crack in the earth.

Jarrold looked up to feel the sun on his face, the breeze against his forehead. He felt like a Native American, an indigenous person bronzed by the evening light. He curled his hand into a fist and flexed his ropey forearm. When he looked again over the edge, the boy was nowhere to be seen.

Seconds earlier the kid had been exultant, so pleased with himself.

Jarrold smiled.

Cosmic justice.

The boy had followed his piss into the great beyond.

CHAPTER ONE

OCTOBER: ANN ARBOR, MICHIGAN

IT FELT good to be coaching again, back in the wrestling room with the hot short breaths stinking like an old blanket, the mat like a giant fish sucking its lips, pulling me in.

Every new season was a chance to rebuild myself, to bury my screw-ups a bit deeper, and I was wishing practice could have been longer, another twenty-four minutes of three-man groups—two minutes on, one minute off—the kind of lung-tearing agony that makes these gritty boys grittier.

We had fewer people on the team this year—a lot of kids had to work and couldn't come out—and the walls hadn't been repainted in decades. The mats were old too, hard and cracking on the edges. They needed to be reconditioned or kids were going to get shoulder injuries, or scratch a cornea if they landed wrong on a jagged corner. Half the ceiling lights no longer worked. Dust and grime lay caked in every crevice and the only person available to do any cleaning or maintenance was me, even though my coaching stipend had been cut forty percent.

That meant practice got cut too, by fifteen minutes every

evening so we had time to mop the mats and rid the room of any bacteria that would give the kids a virus or impetigo. Tonight, I had to cut it even earlier, a full half-hour, a decree which occasioned numerous smiles and high-fives from the wrestlers. But other teams with coaches who didn't have to pull nightshifts were still grappling, and that meant their athletes would have more fuel late in matches, fuel my kids wouldn't have.

Still, shortening practice couldn't be helped. I had to run home through campus, eat dinner, hustle to work. The night before the Michigan-Michigan State football game, rank didn't matter.

No one in the police department got time off.

After a half-mile down Main, I turned right on Hill for the toughest part of the run, first the jarring downhill that hammered at my knee with the missing cartilage, then the long uphill until I reached State Street. Typically about two-thirds of the way up the slog, with my knee screeching like a dying raccoon, I told myself that's it, no more running. I was old. I should be driving. I'd spent money on a car. But I was also not old. Not decrepit enough to be the kind of dad who brings a folding chair to his kid's soccer games, who sets up camp on the sidelines as if his weary bones can't possibly hold him up straight for a single additional minute.

I gnashed my teeth against each other. Kept running.

On rutted sidewalks that needed repair.

Across potholed roads that needed repair.

Thank you, State Government, for giving a two-billion-dollar tax break to corporations that aren't creating jobs, and leaving our thoroughfares as mottled as some freshman's acne-scarred forehead.

While thinking that lovely thought and dodging a gash in the road the size of a medium-sized moose, I inhaled a metric ton of exhaust belched from a passing city bus.

Smiling at me through the choking fumes were a pair of children, an African-American boy and an Asian girl, each with happy gaps of missing teeth. They wore burgundy golf shirts and bright excited eyes and the text next to them proclaimed, "Achieve Academy. Apply now. Spaces Filling Quickly."

An advertisement for an elementary school on the back of an AATA bus?

An additional tagline said, "Individualized Instruction With A Moral Focus."

What the hell did that mean? Talk back to a teacher and get yourself whacked with a personalized paddle in the principal's office?

I tried not to worry about the toxic cloud entering my lungs, about my broken knees, about the creepy children and their digitized smiles.

Kept grinding.

Bone on bone.

The smells of restaurants at the corner of Hill and Packard—pepperoni grease from pizza places, fresh-baked bread from sub shops—pushed my gnarled legs to keep pounding.

To keep my mind off the knives in my knee, I liked to speculate about the students with take-out sandwiches or plastic platters of sloppy nachos. Were they celebrating finishing a big paper, or heading out to avoid one? Were they eating a big dinner now in hopes of achieving higher tolerance during beer pong later?

The streets of Ann Arbor were always thick on football Fridays, but never thicker than when Michigan hosted State.

Elbel Field was a concert of kids playing two-hand touch. Teams ran intricate slip-screens that evolved into elaborate hooks-and-ladders and backward laterals. The choreography of complicated plays was a kind of religion, a ritual of practice, prayer and redemption. If I weren't in a rush, I'd have stopped, watched for a few minutes, tried to remember what it was like to have friends you could count on to forgive you even if your pass was short and the opposing team—those jackasses—intercepted and ran it all the way back.

Other students were already drinking, red-cupped beer in one hand, Frisbee in the other. Mostly I left kids like that alone. The Frisbee kids tended to drink too much too early, be exhausted by ten, fall asleep before midnight. The touch football kids, the ones I'd admired, they'd be worth watching later.

In a few hours, kids would be trying to have sex in that park. Especially on a warm night where thousands of students had road tripped fifty miles and the party was supposed to be epic. Everybody wanted to make a memory. Mostly I'd leave those kids alone too. Let them practice their under-the-stars sorcery and attempt to do what their parents did thirty years ago. Except, there'd always be some girls who were so stumbling drunk, they'd be forging something different, a lead-stomach nausea they'd rather forget. Those interactions were tricky. If a girl couldn't hold herself up, and the boy was half-dragging her into the field, then it was obvious—step in, try to get her to the emergency room before she passed out. But when a girl was still loud and brash and full of *leave us alone, officer, we know what we're doing*, what could we do?

Be careful, I told girls like that, speaking slow, looking them in their blurry eyes.

Remember who you are, what you're good at and proud of.

Make sure you want to do this.

Make sure.

Past the park and toward Packard, the noise escalated. State Street was a festival of yellow and green t-shirts, many of them shredded and refashioned to show additional skin. Tattooed blue M's and white S's decorated shoulders, ankles and biceps.

Girls wore cheerleader skirts, or shorts that looked like bikini bottoms. Footballs crossed the street in wobbly parabolas. Cars stuck in traffic vibrated with over-decibeled hip-hop. Windows stayed open and backseats stayed stuffed with boys in backward baseball hats chewing tobacco. Most students would have a good time, but not a great one. Would eat a carton of fried food and drink to excess and look at other kids and think those kids were having a better time than they were and would feel melancholy for a few minutes, maybe have a conversation with a squirrel or the trunk of a tree, then look back in twenty years and remember the night as the kind of night where they began to grow up.

But there would always be other kids who wanted it all right then. Kids who'd be the most dedicated beer pongers, who'd suck thirty-two ounces from long funnels and wind up loud and red-faced and throwing up at the thin end of the night, or throwing fists.

On State Street, the parties were already amped, lawns in front of frat houses packed. Hundreds of kids milled in netless volleyball sandpits, all with cups held chest-high. From one porch, a line of six girls danced in unison to the new hybrid hip-hop / country, their asses in high-waisted jeans shorts quaking toward the street.

I'd be lying if I said I wasn't riveted.

The house had a professional sound system, the bass thump echoing for a quarter-mile. On the sidewalks, street vendors sold ten-dollar t-shirts that said "State Sucks" and pictured Sparty on his knees with his mouth open in a gaping oval. Other shirts said "Ripstick 19," referring to Michigan's scrambling quarterback LeBannon Williams.

The makeshift booths were crowded, shirts were selling briskly.

I turned when I heard what I knew would be coming at some point, what always comes on these weekends, the kind of shout that splits the revelry with its discordant bite and means only one thing.

Fight.

The guy shouting was big, six-three, pushing two-seventy, a lot of it fat. In a bright yellow t-shirt, he looked like a grapefruit wearing madras shorts. The guy's face was pink and bloated with drink, his dark hair stuck to his sweaty forehead. In one hand, he gripped a half-filled plastic pitcher stolen from a dining hall. Cheap-looking beer sloshed around inside it as he gestured, splashing over the sides.

I couldn't bust him for the beer because he wasn't on the sidewalk but inside the frat house yard, shouting toward the street from behind a brownish split-rail fence. Maybe he was underage, maybe not. If I started asking students for IDs with this many kids at a party, that's all I'd do for the next three hours.

"Get the fuck out!" he yelled. "I'll kill you, you fucking woman!"

The guy he was yelling at was smaller, but didn't look so easily killable. Half his face was painted white, the other half green, a quality paint job, his face divided neatly with a vertical line bisecting his nose so it looked like the border on a map. White country, green country. He tore off a green and grey flannel shirt to reveal a white, ribbed tank top around a lean, flat torso and arms that were well-developed. He might have been a wrestler, maybe in the 167 pound class. It'd be pushing it for him to take on the grapefruit with the beer pitcher, but, then again, wrestlers had that hunger.

"Let's go, you fat fuck!" he shouted after the flannel shirt was a pile on the sidewalk. "Get your fat ass out here!"

Part of me, still off-duty for another forty minutes, felt compelled to join the students forming a circle half inside the fence, half outside it, to watch. I would have bet on the smaller guy.

Then again, I always do.

"Eat a dick, you homo-faggot!"

"Come on, you shitbag fat slob bitch!"

Showing off their fine higher education, clearly.

I pushed through the crowd of mostly yellow shirts, and a growing number of green shirts.

The kid in the tank top rushed toward the grapefruit. His hands were bigger than they should have been for a kid his size. His fists looked like cannonballs.

I stepped between him and the fence.

"Gentlemen," I began. "I am identifying myself as Detective James Harrow from the Ann Arbor Police Department. It is 6:20 p.m. on a Friday evening of uncommonly balmy temperature. Have you noted the architecture surrounding you? Look at Angell Hall. Built in 1924. Designed by Albert Kahn, the famous architect from Detroit. Have you had time to explore the Hopwood Room on the first floor? It's open to the public."

"Eat a dick, you homo," the big guy yelled to the kid I was now holding back with one arm, his heaving chest hard and quivering against my palm. I could hold him for maybe ten more seconds if I couldn't get him to calm down.

"Look at your stomach hanging over your pants, you shitbag," he said to the guy behind the fence, his words spitting saliva into my hair.

"Imagine this," I said, trying to sound cheerful. "LeBannon's got the ball. The afternoon's the kind of day where the sky's a gift and the stadium's filled to the brim.

Everybody's standing. The stadium's rattling. State is up by three. It's fourth and seven, two minutes left. Michigan needs a first down or this thing's over. State's rushing LeBannon like a huge green forest with feet. He jukes left and a linebacker flies past him, but two more green shirts are in his face. He's got maybe an eighth of a second to make a move or he's buried, so here's my question, gentlemen, you ready?"

The guy behind the fence looked bored with my babbling, like he wanted to refill his pitcher and move on to something different. The guy with the muscles was still wired, but I could feel energy seeping out of him.

"Are you ready for my question, gentlemen? I need affirmation. Gentlemen, nod your heads if you're ready for my question."

The kid I was holding back from the fence nodded, sort of. More like a slight jutting of his chin. The big guy in the yellow shirt just stared. As if he could figure me out if he felt like making an effort, but, frankly, wasn't all that interested.

"Excuse me, sir," I told him. "The question you need to think about is this. When LeBannon's either shaking free and heading for daylight or getting flattened by a green tsunami, where are you going to be? And I don't mean that in a philosophical sense of whether your life has meaning, or whether football itself is a worthy cauldron for the swirl of human passions. I mean where will your actual body be situated? Will it be in the stadium with the rest of its peers? Or will it be stuck in a holding cell playing with its package, wondering why its brain was stupid enough to propel it into a fistfight in the presence of a peace officer?"

Typically, this kind of blather bored everyone in earshot and evaporated the tension. But every so often there was a kid who didn't like being pacified. Who wanted to puff himself up in front of his friends and strut into his econ class Monday morning feeling like a legend.

"Fuck you," the big kid said, staring directly into my eyes. "What kind of midget faggot cop are you?"

The kind who will make you eat that pitcher, I thought, but he was already swinging it, rocking it backward then angling it upward so a stream of beer arced toward me, like a great swath of foamy urine, splattering against my chest.

My ratty Pioneer Wrestling t-shirt was already drenched with sweat and destined for the washing machine before 6:30. I had another dozen of them folded in a dresser drawer in my bedroom.

Still.

I jabbed a sharp kick to the shin of the kid in the tank top, sending him sprawling on the sidewalk, then spun over the fence and grabbed the fat kid by the back of his neck. With my other hand, I slammed the beer pitcher into the bridge of his nose, showering it with blood. Yanking the kid's hair and pulling him to his knees, I pushed as hard as I could against the bottom of the pitcher so beer, backwash and blood flooded his nostrils and mouth. He tried to scream, but the sound was muffled by the plastic encasing his face. He was heaving and using up air, and in about a minute, he'd drown.

"Here's what's going to happen," I said, shoving with maximum pressure both against the bottom of the pitcher and the back of the kid's head. "When I let you go, the first thing you're going to do is issue a public apology for assaulting an officer of the law. It will be humble and sincere. Then you will regrettably take your leave of these festivities. You will not stop at any bars or restaurants or anywhere else on your way back to your dorm. When you reach your room, you will not play videogames or waste time on any social network. You will catch up on the homework you haven't been doing for the past month. You will not venture out again into this night. If I catch you outside before game time tomorrow, you will spend the rest of the weekend incarcerated. Nod your head if you understand what I'm telling you."

Pulling the kid's hair again, I nodded his head for him. His breath fogged up the inside of the pitcher. He gagged on beer and blood. I pulled the pitcher off his face and let go of his hair. He fell backward. His head hit the ground with a thunk.

"Apologize to the officer of the law," I said.

"I'm sorry, Officer," he said, blubbering.

"Go home," I said.

He scrambled to his knees, then grabbed the fence rail to hoist himself up. His nose continued to gush and he tilted his head back and tried to plug his nostrils with his shirt.

"Start walking," I said.

"Can I have my pitcher back?"

"No."

"I'll get it," a girl behind me said, like she was some kind of saint.

The fat kid made his way over the fence and began to walk south, toward the Packard intersection, his head still tilted backward with his shirt pressed against his nose. He ignored the kid on the ground in the tank top. That kid stayed quiet too. When he looked up at me, his eyes were moist.

"I suggest you also make it a mellow night," I told him. "Put your shirt back on and pretend you care about your education. Next to Angell Hall is the remodeled art museum. There's an exhibit on the second floor. African walking sticks. Intricate patterns and runes carved into the handles. Each stick tells a different story. Make yours one you won't be ashamed of, you get me?"

He nodded.

I turned to the girl who said she'd take the pitcher.

"You really want this?" I asked.

"No."

"Good."

I hopped the fence and started jogging again. A block later, my knees throwing a tantrum, I stopped and tossed the pitcher into a recycling bin. Another city bus stopped next to me and spewed a cloud. From its side panel, three children in forest green golf shirts smiled at the officer of the law. The ad said, "Bright Futures Academy: Featuring Innovative Personalized Instruction. Apply Now. Spaces Filling Quickly."

I could still hear the bass thumping from the frat party and looked back at the porch.

No one was dancing.

CHAPTER TWO

STATE BLEW US OUT.

The green forest with feet swarmed LeBannon every down. He managed to break free a couple times and eventually put a few points on the board, but Michigan couldn't stop the bruising backs of the Spartans and we were down twenty at the half.

Nonetheless, I was having a blast. I hadn't been to many games in the past five years. Molly got our season tickets in the divorce and I'd spent most of my fall weekends since then carting our daughters all over the Midwest to play field hockey. I didn't begrudge that time. What was better than watching Jenna and Lisa go after bigger girls with that tiger spirit they had, jutting their faces with only those tiny eye guards to protect them into what seemed like the direct paths of swinging sticks and the vicious flights of a ball that was as hard and compact as a plastic grenade?

Look, when your twins are the kind of kickass athletes that compel opposing coaches to tell you after the game, win or lose, that they wished they had them on their team, it's tough not to fan your shoulders as wide as a small airplane hangar and think you didn't do something great as a father.

Still, to be back in The Big House, to pump my fist and hail the Victors even if the Victors were headed toward an epic beatdown, that's when my love for this city overwhelmed me.

I was a cocktail of contradictions. The only son of two English professors who grew up to daily recitations of Pound and Elliot, yet I constantly had to check my desire to injure people. Maybe that's why I loved football Saturdays, this odd mix of book lovers who came together to celebrate violence amidst the smells of toasted cinnamon almonds sold in nine-dollar bouquets at vendors' booths, and homemade bratwursts stuffed with Michigan cherries sizzling on hibachis.

It was crazy how normal it seemed that neighborhoods around the stadium could flood with a torrent of grown men and women with real jobs and real money and real preferences for organic produce, all of them shaking maize and blue pom-poms and singing fourth quarter lyrics to a thirty-year-old Journey song.

My heart swelled at the sight of hundreds of buses and RVs with big-screen TVs, and three generations of families building temporary living rooms in parking lots, and people leasing space in their front yards to strangers for twenty bucks a car. This was the community I swore to protect, the city in its most fanatic, pigskin-worshipping finery. I'd never begrudged working Friday and Saturday game nights because I grew up watching those games with my own dad, and his dad, the three of us living and dying with every fumble and dropped pass.

I also knew the games paid my salary.

This crater in the ground ringed with ninety-five rows of wooden benches was clearly the city's economic engine. Every home game brought in fifteen million dollars for the

University and probably another ten million for the city. Every hotel within fifty miles filled every room. Every restaurant boasted a waiting list of forty minutes. Every store that sold beer by the keg sold enough kegs each season to put the owner's kids through college.

How often did a hundred and fourteen thousand people gather in one place for close to four hours, almost all of them smiling and excited, even when we weren't winning but especially if we were? I was a detective in a medium-sized, highly livable city, but every day, I knocked on doors that opened into homes that stank of misery. People stumbled into our lobby beaten down by lives that dropped tree limbs through roofs and cancers through colons and layoffs and car accidents and children gone horrendously wrong week after mind-numbing week. I fielded countless phone calls where the voices on the other end sounded like the air had been slowly wheezing out for half a century.

But then came these Saturday afternoons where a nineteen-year-old kid from some small town in Michigan kicked an egg-shaped brown object end over end through the air and a hundred and fourteen thousand sets of eyes glued themselves to its flight, and a hundred and fourteen thousand hearts pressed like convicts against the bars of their rib cages, and the clanking machinery of a hundred and fourteen thousand unique apparatuses of problems were—for the length of that football's soar—stilled.

What I mean to say is The Big House was packed, and I was lucky enough to be there because Mike Bednarsky, my former teammate and U-M's current wrestling coach, gave me his extra ticket. He got four seats and usually took his family but his wife and kids were up north so I was sitting —standing actually—prior to the kickoff, right next to Mikey and on his other side his dad was standing, albeit more crookedly because he's maybe eighty, and his dad's golfing buddy, also maybe eighty, was next to him, and the bleacher seats offer each person roughly eighteen inches of space. The thing is, a lot of people possess a lot more than eighteen inches of girth, so real estate tends to get precious.

Especially when a dude who looked around six-four and three-fifty jostled through the crowd and landed the mammoth airship of himself next to me and informed me, politely at first, "Man, I think you're in my seat."

Which was technically true because, yes, what with the whole accumulated mass of thirty-plus people on the other side, I had drifted slightly into his assigned territory, but that's just what happens at Michigan games. The courteous and proper thing is to try to squeeze in where you can.

"Hey, man," he said again, "that's my seat."

There was maybe a quarter-inch of space between me and Mike, and the same between him and his dad, and for all the people down the rest of the row, and I turned and looked at that negligible space, spent a solid five seconds examining it, and then looked back at the big guy who, I realized, had an even larger guy next to him on his other side, a dude who was probably his brother because he had a similar facial structure. They both had a huge swollen mass of red cheek and broken blood vessels on their noses and a receding but still-thick hairline and ears the size of frozen waffles. I sort of shrugged at both of them like, sorry, I'd move, but there really isn't anywhere else to go.

"Hey, man," he said, his voice starting to growl, "you need to check your ticket. I'm telling you, this is my seat."

I tried to angle my torso and legs into as slim a space as possible and told the dude, "Look, there's nowhere for me to go, okay? The stadium's full. There's nowhere for the people next to me to move. We're just going to have to figure out a way to squeeze."

"But that's my se— " he started to say, but then the drum roll rumbled and the kick went upward and we both watched it and the State kid caught the ball with forward momentum and broke loose for twenty yards before being forearmed to the chin after he'd already stepped out of bounds, which tacked on another fifteen for unnecessary roughness, and the faithful shook their heads and muttered, and we shook our heads and muttered too, and when everyone sat down the enormous dude and I sat down with them and we were practically in each other's laps, our genitals not six inches away from initiating contact, and this big, billy-goat-gruff of a man did not jab an elbow into my ribs or spread his tree trunk thighs wider to squeeze me smaller, but instead broke into a face-splitting grin and said, "Oh, well, sharing is caring, right?"

And that, right there, is why I loved Ann Arbor.

After much sharing and caring with my new friend for life, most in the form of lamenting Michigan's willingness to allow State's receivers the kind of wide open territory associated with vast swathes of prairie, he headed off at halftime with his man-mountain brother in search of sustenance that would help them increase their bulk.

"Bro," he said, handing me his business card, "I'm a contractor. You ever need any work done, new roof or anything, give me a call. I'll take care of you. Get you a deal."

"Can't. I'm a cop. Don't do deals."

He nodded, smiled that big goofball grin, then gave me a high five that nearly broke my wrist. On the positive side, their leaving opened up enough space for me to reach into my pocket and retrieve my cell phone.

I had texts from both my daughters. Jenna asked if she could use my truck to drive to a party, and Lisa cursed Michigan's defense. I didn't have to ask why Lisa wasn't going to the party with Jenna. After a Wolverines loss, she wasn't presentable to the public. Didn't like to do anything except stay at home and rearrange the furniture in her room. Clean out the garage.

The third text was from my friend Danny—It simply said, "17."

Again, I'd underestimated.

Danny Root worked as a nurse in the U-M Hospital emergency room. Earlier that morning, I'd texted my guess: eleven. It was a game we played on football weekends. We each tried to predict how many students would get their stomachs pumped for alcohol poisoning. Seventeen in one night was the highest number in the six years we'd been playing the game.

I tried to imagine what would happen on a night after the Spartans stomped us. State kids would celebrate heartily, rubbing our faces in their victory. Michigan students would drink harder, suck down more funnels, attempt to prove they were still the better partiers despite their team looking like over-cooked spaghetti when it tried to tackle people.

"Beers at Grizzly Peak?" I texted back.

Those were the stakes. If my guess was off by three or more in either direction, I owed him beers. Looks like I had to pay up.

An advertisement for Blue Skies Success Academy flashed on the video screen affixed to the scoreboard. Students wearing golf shirts smiled at the camera. An Asian boy said, "I used to hate school because it wasn't challenging. Now I love going to class because I learn at my own pace."

At the end of the commercial, a tagline said, *Make Personalized Instruction available for all children. Vote YES for Education Fairness on November 4th.*

I was thinking about how these charter schools, if that's what they were, must have a ton of money to spend on advertising when, seconds after the commercial ended—clearly in a coordinated effort —an airplane flew over the stadium trailing a banner that said *Vote YES for Education Fairness!*

I finished my text to Danny Root.

"22 tonight," I wrote. "Gonna be bloody."

It was.

By two a.m., we'd already broken up twelve parties and nine fights. Every one of the fights started because one person said *Go Green!* and the other insisted *Go Blue!* I'd written forty-six MIP tickets and confiscated nineteen fake IDs. My partner and I were in the process of cleaning up detritus from fight number ten when I heard the saddest phone call of my life.

I don't mean sad in the tragic sense, I mean sad in the pathetic sense. A kid in a Michigan t-shirt stained with blood was talking to his girlfriend on his cell. She was having a hard time understanding him because I was in the process of retrieving several of his teeth from the sidewalk and depositing them in a plastic bag.

Apparently, the fight had lasted only one punch. A kid in a State sweatshirt had bombed the Michigan kid in the mouth, then scampered away. A witness, a cello teacher who lived across the street, heard what sounded like a loud smack as he was opening the door to his house after hearing confrontational shouts. He emerged in time to see a guy in a green sweatshirt running down the block. The neighbor helped the kid sit up and checked his vitals, then called the police. The kid was still sitting on the sidewalk holding his mouth two minutes later when Karen and I rolled up in a squad car.

"You smell something burning?" Karen said when we got out of the car.

I did, but stuff was always burning on party nights. Mostly weed and cigarettes.

"What happened?" Karen asked the kid sitting in his blood.

"I don't know," he said. "A guy hit me for no reason."

Due to his lack of teeth it sounded like he said, *a guy hith me for no reathon.*

I stifled a snicker. So did the cello teacher. Karen was better than me and didn't laugh in that kind of situation.

In fact, Karen was better than me in most situations. Solved the majority of our cases and the field hockey team she coached at Pioneer was in the state championship game every season, while my wrestlers were lucky if we won half our matches. My daughters adored playing for her and she loved coaching them.

Karen and I had gone to school together at Pioneer, then U-M, and had been partners on the job for fifteen years. We were basically the same person, only she was better at being it.

Did we date?

No.

Ever slept together?

Yes, one time.

Two days after Molly left.

We were supposed to go for a beer. Partners, right? That's what we did whenever either of us was struggling with a personal matter. We drank beers and got sad as a twosome. She dropped me off at my house and I was going to go for a run and meet her later but she followed me inside and we ended up never making it to the bar. I remember it as the most incredible night of my life. In the morning she said, "If we do this again, you will kill me. I am too young to die. Therefore, we are not doing this again."

We haven't.

The cello teacher told me what he knew.

The State kid had walked past the Michigan kid and the standard "fuck yous" resulted. The State kid punched the Michigan kid and broke his face. Then he ran down the block.

"Did you see the attacker at all?" I asked the cello teacher.

"I only saw his back. It seemed like a blocky, muscular back but he wasn't that tall. Taller than you, but still only maybe five foot eight."

I had the guy write down his name and contact information while I scooped the teeth into an evidence bag. I figured I'd give them to the guy from whose mouth they'd been jettisoned. I didn't think they could be reattached but maybe he could frame them, keep them as a reminder not to be a moron.

Karen had finished questioning him and now he was on the phone. Calling his girlfriend so she could take him to the hospital.

"I'm in Ann Arbor," I heard him say, "but you're not going to like it when you *thee* me." Then he paused, started to sob.

"I got in a fight," he said. "You, you're, uh, you're not going to want to *kith* me anymore."

I tried not to, but I think the cello teacher and I both snickered in a way that was audible. Karen shot me a look that said *this is why we'll never sleep together again.*

"You sure you don't smell something burning?" she asked.

I looked down the block toward State Street. Above the trees and slightly northward, the sky was lit with an orange glow.

We heard a siren.

Our radios crackled at the same time.

CHAPTER THREE

PAR-TAAYY!!!!

It was so fun!

Hanging out with college kids—drinking and dancing! —throwing *down,* partying *up* in a way he never had when he was in school.

It was like a do-over.

Jarrold had been so bland at the land-grant university where he'd almost gotten his bachelor's in economics: classes, the gym, his gloomy room, jujitsu training. To the hot sorority girls, he'd been just another loser from a small town in a flyover state, a kid who took up space. In fact, he'd only dated one person his whole time in college, and she was dead now. Oh, Kimmie! So sweet. So trusting. The only girl who'd paid him any attention at all, and only because they'd been forced together into a study group by their professor and, consequently, she'd realized how smart he was.

He hadn't wanted to kill her.

It'd been senior year, dreary February, and they'd been cramming for midterms in her cramped dorm room, and he'd just made her climax for the second time though he hadn't orgasmed yet, but he'd wanted to. Oh, yes, he felt like he was going to burst, his groin swelling like overripe fruit, and he'd pleaded, but she'd waved him away.

"In the morning," she'd said. "I'm exhausted."

In the *morning?*

That was unacceptable. He had tests in the morning. So did she. Not that it mattered if she passed them. She'd be taking over her father's million-dollar airline catering business regardless. Exhausted? She'd been pampered since birth. She didn't know what exhausted was. She wasn't going to do anything for him in the morning. She was lying.

"Not the morning," he'd said. "Now."

She'd looked at him first with fear, then anger.

"I think you need to go home," she said.

"Not like this." He pointed to his need, so large and full.

"I can't anymore tonight. You need to go."

He looked around her room, the pretend poverty of her dust-ridden windowsills, the lavender duvet that had fallen from bed to floor. The film poster of *Henry and June* on the wall.

What bullshit.

She was no Anaïs Nin.

She had no hunger.

"Now."

"No."

He'd grabbed her hair then, wound it around his wrist, forced her face to his hips.

She'd tried to pull away and he'd put a hand around her neck and shoved himself in her mouth. She'd gagged but he'd kept pushing. With tears leaking down her face, she tried to bite him and he shoved her away, all his muscles taut as he felt his blood rushing through his body. Her temple slammed against the corner of the desk where she'd been studying a half hour earlier and a grunt escaped from her throat just as he exploded into the sheets.

Then she didn't move.

He turned off the lights and sat in the dark.

Anyone who'd heard any noise would have thought a book had fallen from Kimmie's shelf. It was too bad. She was a nice girl. Round, firm hips and that friendly smile she liked to wear when she was in a good mood. He sat up for hours, brushed her hair away from her face. She looked more beautiful in death. Like a statue made by one of the masters in her art history class.

Before dawn, he wrapped her in the duvet and carried her out of the dorm. Her body was surprisingly light. Then again, he was surprisingly strong.

He took his nine o'clock midterm with his dead girlfriend in the trunk of his car. Aced it, then drove away from campus, his own room hastily packed up, most of what he hadn't thrown away stuffed in the back seat. Three hours later, he pulled off the highway onto a dirt road by an abandoned farm. He drove a few more miles, then parked near a wooded area that looked like it hadn't been explored for years. He carried Kimmie deep into the woods and threw her into a culvert that could have been a dried-up stream bed, then covered her with leaves and grass.

He wouldn't be going back to college, or graduating. Would never become the financial analyst he'd planned to be.

He'd have to find something else.

He found something else.

Six months after killing Kimmie and unable to establish anything other than washing dishes in a hot kitchen, he'd wound up in Chicago and met a guy who could give him a false identity—a new driver's license, a new social security number and passport, even the undergraduate degree in finance he'd never finished. It would cost him three thousand dollars though, and he didn't have it.

"There might be a way," the man said. "You look like you could pass for a college kid, if you cleaned yourself up."

I just *was* a college kid, Jarrold wanted to say, but he'd stayed quiet. A powerbroker who ran a commodities firm had a daughter at Northwestern. She'd fallen in love with a third-string catcher on the baseball team. *Guy warms up pitchers in the bullpen, for God sakes,* the rich man lamented when they'd met in the library in his gigantic house, his disgust obvious. The boy was a bit of a radical too, a participant in a number of anti-police rallies. He was dragging the guy's daughter into his seamy world of hating the man—her father *was* the man—and probably of late-night sex in his filthy off-campus apartment.

"I want this kid dead," the man told Jarrold, "but it has to look like an accident. I don't want him to be some martyr my daughter pines over until she's forty. The kid's got to do something stupid, make some horrible choice that lets her know he was never worth her time in the first place."

Jarrold had nodded slowly, thinking of Kimmie's body decomposing in the woods.

He'd spent months setting it up, fending off the father's impatience as he earned the pathetic kid's friendship, first by meeting him at rallies for so-called liberal causes, then by drinking with him in a dark bar, talking late into the night about how to start a fantasy revolution. The boy was hopelessly naïve, speaking in baseball metaphors all the time, believing he could save the world by shining a spotlight on all the hard-working bench-players who never got their due.

"We're the ones who make the stars better," he'd

insisted. "Without us willing to bruise ourselves by blocking their balls in the dirt, where would they be?"

Finding some other sucker dying to squat for them, Jarrold wanted to say, but instead he toasted the kid with cheap beer.

One night after a long bout of drinking and toasting and building the kid's anger to a fever, he guided him downtown to a train yard and produced a couple cans of spray paint. "Let's write on the trains," he suggested. "Get our message out to the whole city!"

"Let 'em know!" the boy echoed.

They sprayed ridiculous sayings like *Absolute Wealth Corrupts Absolutely!* and *The People Shall Rise!* splattering the sides of several trains with sloppy and amateurish black paint. Jarrold knew the cops would come. In Chicago they always did. Couldn't be bothered with commodities traders ripping off pension funds, but a kid with spray paint, that was a crime that had to be obliterated. So they chased. With guns drawn. Jarrold pulled the kid along with him and they ran through the yard.

It was only a matter of time.

The kid was drunk and stumbling and Jarrold darted between trains, following the course he'd been practicing for weeks, and the boy—as Jarrold knew he would—eventually made a wrong step, or didn't make a right step quickly enough, and when he fell onto an electrified third rail, the result was immediate. The kid screamed and the shock jolted all the way through him. Then, with a loud crackle and spark, he fried. The police stopped and spoke into their radios but wouldn't touch him because they didn't want to die from the current. The kid twitched like an epileptic for almost thirty seconds, body smoking.

Jarrold slipped between the trains, hopped a fence on the other side of the yard and was gone.

Two days later, he had a new identity, forty-seven

thousand dollars in a high-interest mutual fund, and a reputation that grew into an avenue for him to grow richer than he'd ever dreamed.

And now—throw your hands up!

Throw your hands up!

Ann Arbor was so fun! There was so much to do!

Sure, it'd been a drag to trundle from store to store, restaurant to restaurant, coffee shop to coffee shop and fill the vending boxes, empty the vending boxes, hand out the twenty bucks, smile his stupid up-and-comer grin, say, *see ya next week* as if nothing were more important than the ridiculous "festive events" he was promoting, but the drudgery had paid off, the plan worked.

Here he was drinking beer in a plastic cup.

Cheap beer from a keg!

He'd already had one blowjob in the pantry nook in the kitchen. He loved these old houses the landlords chopped up to sardine as many students as possible into bedrooms the size of shower stalls. So many angles and crannies and places he could steer these young girls into and do what he wanted. The first one tonight couldn't have been more than nineteen. "You're such a good-looking guy," she'd told him, her knuckles brushing against his cheekbones, the cleft in his chin. "How did you get to be so good-looking?"

"Surgery," he'd joked, though it was the truth.

She'd laughed, a musical giggle that shook her ample breasts, then shrugged as if she needed to reassure him, as if she were the expert on evaluating handsomeness, "whatever, you look really good to me."

"You're the one who looks good," he'd insisted, moving her hands toward his belt, the kind of fratboy preppy belt made of canvas he could potentially use to strangle her if necessary, "and you feel good too."

The pantry was stocked with bulk rations of cheap pasta, some packets chicken-flavored, some shrimp. There were canned soups and vegetables. More pretend poverty. He was learning something about what people were willing to settle for, his eyes landing on a half-eaten sack of dried garbanzo beans as he neared his climax. Most of the soups were high in sodium. Oh, oh!

Their transaction complete, he palmed the top of the girl's head, rubbed it as if it were a cantaloupe, and they squeezed out of the kitchen and separated, he drifting toward the beer pong table, she casting her glance around the living room, looking for another boy who would extend her fifteen minutes of devotion.

He considered beer pong a gift from the higher power. How had he never played it when he was a student? He'd been such a bore then, such a dull stereotype of Midwestern work ethic, all problem sets and anonymous workouts in the gym. No wonder Kimmie claimed to be tired. She'd been tired of *him*. He'd been such a loser. But now he was the beer pong king!

How many among us, he wondered, truly appreciate the sheer elegance of a ping-pong ball? It was becoming increasingly evident that the more time he spent with the empty, airy, egg-white spheres, the more spiritually closer he grew to them.

Their opaque, delicate shells.

Their ability to bounce and then almost to float, to defy gravity and hover like hummingbirds, but more peacefully, without the violent happenstance of wings.

How he could crush one between his fingers if he exerted too much force.

So fragile!

He'd taken to sleeping with one cupped in his right

hand, just so he could brush it in the early morning, know it was safe. As he walked through Ann Arbor's crowded streets, weaving in and out of hipster wannabes and frat-people, he thrilled to finger one in his pocket, furtively spinning it back and forth from palm to thumb.

When he'd initially been given the assignment in Ann Arbor—or "Ace Deuce" as the half-stoned townie kids on the Diag referred to it—he'd done his research. The city was a beer pong hotbed. If he were going to fit in, he'd have to know how to play. He immersed himself in trying to learn. It was surprising how many well-made instructional videos appeared on YouTube. After watching for several hours, he'd cracked open a six-pack of balls, set up cups on the dining-room table in his rented apartment and begun to practice. For the better part of two months, he honed his skills. Overhand. Underhand. With lean. Without lean. Straight lob. On the bounce. Double-bounce. Overhand hook grip. Backhanded shots. Blindfolded shots. Two balls at a time. Three. Bounce them off the staircase. Off the wall. Off the spinning blades of the ceiling fan. Toss them in after drinking one beer, two beers, eight beers.

Can he make it in the cup ten straight times without missing?

He can.

Twenty times?

He can!

Now that he was so good at it, it was astonishing how popular he'd become. When he was at the table, boys bro-hugged him and cheered him on, even "what-up-Dawged?" him if they ran into him on the street the next day. And the girls. The girls! Just because he demonstrated a facility to bounce a ping-pong ball into a plastic cup, he became the good time they wanted so badly to be part of. They could hang onto him, breathe into his neck and shoulders, clap their adorable prayer-hands claps when he bulls-eyed the ball into the cup, and the party would revolve around them. They'd be at the center of the action. The college experience!

No wonder it was so easy to direct them toward closets and vestibules for a quick physical release.

And now, with Waka Flocka bass beats vibrating the thin walls of the house, he was almost ready to steer the night's second conquest toward a more intimate encounter. She was a cutie too, with large fawn eyes that reminded him of Kimmie. Full lips and what a posterior. Divine! Slim-hipped yet lush. He couldn't wait to get his hands on all of it.

But where?

Somewhere far from the top floor.

The basement? A laundry room?

Somewhere that would leave him distant from suspicion while events transpired in the target's bedroom. Not that Jarrold really needed an alibi. He planned to be long vanished from Ann Arbor if the police ever got around to inquiring about him. Still, it wouldn't hurt to be in a totally different part of the house, to leave a collective impression in case any of the kids at the party began to wonder what he'd been up to—the champion beer ponger!—*oh, yeah, he'd disappeared downstairs with that girl who'd stuck her mouth to his neck like a suction cup.*

He'd have to time it right though. Monique seemed to be doing what she was supposed to—drinking, dancing with the target and whispering in his ear. Jarrold smirked, wishing he could wink at her, then bounced another ball into the cup on the opposite side of the table. His fifth bulls-eye in a row. A kid on the opposing team downed his beer, then spit most of it back out. The crowd surrounding the table booed. The girl with the terrific ass slipped her hand into his front pocket and squeezed his thigh. He'd trounced Monique and the target twenty minutes ago—just to throw anybody off who might think he knew her, and also so he could impress the hell out of her—and sent the two of them off happily sloshed to mesh tongues on the couch on the front porch. How ironic! The couch on the porch! If all proceeded according to plan, in another few minutes she'd return inside and lead the target upstairs. Then Jarrold would have to abdicate his throne and leave the table, usher the girl with sticky lips and probing fingers to the basement.

For now, though—par-taayy!

Bounce the ball off his cement-slab chest and smack it with a backhand and still dunk it in the cup. Goddamn, he was good. The key—always aim for the closest cup. Don't go for the big mass. People think that makes it easier, that even an errant toss will find a home. It won't. Better not to make any errant tosses. Better to shorten the distance and zero in on a specific target. It was always better like that. Find your target and laser your focus. Then you never miss.

He dunked six more in a row and felt the crowd growing bored. The kid who'd spit up his beer had spit it up six more times, each successive eruption less compelling to witness. The girl with the great ass had her tongue in Jarrold's ear, but it felt lackluster. Where were Monique and the target?

Ah, there they were, sliding through the crowd on their way back from the front porch.

Perfect timing.

She looked good too. So much better than the girl now slobbering onto his clavicle. Jarrold checked his watch. Everything was still happening within range. He nodded at her as she pulled the geek up the stairs. She ignored him, or seemed to, but held up the six-pack he'd told her to be carrying. "Why do I need more beer?" she'd asked. "Won't we already be drunk?"

"You don't need to understand that," he'd told her. "Your job is to bring him to his room. Make sure he drinks at least one of the beers, finishes the whole can—you can talk about whatever bullshit you want while he's drinking—and then if anything physical happens, that's up to you. Just don't leave until he falls asleep."

With the geek looking like he'd never had a better night in his life, Jarrold congratulated himself on recruiting Monique, first for the job last year at Western, and now for this one at U-M. He bet she was whispering all kinds of shit in the kid's ear. Blowing his nerd mind to pieces. Drunk and slap-happy, the kid trailed her like a drooling dog, one hand holding hers, the other on her hip. He was practically dancing up the stairs. Doing a goddamned Fred Astaire to the commercial bass beats. Jarrold almost felt sorry for him. He hoped Monique—with her fake French name because her trailer park family wanted to seem sophisticated—did screw him before he passed out.

"Sorry, guys," he said to the clowns across the table, "gotta bounce."

They didn't even try to hide their relief. The bored flock perked up. Now other people could attempt to win, even if they threw and missed, repeatedly, exactly like the forever-losers their sad parents suspected they'd become.

Jarrold, on the other hand, had drunk the perfect amount. A side beer here and there while delivering his opponents to pukedom. His senses remained sharp. He felt himself aroused as he hustled the ass-girl down the stairs. Thinking about what would happen in the target's bedroom, about Monique slipping out of her jeans, about the nerd not believing his luck, all made Jarrold even more excited. He felt huge. Porn-star huge! Everything had been calculated. He had thirty minutes to accomplish what he wanted to in the basement and then the beer from the kegs would run out and the party would shut down. He'd say goodbye to the girl he was with, maybe even act the gentleman and walk her to her dorm. Then grab a sandwich somewhere.

Then he'd come back.

Everyone would be asleep, the house quiet. His other employees would have already hauled away the gear they were supposed to, and he'd take care of his part of the job. Do it precisely right.

The girl whispered to him, "You're beautiful."

"Not half as beautiful as you," he said.

She smiled. Squeezed the rock in his bicep.

He smiled back, tried to bathe her with his glow. "You are limitless," he told her, slipping a hand beneath her shirt and thrilling at the warmth of her skin. "Don't ever let anyone put limits on you. You're not like these other fools here. You're different. You're everything the galaxy hungers for with its cosmic hum."

She squeezed his arm harder and made a purr that sounded like nothing could ever be more magical than the present moment.

He couldn't have agreed more with the insipid song thumping through the industrial-sized speakers—tonight was going to be a good night. Tonight was going to be a good, good night.

CHAPTER FOUR

WE GOT THERE JUST as the firetrucks arrived.

All of us too late.

The house was already engulfed, the front porch a wall of orange. The firefighters got busy soaking the homes on either side, tried to keep the blaze from claiming them too.

The lawn was littered with red plastic cups, the proud mark of a well-attended bash. Karen tried to move the crowd across the street, shouting, "Get back! Get back!" Any second, the house could spew burning debris all over the sidewalk. I added my voice to Karen's but it felt like we were shouting into a wind tunnel.

A group of students jumped up and down, resisting Karen's efforts to marshal them to safety. One pointed toward the upper floors where black smoke swirled behind closed windows. A rock lodged in my throat.

There were people inside.

Just then a second-floor window blew out, shooting glass and wood into the crowd. The roar vacuumed up the new oxygen, devouring it. "Get back!" Karen yelled at the students again. More glass shattered and then—like something you'd see in a Bruce Willis movie—two people wrapped in a blanket tumbled out another window on the same floor and fell into a leafy hedge. Branches slowed their fall but couldn't hold their weight. Karen and I rushed over and kicked through the shrubbery to pull them out. One male, one female. They weren't burning but they were badly scratched and the boy's arm was bloody and soot-covered. The blanket was soaking wet. He emerged from it wearing only his boxers. The girl was in a too-big t-shirt that said Michigan School of Engineering. She appeared to have twisted her ankle in the fall.

Karen helped her up, tried to make sense of her sobs. The boy looked disoriented and let me pull him across the street. He was Indian, possibly Pakistani. His face was shiny, his eyes tearing. "We tried," he told me between coughs. "I swear."

The girl, nearly collapsing in a coughing fit, pointed back to the top floor where flames danced inside the smoke.

Son of a bitch.

"Is somebody still up there?" I asked.

The firefighters finally turned their hoses on the burning house, tried to tamp down whatever they could, but there was no way anyone was going back in.

"It's Sanders," the boy said, his voice more lucid. "We yelled for him but he didn't answer."

A window exploded right where the girl was pointing, and there was a great whoosh and suck of wind. "Oh, God," I said.

With a tremendous crash, the roof blew off the house, flames and smoke breaking free.

The entire top floor was gone.

Wood, glass and metal shot out in a shower of flames and sparks.

A charred black body thudded to the ground.

Incredibly, neither the girl nor her boyfriend suffered significant injuries. She had a high ankle sprain and a few cuts on her face. He had a nasty gash on his elbow from breaking the window they'd jumped through. They both had minor smoke damage in their lungs but nothing that required further hospitalization.

As Karen questioned them in the ER, I stepped outside to call the fire chief. "Any confirmation on the body?" I asked him.

"We have to wait for the dentals since he was burned so bad, but every indication says it's Sanders Bolgim, just like his housemates said. Same height and build and the body definitely fell from his bedroom."

I walked across the street from the ER bay and gazed down the hill over Fuller Park. Early light made the dew on the soccer fields sparkle. The pool, closed for the winter, looked abandoned, its long surface hibernating until Memorial Day when the sunrise swimmers would return. On summer afternoons, the pool deck at Fuller was a strange combination of families with small children, and college kids stuck in town to retake classes they'd failed during the regular term. We got complaints every year about couples trying to have sex on the pirate ship in the playground.

"Fire out yet?" I asked the chief.

"Mostly. Only sidewall damage to the neighboring houses but the primary site is history."

"Kid's bedroom?"

"Nothing left."

"That unusual? For the roof and top floor to explode like that?"

"It happens. Especially in these old skinny houses that have been subdivided to maximize occupancy. All those closed doors on every floor. Pressure builds up. Fire's got to go somewhere."

Frank Myers was a stand-up public servant. He'd been chief for twelve years and ran a department devoid of scandal. I'd coached two of his sons, the younger one all the way to regional finals, the older to semis. Anything he was telling me was truth.

"Start on the porch?"

"Looks that way. They had a couch."

Damn.

Both the police and fire departments had been advocating for years for a statute banning indoor furniture on outdoor porches but two fierce libertarians had been voted onto City Council since the restaurant smoking ban went through and any new safety laws were quagmired. "Any chance it was deliberate?"

"Nothing's indicating that right now. Landlord's current on his mortgage and was raking in a ton, so no financial motive. Witnesses say the party was huge. Broke up when the keg tapped out. Could have been anything, a cigarette, somebody drops a smoldering blunt. You know how these things go."

I did.

"I'll tell you one thing, Jim." Meyers' voice got tight. "Whether the fire was an accident or not, that kid's death was politics."

"What do you mean?"

"You saw when we got there. How long did you smell smoke before the trucks showed up? In the state capitol? Those bastards cutting services, trying to bust unions? This is the consequences. We don't close the station on Stadium like we did last year, we're there six, maybe seven minutes earlier."

"You think that would've made a difference?"

"Trust me, Jimmy, that kid was collateral damage."

On my way back to the emergency room, I saw Danny Root signing charts. He mouthed the number *fifteen*. Which was good, fewer stomachs pumped than I'd envisioned, but my beer debt was beginning to pile up.

In the small side room where I'd left the students, the girl, now in a light blue hospital gown in addition to her t-shirt, was sobbing into Karen's shoulder. The boy, also in a gown, was crying too, sitting on a chair, head in his hands.

"This is Kaitlyn," Karen said. "And he's Nash, short for Avinash."

"I'm sorry about your friend," I said.

The boy nodded, his face a pool of anguish. "It's my fault," he said. "I'm the one who wanted to have the party."

Karen reached out and put her hand on his. It wasn't good cop, bad cop. She's just compassionate. I'm a troll.

"You can't blame yourself for an accident," she told him. "You two risked your lives. Tell Detective Harrow what you told me."

The morning light inched through a set of slatted blinds covering a medium-sized window. The way it caught Karen's profile sharpened her cheekbones and lit up the hues in her hair, alternately brown, auburn, and sandy blond. The night we were together I'd asked her what color to call it. "Stripey," she'd said.

The boy told me he and Kaitlyn had gone to his room on the third floor as the party was winding down, maybe a little after twelve-thirty. They were on the verge of sleeping when they smelled burning and leapt out of bed. When he opened the door to the hallway, smoke was already creeping up the stairs. He ran to the bathroom at the end of the hall and turned on the shower then grabbed the blanket and told Kaitlyn to put a shirt on. After throwing the blanket into the shower, he knocked on the two other doors on the third floor, rousting David and Lourdés, two of their housemates. They ran down to the second floor, then the first, and cleared out anyone left in the house. Everyone could still skirt the hottest part of the fire and escape through the front door, but barely. Flames crawled up the walls. Their lungs gasped for air. They were about to make a break for the yard when Kaitlyn said, "What about Sanders? What if he's still upstairs?"

"He's not. He's probably not home."

"But he went upstairs with that girl."

"*Sanders* went upstairs with a girl?"

They ran up two flights with flames licking after them. On the third floor, Nash ducked into the bathroom to grab the soaked blanket. The top of the house held only one small room. Sander's Perch, everyone in the house called it. Sanders Bolgim, a doctoral candidate in the School of Education, was known to sequester himself inside for hours and work on his dissertation. The door was locked. They shouted, kicked and pounded with their fists but got no response.

"He's not here. Let's go!" Nash said.

"He's in there!" Kaitlyn insisted. "I know it!"

The flames grew louder. Their breaths rasped. A window exploded on the second floor and the fire swallowed the air, bellowing with triumph.

"We have to go, Kaitlyn! Right now!"

"But, I thought I heard—"

"Now!"

He wrapped the blanket around their shoulders and they hustled down the stairs. A mouth of flames stopped them before they could reach the first floor. He smashed the closest window with his elbow and they dove through and crashed into the hedge.

"You did everything you could," I said. "You couldn't have saved him."

The boy looked up and turned to his girlfriend, shook his head.

"Before we ran," he said, his voice breaking, "it sounded like a groan. I didn't tell Kaitlyn at the time, but I heard it too. I did. I heard it too." Nash put his head back in his hands and Kaitlyn resumed sobbing.

"I know you're sad about Sanders," Karen said. "But think of all the other people in the house. If it weren't for the two of you waking everyone up, they'd be dead."

I nodded in a knowing way and the kids seemed to feel better. There really wasn't any reason to continue the interview. The fire was an accident. I was exhausted, my body aching for a shower. Karen, though you couldn't tell by looking at her, must've felt the same. Still, it seemed wrong to leave these kids alone, like we needed to keep talking to them, make them feel they were worth our time.

"Tell us about your friend," Karen said. "What was he like?"

"Honestly, we didn't know him that well," Kaitlin said. "He was so busy with his dissertation. He never really hung out."

"Yeah," the boy agreed. "Our house was organized like a co-op, but Sanders was mostly removed from it. He did his jobs in the rotation, like he cleaned the kitchen and the bathrooms when he was supposed to, and he cooked for us sometimes, but he almost never ate with us and you never saw him in the living room watching television."

"He just stayed in his room and worked?"

The kids looked at each other and the girl shook her head and I knew I'd asked the wrong thing. I shouldn't have said anything about the room the kid died in.

The boy soldiered on though, as if his answer was integral to an official investigation and he insisted on doing the right thing.

"He did a lot of work in his room, but he was gone a lot

too. Sometimes he'd be gone all night. Sometimes we didn't see him for days."

"He worked at the library?"

"He never really said. It was weird because we never saw him at a coffee shop or the Union. He had a place where he worked, obviously, because he'd leave with his backpack stuffed with books. But it wasn't the library, and he didn't have an office anywhere. He just had, like, a secret outpost, a hideaway somewhere. That's where I thought he was during the fire."

"Even Saturday night he might be working on his thesis?" I asked. "After a football game?"

"Weekends were the same to him as any other day. Like I said, he didn't have classes, or a job. Didn't teach undergrads. His schedule was totally based on his research. He didn't like football either. I don't think he knew if we'd won or lost yesterday."

"Did he have a girlfriend?" Karen asked. She hesitated. "Or a boyfriend? Was he seeing anyone?"

Something was off. Grad school co-ops with engineering students and researchers didn't normally host red cup parties. And the kid didn't follow the *football team?* Sure, I'd heard rumors some folks thought The Big House was a big cancer, everything wrong with university culture, but I'd never heard anyone voice that opinion in public, and even if Sanders were one of those people, why go to a post-game party if that was what you thought?

Karen felt it too. The tone of her questions had changed. The official investigation had resumed.

"He could have been," the girl said. "I mean, he was a cute guy in a *Big Bang Theory* kind of way, but he never talked about a relationship."

"He definitely wasn't seeing anyone," Nash broke in. "We ate lunch together maybe twice a week. I was probably his closest friend. He would have said something if he were dating someone. He wasn't a recluse, just insanely dedicated to his work. It was his reason for living."

And maybe his reason for dying.

Nah, that was crazy.

The fire was accidental, the unfortunate product of a chaotic night. A million drinks. A couch in flames. The kid in a dangerous top-floor room. A tragedy, maybe even a civil claim against the landlord, but miles away from an act of malice.

"What was his thesis about?" Karen asked.

"That was weird too. He never specifically said. I mean, educational policy, charter schools, test scores, something like that. He thought he was onto something important, but to be honest, the rest of us weren't all that interested. He'd go on one of his 'Life of the Mind' rants and we'd tune out."

"Where'd you guys eat lunch?" I said.

"Blimpy Burgers. He loved the triples. He always asked for extra grilled peppers, spicy, and onions."

"Let me ask you one more question," I said. "I don't want to be insensitive, but you two seem like smart people. You're all grad students in that house, correct? And you're an engineer, right?"

The boy smiled for the first time since I'd met him. It was an uncomfortable, excuse-me grin. Still, it was welcome.

"Um, no," he said, "Kaitlyn's the engineer. I'm in the MFA program."

Two daughters who were big-time athletes and a partner who was the most competent investigator I'd ever been around, yet my sexism was still on parade like it was the Fourth of July. Karen glared at me. I snorted.

"Sorry, I'm a Neanderthal. What's the MFA program?"

"Master of Fine Arts. Creative Writing. I'm a poet."

"Like you read down at the Heidelberg? At Sweetwaters?" I tried to redeem my humanity by dropping names of local poetry venues I only knew about because my daughters had mentioned them.

"Not that kind of poet."

He said it like that kind of poet wasn't really a poet at all. Like doing readings at coffee shops meant you were a fraud. I began to feel less sorry for him.

"Like I was saying, you guys are smart, right? Everyone in your house, advanced intellect and all that?"

The two kids nodded, not sure where I was going.

Karen flashed me a warning look. I ignored it.

"You had to know the danger. Why, for God's sake, was there a couch on your porch?"

"That's the thing," Nash said. "It was only there for one day. It wasn't our couch."

"What do you mean?" Karen said. "How was it not your couch?"

"We won a contest. Take-Home Tailgate."

Take-Home Tailgate? Where had I seen those signs?

"They bring the whole party to your house," Kaitlyn said. "That's their slogan and they weren't kidding. Three kegs, a big-screen TV they set up on the porch, a couch to sit on, a thousand cups, some food and soda, a beer pong table, professional sound system with excessively loud speakers. They brought everything and set it all up and hung a huge banner. People came over to watch the game and the party kept going until the beer was gone. Then they broke everything down and took it away."

That's where I'd seen the sign, a banner on some house somewhere. Maybe one of the frats in my neighborhood.

"They didn't take the couch?" Karen asked.

"They said they'd come back for it tomorrow. Today, I guess."

The kids got sad again, thinking about their burned-up house, their burned-up friend.

I gave them a few seconds but didn't want them to get

stuck wallowing. They'd have more than enough time for that over the coming months. "I don't get it," I said. "You guys are all serious students. Sanders didn't even care about football. How'd you win the contest?"

"It was random," Nash said. "They have sign-up cards everywhere. Downtown, the Union, Blimpy's. I filled a couple out and made Sanders fill one out once. Just for the heck of it. They draw a winner every weekend. His card was actually the one that got chosen. I mean, we haven't ever had a party, not even a wine-and-cheese. Our house seems so gloomy. I just thought it'd be fun."

"You don't have to justify it," Karen said. "People have parties. It's not your fault."

"But we even had a house meeting about it," Kaitlyn said. "It was, like, two hours. A lot of people wanted to turn it down, Sanders included. He had zero interest in a party."

"That's why I wanted it," Nash said. "Somebody like Sanders who had no social life—how can you go to school for so many years and never host a single party? That's what I said in the living room. Come on, one party, what's going to happen? What do you think, it'll kill us?"

Nobody said anything. Nash shook his head, dramatically, like the whole tragedy was his fault. Part of me thought it was bullshit. Like he was concocting irony for a future poem. Kaitlyn reached for his hand.

"The thing is," she said, "Sanders was having the best time of any of us. He played beer pong for, like, fifteen minutes. I didn't even know he knew what beer pong was. He was so drunk and this girl—she had dark hair and was really pretty, I think she was from State, undergrad or something—she was all *over* him. They were laughing and dancing, and they went upstairs together. That's why I thought he might still be up there."

Karen scrunched her eyebrows together.

"But she left before the fire?"

"She must have. Wham bam thank you, sir, I guess." Kaitlyn blushed then, embarrassed to make a flippant remark about her dead housemate.

"She'd never been at the house before?"

Nash shook his head again. "God, no."

"It seemed like a random hookup," Kaitlyn said, "which was crazy because Sanders doesn't do that, but the whole night was insane."

"How about pictures?" Karen asked. "Doesn't every party end up on Instagram?"

"I don't have an Instagram," Nash said. "That's what, like, political poets have."

Kaitlyn looked at him like he needed to be slapped. He did. "Honestly," she said, "the party was a bit much for us. We were too busy wiping up spilled beer and making sure nobody snuck into our bedrooms. We didn't have time for pictures."

"So there's nothing else about this girl you can think of?" Karen asked. "Strange tattoo? Unique sense of fashion?"

Kaitlyn put a hand on her chin, thought for a few seconds. I was starting to feel claustrophobic in the small room. Karen was asking a lot of questions about a death that was still likely accidental.

"Well, one thing was, they were both so drunk already, but when they went upstairs, she was carrying a whole other six-pack of beer. One of those kinds with the extra-tall cans. I remember thinking, are they really going to drink that too?"

Karen nodded as if that detail might be important, but I doubted it was. Drunk people don't exactly demonstrate good judgment regarding how much more they can drink.

"Anything else?" Karen said.

"Just that she was ridiculously pretty. Sexy pretty. Like she carried herself differently."

"How so?"

Kaitlyn looked at Karen for a long time and I got the distinct impression that what she wanted to say was, *she carried herself like you do, as if she were so confident in her looks she knew she could wear stripey hair and get away with it.* Instead, she said, "Sanders was the biggest geek on campus. That girl could have had any guy at the party. She chose Sanders like she'd been looking for him all along, and the way she hung on him, she *made* him better-looking than he was. By the end of the night, other women were flirting with him too. Not that he noticed. He seemed stunned anyone that beautiful cared about him at all."

"And you'd never seen Sanders act like that?"

"Never."

We left the hospital just before nine. Karen drove, jaw set, teeth grinding. Finally, she looked tired.

Kaitlyn's parents came from Saginaw to pick both kids up and bring them back to the family home for a few days. The deans of their respective programs had been contacted, everything smoothed over for any classes, or non-political poetry readings they'd miss.

"You hungry?" I asked, thinking an omelet and cherry-walnut toast at The Broken Egg.

"Yeah, but I need to sleep first. Why don't we meet for dinner later? Talk over what we've got."

"You're not thinking accident?"

"I'm thinking accident."

"But?"

"Nothing. Accident."

On the way out of the ER we'd passed the room where the boy with missing teeth was sleeping off his drunk. Snoring. It sounded like a high-speed dryer with a brick rolling around inside it. His girlfriend sat in a chair reading a magazine, tapping her phone against her thigh like she was pissed off. No doubt, the snoring kid had been right. She wasn't going to *kith* him anymore.

"You think the Tailgate people will come back for their couch today?" I said.

Karen didn't answer. We were stopped at the light at Huron and State, on the way back to the station so we could trade the squad car for our personal vehicles. A student in a black dress and high heels crossed the street, looking haggard. The walk of shame. She held a bag from the drugstore. She was not carrying herself as if she didn't care about what people thought about her choices. I stared. Karen didn't seem to see her. Drummed her fingers against the steering wheel.

"I'm not thinking accident," she said.

CHAPTER FIVE

DINNER WAS AT THE GRANGE. We found ourselves in the more intimate upstairs room, ordering appetizers in a corner where we could talk freely.

A candle lit up the glints in Karen's hair. Freshly showered, she wore a thin grey sweater and a pair of blue jeans that clung to her rock-hard lower body. She was, without a doubt, the most gorgeous woman in Ann Arbor, possibly the entire Midwest.

"You look terrific," I told her.

"Stop dicking around," she said. "We've got work to do."

"Why can't you take a compliment?"

"Why can't you cut the bullshit?"

"Is there something going on I don't know about?" I said. "Because I'm not sure I deserve this level of animosity."

"I don't want to talk about it, Jim. This isn't a date. A student died. Let's work on the case."

"Am I keeping you *from* a date? Is that it?"

"Not your concern."

She stirred her glass of iced tea. Except when I owed somebody beers, that's pretty much all we both drank. I liked mine more weakly flavored than she did.

I looked out the window to the sidewalk below. The bustle from downstairs floated upward and Karen kept her voice low like a movie gangster issuing a threat. It was a bit puzzling. The streets outside were thick with people in sophisticated clothing and expensive footwear. Once again, I was struck by how many restaurants seemed to be thriving despite the dismal state of our roads, the cuts in schools, police and fire. Why wasn't any of the bounty translating into better social services? The mayor had told me the same thing on two occasions, if the Michigan economy is a train going over a cliff, then Ann Arbor is the caboose, the last car that will plummet. I wondered if it could work the other way, if Ann Arbor could be a lead engine and pull the rest of the state out of its funk.

"You really think there's a case to work on?" I said. "Somebody planned this fire, planned for one specific person to die in it?"

"It seems far-fetched, but too much makes me uncomfortable. A party gets set up by somebody else, a beautiful woman hits on a geeky kid, then disappears before the fire starts. That doesn't strike you as sketchy?"

"A thousand sketchy things happen here every weekend. You're telling me you never hooked up with somebody and other people couldn't understand why you were interested?"

Karen swallowed a laugh. "Only once."

"Nice."

"Come on, Jim, we're not talking about me."

"We have to, Karen. At some point we're going to have to talk about you. About you and about me."

I knew it was unfair to transition like that, to stray from discussing the case which might not be a case, to discussing the us which might not be an us, but something about the way we were lately, together, was off. She seemed preoccupied when I joked around, only laughed reluctantly, or worse, ignored me. I couldn't act like I didn't care about that.

"Jim, we're partners. *Just* partners. If we're not focused on what we're doing, we could get hurt. We can't be distracting each other out there."

"Out where? On these violent thoroughfares where professors go for gourmet ice cream and students drink too much tequila and pass out in their puke?"

"Don't be an asshole."

"I'm just saying, don't you think I'm distracted already? Wondering every time I look at you whether we're going to be together again?"

"Stop wondering. We're not."

I reached for her hands across the table. She let me. They felt warm, like the fresh nine-grain bread our server had brought us moments earlier.

"Look me in the eye and tell me you don't wonder the same thing, at least sometimes."

Karen looked at me. She did not flinch. My shoulder joints, rubbed raw from the socket ball popping out and being popped back in maybe forty times over the past three decades, squealed like tires pealing around a sharp corner. She reversed our hands so hers were on top.

"Actually, I don't wonder about it at all, Jimmy. What happened was a fluke. A nice fluke, but it won't ever happen again."

I did not get discouraged when she said this.

I'm a detective.

I know when people are lying.

After dinner, I drove to Dykman Metro Park.

Jon David Dykman had been an early investor in Henry Ford's Model T and quintupled his fortune as a result. In the strange way people thought back then, he sought to ensure there would always be a swath of wilderness where people could go for drives in the country, so he purchased twenty-five thousand acres just south of Ann Arbor, and gave it to the state on the condition it never be developed.

A lot of the park, barely maintained these days, had turned to swamp. A couple years ago when two students from the U-M Business School disappeared, rumor was they'd been buried there. The department rented dredging equipment and searched for a few days but we never found anything. A month later, the two kids—Jonathan Harwell and Andrew Lombardozzi—turned up in Kazakhstan as co-proprietors of a brand-new brothel. Reportedly, they'd developed a computer program to categorize fetishes and track data. They were millionaires.

I pulled over next to a large marsh. Could I do it? Open a homicide investigation based on nothing but a hunch?

The dental records had come in and the body had been confirmed as Sanders Bolgim. Treetown.com, the web site that masqueraded as our daily newspaper, made his death the lead story. With Kaitlyn and Nash in Saginaw, the writer interviewed a bunch of other housemates and they'd all said the same thing: Sanders was a nice kid who kept to himself and worked hard on his thesis. No description of the thesis itself, only a mention that Sanders was a PhD candidate in the School of Education.

The fire was treated as an accident. Started with the couch on the front porch. No mention of Take-Home Tailgate. Though his housemates testified Sanders rarely drank, several witnesses described seeing him inebriated at the party. "Blasted out of his skull," a kid named Jonas Warren said.

Like Karen, I wasn't buying it.

Too many unexplained elements.

The fact that nobody knew what the kid was working on, or where he was spending his waking hours.

The fact that he never partied and all of a sudden, a girl nobody had ever seen gets him looped and brings him upstairs, then disappears.

The fact that there happened to be a couch on the porch ready to burst into flames.

We had no evidence.

Just a feeling.

But we both had it.

The number of reported homicides in Ann Arbor this year: zero.

The number last year: one. A drug deal at a motel turned into a stabbing. There were witnesses and we caught the guy, who was remorseful. There was also a rich kid, this January, Hayden Brickerman, who drowned while snorkeling in Hawaii just after New Year's, but that was out of jurisdiction and nobody investigated. He had a high blood-alcohol level, so accidental death seemed the appropriate conclusion.

That's why both Karen and I can be full-time detectives and also coach a varsity high school sport. It's not that crime doesn't happen in Ann Arbor. Drug use is rampant, mostly weed, and so is underage drinking. There's always an extravagant teenage party New Year's Eve and we always break it up and issue anywhere between fifty and seventy-five MIP's, and a couple dozen kids return to class wearing ankle bracelets and having to blow into tubes stuck to walls in their kitchen every twelve hours.

We get lots of home invasions, arsons on occasion, a fair

amount of embezzlement and stolen cars, and the fights on football weekends. Our most violent crimes are sexual assault and rape. Most of that happens on and around campus, but not all. Lots of snide commentary and backstabbing also occur during tenure reviews, but little of that's prosecutable. The last Ann Arbor police officer to die in the line of duty was in 1936.

We enjoy being named "America's Most Livable City" and "Best Place to Raise Your Children" by prominent magazines. Such accolades drive up property values and make us feel smug. It's my job to protect that smugness and maintain our magazine rankings. No doubt, I'm cynical about it. Too many self-satisfied Thurston Howells in maize and blue wear ascots and boat shoes to football tailgates, sip hot toddies before kickoffs, and refer to the players with racial slurs. Yet, there's also no other place I'd rather raise my daughters. For a city with a population of a hundred ten thousand and close to a hundred fifty thousand when the students are in town, our crime rate is far beneath the statewide average. We solve most of those crimes too. In a college town, somebody always sees something and blabs about it. Living here means your physical person is generally secure.

Nor, as Chief Taylor emphasized Monday morning, did we have any proof to suggest the death of Sanders Bolgim was anything other than an accident. "I'll give you forty-eight hours to dig around," she told Karen and me. "But keep it on the downlow and I want documentation of everything you do. If nothing turns up after two days, we're closing it.

"Oh, and, Jim, a call came in about a guy who identified himself as a cop at a frat party Friday night, then smashed a kid's face with a beer pitcher. Know anything about that?"

"I was breaking up a fight. It was a defensive maneuver. The kid assaulted me."

"That's pretty much what the witness said, but I didn't see a report. I want one on my desk within an hour, got it?"

"Got it."

"And, Jim?"

We were headed out the door. This was one of the chief's favorite control techniques. Halt your momentum when you're on the way to doing something else. Break you out of your rhythm.

"Yes, Chief?"

"Your next defensive maneuver?"

"Yeah?"

"Make it less offensive."

I hit the streets, Karen hit the phones.

My job—find out everything I could about Take-Home Tailgate and a pretty girl with dark hair who claimed she went to State. I finished the report on the beer pitcher incident by ten, too early to head to Blimpy Burger, so I walked down to the burned-out house.

The top half was completely missing, as was most of the porch and front door, the remainder of the edifice covered by a black sheet of canvas with the orange logo of a catastrophic cleaning company. Hundreds of red cups still littered the yard but there was a makeshift shrine leaning against the most stable corner of the house. It was surprisingly paltry. A single Hallmark Teddy Bear, a couple gas-station carnations that looked dead, a framed photo of Sanders that appeared to be a printout of the same high school yearbook picture used in the Treetown article.

A trio of thin and attractive girls strutted past in yoga tights and calf-high boots, all three talking on their phones. None so much as glanced at the house. A pair of nerdy kids clipped by in the other direction and ignored the house as well, though their necks swung to allow for thorough examination of the yoga tights. A jogger with broad shoulders and a hooded sweatshirt —a figure I recognized as my friend Danny Root—started to veer around the nerdy kids, then stopped. For a full thirty seconds, he looked at the husk of the house and the scant memorial and briefly restored my faith in humanity.

"Were you at the party?" I asked Danny. "Seems like it was at the kind of nerd nest you might frequent."

He laughed. "No. Read about it online."

"Ever hear of an organization called Take-Home Tailgate?"

"Brings the party straight to your front porch?"

"That's them."

Two more girls walked by without looking at the house. Both texting.

"I have philosophical issues with that concept," Danny said. "The whole point of tailgating is to bring the party from your home to a shared location. Be part of the arterial flow that attends the game."

Arterial flow? Nurse-speak, I guess.

"Did you know the kid who died? Graduate student named Sanders Bolgim?"

He looked more closely at the picture leaning against the house. Shook his head. "Nah, but I think I've seen him a few times, maybe at one or two in the morning, when I run after working the late shift. I've seen him near Angell Hall."

"Coming from the Fishbowl?"

"Could have been."

The Fishbowl was U-M's communal computer lab. It featured five hundred computers, fifty printers and 24-hour access. Connecting the backs of Angell and Haven Halls, and enclosed by glass windows, it buzzed at all hours with a frantic school of procrastinators attempting to print last-minute papers.

"Any idea what Bolgim might have been working on?"

He shook his head again. "Like I said, I didn't know him, never actually spoke to him. Just waved if he passed by close enough. The fire was an accident though, right?"

"We're just double checking. Trying to confirm the circumstances. Make sure we didn't miss anything."

"Think you might have?"

"Probably not."

"I'll tell you one thing," Danny said, bending down to pick up a plastic cup stuck to a hedge. "He always seemed like he was in a hurry, nervous too."

"How so?"

"Those kind of quick feet, walking with his head down, looking backward to see if someone was following."

"*Was* someone ever following?"

"Not that I saw. Maybe the kid was just anxious. It was the middle of the night, right? And he was alone. That's why I waved. You know how you can sense someone might be scared of you? I'd try and reassure him I didn't mean any harm."

"But he was definitely coming from Angell Hall?"

"Not definitely. I got the impression he was, but I can't say I saw him actually coming out of the entrance or walking down the steps from it."

I nodded and we both looked around the yard, at the cups that seemed like a leftover fuck-you to the kid who'd died there. "You want to give me a hand cleaning these up?"

"Sure."

I walked over to grab the recycling bin in the neighboring driveway and by the time I'd wheeled it in front of the house, Danny had already gathered a stack of cups. In less than ten minutes, we cleared the yard.

I was about to roll the cart back when I noticed several scraps of paper stuck to the hedge by the sidewalk. They were partially burned but it looked like some text was still legible. Maybe they'd blown out of Bolgim's room when it exploded. I put gloves on and picked them from the branches and stuffed them in a plastic bag, then thanked Danny for helping clean up.

We stood and looked at the burned-out house.

More students walked by and didn't look.

"Did I ever tell you I saw you win the Big Ten when I was a kid?" he said. "My dad took me to Crisler. You were awesome against that Minnesota guy."

Nestor Reagent, defending Big Ten champ. Took him out with a first period fall. Less than forty-five seconds. Dude was furious.

"I watched the NCAAs on television too. Your match against Lockha—"

"Hey," I interrupted, and extended my fist. "Look, I gotta go follow up some other stuff. Text me some options for when you want me to buy you those beers."

He looked at me as if I'd said something ridiculous, then shrugged.

"All right, man." He bumped my small fist with his larger one and resumed his jog.

Krazy Jim's Blimpy Burger is an Ann Arbor institution.

It is not named after me.

Everyone drops the "Krazy Jim" when referring to it anyway. The hamburgers are served in small patties, each about the size of a cookie, and they're meted out as singles, doubles, triples or quads. Only gymnasts and figure skaters order singles.

Vapors from the deep-fryer and grill imbue the cramped restaurant with a swampy grease fog that the clunking overhead fans do little to dispel. The smell of the place waters the mouth of anybody within a two-block radius. From open to close—which is around four a.m.—the place clocks a steady business, and on football weekends, boasts a line of hundreds of salivating alums.

The manager and part-owner, Alonzo Metry, was one of the city's all-time great people, a tall, slender widower with a large open face. After the first substantial snowfall each winter, he carved a smiling polar bear in the snowdrifts below the restaurant's front window. Passersby posed for pictures in front until it melted. His kid went to school with my girls.

We met in his office, decorated by scores of autographed sketches of famed U-M athletes and coaches, including Gerald Ford. I showed him my enlarged printout of Sanders Bolgim's photo and he nodded sadly. "That's the kid who died, right? He came in here all the time. Mostly with that Nash kid for lunch, but sometimes I'd see him late at night."

"With Nash?"

"Nah, it'd be around two in the morning, and he'd be alone."

"*You're* still here at two in the morning?"

"Someone has to be."

"Kid ever seem nervous?"

"Not particularly. Always writing, though. Would gobble his food and type into his laptop like he had a deadline."

"Any idea what he was working on?"

"No, but he didn't seem like the partying type. It shocked me to read about that in the online cesspool of a newspaper. Never came in drunk or loud. Nash either."

He shook his head then, as if wondering why out of all the knuckleheads who stumbled in to eat cookie-sized patties, the fates had to claim someone who'd never puked in his bathroom.

"Why are you asking me these questions? The fire was an accident, right?"

"We're just following up to make sure. Anything else you can tell me about him?"

Not really," he covered his large mouth with an even larger hand. It looked like someone covering a swimming pool with a tarp. "Wait, one time I did ask him what he was talking about, because I heard him say something Nicky talks about in his Philosophy Class at school, yeah, *Life of the Mind*. Your girls take that class? They should. Nicky loves it. He came home one day talking about how school doesn't try to make you think anymore. How it's all about producing factory-model employees who won't question their superiors. First, I thought Nicky was trying to make excuses for not doing his homework, just bullshitting, then I heard the Sanders kid telling Nash something similar so we got into a conversation."

"About homework?"

"Sort of, but more about how corporations sell school districts all kinds of mass-produced materials. Pre-packaged worksheets for math and reading, but made for computers. Digitized worksheets, he called them. He was getting heated. Said teachers aren't allowed to create their own lessons and it's even worse for online classes. Nash was kind of rolling his eyes and I couldn't get into it deeper because it was lunch rush, but it made me think. Nicky pretty much hates school except for Philosophy. He's a bright kid but he's bored as hell."

"Tell him to take creative writing. Jenna and Lisa like it."

I didn't want to ask the next question because I knew what would happen, but I didn't have a choice.

"What can you tell me about Take-Home Tailgate?" I said, gesturing in the direction of the sign-up box by the cash register.

"The party place? Guy comes in named Jarrold. Good-looking dude. Once a week, he empties the box of any sign-ups, puts out a new pad of blank ones. Says he's supposed to pay us twenty bucks a week to keep the box out, but I tell him to keep his money, buy his girlfriend some doubles."

"Can you describe this Jarrold?"

"Maybe six inches taller than you. Blond with one of those sharp-angled haircuts. Handsome kid, like I said. Sculpted face. Those watery blue eyes that seem like they don't care about anything. Could be a model for tuxedoes. Smiles a lot."

"Student, you think?"

"I didn't really get that vibe."

"Older?"

"Maybe. Could have been twenty. Could have been thirty. One of those guys it's hard to tell. Wait a second, you're not saying?"

"The party? Yeah, it was Take-Home Tailgate."

"From here?" he gestured toward the front of the restaurant and I knew he was asking if he were responsible, if Sanders Bolgim had filled out the contest sheet and signed up for his death while waiting to pay for a triple.

"Could have been anywhere," I lied. "Boxes all over town."

"But it could have been here?"

I didn't say anything.

"Oh, man." He pressed his big palm against his forehead. "Oh, man."

I gave him a few seconds. The grease smell felt oppressive. I could hear somebody open and close the refrigerator out front, grabbing a soda. "This Jarrold dude leave any contact info?"

He fished a business card from his desk. It said, "Take-Home Tailgate! We Bring the Party to You!" There was an 800 number and a designated extension.

"You ever see him with anyone else? Maybe a dark-haired girl, attractive?"

"Nah," like I said, "he didn't have that student vibe. Always came in alone. Took care of the box, took off."

"Ever see a girl like that otherwise, just hanging out here?"

"Every day. Hundreds."

"Of course." I felt like smacking my own damn forehead. "If you can think of anything else, call me." I gave him one of my cards and waved Jarrold's. "Can I keep this?"

He nodded.

"Jim? It was an accident, right? The fire?"

"Yeah," I told him, "it was."

First thing after leaving Blimpy's, I called the 800 number on Jarrold's card. The automated response welcomed me to the global home of bringing the party to your house and informed me I could press the extension of the party I was interested in if I knew who it was. I pressed. A robo-voice informed me Jarrold was unavailable but I could leave a message and he'd get back to me as soon as he could. I left a message. He didn't get back to me.

Downtown, a dozen additional establishments repeated the same mantra I'd heard from Alonzo. A guy named Jarrold, youngish, model-handsome, stopped in once a week to pick up filled-out entries and supply blank ones. He gave twenty dollars to whoever was at the register. Nobody saw him accompanied by anybody else. He could've been a student but didn't quite seem like one.

Nobody recalled seeing Sanders Bolgim either, though a barista at a coffee shop said she might have recognized him but wasn't sure from where. I left her my card in case she remembered. When she took it, I noticed what looked like track-marks on her upper forearm so I doubted she'd be calling me any time soon. A moron behind the counter at a deli never stopped texting while we spoke. It was almost impossible not to make him eat his phone.

It had been a couple hours since I'd called Take-Home Tailgate, so I tried again. Left another message.

Hit a few more restaurants and coffee shops. Same deal.

After I left a third message for Jarrold, I chose the option of pressing zero to speak to an operator. The call disconnected. I redialed and tried again. Same result.

I called back and listened to the extended options from the original menu and pressed one since I'd suddenly become interested in purchasing a Take-Home Tailgate package for a future home game. I was then informed I was being transferred to a sales representative. I heard waiting-for-a-sales-representative music for thirty seconds. Then the call disconnected. I tried again to purchase a Take-Home Tailgate package for a future home game. Expected identical results and got them. Tried one more time to explore additional options on the main menu. Pressed two because I had a question about the Take-Home Tailgate package I'd previously reserved. Heard thirty seconds of waiting-for-the-agent-who-could-answer-my-question music. Disconnected.

I switched over to my web browser and clicked the "Contact us" option. Was directed to the 800 number. Returned to the home page. Clicked on the staff directory. Was told that the page was under repair. Clicked on "Purchase a Tailgate." Was directed to the 800 number. Clearly, no one at Take-Home Tailgate wanted a damn thing to do with me, or, apparently, anyone else.

My cell rang as I was returning it to my pocket—a number I didn't recognize, but local.

"Detective Harrow."

"Jim, this is Bill Burkett from Treetown.com."

Treetown? What did this clown want? And why was he calling me *Jim* like we were fishing buddies?

"You looking for click-bait, Bill?"

"Depends. Is that what you consider your investigative practices? Because I heard you've been snooping around everywhere, asking about Take-Home Tailgate. That have anything to do with the party where the Bolgim kid was killed?"

Like I said, in a college town, someone always talks.

"Just out for a stroll, Bill. Absorbing the ambiance of our fair city."

"You just happened to be asking questions about Take-Home Tailgate? We know they did the party where the fire was."

"You didn't discuss that in the article."

"Should we? It was random, right? Take-Home had nothing to do with it."

"Yup."

"I can quote you on that?"

This frickin' guy.

"Look, Bill, why don't you call the Public Service Officer like you're supposed to? You know I can't talk directly to reporters."

"Can I request that person connect me to the chief? So I can ask about a story I heard about an officer beating up a fratboy?"

"That discussion's already been had."

"So you admit it was you?"

"Talk to Public Service."

"Tell me about Take-Home Tailgate."

Something occurred to me. Because we'd rushed Nash and Kaitlyn to the ER, Karen and I hadn't gotten contact information for any other housemates. "Look, Bill, you help me, I'll help you. Give me a way to contact the people you talked to who lived with Bolgim."

"I'm sorry," the douchebag said. "It's our policy not to reveal our sources."

I wasn't aware the site actually had any policies regarding the conduct of its so-called writers but I managed to refrain from elaborating on that opinion.

"The sources are already revealed. You named them in the article. I'm just trying to reach them so I can ask follow-up questions."

"Same thing."

"Not remotely."

"Look, if we managed to find those kids, so can the Ann Arbor Police. I'm not here to do your job for you."

Was this guy serious?

"Are you telling me you're willing to impede a possible homicide investigation?"

"Is that what this is now? A homicide investigation? Is that for the record?"

I hung up.

CHAPTER SIX

I TOOK my anger out on the heavyweights. One of them outweighed me by fifty pounds, the other, closer to eighty. I wrecked them, shoved their faces into the mat and yelled at them to get up while I was doing it. Three-man drill again. Two minutes in, one minute out. Except, I stayed in the whole time and let them alternate battling against me. For forty-five minutes.

At the end, the room was thicker with sweat and funk than Blimpy's was with burger grease. Both heavies slumped against the wall with their heads hanging between their knees, sucking breath. Did getting beat on so severely help them? I believe it did. Hugo, the bigger one, got in on me with a sweet firemen's carry. I managed to wriggle out, but if he could shoot it that well in a match, it would work. Javon, the smaller at about two fifteen, was dogged in his pursuit of his bear hug. He wound up on his back fifty times, but never stopped trying.

These guys needed to be pushed. They were both easy-going kids and if nobody was in their faces, they had a tendency to lean against each other like enormously bloated ballroom dancers and waltz through practice. I wasn't having that. Blistered their ears to take the old man down. Dumped them on their backs if they showed any signs of quit.

I ran everybody for twenty minutes after a water break, then finished the workout with an intense series of push-ups, sit-ups and hit-'ems where the kids sprint in place then dive to the floor and scramble back to their feet as quickly as possible. Me too. We clapped it up hard at the end and the room felt alive with pride.

After the team left for showers, I mopped the mat with disinfectant. When it was as clean as I could get it, I sat against the back wall, mimicking the heavies, mixing my exhaustion with the residue of theirs. I figured, if my legs held out, I had another ten years to beat on big kids like that, after which I'd have to get by on reputation. My name, after all, block-lettered on the wall above the door, still held a bunch of team records.

Most career victories: one hundred and forty-four.

That was the number I liked to stare at until it cleared away the fog of my tired, let me think for a moment before I hobbled from the room to start my run home.

Something I'd heard today was knocking at the doors in my brain, trying to work its way in, but I couldn't figure out what.

"It smells disgusting in here."

I broke my gaze from the numbers. Olivia Waterman, my daughters' creative writing teacher, stood in the doorway.

"What are you doing at school so late?" I asked, my words sounding garbled, like I had stones in my mouth.

She made a dismissive motion with her hand. "Grading poetry portfolios."

I nodded as if I understood the burden, as if perusing poems were equivalent to throwing around five hundred pounds worth of sweaty high school kid for forty-five minutes.

"I love reading them," she said. "It's certainly time consuming, and especially so with classes so big because of the budget cuts, but it's beautiful too. Also emotionally devastating. That's what I wanted to talk to you about. Do you have a minute?"

Olivia wasn't what you'd think when you heard the words *English teacher*. No earth-toned sweaters, grey flannel skirts or trendy glasses. No wedding ring either. She was probably my age, maybe a few years younger, but her hair was chalk white and cut in a military buzz, a look she could only pull off because of her high sharp cheekbones and huge brown eyes. She was wearing black jeans and a mahogany-colored t-shirt with the words "Teaching for Social Justice" emblazoned across her chest in graffiti-style writing. Jenna and Lisa worshipped her. Not as much as they worshipped Karen, but almost.

"My daughters write something I should be concerned about?"

She shook her head.

"One of the wrestlers?"

"I only have Hugo and he's a doll."

Nice kid, but, *doll* was not how I would have described the two-hundred-and-fifty pound behemoth who'd spent much of the last hour trying to pulverize me.

"What do you know about heroin use in the city?" she asked.

What do I know about *heroin* use?

I pushed into the padded wall with my upper back and rose to my feet, hoping she wouldn't notice me wince.

"Not much actually. It's getting worse than it used to be,

but it's still not as bad here as, say, rural areas in Indiana, or the way it is up north. We catch a few hopheads nodding out in the Arb. Some hardcore addicts live at the shelter on Washington. We run them in twice a year for shaking down other homeless people. Try to get them cleaned up but it never works."

"How about teenagers?"

"You know something I don't?"

She shook her head again and unshouldered a faux-leather bookbag. It looked heavy as it settled into the mat.

"I wish I did know more, but it's like I said, I've got thirty-six, thirty-seven students every hour. I feel like I don't know any of my kids the way I used to know *all* my kids. Or maybe I just don't care as much."

"I doubt that. It's six-thirty at night and you just finished grading papers. Looks like you're bringing another stack home."

She was quiet for a moment, gazing at the numbers on the wall, the cracks and stains. She looked tired, but seemed to grow prettier each minute she hung around to talk to me. I was going to have to hustle if I wanted to catch the second half of the girls' game against Grosse Pointe South like I'd planned. It started at seven and I still needed to run home and shower, grab a sandwich somewhere. Maybe I could ask Olivia for a ride and save myself fifteen minutes.

Then again, my t-shirt was basically a bag of sweat. She didn't want that in her car.

"You set a lot of records," she said.

"Ancient history."

"I have two kids—" her voice caught. "Let me try that again. I have two *students* this semester who've been sent to rehab for heroin use. Supposedly, their parents had no idea. Now I have a third kid—I was just reading tonight, a poem —well, here, let me read it to you."

She picked up her bag and dug around for the folder she

was looking for. I remembered the barista with track marks. She'd said she recognized Sanders Bolgim but couldn't recall where she'd seen him. Was he a junkie? Doubtful. Somebody at the co-op would have known. Money and electronics would have disappeared. Sanders was a kid who rarely drank. A dealer? Is that what he did for money, since he had no job? Is that why Danny Root said he looked nervous?

Again, I was skeptical. If, as Karen and I suspected, the fire wasn't an accident and Take-Home Tailgate was a scam, then somebody had created a sophisticated operation to murder the kid. Why do that for a user? Or a two-bit dealer?

"Ah, I got it," Olivia said. "You ready?"

I nodded.

Turns out, I wasn't.

Even though her voice was quiet, Olivia read with startling intensity. It was just the two of us in the hot, dimly-lit wrestling room, but her face was filled with emotion and I felt like I was in an alley crawling with rats and zoned-out high school kids with needles stuck in their ankles.

I'm riding the horse and nobody can stop me
I'm riding the horse and I'm soaring
I'm fucking her for the horse and it's getting darker
I'm riding the horse from my balls to my brain to my feet
I'm riding the horse in a dirty motel room with fifteen other people.
I'm nodding out in the bathroom. I'm fucking him for the horse
and it's almost daylight
I'm wearing nobody's clothes
I'm working nobody's job
I'm tapping my arm for a vein
I'm sliding in the needle

I'm nodding out under the bridge
I'm hearing nobody's music
I'm nodding out in the tunnel
I'm tasting nobody's fucking baked ham at the family dinner
I'm fucking myself for the horse
I'm riding the horse and I'm nobody now
I'm nobody.
I'm nobody.
Now, I'm nobody.

"Wow," I said, "that sounds really desperate."

Olivia didn't answer. Seemed to need a moment to drift out of the voice she was using to read the poem.

"We were doing an exercise with repetition," she finally said. "Pick a couple phrases and work them into the poem two or three different times. Use a first-person voice that may or may not actually be your own. Obviously, this writer succeeded. I thought it was terrifying. It's a side of Ann Arbor I don't know about."

"You think the kid might be making it up? Trying to get attention from his peers? You said it could be in a voice not his own."

"Possibly, but it doesn't seem like it. There's an honesty that feels real. He's a good kid, quiet, not the kind who generally seeks the spotlight. But he's missed some class lately. In fact, the day we did the exercise was the only time I saw him last week."

"What do you do when you get something like this? Call the parents?"

"I'm supposed to send an email to his counselor. Technically, she can handle it from there and inform his parents, but that doesn't feel right to me. Usually, when a student writes something this dramatic, it's a way of revealing something to an adult he trusts. So it seems like I should be the one to tell his parents, or his mom, actually. I don't think his dad's around. I'm dreading making the call. It won't be easy."

"I bet."

"I'm not sure of the legal ramifications either. Is the kid committing a crime? That's why I came down to talk to you."

"And here I was thinking you just wanted to get to know me better."

She smiled. Was there the hint of a blush?

"Is he in trouble?" she asked.

"It sounds like he is, right? The drugs, possible sexual exploitation. I'm not going to swoop in and arrest him based on a poem if that's what you're worried about, but I'd like to talk to him. See what's going on. Can you make me a copy of this?"

"I can do that in the office on the way out."

"You did the right thing showing it to me. If there's a surge in opioids among teenagers, that's not a joke. We need to find out who's spreading it around."

"You know Tammy Binder?"

"Of course." Tammy was on the team with Jenna and Lisa. She was a grade younger and didn't get off the bench much because she wasn't quick enough. Played tenacious defense. Just got beat sometimes because she was too slow. Nice kid. Used to come over and bake brownies with the girls. Parents went through a nasty divorce last season.

"She's one of the kids in rehab."

"You're kidding."

"Wish I were. Rumor is she was also supplying other students. She's only fifteen, you know, because she skipped a grade. Has maturity issues but I never thought she'd be involved in hard drugs."

I hadn't either. Why hadn't Karen said anything to me? Or the girls?

"Come on. I'll walk you out. You can give me the photocopy."

Olivia's stride was brisk, even with the overstuffed bag once again hanging from her shoulder. I struggled to keep up, my left knee locking and unlocking with each step. In the parking lot, she thanked me for talking to her as she opened the back door to her car and tossed her bag on the seat. She drove a Prius the color of her mahogany t-shirt, with a dent above the rear fender and a bunch of bumper stickers on the back that said things like, "Any book worth banning is a book worth reading."

She unfolded a piece of paper from her pocket, an agenda from an old staff meeting, and wrote her name and phone number in handwriting as sloppy as a doctor's. I could barely make it out. "Let me know if anything happens with Kevin, okay? Despite what the poem seems to suggest, he's a really good kid."

"Okay," I said, "but hold off on calling his parents. Give me a couple days to follow up before you talk to his mom. I'll probably find out more if he doesn't expect me to come see him."

She hesitated for a moment.

"I don't want to be the one who gets him in trouble."

"The idea," I said, "is to keep him out of it."

Jenna scored three goals and assisted on a fourth, scored by Lisa. With ninety seconds left and Pioneer ahead 5-2, the Grosse Pointe coach called time-out. After circling his team around him to discuss strategy, he inserted into the game a mammoth girl who could have been Hugo's twin sister. Up to now, she'd been sitting glumly on the bench. It was an odd move since he substituted her for the player who'd scored both goals for them, but that girl had also been tasked with guarding Jenna, a job at which she failed remarkably, so I kind of got it.

And then, because I arrest too many people who appear totally indifferent to the effect of their crimes on the remainder of the human population, the true plan hit me, and I felt sick.

I tried to signal to Karen what I was thinking, hoping she'd call her own time-out and prevent the carnage from happening, but she didn't see me and it was too late anyway. Lisa forced a quick turnover and passed the ball to Jenna sprinting up the right side of the field. The large girl—who moved surprisingly quickly for her size—didn't run at an angle to put herself between Jenna and the goalie, as most defenders would. She aimed directly for Jenna herself. Jenna, sensing the girl's approach, passed back to Lisa, but the girl didn't reverse her path and follow the ball. Instead, she kept coming, then, just before impact, crouched like an offensive lineman and exploded upward, hurling her massive shoulders into Jenna's chest.

My daughter flew backward for what seemed about eight feet in the air, landed on the turf, and slid another ten. The referee blew her whistle and the Pioneer trainer ran out toward Jenna, who sat up and shook her head groggily. Karen ran toward the other coach, yelling and pointing her finger. I watched Lisa and felt sicker.

Amidst the chaos of Karen shouting and the additional barking of parents and students in the stands, my other daughter isolated the big girl and did exactly what I would have done. In fact, the sickest part of me was cheering her on. As the big girl loomed over Jenna on the ground Lisa reached up, grabbed her ponytail and yanked her face within range, then clocked her with a right cross. The crack of fist to jaw was audible above the shouts. It sounded like a car accident.

The girl collapsed as if her legs had been hacked off at the knees and slammed to the ground.

She did not slide.

Not an inch.

The aftermath was swift. Both Lisa and the Grosse Pointe South girl were thrown out of the game and, by league rules, would have to miss the next one too. In Lisa's case, the point was moot since Karen suspended her from the team for two weeks. No games, no practice, nothing. "I don't want to see your pretty face," she told her. "Not for one second."

Since I hadn't had time to eat before the game—and to cheer the girls up following Lisa's banishment from the team—I took them to Zingerman's Roadhouse for a late dinner. It was crowded so we ate at the bar.

"Karen's right," I said to Lisa while we were waiting for our food. "You can't let your emotions get the best of you. You've got to be able to control yourself." I didn't say *unlike your dad, who disqualified himself from an NCAA championship.*

On the television above the bartender's head, our governor, Bill Lambright, was holding a press conference to announce another corporate tax cut. He had a manicured coif of thick blond curls that had to be a dye job and an expensive pinstripe suit. Like most public servants, I was not a fan. Our department had seen a slew of early retirements since he'd taken office and we hadn't hired anyone to replace them. So far, we'd managed to avoid layoffs but the force was still shrinking due to attrition and the lack of new blood was hurting us. You need at least a handful of novices around so we older folk can feel like we have a measure of wisdom to share. Granted, Karen and I spend a lot of time with high school kids so I don't totally feel like an extinct species, but I'd still been blind-sided by what Olivia said about heroin. Maybe somebody younger would have noticed something sooner.

The bartender brought us a basket of fresh-baked sourdough, which at Zingerman's, was akin to a benediction. Lisa tore into a piece as if she hadn't eaten since she turned into a teenager.

"What do you think about what your sister did?" I said to Jenna.

She didn't answer right away, which isn't unusual for her, so I wasn't worried about her having a concussion. I could feel her thinking as I smelled the bread steaming under its napkin. The governor wrapped up his speech by urging the good people of Michigan to vote *Yes for Education Fairness!* because every child in our state deserved a chance for success, and then coverage switched to a story about a trio of autoworkers who'd been busted selling weed before their shifts at a Ford plant. The reporter asked a spokesperson why their union was protecting them from being fired.

"Nobody's defending rogue behavior," the spokesperson said, "but there's a process that needs to be followed. After the process runs its course, we will determine our direction in regard to whether to initiate a new process."

No wonder everybody hates unions.

"I think I can fight my own battles," Jenna finally said. "I also think my sister is the most amazing person in the world."

Lisa put her arms around Jenna and hugged her.

It's impossible to describe how much I loved them both.

"And that, ladies and gentlemen," the reporter said to the camera as he wrapped up his story, "is why the President had to use your tax-dollars to bail out the auto industry." Completely ignoring the fact that Ford didn't take any federal money during last decade's debt crisis.

Instead of throwing my glass of home-brewed herbal iced tea through the TV screen, I asked the girls why I hadn't seen Tammy on the field.

"She's not on the team right now," Lisa said.

"Did she get in a fight too?"

The girls looked at each other. "I hate when you ask a question when you already know the answer," Jenna said. "You're violating the agreement."

Busted.

We'd made a pact when the girls entered high school that I'd never treat them as informants and interrogate them about their friends. Their half of the deal was to come to me on their own if they ever discovered anything important enough for me to know. I was supposed to trust their judgment. Most of the time, I did.

"Heroin's serious," I said.

"We *know*, Dad," Lisa said with the kind of eye-roll that made me temporarily love her a little less. "And we didn't know about it until today, either. Coach told us right before the game. That's why—" She stopped.

"That's why what?"

"Nothing. I was pissed off, that's all. I shouldn't have hit that girl. I'm not going to make excuses."

"We're both angry, Dad," Jenna said. "The point is we *should've* known. Tammy missed a bunch of practices, but we all thought she was still upset from when her boyfriend broke up with her."

It never failed to astonish me how such talented, high-achieving young women could go to pieces over their boyfriends, half of whom were the kind of mopes who had no greater ambition than to wind up like the autoworkers in the story, getting stoned before work in a parking lot.

"We were shitty friends," Lisa said. "We should have talked to her more."

"Karen didn't know either?"

"She found out right before she told us. She said we wouldn't be able to contact Tammy right now, but at some point, she'd be able to take calls and then we should reach out to her. She's probably going to miss most of the season but Coach said she'd need friends more than ever when she gets back. She told us to take care of each other, that was the most important thing."

"Have you heard anything else about heroin? Lots of kids doing it?"

Jenna shook her head. "I don't think so. Maybe some of the hipsters."

"I heard a piece in creative writing class," Lisa said.

"The one with all the repetition in it?"

The girls looked a question at me.

"Ms. Waterman came to see me at the end of practice. She read it to me."

"She went into the *wrestling room?*" Lisa asked.

"Did she throw up?" Jenna asked.

"Not funny. Nor was the poem."

The newscast came back from a car commercial with the sports guy. His hair looked similar to the Governor's. He started with a story about a Lions running back with an ankle injury.

"Actually," Lisa said, "I think it was a different piece."

"*Two* kids in your class are writing about heroin?"

"Could have been the same kid writing about it more than once. The hockey players write about hockey every time."

The sports guy moved on to previewing Michigan's upcoming game at Iowa. The Hawkeyes had a defensive end projected as a first-round draft pick. LeBannon Williams would be scrambling all afternoon.

"But you've never seen it?" I asked the girls. "At a party or anything? The poem referenced a motel room, and a bridge people hang out underneath and something about tunnels. Any of that make sense to you?"

Jenna shook her head.

"Maybe the railroad bridge downtown," Lisa suggested, "with the graffiti?"

I knew that bridge. That'd be a good place to start.

"What'd you think of Ms. Waterman?" Jenna asked.

"I've met her before. It was pretty cool when she read the poem. I can see why you guys like her."

I didn't say she'd given me her number, albeit not for social reasons.

"And finally, from Ann Arbor," the sportscaster said, "a high-school field hockey game turned into a boxing match when the daughter of a local police detective punched an opponent in the face."

All three of us stared at the screen.

"We have amateur video from a cell phone," the sportscaster continued. "Be prepared, the images are graphic."

The clip started with Lisa throwing her stick to the turf. It didn't show Jenna getting hit. You couldn't even see her on the ground. All you saw was Lisa grabbing the big girl's ponytail, pulling her fist back and cold-cocking her jaw. The girl fell out of the frame as if a sea serpent had coiled around her ankles and wrenched her underwater.

They showed the video three times. Then cut back to the main anchor saying, "Wow, Bob, that's disturbing. I had no idea girls' sports were so violent."

"Here's the irony," Bob the sports guy said from beneath his shiny hair-helmet. "The police detective who's the father of that girl? It's James Harrow. The guy who was disqualifi— "

I looked away from the screen and none of us talked. The silence was a giant fishing net with no holes.

"Can you change the station?" I asked the bartender as he handed us our meals.

The girls split a large spinach salad. I had oven-baked macaroni with Wisconsin cheddar, caramelized onions and applewood smoked bacon.

We ate. I pretended I could taste the food.

Lisa spoke, her eyes glued to her plate.

"I'm sorry," she said.

"It's not your fault some idiot was filming, or that the news loves bullshit."

CHAPTER SEVEN

BY THE TIME we got to the car, the story was leading on Treetown.com.

The image of Lisa's fist connecting to the other girl's jaw had been frozen into a still photo, though a link to the video on YouTube was also available.

At least the story mentioned Lisa's punch was in response to the nasty check on Jenna. Karen had so far made herself unavailable for comment but the Grosse Pointe coach said, "The whole incident was an unfortunate situation where players on both teams used poor judgment. Nobody's a bad guy here. They're all good athletes and good people."

Nice try, Bub. Tell me you didn't direct your player to blindside Jenna.

The rest of the story identified Lisa as my daughter and rehashed my many failings. Pioneer was looking into further disciplinary action against Lisa. There were already forty-seven comments in the feedback section, which I didn't read.

Never read the comments.

By next morning, Lisa's video on YouTube had already spawned nine thousand views. One of Lisa's classmates had even made a companion video, a mash-up called "Field Hockey Gyrrrrrl vs. Mike Tyson" featuring Lisa's fist connecting to the former champion's jaw, his face shattering like a flower vase dropped onto a cement patio. The piece was set to LL Cool J's "Mama Said Knock You Out," except "daddy" had been dubbed in for "mama."

Cute.

Lisa never made it out of the parking lot on her way into school. Two assistant principals escorted her to the office. She was suspended for five days. "Don't let this be the thing people remember you for," I told her when she texted me.

Karen was also suspended from coaching, pending a meeting at the end of the week with the athletic director, the principal, and the superintendent.

We commenced the remainder of our lovely day in Chief Taylor's office.

"We don't need this shit," she said.

I have a lot of respect for Aricka Taylor. She's smart and fair. Grew up in Detroit. Went to law school. Graduated and then went to the police academy. Did it, she said, "because Detroit is a city with too much heart to die and I want to help it live."

She walked a beat for five years then became a detective and eventually a homicide chief. She said she'd return to Detroit after she got experience running a smaller city. She also had a daughter who was President of Pioneer's nationally renowned Theater Guild and her son played soccer at Tappan Middle School.

It didn't escape me that her stint living here coincided with the key developmental years of her children.

"I've already fielded ten calls demanding to know how two detectives can have enough time to moonlight as high school coaches," she said. "They're threatening to vote against the millage to fund the station remodel. Said they'll support any initiative to keep cutting staff unless both of you are fired."

"Do they know we work overnights during football weekends?" Karen said.

"I told them that. They didn't seem pacified."

"It's the same gang of dickwads who write comments on Treetown," I said. "They're just bitter because they live in a community where no one buys their rightwing quackery."

"I thank you not to use that particular insult in my presence, Detective Harrow."

"Rightwing quackery?"

"You know what I meant. And you've got other problems. The kid whose face you decorated with a beer pitcher hired a lawyer and is suing the department. Says he gets headaches and can't concentrate. Claims to be failing his classes because of your defensive maneuver."

"He didn't, all of a sudden, start failing classes this week. He's failing because he's a drunken moron."

"Doesn't matter. It's another hassle we have to deal with. I'm half-tempted to cuff you to your desk for a month just to avoid any additional fuckups."

I looked out the window of the chief's office into the greater squad room where I could see my desk. On top of it sat a pair of clown-sized boxing gloves, a gift from fellow detective Johnburt Standish, along with a note that said "For self-defense during family arguments."

Funny guy, that Johnburt Standish.

"As it is," Chief Taylor said, "I'm cutting short your investigation. You've got, essentially, speculation and nothing substantial, some guy named Jarrold who collects contest forms and your nurse buddy who says the deceased might have looked nervous when he was walking around by himself late at night. That's not enough."

She flipped through the reports Karen and I wrote about yesterday's progress. Even before Lisa thumped the Grosse Pointe girl, Karen's day had been as frustrating as mine. She'd spent hours trying to research what Sanders Bolgim had been working on and been thoroughly stymied. He had no social media presence, no published research online, nothing she could find hiding up in the cloud. Nobody in the School of Education wanted to talk either. The few who said anything claimed not to know what the kid's exact project was and pointed her to his thesis adviser, currently on sabbatical and unreachable, thought to be backpacking in Nepal.

She'd also had no luck finding Sanders' work hideaway. She confirmed he didn't have an office, and nobody at any of the libraries, or at the Fishbowl, could remember seeing him.

"I can't have staff wasting shifts poking around an accidental fire based on so little," Chief Taylor reiterated. "Not when we've got everybody looking at both of you with a microscope wondering how we're spending the people's tax dollars. I'm getting lots of complaints about home invasions on the West Side. People are breaking in and stealing flatscreens and laptops. I've got three different neighborhood associations demanding we devote more resources."

"Can't you put Standish on it?" Karen asked, at risk of his smacking her later with the oversized boxing gloves. She and Johnburt hadn't gotten along for years, since he'd gotten smashed at our annual barbecue at Allmendinger Park and pawed her while she was pushing Jenna and Lisa on the swings. She'd put her knee into his crotch and he'd vomited into an oil-drum trashcan. Nobody else in the department knew what happened except me because I'd had to drive him home. He basically cried the whole time. His wife had been having an affair and was leaving him for a geology professor. I refrained from joking about how the guy was probably rocking her world, or that she was getting his rocks off. In fact, I empathized, since Molly had recently told me she was unhappy and had also met someone she was interested in getting to know better. Thus, even though Johnburt's sense of humor was bleak, we continued to share a kind of cuckolded-cop kinship, which was awkward since Karen continued to dislike him.

"Already is on it," the chief said. "Gumpert too. Look, I appreciate you two think something's wrong with the fire, but you're telling me this party company doesn't exist? Somebody created a shell corporation just so they could kill a PhD student? That's absurd. The party, after all, actually took place. The company was legit enough to make it happen. Previous parties too, right?"

"What about the sketchy website and phone system?" I asked. "Can't we at least have True North check them out, see if they were intentionally set up as a feedback loop to nowhere?"

Truevayne Norowitz, whom we called True North, was our resident cyber-genius. He probably could have cracked the Take-Home Tailgate website in two minutes.

The chief shook her head. "He's busy with the library funds embezzlement case. The DA wants an arrest by Friday. True's tied up 'til then."

"This thing stinks," I said. "Why would a company claim to sell blowout parties but make it impossible to purchase one?"

"Maybe they shut everything down after the fire because they're afraid of a lawsuit."

That sounded plausible.

"Can't you just give us today?" Karen said. "Like you originally planned? If we can't find anything—"

Her plea was interrupted by the theme song from *Gilligan's Island* emanating from the pocket in her sweatshirt, which was underneath a fisherman's type sweater.

"Tell me you didn't come to this meeting with your phone on," Chief Taylor said.

"I'm waiting for a call from Roland." Karen checked the screen. "Can I take it?"

Annoyed, Aricka shooed her out of the room with a backhand air slap, then turned toward me.

"Can you enlighten me, Detective Fuckup, as to why I have three messages this morning from that buckethead Burkett at Treetown?"

"The Public Service Officer's not screening calls?"

The stare she gave me could have sliced a diamond.

"Sorry, I blew it. I was trying to get information."

"You said the fire was a homicide investigation?"

"I may have suggested it was possibly one, I think."

"It's not. It *was* a preliminary inquiry into whether we should undertake an investigation. Now it's not even that. He said he's going to post a story this afternoon claiming a respected AAPD detective thinks the kid got murdered, unless he hears otherwise from me. He's *going* to hear otherwise from me. With the millage next week, we can't afford to have the city hysterical because we said somebody's killing students when it turns out we've got an accidental death. I'm shutting this thing down."

"You might want to rethink that decision," Karen said, ducking back into the office. "The tox screen came in. Bolgim was stumbling drunk like everyone said, but that's not all. His blood shows significant levels of GHB."

Thank God for Dr. Roland Roethke, Washtenaw County Medical Examiner. You'd never know it looking at him, but the guy knew what he was doing. He was nearly fifty but looked twelve. He was about five-foot-two with a wild bush of brown hair, a pair of ruddy cheeks and a slouching happy-go-lucky manner that made it seem like he was perpetually stoned. He moved and talked with the laconic ease of the long-term jobless and tended to wear beat-up basketball sneakers and faded t-shirts featuring lesser-known *Sesame Street* characters such as The Amazing Mumford.

He also never made mistakes. If he said there was GHB in Sanders Bolgim's blood, there was GHB in Sanders Bolgim's blood.

"Doesn't matter," Chief Taylor said. "My decision stands."

"But the kid was drugged," Karen protested.

"So are dozens of other students every weekend. You're telling me it's not hormone central around here? All the drug tells us is maybe your dark-haired mystery girl wanted him zonked. Doesn't mean it's connected to the party company. Doesn't mean he was murdered. Doesn't even mean she was the one who put the stuff in his drink. Who knows what cup he picked up and swigged?"

"But that makes no sense," I said. "By all reports a big night for this guy is when he orders a quad instead of a triple at Blimpy's. I'm betting the last time he saw a female sex organ was when he came out of one. Why would a supposedly mega-hot girl need GHB to get a guy like that to bang her?"

"Maybe—if it even was her—she wanted to rob him?" Aricka suggested.

"A grad student who basically lived in a closet?"

"Look," Karen said, "the woman Bolgim was with didn't drug him so she could sleep with him, or rob him. I know it sounds crazy, but she drugged him so he'd pass out and sleep through the fire. That's why, when Nash and

Kaitlyn were kicking his door and yelling at him, he didn't respond."

Chief Taylor shuffled through our notes again, appearing to consider Karen's theory. Even when she was hacked off at us, even when we were being juvenile and embarrassing ourselves, she was willing to envision a scenario where her top two detectives might be onto something.

"All right," she said, her shoulders slumping in defeat like a parent about to let her kid eat ice cream despite his failing to do more than nibble at his asparagus. "I'm giving you twenty-four hours to keep this case alive, but that's it. I'll talk with Burkett, try to stall him, probably have to promise him an exclusive if anything juicy turns up."

She didn't have to tell us how much she hated negotiating with a sleazy prick like Burkett, who probably drank fourteen-dollar mochas. "And, Harrow, keep your damn mouth shut. We can't have another situation like when those kids ended up owning the whorehouse after we dredged the swamp. You remember all the accusations of wasted man hours? City Council, in case you forgot, cut our budget by two patrolmen after that."

She made a sweeping gesture toward the squad room, arcing her hand in a curve to encompass our shabby walls suffused with the odor of old coffee and cigarettes, the water stains in the ceiling's asbestos-laced tiles, the decade-old boxy computers that growled and clunked on our battered desks. "We need this remodel to move into the twenty-first century. Do not give the voting public a reason to dislike us. You understand me, Harrow? Do *not* fuck this up."

"*Gilligan's Island* ringtone?"

Karen sneered and kept walking at a hurried pace, her jaw jutting in front of her like the blade of a snowplow. We were cutting across the Diag on our way to East Quad. It had grown distinctly colder, not just the air, but Karen's demeanor. Beyond our little tiff in the chief's office, I wondered if she blamed me for Lisa's unpredictable temper, or for her own subsequent coaching suspension.

"I used to have a crush on the Professor," she said without lightness, a sort of hiss from the side of her mouth.

"I would've figured you more for the Skipper. He was brave and sure, much like someone else you know and love."

She stopped.

"Look, Jim, we need you to stay focused."

We were standing outside Hatcher Graduate Library, where a dozen students floated past, each oblivious to their surroundings, every one of them texting.

"I'm sorry. I didn't realize I couldn't joke about old television characters. Did you know, by the way, the Professor was actually a high school science teacher, not a university professor? Also, in case you're wondering, I didn't teach Lisa how to grab someone's ponytail in order to slug her."

"This is bullshit. You need to stop acting like you have some sort of claim on me."

"Pardon?"

"We meet to talk about a case and you treat it like it's a date. You think you have some smug idea about the kind of person I'm interested in. We don't have the same brain, all right? Back off."

The sky was threatening to become the kind of grey that marries Michigan from late November to May, an oppressive weight that feels like an unshakeable bad mood. I didn't deserve Karen's fury.

"You want another partner," I said, "get another fucking

partner. In the meantime, whatever shit you're going through, don't take it out on me."

She started walking, even brisker than before, then stopped again, and turned with one hand on her hip, the other pointing a finger at my face the same way she did to the Grosse Pointe coach. Any student who looked up from texting would have thought she was a mother scolding her child.

"Let me ask you something," she said. "When we were at that stop sign yesterday and that woman walked past us? Looked like she had her clothes on from the night before? I'll bet you thought she was regretting what she'd just woken up from, that she wished whatever she just did she hadn't done. Tell me you didn't feel that way."

I shrugged, knowing where this was going. Two kids with tape guns were hanging posters on the kiosks surrounding the plaza that advertised tutoring for GREs and LSATs. Guaranteed a triple-digit rise in your score or your parents' money back.

"You think this city is the happiest place on earth," Karen said, "but only because you're the designated savior of every female in it. Well, guess what? You can't protect us from every dirtbag and you can't smash every potential date rapist in the face with a beer pitcher. Maybe that girl was anxious because she had to go to track practice. Maybe she *loved* what she did the night before. Maybe she did it with another woman. Or maybe she didn't do any goddamn thing at all. Sometimes I feel like you make all these bullshit assumptions because you believe any woman who's not dating either you or Mike Bednarsky is committing a colossal blunder that will permanently torpedo her life."

"Wrong. Dating Mikey would be a blunder too. He doesn't understand losing like I do. No empathy."

"Not funny."

"Karen, don't tell me you're buying into this soundbite that Lisa punched that girl because she wants to be just like her father."

"Now you're wrong, Detective Fuckup. Lisa doesn't want to be just like her father. She only wants to prove to her mother that her take-no-shit dad was the best thing that ever happened to her and she screwed up epically by divorcing him."

Two white women in their late fifties walked past. Both had rolled-up yoga mats tucked into canvas bags hanging from their shoulders. Each sported a mass of grey hair contained by a funky hand-knitted hat, circa Greenwich Village 1982. One mauve, the other taupe.

"You're not worried about Lisa, are you?" I said.

"Angry at her, yes. Worried about her, no."

"Tammy then?"

I didn't know what prompted me to ask that, maybe it was the guys still at it with the tape guns, spreading the gospel of test-prep specialists. Maybe it was the weight of the sky, maybe it was Karen's calves humming like eight-cylinder engines inside her boots.

Her face sagged and for a moment I thought I saw what she'd look like in fifteen years, how the fist the world swung would sometimes connect. How she couldn't duck everything.

"I don't understand how I didn't know."

"How *we* didn't know, you mean."

"I saw her every day, Jim. When she didn't show up for practice, I didn't call home. Didn't follow up in any way. Maybe the critics are right. Maybe we shouldn't be doing two jobs."

"Karen, you're the best cop I know and the best coach anyone's ever seen. Like you just said, nobody can be everybody's savior."

She shook her head. Any hint of face sag had vanished.

"What I said, Jim, was you need to stop thinking every woman who doesn't date you is messing up both her life and the cosmic tilt of the universe. Listen, I've known Tammy since she was eight years old and playing Rec & Ed with a ten-dollar used stick. I've seen her crying with two bloody elbows and third-degree turf burn. I've seen her sleeping on six-hour bus rides with her mouth wide open like she trusted every molecule of air to love her. I've seen her run harder and longer than she ever believed she could and I've seen her get beat by a slick center forward and gaze at the ground as if the planet had spun in the wrong direction and fooled her feet just to make her feel too fat and too slow. There's no way I shouldn't have seen she was sticking needles in her arm."

I felt weary all of a sudden. Maybe my own face was sagging.

The kids posting fliers made a screeching sound as they stretched fifteen feet of tape around a kiosk and I wanted to grab the two of them by their ears and bounce their heads together like basketballs.

"So let's do what we need to buy ourselves some time on the Bolgim case, then go bust whoever's selling heroin to our children."

"Agreed," Karen said, "but then I really need to think about whether I can keep doing all this, and if I can't, which do I give up, the job or the team?"

"Meaning whom do you quit on, right? Me, or my daughters?"

Karen started walking again.

Didn't answer.

Jarrold was bored.

He'd been promised there'd be more jobs, but waiting

was no fun. Not after the high of what he'd just done, and not in his nondescript apartment in the nondescript mid-sized town where he pretended to be the kind of person who went to mediocre sandwich shops and ordered lukewarm soup. He did enjoy visiting the ATM every morning. It was satisfying to check his balance and admire its size.

But what could he spend the money on?

He had no friends to speak of.

He couldn't take a vacation. His employers might call at any time. Tell him he had a new assignment. Then what? He'd have to drop the tropical woman he was holding, drop his fruity drink with the paper umbrella, then hustle off to whatever school they wanted him to go to and start planning.

Plus, he was trying to save his money. He had only another year or two where he could blend in on college campuses. After that, he'd have to find something else to do. Maybe he could do similar work with young go-getters on Wall Street, get rid of whomever needed downsizing, but did he really want to? Did he really want to kill people his whole life? Was that a sustainable way to make a living?

He most assuredly did not want to. He wanted what he was doing to be a phase, a young man's foolish—if lucrative—follies to be put away and forgotten. Like anyone else, he wanted a family. Wanted to invest his savings in a cutting-edge beverage boutique, with exotic teas, and with a martial arts center and weight room. A place where he could settle down, and own a house not too far away from his teashop, and raise some boys not to be nerds. Teach them how to be tough guys, outstanding beer pong players.

Beer pong!

He missed the frenzy. Practicing at home now, without any impending party on the schedule, was too dull. He knew he needed to keep his skills sharp, so he still played with ping-pong balls as faithfully as he spent hours at the gym, but the plunk of ball into cup in his empty apartment sounded hollow.

It had only been a couple days, but he already missed Ann Arbor. What a playground. What a place for him to find himself, to grant himself a do-over and live the kind of college dream life he'd never had.

The truth, though, was he didn't miss those college girls he could so easily slip out of their panties. He missed Monique.

Not just the sex, though that had been tireless and her skin had smelled like a gooey cinnamon roll. He'd enjoyed her even when she wore clothes. When he'd taken her to breakfast at the gourmet deli and paid for her seventeen-dollar organically farmed corned beef hash, and then explained to her what he needed her to do, he'd loved just looking at her, spending leisure time with her, and found himself mumbling, bumbling in his speech, unsure whether he could really request what he intended.

She'd laughed, the music of her guffaw the kind that attracts other guffaws so that a three-year-old brat who'd been whining to her mother that the potatoes on her plate weren't crunchy enough, stopped whining and started chuckling and the mother flashed Monique a look that said thank you, my morning is better because of you and your joy.

"Is that what you're saying?" Monique had asked, still half-laughing, her eyebrows raised like a garage door. "You want me to hook up with this pathetic geek boy?"

"Why not? You hooked up with that professor."

"Please." She laughed again. "He was cute *and* married. A double bonus."

The mom heard that remark too, and looked at Monique in a different way, as if she'd like to stab her with a bread knife. Then she yanked her three-year-old by the wrist and hauled her out of the deli, the girl bawling and unsuccessfully reaching for a last slice of sea salt cured bacon from the plate she was being forced to abandon.

"Looks like you pissed off the wife of a cheating professor," Jarrold said.

"Not my fault she makes everyone around her as miserable as she's making her daughter."

In that moment, Jarrold felt Monique's fingerprints from the night before on his chest, a palimpsest that jolted his heart. Lord, he wanted a woman like her to settle down with, a woman who wasn't apologetic and wasn't afraid to make other, less prettier women angry.

"You don't actually have to hook up with the nerd boy," he said. "You just have to get him smashed, and make sure he winds up in his room."

"*Can* I hook up with him if I want to?"

"Not my business."

Three high school students had breezed in then, all boys, loud and confident, two of them wearing t-shirts advertising an underground hip-hop group that looked like a conglomeration of rich, white college kids with Jew-fros and undeclared majors. The boys each carried expensive coffees and were tall and slim, the boisterous curls of their hair smothered by backward baseball hats. They were talking about the Arboretum—"the Arb"—as if it were a holy shrine, something Jarrold had noticed Ann Arbor locals liked to do when they were planning where to spend a lazy afternoon smoking marijuana.

"What happens to the nerd afterward?" Monique had asked.

"What do you mean?"

"I mean that professor lost his job. What's the geek going to lose?"

Jarrold hadn't answered. Two girls, twins even if they didn't look exactly alike, walked in and joined the boys. The energy in the room changed immediately. Even Monique noticed it. The baristas behind the counter stopped frothing their whipped cream. The middle-aged quartet of women plotting the advent of a social justice book club forgot which injustice they were most interested in exploring. Entrepreneurs playing on their tablets looked up from their spreadsheets and remembered, for a moment, the delight of first loves. The girls, blond-haired and lithe, moved like athletes, sure of themselves, aware of the spacing of every chair, table and customer in the crowded room. Their taut thighs pushed against the skin of their shorts and they laughed like Monique, loud and free, smiling at a joke the slightly taller one made, as they slid toward the boys.

Jarrold felt like getting up and backhanding each boy in the cheekbone. Out of all the people in their vicinity, the boys appeared to be the only creatures who failed to appreciate the loveliness of the girls. They barely paid them any attention at all, miming instead the motion of squeezing the end of a joint and sucking in a hit.

"Fucking idiots," he said, shaking his head, angry at the thick smell of their coffee drinks.

"Don't hate," Monique said. "You were once like that."

Jarrold stared hard at her, seeing right through her clothes to the nipples he'd spent so long kissing the night before. She blushed, squirmed a little in her chair, and he knew she wanted him again. Right then.

"I was never like that," he said, throwing forty bucks on the table and grabbing her hand. "Not for a second. Let's go."

He could feel the eyes of both twins following him as he guided Monique out the door, his palm massaging circles between her shoulder blades.

"You don't need to worry about the nerd," he told her. "Whatever happens to him after you leave his room is not your concern."

Even then he'd known it wasn't going to be that easy.

He couldn't ask her to seduce the kid, then expect she wouldn't be freaked out when he set fire to the house. Burning that kid alive meant he was also burning any chance for a future with Monique.

At the time, he'd accepted that result. The paycheck was legit. There'd be other Moniques.

Now, two days down from the high of the operation's success, he was no longer sure. Tossing ping-pong balls into a cup with his eyes closed wasn't making him feel better. He missed her with a searing pain in the lower part of his throat. He needed to see her, explain.

The local news website was calling the fire accidental. What could it hurt to slip back into town and talk to her?

He'd messed up with Kimmie.

Poor Kimmie.

Rotting in the creek bed.

He flipped the ball he'd been holding behind his back and watched it bounce off the wall, skip once on the counter and plop in the center of the cup sitting on the table. Then he drained the cup of its beer and lolled the ball around on his tongue, careful not to crack it with his teeth.

How could he let Monique go without at least giving it his best shot?

CHAPTER EIGHT

"I WAS THINKING about the sexy dark-haired girl," I said. We were drinking coffee in Espresso Royale on South U. I was eating a maple scone that tasted like the Swiss Alps. It seemed odd there were no contest boxes for Take-Home Tailgate near any of the cash registers. In fact, even though we were close to the fraternities, I realized I hadn't seen any boxes at all on this side of town.

"I'll bet you were," Karen grumbled.

"Come on, not like that. I was thinking about how nobody took pictures at the party."

"Kaitlin and Nash said their housemates were too nerdy."

"Right, so we need to find someone not-nerdy, more of a seasoned party veteran, someone more likely to engage in social media."

"But if nobody took pictures, we don't know who else was there. It's not like they had a guest list."

I fished my phone from my pocket and pulled up the click-bait newspaper's website. "On the contrary, my dear Evans, we do know someone. This guy."

I highlighted the quotation where Jonas Warren had described Sanders Bolgim as *blasted out of his skull.*

"Tell me this dude isn't the accomplished party type we're looking for."

Karen smiled. Almost. "Should we head to the registrar's, see if they'll help us locate him? I'm not sure they're still open."

"We're about ten feet from frat house row. Fifty bucks says he's a brother somewhere. Let's knock on doors until we find him."

We found him in House number three.

Sitting on a huge manicured lawn on a side street just off Washtenaw Avenue, the Sigma Chi Omega Palace was the most opulent frat in the city. It looked like an antebellum mansion. The alabaster paint shone orange in the declining sunlight and the expansive front porch, circular and porticoed with fifty-foot Ionic columns, made the place resemble a taller, more obese White House. About forty wicker chairs crowded the porch, with intermittent side tables holding ashtrays stuffed with cigar butts and blunt wraps. Female students, at least those who didn't seek detailed commentary on their appearance, avoided walking past the porch.

The brothers of Sigma Chi Omega, who called themselves the Psychos, were cozily familiar with Karen and me. Over the years we'd pronounced the adjournment of countless house parties attended by underage Ann Arbor girls, some as young as middle-schoolers. We'd also broken up a sophisticated Adderall drug ring, four illegal sports-betting operations, a pseudo Fight Club in the basement which had resulted in numerous concussions and two fractured supraorbital ridges, a so-called Slave Auction fundraiser that sold the sexual services of pledges at a sister sorority, and an identity-fraud specialist who recruited his bros—at $500 a pop—to pose as high school kids and take their ACTs.

In addition, we investigated date rape accusations at least twice a month, knocking on doors that opened into bedrooms with 60-inch flatscreens and full wet bars and knowing that even if kids straight-up admitted it to our faces—as one boy once had, saying he'd *spread this girl's legs so wide it was like fucking the goalposts at the stadium and she was passed out the whole time too, a limp-ass dead fish*—none of them would ever be prosecuted. They knew it too. For the same reason they knew neither the university nor their national charter would ever shut them down. The average annual income of their parents was $1.7 million according to the bragging on their very professional-looking website. They bought people the way I bought baked goods. They were all headed to big jobs on Wall Street regardless if they ever passed a class at Michigan.

We were there so often, we had nicknames. They called Karen THC or The Hottie Cop. Me, they just called Napoleon, as in short dude who wanted to administer beat-downs and rule the continent. The governor's son had come up with the name when he'd been social chairman five years ago.

"Is there a brother named Jonas Warren who lives here?" I asked the kid who answered the door.

"Yo, Napoleon," he said by way of an answer. "Hook it up! Hook it up! I heard you smashed that blimp Morris from Tri-Delts in the face and then told him to go to the art museum. That's some mad-ass shit, Bro. Bumpity-bump, yo. You're one deranged fucking midget, Mr. Officer Napoleon Harrow. Art museum? What are you talking about, art museum? Hook it up!"

I ignored his offer of a high-five.

"You're wasting our time," Karen said. "Do you know Jonas Warren, or not?"

"J-Dubs in the Hot Tub! Hook it up! That dude's a legend. Three chicks in the hottie-hot tub. Bumpity-bump! One time! Hook it up! Hook it up!"

The Psychos boasted an exorbitant hot tub on their back porch that was capable of accommodating thirty-six people. I did not want to know what Jonas Warren had done in its bubbling foam with three girls at the same time. Nor did I want to know how many other people had been watching. I did appreciate that the brothers of Sigma Chi Omega were so nonchalant about not protecting each other from officers of the law. It was a cockiness actually, a belief we didn't have the power to do anything but deter their wanton behavior for brief intervals, a belief so far proven accurate.

"Where can we find said J-Dubs?" Karen asked. "Not in the hot tub at the moment?"

"Hottie Cop of the Ace Deuce in the hizzouse! You know I'd never lie to you, Sweet Tomato Sexy! Hook it up! I'll do it right here! Bumpity-bump! On the pizz-orch! Nappy can wait in the car. Brother Jonas is chilling in his room upstairs. Third floor. Number 309. Hearken to the smell of the sweet, sweet herb and you'll know you're near his domain. J-Dubs! Bump-bump! One time!"

We left the kid on the pizz-orch as he fired up a cigar. The inside of the house always smelled like a bar at six a.m. after a hard-driving Saturday. Two boys and one girl were passed out on the mammoth couches in the Great Room while two red-eyed brothers played a militaristic videogame on a giant flatscreen. It was the game where everyone gets to pretend to be a soldier with an AK-47 in one hand and a rocket launcher in the other and shoot at people in turbans.

The brothers high-fived each other after one scored a direct hit and separated a turbaned head from its white-robed body, sending it bouncing across the screen like a soccer ball.

The kids passed out on the couch stayed passed out.

The reek of Jonas' room was evident fifty feet before we reached it. The door was open and Bunny Wailer was playing loudly through a set of small but expensive speakers shaped like bratwursts. Jonas Warren was wearing a navy-blue golf shirt and plaid-patterned boxer shorts. His sizable phallus was visible through his fly as he leaned over his desk, a gold American Express card in his mouth, and searched for a paper to download from foolmyprofessor.com. The search box on the site said, "1990's Savings & Loan scandal."

"What you working on, J-Dubs?" Karen said, just as the boy reached inside his shorts to stroke his member.

Unstartled, he left his hand where it was and spit his credit card casually onto his desk. After pressing the mute button on his computer to silence the music, he turned his bloodshot eyes toward us. "Not your business, Hottie Cop."

"Don't worry, Jonas," I said. "We don't care about the weed and we don't care about the plagiarism, though I must admit the latter displays a distinct lack of character. We want to talk about the Take-Home Tailgate party."

He took his hand out of his boxers and put it on his hip. Then he pointed his other hand at us as if he were a back-up diva in a Motown band and began to gyrate his hips as he sang in a voice surprisingly on-key, *"I didn't start the fire. I didn't start the fire."*

Karen retrieved her phone from her pocket and started to type on it. The kid had dark hair parted neatly. His arms were skinny and hairy and he was eight inches taller than me. His lips were full and he made a saucy pout with them as he sang. He had a tattoo on the back of his left calf of a hot tub with a fat number three under it, the kind of number you could buy at a grocery store to stick in a toddler's birthday cake.

If he ever got within a hundred yards of my daughters, I would beat him with both fists.

While waiting for his dance to play itself out, I looked around the room. His television seemed smaller than normal for a Psycho brother, maybe only fifty-six inches. His king-sized bed was neatly made. There were no bookshelves or books anywhere. Much of the room appeared to be a shrine to his favorite plant, with five framed paintings of cannabis leaves dotting the wall not taken up by the TV. A bong the size of a medium-sized child sat in one corner, the water in its base the color of roadside slush. Centered on the headboard above his bed, a sterling silver sculpture of another pot leaf was at least two feet high and looked like it was worth several thousand dollars. He saw me gazing at it and said, "It's an original Molvoran. One of four in the world. Valued at a hundred grand. At least."

A hundred grand?

I hated this silver-spooned fuckboy with his fake-tanned legs and tattoo he deserved to be beat up for. I felt like sticking the pointy leaf of his pot sculpture into his ear canal. My hatred was growing tangible and eating the air in the room and Karen knew it and glared at me to calm down. I didn't want to calm down. Above the transom was a framed photo of the two Business School jerkoffs standing in front of their brothel, arms around the shoulders of blonde girls who looked twelve. Hanging from each of the upper corners of the photo was a pair of satin thong underwear, one sky blue, the other mint green.

"Those guys weren't Sigmas," I blurted as I turned my chin toward the picture. "They didn't even go here for undergrad. Why are they on your wall?"

"Are you kidding?" Jonas Warren said as if I were a five-year-old. "They're heroes, man. You need to follow them on Twitter. You know how many girls they get? Like ridiculous-looking models who say the funniest shit because they can't even speak English. I mean the hottest fucking million-dollar models in Siberia. You don't even know, man. You don't even know."

I was on the verge of professing to Jonas exactly how bountiful was my desire to hurl him through his window when Karen stepped between us.

"Listen, J-Dubs," she said. "We get you're the big ladies' man here. We're not trying to hold that against you."

"You can hold anything you want against me, Hotness."

"Not today, Jonas, we just want to talk."

"That's good, Hottie, because it seems like Napoleon Pygmy is about to go ham on my ass. I don't want that crazy police brutality motherfucker trying to murder me because he gots that little man complex."

"Don't worry," Karen said. "I'll keep my partner in check. We just want to ask you some questions about the party."

Jonas, whom I was beginning to understand, was high out of his mind, jumped up and down, his junk flopping in and out of his boxers, and shouted in a fake Mexican accent, *"Questions! I don't need no stinking questions!"*

"Jonas," I said, "settle down."

He stopped jumping and jostled his shoulders, then walked toward me and put his finger in my face. When he spoke, his voice had grown deeper and switched to an attempt at an urban accent, something faux African-American mixed, I think, with Native Hawaiian. "Don't be violatin' my rights, bruh. If y'all two don't jump off my jock right now, my pops is about to sue you for harassment. We got some expensive lawyers too, bruh. They mob deep."

"That's not going to happen," Karen said. Her voice was the one she used at halftime when she didn't like the effort she saw from her athletes, the one that made every kid in the locker room swallow any potential question and ask it inward. "Seems like your father's lawyers have their hands full."

She turned the screen of her phone toward Jonas. "Let's assume the *pops* you're talking about is one Walter Wallace Warren—otherwise known as Dot Warren because of the WWW—currently serving twenty-one months in upstate New York for insider trading. Doesn't look like he'll be suing anyone anytime soon. We've got you caught in the act of downloading a paper for a finance class you're probably failing. If we search this room, how much pot are we going to find? It is most definitely in your best interest, Brother J-Dubs, to answer our questions. Jim, would you agree?"

"I would. Jonas, the quicker you answer, the quicker you can go back to worshipping your original Mol-doughboy."

"Molvoran."

"Sorry, so did you know Sanders Bolgim, the kid who died in the fire?"

"Why would I know a loser like that?"

"Jonas..." Karen waggled her finger.

"Nah, I didn't know him. I just went to the party because I saw the banner and that means free beer and I figured there'd be girls there. They were heinous though. I mean, *gorilla-ugly* with that fucking sundress hippie look. Like, shoot me with an Uzi if I ever stick it into a swamp rat like that. I only noticed the Sanders dude because he was a monster geek with one of the few hot girls at the party and he was blasted, yo, I mean, dude was fucking *blizzowwww!"*

"Did you happen to take a picture, or record anything?"

"Hells nah! Why would I need a nerd like that on my phone?"

"How about the girl? You said she was hot."

"Dude, I said she was hot *relatively.* Also, I got her on my phone already. And not in no fucking sweatshirt neither. Half the dudes in this house have hit that dime piece. She be one serious fro."

"Tell me that does not mean frat-ho," Karen said, her face an incipient storm.

"You is correct, Hottie Cop! I done did that girl so hard she couldn't walk for forty days and forty nights. That shit was biblical."

"So you know this girl?" I prodded. "I thought she went to State."

"State? She *was* going to Western. Or Central maybe, but she failed out. Now she's a waitress at Minty's, that shitty diner on Washtenaw. Maybe she takes some classes at WCC, but she's not exactly Bill fucking Gates." He mimed giving himself a blowjob, bulging his cheeks in and out and opening his mouth with his fist cupped around his lips. "So I doubt it."

"You know her name?"

"Yo, that shit insults me! You think I'm the kind of asshole that does girls so hard they turn into bible verses and don't even know their names? Hells, nah! Monique. Yeah, inscribe that girl into the J-Dubs Book of Life! Monique with a last name that's got a V in the middle of it somewhere, I don't know, I just think it's funny because V, you know, in the middle, like for, you know, vagina?"

"Yeah, J-Dubs, I get it."

"Not a lot of it though, right?"

Jesus.

"And works at Minty's on Washtenaw?"

"As opposed to Minty's in your mom's house? Yeah, man, Minty's on Washtenaw. That's the shit I said. That's the shit I meant!"

"You got anything else?" I asked Karen.

She shook her head and I walked over to the desk and quit Jonas' computer out of its browser.

"Yo, bruh!" he said, grabbing at my arm. "What the fuck?"

"Listen, Jonas, I'm not your brother and you strike me as a pretty severe scumbag. On the other hand, your father's in prison and you're young. Perhaps today will be the day you turn everything around. To do that, you'll need to develop a foundation of integrity. Start by writing your own papers. Do yourself a favor and pretend you care about the kind of person you want to become."

I was hoping the kid wouldn't say anything and would begin typing whatever essay was probably due the next morning. But Jonas being J-Dubs, and the Psycho House being the Psycho House, that's not what happened.

"Come on, Nap," he said, his voice soothing like a car salesman's. "Don't be all hostile. I heard your daughter likes it rough. Bring her by the hot tub one night. She won't care about becoming any kind of person after that. She'll be barking like a wild dog, begging for this bone right here, you feel me?"

Karen threw an elbow into his sternum as if she were boxing out Charles Barkley and the kid buckled over. She then slapped his ear with her open palm and sent him sprawling onto his bed. His shoulder banged the headboard and the sterling silver marijuana plant, which looked like it weighed at least twenty pounds, toppled onto his pillow, one of its sharp leaf-points missing putting a hole in his neck by maybe half an inch.

"Next time a comment about one of my athletes comes out of your mouth," she said, "you won't have a mouth to comment with. Nod your head, bruh, if you feel me."

Before he rubbed his ear, J-Dubs in the Hot Tub nodded his head.

"Not a single word," Karen said.

We were walking back toward campus, but I wanted to convince her to look at one more thing, and then I'd have to head to practice. "I was just going to compliment you, Hottie Cop, on how well you managed to control your partner's temper."

"Call me Hottie Cop again and you won't have a partner."

"Regardless, thank you for defending the honor of my daughter."

"Didn't matter it was your daughter."

The traffic on Hill Street was congested. Students in packs walked to afternoon classes. Mothers, phones pasted to their ears, picked up their kids from preschool in sparkling Subaru wagons or Priuses. *Priui?* The cars made me think of Olivia Waterman.

"Anything strike you as odd in that room?" I asked.

"Besides the moron in boxer shorts?"

"I'm thinking of the picture of the Business School kids, Harwell and Lombardozzi. Correct me if I'm wrong, but they had, what, six weeks left before graduation when they left? They were in good academic standing and they chucked it all to open a whorehouse. That make sense to you?"

"They seem to be doing all right. They're legends, after all, according to Brother J-Dubs. Looks like their investment paid off."

"Exactly. Their *investment.* We're talking about two students. Where'd they get the money to buy a brothel?"

"What are you saying?"

"I'm saying I have to go to practice, but we're a block away from the B-School. How do you feel about poking around, trying to find out what Harwell and Lombardozzi were working on when they dropped out?"

"Why?"

"I'm thinking there are two ways to get rid of people. One is to kill them. The other is to pay them a lot of money to move to the other side of the world."

When I got out of practice, there were two messages on my phone.

The first was Molly telling me she was dropping Lisa at my place in the morning. With no school and no field hockey, the girl had spent the entire day burning restless energy. She'd emptied old clothes from her closet, stuffed them into bags and dropped them at the PTSO Thrift Store. Rearranged the pantry in the kitchen. Rearranged the silverware drawer. Baked six dozen chocolate chip cookies to drop off at the battered women's shelter. Rearranged the bookshelves in the living room and returned to the shelter to donate used books.

It's not that Molly, who'd been working at home, didn't appreciate what Lisa was doing. In fact, she appreciated it too much. "It's making me remember what a lousy homemaker I am, not to mention an absolutely selfish human being," she said. "Please take her for a couple days so she can make you feel guilty."

Guilt was not something I needed additional inspiration to feel, but I was happy to have Lisa stay with me. I imagined preparing buckwheat pancakes for her the way I used to, fresh Michigan blueberries swirled into the batter. It'd be weird without Jenna, but maybe she'd come too. The two of them sleeping overnight at my house hadn't happened for a couple years. I saw them all the time, and they liked hanging out with me, but they were so busy with school and sports, we'd scrapped the three-days-here-four-days-there itinerary after ninth grade and permanently situated them with Molly.

The other message was from Karen. "You're earning your keep, Detective Fuckup," it said. "Meet me for dinner at Minty's. Eight o'clock."

After I jog-limped home and showered, I straightened the place for Lisa. Wiped the kitchen countertops, vacuumed the living room, cleaned the bathroom, put fresh sheets on the bottom bunk in the guest bedroom. Made a note to stop at Whole Foods on the way to the restaurant and pick up blueberries, butter, pancake mix, milk, eggs.

Chocolate chips too. And flour.

In case she wanted to bake more cookies for the shelter.

CHAPTER NINE

KAREN WAS WEARING the same clothes she'd been wearing all day but they looked rumpled, as if she'd napped in them. I hoped she'd been able to catch a few hours of sleep somewhere. Maybe she'd snoozed in the plush B-School lounge.

When I sat in the booth, she slid a brown 9 x 12 catalog envelope across the table. On the front of the envelope, it said *Your Keep.*

"Cute," I said.

"Open it." She smiled, as if it were some kind of cheesy Valentine's Day gift.

She seemed more cheerful than she should have after elbowing and slapping a frat kid, even if a few hours had elapsed, so I didn't open the envelope, not right away. "I'm sorry you got suspended from coaching," I said. "I wish it hadn't happened."

"I'm sorry too. Pretty awful when you left for your practice but I couldn't go to mine. Is that why you gave me something else to do? Keep me occupied instead of brooding?"

"Actually, I was interested in what you'd find out."

"So open the damn envelope."

I'd forgotten how much I liked Minty's. It wasn't great food but it oozed comfort. Booths and tables had absorbed so much grease and human oils, they understood how to welcome you, like you were just another traveler seeking warmth. The menus were the same they'd been since 1991, laminated, also greasy, full of sandwiches and burgers—not *sliders*—and sides of unadorned, unflavored fries.

Hanging above the cash register, a boxy television showed the governor at a press conference in Mackinaw City, announcing a new initiative to loosen regulations on shipping toxic waste across the Great Lakes. "The days of unsafe transport are thankfully in the past," he said, the breeze from the lake behind fanning his thick blond locks like a parachute. "American ingenuity has figured out how to move these materials without risk. I ask the Do-Nothing Democrats in the Statehouse to stand with me and open these shipping lanes so we can create thousands of new jobs."

"You notice Monique with a V in the middle yet?" I said.

"Not funny. It's Harvey. I asked the host. We're sitting in her section. I ordered an iced tea for you, no sweetener. She'll be back any minute. Open the envelope."

I did. Inside was a single sheet of paper. It was titled *Prospectus for Final Project, Strategic Initiatives 401.* Jonathan Harwell and Michael Lombardozzi listed as co-authors.

"What's this?"

"When our geniuses dropped out to start their business in Kazakhstan, they took every scintilla of research with them. I was told that kind of hoarding has actually become common in the B-School because students have grown increasingly proprietary. It's called the Zuckerberg Syndrome. Everyone's terrified someone else will cash in on his idea. Still, two different professors told me it was surprising how thoroughly Harwell and Lombardozzi had eradicated absolutely everything they were working on, especially since they high-tailed it out of town so quickly. The only thing any professor could dig up was this one-pager they had to turn in to initiate their fieldwork.

The subhead for the first section said, *Charter Schools: Increasing opportunities to leverage public financing and create revenue streams for the private sector.*

"Is this saying what I think it's saying?"

"Read on, McDuff."

As I read, my jaw tingled like I wanted to fight. The synopsis seemed to suggest how a combination of the distressed economy and a prevailing anti-government ethos fostered an environment where taxpayer money designated for public education could, with proper legislative strategy, be pried away from union control and funneled toward for-profit enterprises. If demand could be scaled, earnings yield was potentially unlimited.

The growth curve in Michigan alone projected twelve billion dollars in just five years.

Twelve billion.

With a B.

"They were working on a strategic plan to siphon money from public schools and transfer it to private corporations?"

Karen nodded. Two talking heads on the television argued about the governor's proposal. The liberal had a fat neck and looked like he was about to experience cardiac calamity. Spittle erupted from his mouth as he warned about a potential Exxon Valdez, another Three-Mile Island. The conservative, a thin red-haired woman with a surgically constructed nose, accused her opponent of the kind of job-killing attitude that was throttling the middle class. "If we don't handle this waste," she said, "the Chinese will."

"What does if *demand could be scaled* mean?" I said, thinking of the bus and scoreboard ads, the Education Fairness Act.

"It means if enough people enroll their kids in for-profit schools, then the model allows for mass production that increases earnings. Kind of like Ford and the assembly line. The product can be made more cheaply if more people want it, and profits can increase."

"That's disgusting. We're talking about school, not tie rods."

"Exactly. So, what if Harwell and Lombardozzi were studying the other side of what Sanders Bolgim was working on? We know he was looking at charter schools. What if he were investigating the impact on public schools of *losing* all this money?"

"That's a big leap. And aren't charter schools public?"

"That's what I thought too. I did some checking. Yes, charters are public in the sense they're taxpayer funded and anybody can at least apply to get into them. On the other hand, they can be privately owned and can operate as for-profit ventures. In fact, Michigan has by far the highest percentage of for-profit charters in the country. Ready for this?"

No, I wasn't. Already, I felt like brawling. We were talking about kids. About the place we sent our children every morning with lunches in their backpacks and hopes they'd figure out how to be good people. Those places were going to be profit centers? A significant part of me wanted to go outside and empty my pistol into the first Lexus that drove down Washtenaw. I closed my eyes and drew a long breath.

When I opened them, a woman with dark hair was heading toward us with a tray that held a sizeable-looking iced tea and a glass of red wine. At first glance, she was definitely attractive. She stopped for a moment to talk with another server. "Tell me," I said.

"In most states, the percentage of charters that are for-profit is somewhere between ten and twenty percent. In such well-regarded educational utopias as Florida and Texas, fifty percent of their charters make money. In the celestial haven for educational attainment otherwise known as Michigan—get this—it's eighty percent. *Eight-oh.* No other state is even close."

"You're kidding."

"Nope. And the vast majority of Michigan's for-profit charters are run by a corporation that operates almost two thousand schools across the country. Stock values for said corporation have risen over four hundred percent in the past two years. The company's called Learning With Love Inc. Its slogan: *A Wonderful School for Every Wonderful Child.* Reported profits last year—$2.7 billion. I'll give you one guess who the CEO is."

"Donald Trump."

"Close. Two guesses."

"Bernie Madoff."

"God, how do you ever solve anything? Think already behind bars. Think his son has a bruised sternum, a foul mouth, and a tattoo featuring a hot tub."

"Bullshit."

"Nope. The man presently vacuuming resources from the school your twin daughters attend, a man capable of exerting undue influence on educational policy throughout the state, is a man already convicted for insider trading. The one and only WW Worldwide Dot Warren."

I closed my eyes again.

"You guys ready to order?" said Monique Harvey.

Damn it to hell.

What were the cops doing here?

Jarrold recognized the sexy detective with the multi-colored hair—almost as sexy as Monique—and her midget partner from the house after the fire. Their examination of the initial scene had been cursory, routine. Mostly they'd been comforting the housemates after the nerd's barbecued corpse flew out from the exploded top floor like a burned-up dud at a fireworks show. That was pretty comical. He'd had to work hard to hold his giggle inside when he saw it.

So what were they doing here, now, at Monique's place of business?

He was just a lovesick boy trying to drop by to see his girl, and they were screwing it up.

Messing with him.

The ultimate cop-lock cock-block.

Could be they were just getting a plate of meatloaf, some hot chocolate, but Jarrold doubted it. The dwarf was scanning the parking lot as if he wanted to memorize the cars. Good thing Jarrold had taken the precaution to check the place out before going in, to watch from across the street in his nondescript grey rental, a Detroit-made four-door like all boring and anonymous middle-managers drove. The two cops definitely had an on-duty look, a purposeful stride as they moved past the newspaper boxes and into the restaurant. They were after something for sure, and that meant they'd already connected Monique to the nerd.

The nerd-crisp!

How had they done that?

Jarrold had made sure Monique knew not to introduce herself to any of the target's housemates and the rest of the party had been chaotic. He doubted anyone had been paying particular attention to the geek boy. That was half the reason Jarrold made himself the star at the beer pong table. He'd wanted to create something memorable for the partiers to focus on. And he had. He'd been unforgettable! He felt his feet tapping the floorboards of his car as he remembered the night. So fun! The driving bass beats. The girl in the pantry. The even better girl in the basement.

Still, the cops had found Monique.

Why had they been investigating in the first place?

Ann Arbor resources were stretched to breaking. These detectives wouldn't be doing so much follow-up if they were buying the nerd's death as accidental.

He would have to wait and see. He turned on the radio, tuned into the sports talk station he'd developed the habit of listening to. If he wanted to blend into football-crazy Ann Arbor, he had to know what was going on with the Wolverines. The hosts were idiots and the callers were worse, but at least he'd learned about the travesty of Rich Rod and the joke of Brady Hoke. The frustrating enigma of Ripstick.

At the commercial break, he texted Monique to let her know the police were in her restaurant. He'd have to see her later, find out what the cops had asked her about.

And, after what had happened to the nerd, if she could still be trusted.

CHAPTER TEN

WHEN JENNA and Lisa were young, we rented the documentary about penguins. The one where Morgan Freeman narrates how mother penguins trek to the ocean in order to bring back food for their infants. While the mothers are gone, penguin eggs are sheltered by penguin fathers who keep them warm in a stomach pouch that drapes over their feet. In order for the sheltering to happen, the mother penguins must carefully transfer the eggs from beneath their own stomach pouches onto the feet of their mates. The transfer is not always successful and, when it fails, the egg tumbles onto the frozen ground and the chick inside perishes. This is how my daughters first understood the concept of death. They knew a certain number of baby penguins failed to survive when their eggs got stuck to the ice.

When one of their cousins in Virginia died in a car accident a few months later, the girls knew what had happened to him was what happened to the penguin chicks who didn't survive. "Do you think Aaron's cold?" Lisa asked me.

"No," I'd said. "Once somebody dies, they don't stay stuck. Their soul goes to a place that's warm. I'm sure Aaron isn't feeling cold at all."

I hope Lisa believed me.

What I saw behind Monique Harvey's eyes made me think about those long-ago conversations. Something inside her had gotten stuck to the ice and wasn't getting any warmer. I ordered a burger with cheddar and grilled mushrooms and onions. Karen had a bowl of chili and a club sandwich on wheat. Monique wrote down our orders without comment. Despite what felt like a distinct lack of interest in Karen and me, she remained attractive. She was about my height and wore low-slung blue jeans. Her t-shirt was tight, her chest full. As she turned back toward the kitchen, I asked if she might be taking classes at Washtenaw, said she looked familiar.

"Are a you a professor there?"

"No, but I'm on campus a lot." I didn't tell her it was usually to make a drug bust.

"I'm trying to transfer," she said.

"Where to?" Karen asked.

"Florida, maybe. New Mexico. Someplace far away."

She didn't elaborate. Waited to see if we had any more questions. Returned to the kitchen when we didn't.

"Not a happy camper," Karen said.

"Any idea when her shift ends?"

"Midnight, according to the hostess. Should we meet her?"

"Yeah, but what's your theory on Sanders and the B-School kids?"

"Like you said, they were all researching something similar and were successfully disposed of, Harwell and Lombardozzi to Kazakhstan, Bolgim to an urn for his ashes."

"Why not just buy off Sanders too?"

"Maybe Sanders wouldn't be bought. Don't forget the business schoolers were looking to maximize profits. Seems natural they'd drop their research for up-front cash. Sanders wasn't looking for money. He was trying to nail somebody."

"But you found the financial information easily, including the connection to Dot Warren. Why would somebody kill Sanders if he was just looking at stuff already in the public domain?"

"That, Detective Fuckup, is the twelve-billion-dollar question."

After dinner, we stopped by my house so I could drop the groceries in my kitchen and my car in the driveway. We wanted to roll the way partners are supposed to roll so Karen was set to drive us the rest of the night in her car. As soon as I pulled in, I knew something was off in the way you know when someone has been messing with stuff on your desk.

The way you know someone's been fishing through your recycling bin in the middle of the night.

Karen seemed to sense it too and I didn't have to signal her to stay quiet. We crept up the driveway toward the front door. The automatic floodlights came on and everything looked normal. No visible footprints anywhere.

The front door was locked, the way I'd left it.

I walked backward to see if the windows looked secure.

"You smell something burning?" Karen asked, a replay of the other night in Burns Park.

"Sonuvamotherf—" smoke was rising above my roof. It seemed to be coming from the back yard.

We pulled our guns and ran around the side of the house.

A rudimentary dummy was in flames. Basically, a stuffed sheet with stuffed blue jeans for legs, it hung from a branch belonging to the oak tree on the side of my porch. The stuffing in the legs was what was burning. It looked like paper. Probably old homework. Or fliers for a kegger. A noose hung around the dummy's neck. It had no face, but it wore a blonde wig with auburn stripes. A sign hung around the neck said *Hands off the Psycho Bros!*

I turned on my garden hose and showered the dummy until the fire sputtered.

"It couldn't have been burning for more than a couple minutes," I said. "They must have had someone a few blocks from the house watching, waiting for my car to pass by."

"They know where you live?"

I shrugged. "I know where they live. They must have seen me running at some point and followed me here."

"You think it's an actual warning or just a lame attempt at revenge?"

"Revenge. If they want to warn us, they'll come with lawyers. They're trying to shake us up."

"Are we shaken up?"

"No."

"Good."

We searched the rest of the yard and inside the house and found no further evidence of mayhem. I put the groceries away and called Molly to tell her what happened in case she wouldn't feel safe having Lisa stay with me. "You think they'll come back?" she asked.

I told her I doubted it, the fratboys had shot their wad and would probably go practice beer pong amongst themselves, then get back to date raping people. She sighed. "You think Jenna or Lisa will ever get into all that, the frat party scene?"

"Hard to avoid it in this town. They're smart kids

though. I trust them to stay away from sketchy dudes. Or, alternatively, to slug them."

"Not funny, Jim."

"I was only half kidding. A lot of those kids need to be slugged."

"I was going to say I miss you," she said. "Now I'm not so sure."

It was almost ten by the time we got to Kevin Trouma's. Late for us to be talking to a high school kid on a weeknight, but if he were involved in anything his poem described, staying up late was the least of his problems.

On the way to his house, in one of the ritzier subdivisions on the city's western fringe, we heard a story on the radio about a kindergarten class in Detroit with fifty-six students and only one teacher.

Why was the class finally broken up?

Because one boy's mother, after banging her head against the wall of the principal's office multiple times, called the Fire Department to ask if the number of people in the room was above fire code. Turns out it was. Capacity for the room was forty-four. What did the principal do? Instead of hiring another teacher, she took thirteen kids out of the room and added them to a couple first-grade classes that only had thirty-eight kids in them. Made the first-grade teachers handle forty-four kids each and two different grade levels.

"That's why people send their kids to charter schools," Karen said.

"Don't they realize if they pull their children out of a school, it winds up with even fewer resources? That it gets worse for the kids who stay?"

"Not their problem. Think about it, Jim. If Pioneer were

putting fifty kids in a class and you could move Jenna and Lisa to a place where the classes were smaller, wouldn't you?"

I was thinking about what it must be like for a teacher of a kindergarten class with fifty-six children, or even forty-three. How the only way to keep the class from exploding into chaos must be to make all the kids so afraid they stay paralyzed in their seats, trembling whenever the teacher approaches. It wasn't so different for Karen and me. Neither of us wanted to spend time beating up college kids, but we knew the numbers. Our department had dwindled from a hundred and fifty officers to ninety-four. Forty thousand college students lived in our city. On any given weekend, somewhere between ten and fifteen thousand would be drunk. It was like we were dancing on top of a thin lid tamped over a drum of highly combustible fuel. If we didn't keep the lid sealed tightly, the whole city could erupt.

If we wanted to live in a place with high property values, cute cafés and an almost non-existent homicide rate, we had to draw a line. If a student throws beer on you, his face gets smashed. If he makes a suggestive comment about your teenage daughter, he gets slapped. If these kids didn't fear the repercussions of the legal system—and they didn't—they had to fear something else.

Us.

Kevin's mother answered the door looking like she'd been drinking. She was tall and gaunt. Splints of hair spidered across her face. Her eyes were puffy, her shirt missing a button. "About Kevin?" she said when we showed her our badges. "He's a good kid. He's not in trouble, is he?"

"We don't know he did anything, Mrs. Trouma," Karen

said. "We want to ask him some questions about a classmate. Is he doing homework?"

"Might be. Check downstairs."

The house was huge. And spotless. The long sloping lawn had been recently mowed and everything inside was symmetrical and expensive, the floors were polished hardwood the color of dark chocolate. No indication of a Mr. Trouma. Kevin's mother, who ushered us through the enormous rooms quickly, as if she couldn't care less about them, seemed an unlikely candidate for keeping everything in shape. I was betting on a housekeeper.

We passed through a kitchen with more square feet than my house. The appliances sparkled and the refrigerator could hold a herd of cattle. A half-filled wine glass, white, sat on a marble island as big as Aruba, the bottle next to it nearly empty. Mrs. Trouma opened a door to a descending staircase and said, "Kevin, I'm coming down. I have some people with me."

I wondered if she'd walked in on him masturbating on some prior occasion, or caught him rolling a spliff. Karen pulled out her phone again and started playing with it, her signal I should initiate the questioning.

The basement had a ping-pong table, a pool table, a professional-looking poker table, and a massive stone-encased fireplace appropriate for a hunting lodge. From a room to the left, we could hear The Dave Matthews Band.

The kid was alone on a u-shaped leather couch capable of seating the entire fifty-six- person kindergarten class. He was facing a flatscreen nearly the size of the one in the Psycho Brothers' great room. It was not turned on. He looked like a thousand other wealthy white teenagers in Ann Arbor, tall and lanky, blue eyes, tousled sandy hair. He was wearing a lavender golf shirt and droopy cargo shorts. The kind of boy my daughters fall apart over. Maybe the way he held his shoulders indicated an aura of sadness beyond the standard teenage magnitude, but something told me he was a battler, not the kind of kid who gave up.

His long and slender bare feet were propped on a marble coffee table next to a bin of four remote controls, each with a type-written label: TV power, TV channels, stereo, Blue-ray.

Mrs. Trouma took the stereo remote from the bin and muted the music, then introduced us to her son. He'd been writing in a journal, which he closed and put on his lap.

"Is that for creative writing?" I asked him after we introduced ourselves. "My daughters Jenna and Lisa have that class."

"They're amazing," he said, and I wasn't sure if he meant they were great writers, great athletes, nice people, or just really pretty.

"Listen, Kevin, you're not in trouble and I don't want you to be mad at Ms. Waterman. She felt bad about violating your confidence but, after what happened with Tammy Binder and Austin Spoolbaugh, she's worried, so she showed me one of your poems."

"I figured." He looked at his feet on the table, wouldn't meet my gaze. "It's not about me. I've never done that stuff."

"What stuff?" his mother said. "What are you talking about?"

I waited for the teenage explosion. The whipping of one of the remotes toward the giant TV and the shouting that she was the one with the substance abuse problem, not him. It didn't happen. When Kevin looked up, his eyes were misty. "Mom," he said, "would it be okay if I talked to the detectives alone?"

"What are you involved in?"

"Nothing. I swear."

"Does he need a lawyer?" she asked us.

"He's not in trouble," I said again. "Legally, you have

the right to be here while we talk to him, so it's up to you if you want to stay."

"Please, Mom, I don't have anything to hide. How are my grades? Good, right? I'm not involved in anything dangerous, I promise."

The kid's mother looked at me, then over at Karen. She was maybe going to cry if her son had to beg her any further. Karen spoke for the first time since we'd entered the basement.

"Mrs. Trouma, you can trust us. If Kevin starts to say anything that could put him in jeopardy we'll come get you before he continues. Deal?"

"He's just a kid."

"We know it," Karen said. "We've got our own."

Technically, that wasn't true. I mean, I did, but Karen didn't. Maybe she meant her athletes.

Reluctantly, Mrs. Trouma nodded at her son and headed upstairs.

"Tammy and I used to date," Kevin said. He was sitting up straight on the couch now, his journal still closed on his lap.

"You're the boyfriend who broke up with her?" Karen asked.

"Yeah, you're her coach, I know. She loves you. She feels bad about letting the team down."

"The team will be ready for her when she's ready to come back."

"We used to watch a lot of movies down here," Kevin said, leaning back against the couch again but keeping his feet on the floor. He looked at the ceiling as if remembering something. "I really liked her."

"What happened?"

"The thing is," he started, then stopped, looked at the ceiling some more. "The thing is, I didn't love her. Not the way she loved me. Like she started talking about staying together during college and I hadn't even started my senior year. I didn't want to hurt her. You see how my mom is. I mean my dad—" He stopped again.

Karen looked at her phone. "Benjamin Trouma? CEO of Blue Leaf Real Estate?"

Where had I heard those names before? Blue Leaf Real Estate. Ben Trouma. He was the guy who spearheaded the opposition campaign a couple years earlier when the school district was trying to float the county millage for more funding. Spent a couple hundred thousand dollars to defeat it. TV ads that claimed property taxes would skyrocket while lazy teachers sat back and celebrated summers at the lake. Also, unless I was mistaken, he was a big supporter of Governor Lambright, maybe even stood behind him on the stage during his victory speech.

"Yeah, that's him," Kevin said. "Over the summer he was gone for a month. Said he was on business but my mom found out he was in the Caribbean with a woman from Chicago. She drank for two weeks straight. Wouldn't get out of bed. I couldn't watch that and pretend to love Tammy more than I really did. I felt too guilty."

The kid was crying. His hands were flipping open his journal and closing it.

"Then she started dating Austin at the beginning of the school year. I knew that was a bad idea, but what could I say to her? He doesn't love you, but I don't really love you either?"

We all took a few seconds to look at the blank television screen. I imagined Tammy Binder, exhausted after a tough game, coming down here in a pair of sweatpants, curling up next to this kid, watching a feel-good 80s movie.

"Kevin, let me ask you something," I said. "Who cleans this house? I know it's not your mom. You have a housekeeper, something like that?"

He shook his head. "She only comes once a week."

"And the rest of the time, it's up to you, isn't it?"

He wouldn't look at me, but he didn't shake his head again.

"And you wanted your mom to go upstairs so you wouldn't make her feel worse by saying what you just said?"

Again, he kept his eyes on the blank television.

"You're a good kid, Kevin. Whatever's between your parents isn't a problem you're required to solve, you understand?"

He turned to me, nodded, looked back at the screen.

"What happened to Tammy isn't your fault either," Karen said. "I've known her since she was eight. Whatever she's going through, she was going to go through eventually. You probably kept her from doing it sooner."

"She was happy when she was with me," Kevin said.

"Then be happy you gave her that. The problem is she thinks she needs a boyfriend in order to feel she's worth loving. If she doesn't believe in herself, it doesn't matter what anyone else thinks. Same thing in field hockey."

"Kevin," I said, "I don't see any marks on your arms or feet. We believe you about not being involved in heroin, so where'd the poem come from?"

"I smoke weed sometimes."

"Along with half the population of Ann Arbor. Believe me, the best thing you can do for Tammy right now is help us find her supplier."

"I only know what she told me. That she and Austin used to go to the Arb all the time to hang out. A lot of kids do, to smoke or do 'shrooms, but they're usually down by the river. She used to shoot up on the benches in the Peony Garden."

"What about the motel you talked about in your poem?"

"I made that up."

"The bridge too? And the tunnel?"

"No, the bridge is downtown. The railroad one where all the graffiti writers hang out. I don't think she went there a lot, but she mentioned it. Or, I think she did. She definitely talked about how she'd be high and staring at the different tags and colors. The tunnel had something to do with U-M, but I don't know what."

"The tunnel at the football stadium? Where the players run onto the field?"

"No, on campus, something near the Diag."

"Steam tunnels?" Karen said.

"Yeah, that sounds right."

It was always rumored to exist, a network of secret tunnels beneath central campus where all manner of illicit behavior was supposed to happen. I'd never actually been down there. Maybe the kid was bullshitting us. Or maybe Tammy had been bullshitting him. Guess it couldn't hurt to check with Public Safety at U-M, find out once and for all if the tunnels were anything more than campus legend.

"Any idea where they got the heroin?" I asked.

For a while he didn't answer. Picked the journal up and held it over his face like a tent, then started talking, his face still covered.

"She called me," he said, voice muffled. "The night before she ended up going to rehab. It was around 4:30 in the morning and she'd just thrown up. She was scared. Austin's parents had found out about him a week earlier and sent him away so I was hoping Tammy would calm down. For a few days, it seemed like she would, but then she started getting high without him. She kept saying she had nothing to live for, that she was screwing her whole life up. I called her mother. That's how her parents found out. She was upstairs puking in the bathroom and her mom found the needles. But she said something about a guy called Gumby. That's why she said she wanted to kill herself. She told me she—" He stopped talking and pulled the journal away from his face and gazed at the ceiling again, then sighed and tried to finish what he was saying without looking at us, his voice cracking, halting to catch itself every few seconds. Karen and I listened quietly, not interrupting.

"She said she did stuff with him so she could get high. She said she was the biggest whore in the world. I told her she wasn't. I told her I knew her. She'd just made a mistake. She kept saying she loved me. That's when I wrote the poem, right after that."

The kid was crying again. I put an arm on his shoulder. It wasn't his fault what happened to Tammy, but I doubted he was going to believe that any time soon. I'd bet my salary the kid hadn't told his mother anything about Tammy in rehab, about everything he was carrying inside his chest. His journal was probably the only thing keeping him sane.

"Did Tammy say anything else about this Gumby person?" Karen asked. Her voice was tight. If we ever found this dude, I'd have to keep her from snapping his clavicle like a wishbone.

Kevin shook his head.

It was time for us to leave if we wanted to catch Monique Harvey at the end of her shift. I was hoping Kevin's mother had sobered up. I had a thought. His calves looked muscular. He was skinny, but his shoulders felt solid beneath my palm. He was a senior, but it was still early in the season. He could learn. Maybe make an impact by the time Districts rolled around in February. Kid had guts.

"How much do you weigh?" I asked him.

"What?'

"Your weight. What are you, about a hundred-seventy?"

"I guess. A little lighter."

"You know where the wrestling room is?"

"In the pit?"

"Be there tomorrow afternoon. Four o'clock."

"But I—"

"Kevin, get your ass down there. Bring a pair of shorts."

"But—"

"Four o'clock."

Outside, the wind had picked up and the air stung. I felt a cast-iron weight in my stomach. Despite my love for Michigan football, autumn depressed me. Ann Arbor seemed to attract an excessive number of crows each November. They'd crowd the tops of trees in flocks ten thousand strong, making it look like the branches had donned bulky black cloaks. When the girls were younger, I'd make *caw-caw* sounds that would send the whole murder screeching and flapping, rending the sky with a violent ripple. The girls would act amazed and clap their hands but I think they were a little terrified. I know I was, as if I owned a power to send terrible omens shuddering through the calm.

My father died in the fall, long before the birth of my daughters, a heart attack on Tuesday of Ohio State week. He'd been walking with my mother on a trail through Bird Hills Park, something they did two or three times a week, when he turned to her. "I have such an odd feeling today," he'd said, then staggered and clutched at his chest. He was dead before he hit the ground. I was a sophomore in college when it happened and my mom showed up at wrestling practice to tell me. I was working a double arm bar on Mikey when my peripheral vision registered a woman in the doorway. She looked old, as if the day had kicked her in the chin. I didn't realize it was my mother. I was sweating like a faucet and trying to catch my breath when Coach Cox beckoned me over to talk to her. She told me without crying. I listened the same way and then went home so I could help notify relatives and friends, the first and only time I left practice before it was finished. Three years later, she would be dead too. Throat cancer. Hospitalized, she'd miss my appearance in the NCAA finals in March and pass away the following October, also without ever knowing my daughters.

My father was fortunate, I guess, to miss the pasting the Buckeyes put on the Wolverines the year he died, a 21-6 embarrassment. I've always thought the team—without my father in the stadium to cheer them—was as despondent as I was.

He was only fifty-seven when he died, a young man who, despite his obsession with Michigan football, wasn't much of a sports guy. He was everything you'd think of when you imagine a comparative literature professor—calm and measured in his demeanor, careful and precise in his speech, except in the Big House where he'd curse a blue streak if the Wolverine defense faltered.

I don't think he knew what to make of me, his only son who seemed to possess the reflexes of a panther, the strength of a man twice his size. I often wondered what he thought when he sat in the stands and watched me crank on someone's shoulder socket.

In my lowest moments, I think of my mother sitting cross-legged in the leaves and dirt, lit by a shaft of sunlight, holding my father's head in her lap, waiting for the paramedics when she knew there was no hope. His years of pipe smoking probably killed both of them. I don't like to think about that.

I, too, expect to die during the autumn months. Probably with a bunch of crows circling like vultures, laughing.

CHAPTER ELEVEN

INSIDE MONIQUE'S car in the parking garage, Jarrold let her hit him in the upper chest, her fists sharp and fast, knuckles battering him like small stones. He knew he'd be bruised, but what could he do? She was angry.

"How could you?" she kept saying. "You burned him alive. How could you?"

Her tears were hot, her fists flailing. Jarrold leaned back in the passenger seat and let her punch. Finally, exhausted, she slapped the dashboard with her open palm and turned to him, her eyes huge and open, more sad than furious. "You let me sleep with him and then you killed him."

"You didn't have to sleep with him. That was your choice."

This time when Monique tried to slap his face, Jarrold caught her wrist.

"Enough."

With his free hand, he wiped her tears then held his palm against her cheek. Her skin felt feverish and the heat traveled through his body. She didn't push his hand away and her surrender enflamed him. He wanted her more than he'd ever wanted Kimmie, more than he'd wanted anyone.

She sensed his desire and smirked.

"He was better than you'll ever be," she said. "A geek like that, and he made me come harder than you ever could."

Jarrold felt himself so aroused he thought he'd explode. He didn't believe what she was saying, but he wanted her to say more.

"What'd he do to you?" he whispered. "Show me. I'll do it too."

"I could show you a thousand times and you'd never do it like he did."

Jarrold untied the scarf around her neck. It was a light, paisley thing. He'd need it later. "What are you wearing this for? You look like an English major."

She didn't resist and he put his lips against her neck. She moaned and it sounded like she meant it.

He reached into the front pockets of her hooded sweatshirt and pulled out her keys her wallet, and her phone, and placed it all on her seat, then tugged her close to him. "I don't want all this stuff between us," he said. "That's the problem. Everybody walks around with so much gear. I just want to feel the real you pressed against the real me."

"Why are you still wearing your gloves then?"

"My fingers are cold. You know how my extremities get."

"Take them off. I feel like you're going to kill me too. Like you don't want to leave any prints."

He made a show of pulling them off with his teeth, seductively, as if he were a stripper. She giggled.

"Let's get out of the car," he said. "It's a pretty night. Look at the sky, how thick it is with stars. Let's dance."

"To what? There's no music." But Monique was still chuckling and took his hand.

"It doesn't matter. We're here, just the two of us. We can see the whole city."

He started humming. He couldn't have said what song it was, though it probably resembled something by John Mayer.

"You're so cheesy," she said.

He waltzed her around the asphalt. She laid her head on his shoulder and he kept humming. His erection was throbbing and she nudged her hips against it. His heart was breaking.

"I didn't say anything to the police," she cooed, "if that's what you're worried about."

"I'm not worried," he said.

Then, with her back to the guardrail, he lifted her as if she were his bride and he were carrying her across the threshold. She seemed so light. Her sweatshirt smelled as if it had been freshly laundered.

"Do you trust me?" he asked her, looking deep into her eyes.

She nodded.

"Then take your hands from around my neck."

She did and he held her for a moment, rocking her gently as if she were an infant. He got the impression she knew what was going to happen. That made him feel better as he tossed her over the edge.

I had another bad feeling when we pulled into Minty's parking lot. Again, something was different. I searched the hard drive of my memory and tried to pull up a snapshot of what I'd seen earlier. Had there been a car in the now-empty corner opposite the restaurant's entrance? A somewhat battered Toyota, beige, with a bumper sticker displaying the brown and gold of the Western Michigan Broncos?

Maybe I was just imagining it.

It was 11:45. Karen waited in her car. I walked around the building and leaned against a dumpster where I had a clear view of the rear exit. If either one of us saw Monique Harvey, we'd text the other. The wind cut inside my jacket and spiked my chest. Karen sent me a message. "You were great with Kevin."

I guess she hadn't wanted to tell me in person, didn't trust herself to let me see her face when she said it.

"I'm learning," I typed back. "Have a good mentor."

No response.

At 12:30, I texted her again.

"Still inside? Cleaning up? Beer with colleagues?"

"Let's go in," Karen texted back.

The restaurant was mostly deserted. A guy who looked like a tugboat sat at a booth in the back, eating eggs covered in gravy, reading a spy novel. Two middle-aged women in a booth drank coffee and ignored each other while they looked longingly at their phones.

No sign of Monique Harvey.

The hostess recognized us. Didn't seem surprised we had badges.

She informed us Monique had left shortly after we'd paid our check. "She got a text and said she had an emergency. Made me cover her tables."

"Did she say where she was going?" I asked.

"No, but she looked anxious. It was weird. She hugged me like she wouldn't be back. Her shoulders were trembling."

"Did she say anything about the text?"

"Only that she had to go."

"How well do you know her?" Karen asked. "Is she seeing anyone?"

The hostess flipped through the receipts at her station, seemed unsure about what she should tell us. I tried to put on my most trustworthy face.

"She's not in trouble if that's what you're thinking," Karen said. "We just wonder if she knows something connected to a case we're working on. Anything you can remember about her relationships could be helpful."

"I don't know that she's seeing any one person," the hostess said. "Monique's a bit wild. We're not really close because she's only been here a few months, but I've been out with her a couple times. Guys are all over her the second we show up anywhere. She has this way of flirting where she looks like she's not interested, then all of a sudden, she and the guy she was talking to are gone. I'm not sure she ever goes home by herself."

"So not one particular guy?" Karen pushed. "No one she sees on a regular basis?"

The hostess played with her receipts some more. I hunched my shoulders, tried to look like I was easy to beat up.

"One guy met her at the end of a shift once. I don't want to say she seemed happy to see him, but it seemed like he calmed her down about something. This was just a few weeks ago. They were in the parking lot and she was yelling. I couldn't hear what she was saying but you could tell she was mad, like, pointing her finger at him. Then he whispered something and she put her head against his chest and he was, like, massaging her back, comforting her. Then she kind of melted."

"Do you know the guy's name?"

"Jarrold. I don't know his last name."

Karen and I exchanged a look.

"Any idea why she was upset?" Karen asked.

"Probably some other guy she was seeing, or some other woman he was seeing. A lot of her relationships were like that. Monogamy wasn't her thing. The last two days though, she's been more down than I've ever seen her. Definitely in a fog because of the fire where that kid got killed. She really liked him even though she just met him. He was really nice, she said. And also—"

She stopped, embarrassed. Fingered the receipts. Looked at Karen when she spoke again.

"She said he was the best sex she ever had."

Sanders Bolgim? I made a quizzical face.

Karen didn't see it because her phone buzzed—I guess she'd turned off the ringtone—and she looked at the screen. Something twitched on the side of her mouth.

My stomach fell.

When Monique Harvey was found with a shattered skull on the sidewalk beneath the Maynard Street structure, it was assumed she'd jumped from the sixth floor where her car, a beige 1994 Corolla with a mess of bumper stickers—including one professing loyalty to the Western Michigan Broncos—was found with its driver's side door left open, her wallet, jacket and keys on the front seat.

We looked at the body first. Dr. Roland Roethke was taking pictures with a digital camera. Blood and brains were splattered around her skull. Teeth and chunks of bone also lay in the pool of fluids that had leaked from what was left of her head.

"Looks like her head hit the ground first," Roland told us, "after falling about ninety-five feet. Fractured parietal bone, sphenoid bone, temporal bone and occipital bone. Partial fractures of ethmoid and frontal bones. Essentially, her skull exploded upon impact with the sidewalk. She died instantly."

"Is that unusual when a body falls, for the head to hit first?" I asked.

Roland nodded, the kind of slow nod that indicates he'll offer the best answer he can, but it won't be an answer that addresses every complexity of the human experience.

"Most people try to break the fall with their arms, even if they jump. It's instinct. Not that it makes a difference. Usually the wrists fracture too, but a fall from that height will kill anyone."

Part of me wanted to rebel at this statement, as if somehow, if I'd fallen from ninety-five feet, I'd have found a way to survive.

"Does that mean somebody pushed her and she fell backward?" Karen asked.

"Could be." Roland offered another slow nod. "But there's no way to know. Funny things can happen to a body in the air. She could have panicked and flailed while she was falling or she could have intentionally dove and held her hands behind her back. Could have even sat on the railing and rolled backward as if she were scuba diving. There's no sign on her body—no cuts or bruises—that would indicate trauma. I'll check more thoroughly under her fingernails but from the naked eye, there doesn't seem to be any tissue."

"But you can't rule out she was pushed or forced over in some other way?" Karen said.

"No, and there's no note or anything. At least not in her car. But the leaving behind of personal effects, the taking off of her jacket, those behaviors are consistent with suicide. When the tox screen comes back, we'll know if she was pumped up with alcohol or anything else."

Karen nodded. More quickly than a Roland nod. Then something strange happened. She touched his forearm and the two exchanged a look I wasn't supposed to see. I pretended I didn't see it. He was a good-looking guy in an impish, youthful way, with a strong jaw and a thick crop of hair, but I'd never figured him for Karen's type. The hipster glasses and *Sesame Street* t-shirts, the even more pronounced lack of height than my own, the slender build—all that would've seemed to exclude him from her list of prospects.

But I know what I saw.

Three days. Two dead kids.

One body burned, the other exploded against a sidewalk.

I'd never lived anywhere but this city. Never sensed a greater evil in it either. Something was lurking beneath our parade of trendy restaurants, fair trade coffee shops and digital start-ups. I felt ready to punch the first pair of angular cheekbones I saw.

At least if what Monique Harvey had said to the hostess were true, she and Sanders had enjoyed their time together, had spent part of his last night as fully alive as they could feel.

It was also becoming increasingly clear why Karen could so quickly comprehend why a stunner like Monique could go for an intellectual like Sanders, and also why she preferred the Professor over the Skipper. Still, I decided to hold off saying anything about Roland.

We were on the sixth floor of the parking structure looking at the beige Toyota. Lawrence Eagleden, the crime scene technician we shared with Pittsfield Township, was dusting the steering wheel and car door for prints. I expected him to find Monique's and nobody else's. There were no scuff-marks by the railing where she'd gone over, or any other sign of struggle. The security video had shown her entering the parking garage at 10:22, about forty-five minutes after Karen and I left Minty's. We should have just interviewed her after our meal. Maybe she'd still be alive. I guess we'd thought if we caught her on the way out of work, as opposed to mid-shift, she'd be more forthcoming about the party.

The video showed her alone in her car. She looked anguished as she pressed the button to retrieve a ticket, her pretty face tear-streaked. She fumbled with the ticket and dropped it, seemed to consider leaving it on the ground, but opened her door to pick it up. Then she floored the gas and squealed away from the entrance, too quickly to be safe, up the ramp toward the parking spaces.

Downtown was pretty calm late on a Tuesday. No other car had entered the garage within ten minutes before or after Monique, and no car all night had shown anybody who matched the description of the mysterious Jarrold. There were plenty of open spaces on lower levels. Monique had driven up to the sixth floor either to jump, or to meet someone.

"No cameras in the stairwells," Karen said.

"Right, so somebody could have slipped into the garage through the alley entrance to the stairs, which isn't visible to the cashier, walked up to the sixth floor, met Monique and pushed her over, and walked back down the stairs and left, and nobody would have seen him."

"Could have, but why would we think somebody did?"

"It's too much of a coincidence for Monique to kill herself when she knew something about how the GHB got into the body of Sanders Bolgim. Somebody wanted that information to die with her. Especially if that somebody knew we'd tracked her down."

"Except maybe that's why she did it," Karen said. "Maybe she put the GHB into his drink but didn't know somebody was planning on starting a fire. Maybe she really did like Sanders. Maybe the guilt was eating her up and she couldn't handle it. Maybe she even set the fire."

"What about the text she said she got?"

"Maybe she got a text, maybe she didn't."

I looked at the car where Eagleden was working. Monique's wallet and keys were still on her front seat, jacket too. "You find a phone anywhere in the car?" I asked.

"Nope."

I bent down on my knees and peered beneath the car, then made a quick sweep of the area, looking under the only other cars on the sixth floor—a Honda hybrid and a Ford crossover—nothing.

"Roland find a phone on the body?" I asked Karen.

"No."

"You ever know a kid Monique Harvey's age who didn't have her phone with her?"

"No."

"Yet she didn't have it on her when she jumped, or was pushed, and she didn't leave it with her personal effects in the car. What's that tell you?"

"Someone else was here. Someone who didn't want us to know who she'd been texting."

Eagleden had moved over to the railing and was spreading print dust over an area about a dozen feet long. After finishing, he shined an ultraviolet light on the floor beneath the railing, looking for footprints. "That's odd," he said.

"Find something?" Karen asked.

"That's just it. There's nothing. No evidence even of the girl. Unless she took off running and dove over the barrier from six feet away, there's nothing to suggest she ever came near this handrail."

"Somebody swept the floor?"

"Or vacuumed it."

A wave was gathering inside me. It felt like a football

game when Michigan was down six with a minute to go. The Wolverines were marching across midfield and the stadium swelled with a hundred and fourteen thousand roaring voices. I saw my daughters jog onto the field hockey pitch, resplendent in their purple and black uniforms, preparing to shake hands with the Huron captains before the state championship game. I saw myself, and then the girls, years earlier, sledding down Magic Mountain in Burns Park, our faces red and half-frozen, and, on warmer days, all of us pumping our legs on the swings in the playground. I felt the glow of my fifteen-year-old swagger as I strutted through Pioneer's halls on the morning after I'd wrecked some kid from South Lyon in what was supposed to be a tough match.

My chest stretched.

My teeth hardened.

Three days.

Two dead kids.

Somebody was messing with my city.

By the time we wrapped up at the parking garage and filed our reports at the station, it was after three a.m. I was meeting Mikey in less than two hours and I was weary, but I didn't feel ready to sleep. If I went home and tried to wind down, I'd probably get forty-five minutes at most.

"I'm heading back out to dig into the heroin situation," I told Karen. "Starting at the graffiti bridge. Interested?"

"Nah, I—"

She looked intently at the report in front of her, the hard copy of what she'd just emailed Chief Taylor. I felt some of the fire drain out of me.

"Listen, it's just—"

"I get it," I said. "You're meeting Roland."

"I've been trying to find a way to tell you."

Only the two of us were in the squad room. Gumpert and Standish wouldn't be in for at least another five hours. I picked up a miniature maize and blue football from my desk and tossed it from one hand to the other. It had been signed by the six-and-a-half-foot tall quarterback John Navarre a few years earlier when we'd recovered his SUV for him after a couple Pioneer kids took it for a joyride. Fingering the fake laces, I mimed throwing a Hail Mary through the window, then chucked it sideways end over end to the woman who'd worked as my partner for a decade and a half.

She batted it away without trying to catch it. In silence, I watched it roll around on the floor and settle against a filing cabinet.

"Today on the Diag when you bitched me out, you were right." I tried to believe the words I was saying even if they felt like glass shards in my throat. "I don't have any claim on you. Who you see is your business. Roland's a good guy. One of the best."

"He is a good guy."

"That's what I just said."

"I don't want to hurt you."

I reached down and picked up the ridiculous mini football. It felt like all the pieces of my life needed not to be on the squad room floor. Needed not to be resting against a file cabinet.

"Nobody's talking about hurting anybody," I said, squeezing the football.

Karen looked exhausted. But still more beautiful than all the things in the world I would never understand. She was waiting for me to say something that would change everything about us.

"Don't worry about me," I said. "I'm tough."

"Jimmy, that's not—"

I didn't wait for her to finish. Headed back out.
To the street.

The only person at the graffiti bridge when I got there was me. I waited, like a troll crouched in darkness, my hands itching to hit something. After ten minutes, I began to shiver. Since no one was around, I shadow boxed to warm myself up. Bam, bam, bam. Jab, jab, hook. I could feel the thrum of the city beneath my toes as I slid from side to side over a manhole cover. All the clubs were closed, but somewhere, other people were dancing too. Maybe at a frat house. My fists felt like pistons, drumming in the dark, making music on the chins of rich people who sent their kids to private schools and got richer by leeching money from the public ones.

There were fresh tags on the overpass. Somebody with a green and silver bubble style named Quick. Must've named himself after the mutant superhero Quicksilver from Marvel Comics. Probably a kid who thought of himself as a mutant because he couldn't muster a homecoming date. The other tagger favored gold paint and called himself Seep, as if something were leaking from his insides each time he let loose with his Krylon. I didn't subscribe much to the graffiti-ruins-the-city theory. Most of what we got in Ann Arbor wasn't gang related. Kids here didn't mark territory. If anything, they wanted to pretend they weren't representative of the mansions their parents had bought with stock options. They snuck out in the middle of the night to establish new territories inside the landscapes of themselves, to step beyond the cozy shelters their parents had so carefully constructed for them.

A billboard across the street urged me to vote YES! on the Education Fairness Act so all kids could go to for-profit charters and get the individualized instruction they deserved. I thought about what needed to seep from children who were losing chances to make art during the school day when their elective classes were cut due to lack of funding.

I pictured Dr. Roland Roethke and how he might look without his glasses on. How he probably had eyes that were sensitive, full of meaning. How Karen probably stroked his eyebrows with her fingertips. Like she did to mine that one night.

I stopped boxing and pretended to jump rope.

A woman's angry voice cut through the quiet. I slunk back into the shadows as she cursed out a boyfriend over her phone. Something about a car and an insurance check and what kind of bullshit man did he think he was.

She looked fifty-five, but was probably forty, her hair greasy and knotted, her face adhering to the opposite philosophy of wearing too much make-up. Her speech though, was something glorious. Blue with profanity, it was full of rousing spirit, a lyrical barrage against the four a.m. stillness.

She was shaped with one of those torsos too heavy for her legs, like she might tumble backward if the man she were speaking to yelled violently enough through the phone. She obviously didn't care if anyone else felt the vibrations of her anger, her shouts echoing off the arch of the train bridge. She smelled like cheap vodka, a lot of it, and I stepped forward into the light and our eyes met and she kept cursing at her boyfriend and flipped me the finger too.

She must've gotten hung up on because she yelled "Son of a bitch!" and reared back to hurl her phone at the bridge and shatter it against the tropical-colored graffiti, but then stopped herself. Shook her head and commenced muttering, her voice growing lower until all her beautiful noise went silent and she collapsed on the curb, knees drawn against her face, phone flipping back and forth between her hands.

"Ma'am," I ventured, "are you okay?"

"You going to rape me too?"

"No, Ma'am. I'm Detective James Harrow with the Ann Arbor Police. Are you saying you've been sexually assaulted?"

"About five hundred times. What do you want? I'm high, okay? Drunk too. You going to arrest me?"

"Ma'am, I'm just trying to ascertain if you need assistance."

"Where the hell were you when I was getting plowed by my stepfather when I was ten? Or my stepbrother when I was fourteen? Why weren't you trying to ascertain anything then?"

Her phone buzzed and she looked at the screen. "Stupid bastard," she said, and didn't answer.

"I'm sorry for what you've been through, Ma'am. Can I get you a cup of coffee? A ride to a shelter?"

"Do I look like I need a shelter? I don't live in a goddamn shelter. You just want to drop me off somewhere and pretend I don't inhabit your city. I see how it is. I'm not one of those college kids, not one of those Barton Hills people, so I must not have a house to go home to, right? You can just stick me in a shelter and think you've done your good deed for the day. You think I don't pay taxes? You think I don't answer the phone when your Police Benevolent Association calls and holds me up for a sixty-dollar donation? What are you talking to me for? Why don't you go arrest those drug addict kids?"

"What drug addict kids?"

"You haven't seen 'em? They're there right now. Half of them nodded out already, the other just got a bag of weed from me."

"Ma'am, are you telling me you're out here selling drugs?"

"I didn't say anything about selling. I had some weed. Now they have it. Maybe I have a medical condition in my spleen and it's part of my treatment. Maybe there was a bag of something lying on the sidewalk and I was just walking around trying to get some fresh air in this high-quality city that cares about everyone who lives here, and I picked the bag up because I'm a curious person. What's wrong with curiosity? Isn't that what the professors say? We should care about being curious? Did my curiosity end when somebody abused me, Detective Harrow?"

"Ma'am, the kids you were talking about?"

"You're curious about the kids now?"

I wanted to feel tired of talking to this woman but she was blowing her nose into her sleeve and somehow that was charming.

"You got a cigarette, Detective Harrow?"

I pulled twenty dollars from my wallet and handed it to her.

"The kids?"

"They're over in that alley where everybody sticks gum to the wall. Or they were ten minutes ago."

The graffiti *alley,* not the graffiti bridge.

"You see them there a lot?"

"I do not spend a lot of time there, sir."

I had to meet Mikey in an hour. A handful of blocks away a group of teenagers might have been getting high in an alley with gum stuck to the walls. If I left right away and caught them before they moved on, I might learn something about who was selling them poison.

"Can I ask you a personal question?" I said to the woman who'd sniffled again into her sleeve.

"What have you *been* asking me?"

"Impersonal questions."

"Go ahead. You have nice eyes for a short police person."

"What are you doing out here at four in the morning?"

She kicked the heels of her sneakers against the curb a couple times, then leaned her head against her knees again. Her sneakers looked new, and costly.

"My husband left me," she said, without looking up. "Three months ago. During the summer when it was all hot and it wasn't ever raining, you remember that?"

I nodded.

"He took off with this slut from Howell. She's not even pretty and they went to go live in a trailer by Traverse City. For a few weeks, I came out here every night, to get drunk, sometimes to try and get high. My son's away at school at Grand Valley. He was in Europe last summer, Belgium. He wants to work for a museum. He's gay. My husband hates him and won't talk to him. He doesn't know about any of this, my son. I only come out here once a week now."

She seemed sincere when she said that, as if even if she were lying and still going out every night, she wanted, with some desperation, for it to be true. I felt compelled to sit down on the curb next to her. By mistake, I sat a little too close and brushed my hip against hers. Our thighs touched, but she didn't move away. We sat there for a while, quiet, gazing at our shoes.

I put my arm around her shoulder as if we were friends. It was inappropriate but didn't feel like it. We listened to the night. She leaned into my arm as if we were twelve-year-olds at summer camp.

"You have any idea where the kids might be getting the heroin?" I asked.

"They talk about a guy named Gumby. I've never seen him but you know how it is. When kids have a dealer, they talk about him like he's a hero. Like he comes out of a comic book to save them. They call him that because he's tall and skinny and they said he can breakdance like he's made of rubber."

Independent corroboration of Kevin Trouma's assertions, but I was still skeptical. A Gumby made of rubber who sold drugs to high school kids? Then they nodded out in an alley with gum stuck to the walls? Gumby in the gum alley?

"Black guy?"

"Did I say that? Don't go all racist cop on me, Detective. He's ghost white. Gives the high school kids whatever they need. I got the feeling they give him sexual favors in order to get it. Not just the girls either."

"They sleep with him for drugs?"

"I don't care how rich their parents are, none of these kids has enough money to support a heroin habit. You need to catch that guy. Make the streets safe again."

"I'll try, Ma'am. I surely will." I removed my arm from her shoulder and fished into my pocket so I could hand her a card. "Will you call me if you ever see this Gumby character? Matter of fact, you call me for any reason. You sure I can't give you a ride somewhere?"

She shook her head. Looked toward the bridge like she could see through Seep's pink and blue tags and far away, into a different time, a different place.

"My asshole husband," she said. "He never took me to Traverse City one time. All the years I've known him, he never took me. Not for fudge or to sit at one of those cafés by Lake Michigan and eat ice cream. Not once."

"You're better off without him," I said. "I've had a long day. Talking to you has been the only good part of it. I bet your son misses you. I bet he'll make beautiful museums." I pointed to the card in her hand. "Call me, all right? You get stuck somewhere, call me."

A train whistle sounded. It was still at least a minute away. The ground hadn't started rumbling.

"I will, Detective."

We both knew she wouldn't.

The alley.

Empty.

Graffiti everywhere. Seep and Quick and Most Roast and Dig-Dag and Slow Chill and Too Blunted and about a million other signatures zig-zagged and bubbled and criss-crossed and shadowed and bright and blaring and fading.

A ten-foot tall portrait of Marx.

Another of Lenin.

A dozen silk-screened silhouettes of Che Guevara in his beret.

Santa Claus in an airbrushed sleigh belting a swig of whiskey.

R.I.P. Johnny Cash.

Lightning bolts and flying cars and Grateful Dead skulls and peace signs and rainbows and thousands and thousands of pieces of gum stuck to the bricks. A mosaic of gum. Pink mostly, and white and grey and turquoise and beet red and apple green and neon yellow. Enough chewing gum to activate a hundred thousand mouths.

R.I.P. Eleanor Handlebar

R.I.P. Jesse and Melvin Johnson.

Pieces of chewing gum shaped like a giant marijuana leaf. J-Dubs in the Hot Tub would've been proud.

Pieces of chewing gum shaped like a smiley face.

Maize and blue pieces of gum shaped like a rubbery block M.

Gum, gum and an additional fifty collages of randomly placed pieces of gum stuck to the walls like dead bugs. Maybe I could peel every piece that still looked moist off the wall and get it tested for DNA. Maybe somebody would show up in the database resembling a skinny white kid known for breakdancing.

I heard a swooshing noise, like the flapping of pigeon wings, and turned toward the alley's entrance. A tall kid in black jeans and a black sweatshirt with the hood up so it could oval his head, knifed past on a skateboard.

I thought about running after him, but I'd never catch someone on a skateboard and the kid looked kind of hulking, not skinny.

Not Gumby.

I closed my own eyes and pretended I was the kind of superhero who had the power to detect infrared heat molecules of human beings present moments earlier. In my head, I conjured the pale shapes of almost children sitting cross-legged in a circle as if they were playing Duck Duck Goose beneath the portraits of Marx and Lenin. I saw them taking hits from a makeshift pipe fashioned by punching a hole in a beer can, then passing it around the circle to the left. I would start there, under Marx and Lenin, and I'd attempt to limit my gum touching to a six-foot by six-foot square. If I found nothing moist, I'd bang my forehead against the bricks, move on to somewhere else.

On the ground near the portraits—beer cans, a number with holes poked in them. Gum wrappers. Fast food bags.

A couple Red Bull cans.

I kicked one.

Beneath it, a condom.

Used.

I put on a pair of latex gloves—I always had some in my pockets—and picked it up. It appeared to contain a healthy amount of seminal fluid. Carefully, I deposited it into a zippered plastic bag.

Gotcha, Gumby.

CHAPTER TWELVE

FOR NEARLY TWENTY-FIVE YEARS, Mike Bednarsky and I have met at five a.m. twice a week in the University of Michigan wrestling room. He flips on the lights and the room is cold. We warm it up by jogging for fifteen minutes, stretching, throwing down a few sets of sit-ups and push-ups, and then we go at it. Every Wednesday and Friday morning for almost a quarter century, we've snapped on our headgear and tried to slaughter each other. We are still, like we were so many years ago, almost exactly the same size.

When we were on the team together, we beat each other up. He the fishing-hunting-farm-kid from the UP, me the son of two professors who wanted to prove he was too tough for the library. He taught me how to work in deeper on the high-crotch single than I ever knew possible and I taught him how to throw a cross-face with enough force to break someone's nose. The result—we broke each other's noses. Twice. And separated each other's shoulders too many times to count.

Popped them back in and kept wrestling.

We'd never faced each other in high school because I was ten pounds lighter but by the time we got to U-M I'd put that weight on in iron plates across my chest and we wore the same haircut, the same resting pulse rate, the same 5:14 timed mile, the same 325 max on the bench. We wrecked each other for four years in a brutal battle for the varsity spot in the 157 pound weight class, and every year because I was meaner and capable of throwing an elbow into his groin or grinding my forearm into his earlobe, I squeaked out an overtime win. Eventually, he wrestled up at 167.

By the time we were seniors, we knew we'd never face anyone meaner than the son of a bitch we squared off against in practice. Nobody anywhere in the country wanted to mess with us. When spring unrolled the mats for the NCAA championships in Iowa City, we strutted into the finals as a pair of undefeated top seeds.

Here's how it was for me, and is for me still.

When I'm working somebody during a wrestling match, I am a fit of rage. I act and react in a sheet of black that wipes out memory, doubt, logic. The opening whistle blows and my body transitions to a place where it does not think, and when a buzzer sounds to end a period and I look up at the scoreboard and don't know what happened to make the numbers look the way they do, then chances are I'm ahead 12-0. When the referee slaps the mat to signal I have pinned my opponent, I release a hold I don't remember attaining.

I competed in over two hundred matches in my combined high school and collegiate careers. I lost nine of them. I remember almost nothing about the wins. I remember in vivid detail eight of the nine losses. It is *because* I remember, that I lost them. In each of those eight losses, my body did not transition. I saw myself trying to set up the single-leg shot—*I will decoy left, then shoot right.* I saw myself trying to shift my weight so I could stand up and shrug off the guy trying to control me. I saw myself attempting to work one arm free, then the other. I saw these things, thought about how to execute them, and because of that seeing, that thinking, they did not happen. I did not have the speed. I did not have the rage. And I lost.

Twice, as both a sophomore and junior, I was vanquished by Eric Lockhard in the semifinals of the NCAA tournament. He was from Cal-State Bakersfield and his surname was no lie. His hands were vice clamps and his legs were pliers. He locked hard and I could not move. I thought about how to move and I saw myself moving and I was unable to accomplish what I was thinking and seeing. I can remember every agonizing second of those matches. There were no takedowns. He won the coin flip both times to start the second period, chose the down position and, when the whistle sounded, stood up. His broad back expanded as if somebody were pumping it with steel and my arms were too short and his rise was too rapid and I could not clasp my hands around him. Had I been able to keep up with his speed, I could've held him, but he was California quick and I was Midwest grip-and-hold and he was gone. I lost both matches 2-0.

Mikey was the one who told me what I already knew.

"You're thinking too much. You're not in your trance. If you wrestled that way against me, I'd beat you too."

My whole senior year I told myself not to think. I prepared for the season by working for Fingerle Lumber, loading cords of wood onto flat trucks. I practiced, during those months, the art of blanking out, my body moving and shifting and my mind acting as nothing more than a sensor that kept the body in motion. I dated four different women and I don't remember their names, the color of their respective hair, the taste of their lips. They quickly learned to hate me and I didn't blame them. I just kept moving.

They make me think now of a movie I watched when I was half asleep.

When the whistle blew in the finals, I crashed into Eric and I do not know what happened. His face was a mop I swished around the mat. I gave him nothing to lock. His ankles and wrists were mine. I bounced him off the floor and yanked him back up. He escaped and I trapped him again. He tried to stand and I stole the earth from him, held him helpless in the air the way an owl holds its thrashing prey in its mouth. Except, Eric Lockhard wasn't even thrashing. When I watched the tape later that was the thing that stunned me most. Eric Lockhard, defending NCAA champion, was listless, already a victim, defeated and waiting for the clock to tick the match to its inevitable end.

I didn't know halfway through the third period the score was 14-2, that the defending champ was being embarrassed in historical fashion, that the announcers were calling it the most shockingly dominant performance they'd ever seen.

Maybe my body sensed Eric had given up. Maybe my body was angry about his weakness, and wanted to punish him. I don't know why when I held him aloft and all I had to do was lower one knee to the ground and drop him to the mat and contain him for one more minute and walk away with my gold, I did not do it.

Instead, I slammed him down as if he were a bag of trash and I did not lower my knee and his head was unprotected and hit first and that made the slam illegal and the referee blew his whistle and halted the match.

The crowd was silent and horrified that Eric was paralyzed and even though the populace had been rooting for blood all night, when it actually saw it, perhaps my savagery was too much of a reminder of the animal so many of us like to believe we don't harbor.

I will never believe that Eric, now in his seventh term as

a stridently pro-life congressman and recently named co-chair of the House Appropriations Committee, did not sense how quickly the crowd had turned on me, and did not—after accepting his failure—see a way he could win. Maybe he was woozy, but I saw him lift himself to his feet and listen to the people cheer because they knew he was not paralyzed and I saw his eyes. In that moment when the match was paused, Eric's eyes sharpened, then turned to the scoreboard. Anybody can do the math. He could have shrugged off the slam and continued to wrestle and the ref would have deducted one point from my score and he would have been eleven points down with a minute to go and no hope, or he could shake his head, pretend my illegal maneuver had made him unable to continue and I would be disqualified and he would go into the books as a two-time NCAA champion.

If you watch the tape, you'll see him shake his head when the ref asks him if he's all right. He shakes it reluctantly, as if he can't quite believe he can't keep fighting when everything in his heart wants him not to surrender. You won't see what I saw. The face of his coach, who'd been propping open Eric's right eyelid in order to examine the ability of his pupil to focus and squirting water into his athlete's mouth. Who'd been whispering to the best wrestler he'd ever had in his program how he should attempt one last risky move to win. How he should stand up, use that speed and broad steel back to shove me off him, turn and face me and go for a suplex. Try to flip me and pull off a miracle. You will not see that coach's face freeze in disgust when, instead of nodding and preparing for the next whistle, his star athlete looks to the ground and shakes his head at the referee's question, and the referee leans in and says, "Are you sure, Eric? Are you sure you can't continue?"

And Eric appears to consider what he's being asked, and

everything in my brain knows exactly the calculations his brain is making, and he does not look at me. He slowly shakes his head again while his coach looks on in mute revulsion and the referee turns to me and says, "I'm sorry, Son, I truly am," and he raises Eric's hand in triumph and the match is over. Eric Lockhard has beaten me a third time.

The thing I like most about myself is this.

I did not throw my headgear and storm off to the locker room. My best friend was about to wrestle for the NCAA title and I stayed matside and let the sweat dry on my skin and cheered my throat raw. I pumped my fist when Mike Bednarsky got in on the single and when he walked off the mat a 4-2 winner and a national champion. I was the first to kiss his cheek with a joy that was as genuine as his own, and that is why twenty-five years later, we are still meeting twice a week to beat each other up.

We don't ask a lot of questions. When Molly threw me out, I knocked on his door and he let me in. I stayed in his guest room for six months.

On the morning after a night when I did not sleep, when I'd looked for clues on the dead body of a woman who'd served me a burger with cheddar and grilled onions two hours before she died, our routine was no different. There was no mercy, no asking if I wanted an easier go. Mikey yanked at my wrist. I yanked at his. We circled and feinted, locked our arms around each other's heads and pushed and pulled and unlocked, and I was too slow and he caught my ankle. I fell backward as if a sinkhole had opened beneath me, then squirmed to my stomach when I hit the mat. He shoved my face downward and I smelled disinfectant and the residue of shoe-bottom dirt and the deaths of my parents and Sanders Bolgim and Monique Harvey and the failure of my marriage.

That was an unacceptable smell. I inhaled it. Pulled it deep through my nostrils and let it fester. Fanned the wings of my broad back. Mikey tried to break me. Chopped at my elbow. Dug his knee into my hip. I made my back broader. Stood up. Gave him all the granite in my shoulders. Clamped my hands around his wrists. He tried to lift me the way I'd lifted Eric Lockhard but I made my feet lampposts and pushed down on his wrists, and his grip faltered.

I spun to face him and we, once more, tied our arms around each other's heads. We circled and he shot again at my ankle. I sprawled and landed my anvil chest on his head. He tugged on my elbow and spun free. This is how we spent two hours, pushing and bruising, breathing like trains, rarely scoring points. By the time we were finished, I felt a decade older. My shoulders sang an aria of pain. My knees were creaking hinges on the cellar door of a condemned tenement. Sweat climbed in my eyes and made a swampland of my thighs.

"You look like the worst kind of hell," Mikey said.

"You're gorgeous," I told him, ruffling his sweat-drenched hair.

We sat against the padded wall. My knees advised me if I didn't sleep soon they would murder me in premeditated fashion.

We looked at the bucket of disinfectant.

"You going to mop the mat again?" I said after a while.

"In a minute," Mikey said.

"I'll help," I said.

"In a minute."

We looked at the bucket some more.

"Two kids are dead," I said.

He didn't say anything, then after three or four minutes, "You'll catch whoever did it."

"Yeah," I said. "I will."

Mikey levered himself to his feet and extended his sweaty hand. I put mine in it. He pulled me up.

We mopped the mat.

After I showered and shaved, my face sparkled. My kitchen was warm with the smell of frying pancake batter when Molly dropped off Lisa. She kissed the top of her head then held out her palm.

"Really, Mom?" Lisa said.

"Really," Molly said.

Lisa pulled her phone from a pocket in the jeans she was wearing that were so tight I didn't understand how she was able to fit herself, let alone an electronic accessory, inside them.

"And the back-up," Molly said.

"What are you talking about?" Lisa said.

Molly rolled her eyes. They were beautiful eyes. When they rolled, they were like tornadoes darkening the sky. In the soft morning light hazing through the kitchen window, everything about Molly presented itself as dazzling. Her jeans were almost as tight as Lisa's and her figure felt to me like it was seeking to engage in a potentially compelling and lengthy conversation.

"The back-up," she repeated.

"Damn," Lisa said, and fished into the bookbag she'd brought with her, digging out a phone I remembered her using last fall.

"That still works?" I said. "It doesn't have a plan."

"Good enough for internet, though. Wifi." Molly looked like she'd dyed her hair a slightly deeper shade of brown since I'd last seen her. "Don't give her the password to your router. No television, either. You got that, Jim?"

I was tempted to tell her that Lisa already had the password, just as a way of reminding her I was fully capable of making my own rules in my own house. But I had to be in Chief Taylor's office in fifteen minutes and that discussion, a different kind than her jeans were offering, would have taken at least forty-five. "Got it."

"Tomorrow," Molly said, "no pancakes either. Lisa, in case you've forgotten, is suspended from school. She should be punished, not rewarded."

"Those pancakes?" I pointed to the steaming platter. "Those are for the neighbor's son next door. Poor kid's home with a broken ankle. Apparently, he was delivering newspapers on his bicycle and the canvas bag snagged in the spokes of the back wheel. Kid flipped over his handlebars but his right foot stayed stuck in the toe clips, snapped the ankle bone like toothpick. Lisa's getting gruel."

Molly almost smiled. Then didn't. "We don't have a newspaper any more, remember? I need you to support me, Jim."

"I get it."

I don't think Molly believed me, but she left anyway. I watched her walk out the door with a kind of hunger that felt like a chipmunk gnawing the walls of my gut. I piled pancakes on my plate, and Lisa's, to soothe it. "Mom's right, you know."

"I know, Dad."

"I'm resetting the password."

"You're going to switch it from JennaandLisa to LisaandJenna? You won't remember anything else."

"I'm a detective. I remember everything."

Lisa smiled. "These pancakes are good," she said.

With Monique no longer able to open her mouth, Jarrold felt like he'd bought some breathing room. He'd believed her when she said she hadn't told the police anything. She was a good kid, loyal. Still, if the cops talked to her again, they might have tricked her.

His sense watching the detectives leave the restaurant was they hadn't learned much. The midget's glance around the parking lot had been swift, distracted, as if he were thinking about something else. He probably had been. His partner's ass! She'd carried herself as if the two of them were architecting a long-term plan and they'd just gone in to check Monique out, then chow down. Probably on something deep fried because that's what cops ate, though both of them looked gym hard like he was. Still, they hadn't turned that toughness on Monique. That was evident to Jarrold's trained eye. The pair carried no residue of confrontation. They were going to be patient, question her hardcore another time.

Except, there wouldn't be another time.

Jarrold wondered how they'd found Monique in the first place. Opening his laptop, he searched through the Treetown articles about the fire. There had to be something that would let him know what had tipped the police off, made them want to investigate further.

He couldn't focus, though.

He missed her.

He sniffed the scarf he'd used to clean his prints off her wallet and the car door, and he'd used to sweep away the footprints of their dance. Even though he'd washed the scarf, he could smell dust on it, the damp mold from where people left their cars the same way they dropped their children at daycare, excising them from their thoughts until they came to retrieve them. He could smell Monique too, the mix of sweat and the mid-range perfume she liked and the vague echo of burger grease from her restaurant, a combined scent that would soon disappear forever from the earth.

He rubbed the scarf against his chest and felt himself

growing aroused, then pressed it to his cheek. He was full of despair. There were so many women in Ann Arbor he could have, but he wanted none of them. The lady cop maybe. She was pretty, sure, but too old, too wrinkled for the beer pong king. He wanted his women ripe, not close to rotting.

Those twins he'd seen the morning in the deli with Monique. He could picture the striations in their calves, the glints in their hair. Oh, he wanted them both! At the same time!

But how to find them?

He couldn't just lurk around town, inhabit the deli and wait to see if they'd show up again. Someone would mark his presence. It was too risky to haunt public places. He felt his erection growing soft. He needed to get out of Ann Arbor as soon as possible.

But not before he understood how the detectives found Monique. He stared again at the website, scrolled backward to re-read for the third time the initial stories about the fire, then changed his mind and instead typed *Detective James Harrow* into the search bar.

The first story that came up didn't make sense. It was about a field hockey player. A high school kid. He remembered hearing something about it on the sports radio station, a girl who punched another girl, but why?

His smile grew.

He felt the blossoming of a fresh arousal. Dropped the scarf to the floor and grabbed himself.

There she was.

The girl from the deli.

The prettier one of the two.

Smiling back at him from her 11th grade yearbook picture.

Lisa *Harrow.*

CHAPTER THIRTEEN

"TELL me if I have this wrong," Aricka Taylor said. "You have a potential witness to what you think might be a murder even though there's no evidence to support that notion, yet instead of interviewing said witness—just in case she might know something that could support your wild theory—you take off to talk to another kid about an opioid epidemic you think might be happening based on what the kid wrote in a poem his potentially flaky creative writing teacher read to you. Then your original witness winds up dead before you can interview her. Now you want me to believe she didn't jump off a parking garage but was pushed, even though there's no evidence to support that either."

"It's too much of a coincidence," Karen said. "Two kids who sleep with each other at a party die within a three-day span? No way that's random."

"Maybe the girl jumped because she was overcome by despair at the accidental death of her boyfriend. Maybe the grief—"

"I'm sorry," I interrupted. "What exactly makes the creative writing teacher potentially flaky?"

"She's a creative writing teacher. The *point* is no one authorized you to undertake an investigation into narcotics trafficking, especially in the middle of a so-called murder case."

"Chief," Karen said, "I've got one of my athletes in rehab over this. It's real."

"You've got another one who should've been arrested for assault." The chief looked pointedly at me. "I've got complaints against both of you for pounding college kids. Granted, yours, Evans, is anonymous. Whoever you went after in that frat house doesn't want to step up and point the finger. Still, this isn't a wild west movie. I can't have a couple of Clint Eastwoods terrorizing the community. I'm forwarding these complaints to IAD. If they want to suspend you, dock you, you brought it on yourselves."

She paused and Karen and I hung our heads, acting duly chastised.

"Could be, like I said before," Aricka said, "it's time to reconsider the coaching situation. I understand it means a lot to both of you but I wonder if your attention's splintered in too many directions. Maybe that's why you put a potential witness in harm's way."

Reconsidering our coaching duties wasn't going to happen, unless we wanted to do it ourselves. Karen was a coaching legend who had helped more young girls turn around rough lives than any police officer ever could. The fact that we wore Pioneer purple made us trusted figures in the community, even helped us develop leads. Witnesses tended not to clam up when you'd steered their children toward emotional growth.

I knew the chief had to say what she was saying in order to reinforce her chiefly status, but I hadn't slept in twenty-five hours and my willingness to be a punching bag was depleted.

"That makes no sense," I said. "Monique Harvey was either a potential witness eliminated by our killer, *or* a depressed girlfriend. You can't have it both ways. True, maybe we should have interviewed her right away, but we assessed the situation and we didn't think she'd say anything in front of her colleagues at the restaurant. We had no basis to arrest her so we thought we'd try and catch her at the end of her shift. We didn't kill her, the scumbag we're trying to catch, did. If we made a mistake in judgment, it had nothing to do with coaching."

Chief Taylor tented her fingers in front of her. Seemed to let my words circulate from one hand to the other, as if her wrists were considering my argument. Outside, a fire engine turned on its siren and roared away from the station across the street.

"You're discounting the possibility the girl knew something and was *also* a depressed girlfriend," she said. "What if she fed Bolgim the GHB, but didn't know he was supposed to die? Isn't it possible she'd be overwhelmed by grief *and* guilt?"

"Maybe, but how do you account for her phone missing from the scene?"

"How do you account for video showing nobody but the deceased entering the parking garage?"

My brain was detaching from my body. I needed to either sleep or get moving. I had maybe two minutes left where I could sit in the office without punching, kicking or cursing at something.

"You might be right, Chief," Karen said in the voice she had that could mollify a den of hissing snakes. "But either way somebody's out there who's at fault for this girl's death. Either somebody indirectly killed her by involving her in a murder she didn't understand she was being sucked into, or someone pushed her over the railing because she knew too much. I lean toward the second scenario because it fits the M.O. of the first crime. Sanders Bolgim was killed in a way that looks accidental because he knew something. Monique Harvey's death looks like a suicide. Maybe she knew something too."

I felt a humming. It started in both elbows, then shot up through my arms and shoulders. I knew what my partner was going to say before she said it.

"Which means," Karen finished, "there might be more victims. Other deaths tied to this killer we never even bothered to investigate."

As soon as the words floated from Karen's mouth, I knew she was right.

"That girl a couple years ago on spring break in Texas, who everyone said was kidnapped," I mused, "but nobody could find the kidnappers? The one found on the side of the road naked a week later? Wasn't she an early childhood education major?"

"Yes," Karen said. "I remember the comments online. People blamed her because she'd gotten drunk with friends the night she disappeared. Nobody wanted a girl teaching their children who spent her vacation getting wasted on South Padre Island."

"That wasn't our case," Aricka said, waving her hand as if she were batting away the kind of above-the-head insect plume—a chimney of midges—that often haunts the sidelines of Jenna and Lisa's summer tournaments. "We've got no jurisdiction over Texas vacation resorts."

"That's my point," Karen said. "Somebody's killing people and trying to avoid turning the deaths into cases we look into."

"What about that B-School student who died last January?" I said. "The scuba-diving accident in Maui. Wasn't it something like he swam off into deep waters and disappeared? Maybe we should find out what he was studying."

"You guys think you can investigate every time someone dies somewhere in the world? This isn't the Justice League of America. Students aren't *from* here. They do their four-year stint, then go back to where they came from. These aren't our cases."

"They *are* our cases," Karen insisted, "if we can show somebody is targeting kids here and then killing them somewhere else. There's clearly a link. Business students and education students. Money and schools. There's something underneath all this and we're being directed not to look at it."

"It might not just be Ann Arbor either," I said, the thought chilling me. "What about students at Central, Western, Wayne State? I seem to remember some kid falling off a balcony in Vegas last year. A football player. Drunk also, but who knows, maybe he was studying to be a teacher."

"There's no way—"

"I'll tell you something else," I said, as if I couldn't care less whether interrupting my boss would land me in deeper misery. "We need to think about how anyone would have access to what these kids were studying. Who would know that information?"

My question stopped the conversation cold. We could hear coffee machines percolating and photocopiers lying in wait to begin their shuffle. Chief Taylor fidgeted so hard behind her desk her knee thumped into the bottom of it.

"So you're saying?" Karen said.

"You have no evidence to support—"

I interrupted Chief Taylor again. "Evidence or not, there are only two kinds of people who have the juice to monitor what students are studying. Think of the thousands of kids who write papers, or at least plagiarize them. If somebody's red-flagging whenever students are digging into a particular subject, you have to be talking about either a dean of students or some kind of university regent. Either way, that means if there's anything to all this, it goes up high. I don't know what we're tugging on, but if we don't let go—"

This time it was Karen who interrupted, tapping her pen against her notebook as she did it.

"We're about to piss off some powerful people."

"We can rule out the football player," Karen said, pulling her phone away from her ear.

We 'd been burning up the squad room with calls that mostly resulted in additional questions. The girl who'd been kidnapped in Texas was definitely studying childhood education—one of those pure hearts who'd wanted to be an elementary school teacher since seventh grade—but nobody could remember if she'd specifically been looking at charter schools. Nobody knew what the B-School kid who'd disappeared while scuba-diving had been working on either. The Dean's secretary said she could probably find out but she'd have to get permission from the Dean, and he was gone the next three days at a conference. He'd also left strict instructions not to be bothered unless it was a matter of life and death.

"It *is* a matter of life and death," I told her. "We're trying to find out if this student was murdered."

"That's a matter of death only," the secretary said. "The kid's not coming back to life, is he?"

Bottom line, without a search warrant, she wasn't going to help us.

We tried to get a search warrant.

The judge, newly appointed by our big-haired governor,

laughed. "You want me to sign a warrant about an accidental death that's almost a year old and happened in Hawaii? I've got a full docket and I'm headed out of town in two hours. No chance."

I tried not to wonder what kind of judge would cut short his workweek on Wednesday afternoon because we were on the grind and it looked like we might've found four other potential victims. A kid from Kalamazoo College had died of alcohol poisoning at the Burning Man Festival in Nevada a year ago, but we couldn't dig much deeper because there was no report on his major. Since none of these kids had died recently, all their social media had already been excised or made private for their families. We tried the K-College registrar's office, but were again stonewalled. No warrant meant no privileged information including, apparently, the simple fact of what a student was studying. Without any concrete proof to bolster our theory, no judge would grant us a warrant. It felt like a feedback loop as absurd as Take-Home Tailgate's.

A student from Central had died a few months after the scuba-diving kid while on a camping trip at the Grand Canyon. The people he'd been hiking with said he was seriously stoned when he went to urinate over the rim just as the sun was starting to set and he must have fallen. I didn't like it. Again, though, we got nothing from the registrar's office. No info without a warrant. No warrant forthcoming.

The other dead kids were a pair of roommates, juniors at Wayne State in Detroit, who'd been gunned down the previous April on Cass Avenue in what had been labeled a drive-by shooting, but neither kid had demonstrated any prior connection to gang activity. This was undoubtedly our best lead. We didn't know what the kids were studying, but DPD—where we had friends—gave us the names of their mothers and we were scheduled to meet them later that afternoon.

"What'd you get on the football player?" I asked Karen.

She shook her head. "Interesting kid. Art major, way into ceramics. Even had his own potter's wheel in the basement of his dorm. There's a story about him in the school newspaper, and another in his hometown weekly in Big Rapids. A maniac on the field, hardest hitter on the team. Then after practice, he'd go home and throw pots until midnight. Quality stuff too, some featured in art galleries. Two of his teammates were witnesses to his death. He was plastered and leaning over the balcony yelling at a group of passing girls. Made the kind of miming motion to encourage them to take their shirts off and lost his footing, went right over the railing. Sworn affidavit says it was definitely an accident. He slipped."

I pictured this gigantic person, two hundred and sixty-plus pounds with strawberry blond hair, an artist's rough hands, a goofy grin. How he said stupid things to girls—the kind of dumb things I used to say all the time and sometimes still think, even if I no longer verbalize them—then lost his balance, his bulk tumbling like a refrigerator through the night. His buddies must've been terrified, maybe reached for him, their own reflexes dulled by too many beers. Maybe he screamed on his way down, the kid knowing it was all over for him. Or maybe he didn't scream, didn't believe he'd die. Maybe he thought it'd be just one more battering collision he'd walk away from.

I thought about the girls who saw him fall, how surreal it must've looked to see the huge kid topple off the balcony, about his family and friends back home getting the news, his teammates and coaches, his art professors losing their prize pupil.

My body ached. I was going on thirty hours without sleep. My limbs felt like sodden logs. I could sense my own balance teetering as if I, too, would've fallen if I'd been on the balcony, and twenty, and a boy, and drunk, and marveling at a pack of girls below.

"Maybe we're fishing for something that doesn't exist," I said. "Kids die in accidents all the time. Think they're immortal and find out too late they're not. Maybe it's just the lucky ones who survive. Maybe Sanders was unlucky, that's all, and Take-Home Tailgate was nothing but a shady company that vanished to escape liability. Maybe Monique killed herself out of grief, like Aricka said.

"It's like you were saying before, Karen, this information about charters is already public, and no one cares. It's well known these for-profit companies are printing money and not only is there no outcry, people are applauding the politicians pushing for their expansion. They're basically getting away with truckloads of theft from the public trough and earning positive press, happy documentary films that praise them for doing it. Why would they need to murder anyone?"

Karen, who was about to make another call, stopped dialing.

"You're tired," she said, her eyes looking at me as if she'd been with me on the curb when I was talking to the woman whose husband left her for his Traverse City tryst. But she hadn't been, she'd been rolling around with Roland.

"I'm not."

"Right."

"I'm fine."

"You want to give up on this case, Detective Harrow?" Karen said. She said it like she'd quit too, if that's what I wanted, but also like I must not be as vibrant and strong as I used to be, as if there were legit reason for her to date someone else.

I shook my head. "I'm good."

"That you are."

"I meant with the case. I'll tell you what, let's go to Detroit, see what develops, make an assessment on the way back. I'll even let you drive so I can crash a little in the passenger seat on the way."

"Hey, bro," the bum said, tapping on Jarrold's half-down window. "You got a quarter? I want to buy a cup of coffee."

Jarrold couldn't stand beggars. He understood bad luck. He'd been there. But had he ever prostrated himself? Ever pleaded with another human being to hand him money?

"I'm not your bro," he said, showing the loser the skin color of his muscular forearm. "I'm white, you're black and you can't get a cup of coffee for a quarter. You think I'm stupid, you shit-faced crackhead? Why don't you get your lazy ass away from my car?"

"You're impolite, Mister."

"How about if you don't move away from my car right now, I break your face into pieces and scatter them across the sidewalk?"

"I'm going to tell the police you threatened me."

Jarrold got out of the car, shoving the door into the bum's crotch so that he groaned. Before he could make whatever additional sputtering noise he intended to make, Jarrold clapped his hand over the man's foul-smelling alcoholic mouth and hauled him into an alley adjacent to a nearby house, behind a huddle of large recycling bins.

From where he'd parked, he could see the driveway to the police motor pool where he hoped he'd be able to watch Detectives Harrow and Evans pull out so he could trail them and discover where they were headed next in their investigation. He'd chosen the spot carefully, beneath a tree still thick with foliage that dramatically, overnight it seemed, had turned yellow. He couldn't be seen from the station. Not sitting in his car, not beating on this bum.

He popped the lid from one of the recycling bins with his shoulder and inhaled the wet cardboard stench of folded pizza boxes and cases from cheap beer. With a quick heft, he grasped the bum by the back of his fraying pants and tipped him into the bin. With the man's head mashed against the bottom, the sharp edge of a clothing catalogue jutted into his eye. Jarrold made his hand into an axe-blade and slashed at the back of the bum's knee.

The man's body jolted, spasming as if he'd been tasered, and then he whimpered. Jarrold pushed harder on his legs so the man's face pressed more urgently against the bottom of the bin, the edge of the catalogue ramming deeper into his eye. The man yelped.

"Shut up," Jarrold told him. "You're boring me."

The man sniffled once more, then quieted.

"Listen," Jarrold said. "I'm going to stuff your legs in here and close the lid. You can move around if that's possible. Feel free to try and get more comfortable. No reason, for example, that magazine needs to keep digging into your eye. Keep your ears open and after you hear me start my engine and drive off, count to one hundred silently to yourself. That might be a challenge, but try to think back to elementary school. Try to remember which number comes after the other. For example, 44, then 45, then 46. When you reach a hundred, you can climb out. I suggest the best way to accomplish that would be to rock back and forth until the bin tips over. Then you can kick the lid open and crawl out backward. If the bin moves before I leave, I'll kill you. If you tell the police about our pleasant interlude, I'll come back and kill you. Do you understand?"

"Yes," the bum croaked, his voice sounding like he'd spent the last two nights sleeping in the rain.

"Good."

Jarrold shut the lid and the air around him smelled fresher. He inhaled, relished the crispness of the day, the blaze of leaves painting something sublime in the trees.

Then he tucked himself back into his car to watch the cop's motor pool and listen to sports radio.

CHAPTER FOURTEEN

WE LISTENED to sports talk on the way to Detroit.

With the Wolverines and Lions on the road, the morons on the air debated which bar was the best place to watch a game. Then the conversation morphed into whether someone deserved to have his man-card revoked if he brought his wife or girlfriend to the game-watching gathering.

I lost interest because I hadn't been to a sports bar since I was thirty. Outside, the sky was murky. The freakish, friendly blue of just a few minutes ago seemed distant, like winter had kicked it in the ribs and was letting us know the long string of months that chews our faces was looming, rolling toward us like an army of slow moving but merciless troops.

Karen drove. I tried to shut my eyes. Maybe I dozed, I don't know. Something was off, I was jumpy, irritated. Wanted to fight somebody bigger than me.

On the radio, the hosts went to the phones and the first caller insisted if a female could drink without complaining, and if she knew sports well enough not to ask stupid questions, she could be tolerated. "I used to have a girlfriend like that," he said. "She knew everything, like even how many time-outs Michigan had left. You should've seen her shout at the screen if she thought somebody blew a pass interference call. She was ready to murder someone."

"And you didn't marry her?" one host said. "She knew the time-outs and you didn't marry her? What happened?"

"A hundred bucks says she's butt-ugly," the other host broke in. "A girl who knows sports and slams beers, she does it because she wants attention from men. She has to be missing, minimum, three teeth. Probably looks like a hobbled barn horse. I bet she could drop fifty pounds and still look like she swallowed the whole Thanksgiving turkey, and the entire left side of a ham salad. Am I right, or am I correct?"

"What the heck is a ham salad? I never even heard of that," the first host said.

"No," said the caller. "The funny thing was she broke up with me. She was cute, not gorgeous or anything and, yeah, she could lose a few, but who can't? Anyway, I really haven't met anybody else since then. I still go to the bar to watch the game with the boys and we drink, but, to tell the truth, it's kind of lonely."

"That's sad, dude," one host said. "You can't call our show with pathetic material like that. You need to grow a pair and forget about her."

"Why do you listen to these idiots?" Karen said, reaching to change the dial. "Christ, a boy band marathon would be less annoying."

"What do you mean? There's pathos there. Poor guy can't enjoy games at the bar anymore, can't get over his lover who used to bash the hapless referees. Can't you see the guy mooning over her, wearing an old Barry Sanders jersey that's too tight around his flabby chest, crying into his beer?"

Karen turned the radio off. "Are you all right, Jim?" she asked.

"Of course, why?"

"You're not imagining yourself as that guy, are you? Crying in your beer—except alone at your house instead of in a bar—while you worry about what I might be doing with Roland?"

"Feel free to check your ego any time, Detective Evans."

We passed the eighty-foot-tall Uniroyal tire off the side of the highway. When I was a kid, I used to believe the story that there was a Ferris wheel inside it. I wondered what'd it be like to circle around the interior of its rubber guts, as if you'd been swallowed by a giant assembly line. The truth is, I *was* imagining myself as that guy, wearing his outdated Lions jersey, drinking alone. And I was thinking of Karen and Roland too. He was a decent dude, and I didn't want to picture the two of them in an intimate encounter—his hands moving under her clothes, positioning her hips—but come on, even with her fake crush on the Professor, there was no way Karen could really, sincerely, super-deeply fall for a guy like him.

"There's a lot of things you don't know about me," I said.

"Starting with it's an eternal mystery how you can listen to Lunk One and Lunk Two on the radio for more than twelve seconds."

The night we were together she'd dropped me off and I'd gone into my room to change for my run. I was sitting on the edge of my bed, pulling on a sock and heard a click from the front door. I closed my eyes and when I opened them, she was in front of me without any clothes on. Shimmering.

Her body is the blade of a hatchet but when I leaned in and kissed her stomach, breathing in through my nose so I could smell how close she was, it's like she knew how to make all her hardness soften. For a long time, I just held my face against her warmth. Her hands were gentle in my hair and then at some point I was on my back—the place I never want to be—except with Karen, I was safe.

"There's other stuff you don't know," I said.

"Like what?"

"Like maybe I have a date tonight, a dinner date after wrestling practice."

"No, you don't, and trying to make me feel jealous is sadder than these radio idiots," Karen said, then flipped the station back on to prove her disdain for the direction I was attempting to steer the conversation.

"Lisa in Ann Arbor, what's on your mind?" Lunk One said.

"Oh, I have a mind now?" my daughter said to the greater Detroit metro listening public. "Then again, I must be butt-ugly if I have a mind, right? I must look like, what'd you say, a beat-up horse that needs to be shot?"

"Whoa, honey, just hold on there," Lunk Two said. "No need to take it personal."

"Listen, you two d-bags, if I want to watch a game, I'll watch the game wherever and whenever I want, and my husband or my boyfriend or whoever the hell wants to say anything about it, can bite me."

"Bite her?" Karen said.

"There'll be no biting of my daughters," I said. "On the radio or otherwise."

"Can she say hell over the airwaves like that?" Karen asked.

"Apparently." I squinted my eyebrows. Molly had her phones. Was she using my house phone? Did kids even know how?

"I think you need to chill a little bit, Lisa from Ann Arbor," Lunk One said.

Big mistake.

"You want *me* to chill?" Lisa said. "Let's talk about your whole stupid idea of a man-card in the first place. Who are you to revoke anybody's anything? You need to revoke your own brain-card. And when did anyone need a license to be a man anyway? You need a license not to be stupid. How about you need to revoke your own human- being card? Or how about next time you say any girl who likes sports must be missing three teeth, I just come down to your studio and knock *all* your teeth from your disgusting pig mouth?"

"Glad to hear the suspension from school's calming her down," Karen said.

"Whoa," Lunk Two said, "you're not *the* Lisa from Ann Arbor, are you? The cop's kid from the news? The babe who cold-cocked that beastly chick? If you are, you can come to the sports bar any time, sweetheart. I'll buy you a beer. Ten beers."

Shit, I thought, or maybe said aloud.

"She's your daughter," Karen said about the girl who in so many ways—other than biological—was her daughter too. "And she's just dazzling."

"Turn it off," I said, and closed my eyes. "I'm taking a nap."

Jarrold grew increasingly irritated as he trailed the detectives. He'd been trying to stay at least a quarter mile behind and his grey sedan was unobtrusive. Still, his stress levels were spiking. Maybe he'd have felt better if he'd strangled that bum instead of making him eat garbage, but he hadn't and now that felt like a mistake. Killing a drunk no one cared about might have thrown the detectives off, broken the pattern and made them second-guess themselves.

Because if the detectives were headed to Detroit, that changed everything.

He didn't want to panic. They could have been going to Detroit for lots of reasons. Maybe there was a cop convention with a gourmet donut buffet.

Maybe they had another case, a dealer who'd been selling molly to spoiled Ann Arbor kids. He'd read on Treetown that a woman had woken up in her Upper Burns Park mansion and found a teenager passed out on the trampoline in her backyard. He'd thrown up all over the grass and wasn't responsive when she shouted at him. At the ER, it was determined he'd nearly killed himself with a combination of tequila and ecstasy. Maybe Detectives Midget and Beautiful had heard about a pipeline from the D and were following up.

His gut was telling him that wasn't true though, and his gut was generally accurate. He'd never wanted to take out the kids from Wayne with such a flimsy plan. *Gun them down like it's a drive-by,* his employers had insisted, *no one will investigate. Black kids die on the street every day. It's not even news.*

There was truth in that assessment of lazy and stupid officers of the law and it was also true the targets weren't rich kids with vacation plans to exotic locales, so he hadn't bothered to lobby for a better strategy, and now that seemed like another error. The kids, it turned out, hadn't been gang members but honors students with fat mothers who wouldn't shut their fat mouths and kept demanding the Detroit police investigate further.

Still, what did that have to do with Ann Arbor cops?

If the detectives had somehow connected the nerd's death, Jarrold realized, or Monique's, with the fake drive-by, then they must know something he didn't.

He'd been given the assignments as if they were homework, problem sets to be completed before a certain deadline. He didn't know why the targets had been chosen and he didn't need to. But was it possible the cops *did* know? How else would they have found a link?

He tried to figure it out. Didn't like feeling like the cops were a step ahead. His skull ballooned like he'd lost at beer pong and been forced to drink fifty cups of swill. He couldn't concentrate with all the noise in his life, the highway and the careless people revving their engines when they accelerated, and Monique's silent gaze as he threw her off the parking garage, her lack of surprise as if she knew it were coming, as if it didn't matter that it did come, and these nattering idiots on the radio with all their wannabe quarterback bluster. He reached to switch to a music station—maybe something breezy, Neil Diamond or Engelbert Humperdinck—when a girl's voice came on, an angry girl's voice, and he knew.

It was her.

The cop's kid.

Berating the hosts about their stupid opinions, making them look like middle school zit-faces who'd flunked a life quiz.

He laughed because she was hilarious and he felt himself getting hard, his lips parched. He needed something cold to drink. A chocolate milkshake, something thick and frozen that would give him a different kind of pain in his head, an arrow above his eyes. His groin throbbed.

Oh, he wanted this girl, wanted to drill her right in front of her midget cop father, wanted to watch his face when she moaned. Oh, he could burst. Right now. He could!

He felt himself tugging his car off the highway. A McDonald's a quarter-mile from the exit. A milkshake! The girl! Oh!

He steered onto the shoulder. Turned off the engine a

few hundred yards away from the McDonald's parking lot. Placed his hand on his throb.

The girl!

Oh! Oh!

We met Beverly Johnson and Amber Allen in Ms. Allen's apartment, but Beverly Johnson was the one who offered us coffee, ushered us into the kitchen and showed us where to sit. The apartment, though small, was well-ordered, the sink and countertops sparkling. Cereal boxes visible in a glass-paned pantry were of the organic grainy variety found in the overpriced aisles of status stores like Whole Foods.

The building itself, in which both women lived, was an island, the sole edifice on the block that wasn't burned out. It stood between two weed-strewn lots where the carcasses of split-open garbage bags festered and enough broken glass littered the concrete to make a mosaic. We didn't have streets like that in Ann Arbor. We knew they existed just forty miles away, but most of us, I suspect, tried not to think about them. We worried instead about whether the price of our season tickets for football games would rise. Maybe that's something I didn't love so much about my city.

"I'm sorry I don't have any cookies," Ms. Allen said, her tone flat, wary. "I thank y'all for coming out here."

She was, I'm sure, dubious in regard to our motives. Why would we care about the deaths of two kids in Detroit?

Karen took charge.

"We're sorry for what happened to your sons, and honestly, we might be fishing in the dark. There's a slim chance the murders are connected to a couple other students who died under suspicious circumstances. We're trying to figure out whether that connection exists. If we cause additional pain by taking you through this again, or by creating a sense of false hope that we'll find who killed your sons, we apologize."

"Look," Ms. Allen said. "My son was shot down in the street. Whatever you tell me won't make him come back. I don't have illusions. I have two more children. Every day I think about what I need to do so they can grow up in a place like where you live. A place where they can walk to school and nobody's going to shoot them. Please don't come in here telling me what I should allow myself to hope for. I appreciate your caring, but I would like you to just ask your questions and let us worry about our feelings. Nobody in this room has any time worth wasting."

Karen nodded, slowly, and I sipped my coffee, which was dark and rich and tasted as good as anything I could buy in one of the buzzing coffee shops back on South University Street.

"The police couldn't confirm the shootings were gang related," Karen said.

"That's because they weren't," Beverly Johnson said. "Not in the way you think."

"How do you know?" I asked. "Nobody's saying your sons were in gangs, by all accounts, they were terrific students, but could it have been an accident? They were mistaken for somebody else, or in the wrong place at the wrong time?"

Ms. Allen shook her head. "Our boys were targeted. There was no mistake. What did the reports say about witnesses?"

"They all saw the same thing. A lone gunman wearing a black ski mask in a black SUV pulled up next to the boys on the corner, rolled down his window and shot with a rapid-fire weapon. Then he sped off before anyone could get the plate on the vehicle."

"That's because anybody who saw it was still ducking," Ms. Johnson said.

"The point is," Ms. Allen said, "if that shooting were gang-related, you'd have witness reports that were blank. You wouldn't have a description of the car or the shooter. You wouldn't even know if it was only *one* shooter. That's why the police were skeptical, because everybody who saw it wanted to talk to them. What does that tell you?"

"That your two boys were loved by the community," Karen said. "People want to see whoever shot them pay for it."

Beverly Johnson shook her head again, as if she couldn't believe experienced cops could be so naïve. I sipped more excellent coffee, waited. We could hear a DPD siren nearby. It sounded ridiculous, like a child crying because a favorite TV program had ended earlier than it was supposed to, a cry nobody felt like listening to.

"People told the police what they saw," Ms. Johnson said, "because we knew whoever killed Blair and Jesse wasn't coming back. Wasn't somebody worried about keeping us quiet. That's why we're talking to you now. Whoever killed Blair and Jesse wanted to keep *them* quiet, and they already did that so they're not worried about us."

"Why do you think that?"

Ms. Johnson looked at Ms. Allen. The two mothers were similar in appearance. Neither was overweight, or tall. Both had hair cut short to the scalp. Ms. Allen was still in nurse's scrubs from the hospital where she worked.

She pointed to a framed photo that hung on the wall next to an old-school telephone, mahogany with a long cord that curled into itself. In the picture, the boys wore high school graduation robes and smiled, their arms around each other's shoulders, caps in their hands.

"You know what they were doing on that corner?" Ms. Allen asked, her voice trembling.

"The police report said they were registering people to vote."

"That's true. They had clipboards and forms for people to sign and pamphlets telling them which issues were important. As if everybody didn't already know."

"What do you mean?"

We heard another siren pleading for somebody to care.

"Look around you." Amber Allen stood up with her coffee and walked toward her kitchen window. Which was spotless. "Our problems are obvious. Vacant lots and buildings. No good jobs, and the ones we do have cutting wages and benefits. Services terminated. You see that garbage in the yard next door when you came in? That's from the past two days only. Beverly and I clean it up every weekend. It's back by Tuesday morning. Like the roaches and rats in these buildings, the mice and bedbugs and lice. Doesn't matter what you do, you can't get rid of them. You know what it's like to try and sleep at night with scratching in the walls?"

I did know. A raccoon dug a hole through my roof three summers ago and set up a man-cave in my attic. Tore up the insulation and defecated everywhere. Cost seventeen thousand dollars to get everything cleaned out, fumigated and repaired, and to replace the roof. Insurance paid for most of it and I only heard the raccoon in the walls that one night, but it scared the hell out of me. For weeks, I felt like nature was letting me know if it wanted to, it could just roll in with its animals and the thin walls of my house would not protect me.

I could only imagine what it would feel like to hear creatures scratching every night. In a way, that anxiety seemed like a metaphor for the whole city. The human population was losing its hold. Its mammoth stone and steel monuments to the construction of the automobile were rotting under the weight of a global climate angry at too much exhaust spit into its skies, and of white flight decimating the city's tax base for too many consecutive decades. Animals and vegetation were reclaiming what had once been theirs, eager, clawing to make it theirs again.

Amber Allen stared at me.

"I know what you're thinking," she said. "When you look at the filth and crime, you think we don't have a lot of time left. You think the death of this city is inevitable. But that's the attitude that defeats us. That's why the boys were trying to get people voting again."

Karen was quiet now, writing notes in her notebook.

"It's not about blaming white people for the problems we have." Ms. Allen turned from the window and walked toward us as if she were about to sit again, then veered instead toward the cabinet with the cereal boxes and gazed at them through the glass. Beverly Johnson opened her mouth to say something, but didn't. The sound of the siren receded. We could all hear Karen's pen scratching across her page.

When Amber Allen turned to face us again, tears were clouding her eyes.

"What happened to this city," she began again, her voice steady despite the tears, "what's *still* happening, is a policy choice. That's what Jesse and Blair believed. They had ideas. Two boys smart as whips and they never thought about going to school in Ann Arbor or moving to Chicago to live in a fancy townhouse. They wanted to stay and fix things. That's all they talked about. That's why they both majored in urban planning, and did it here, at Wayne State. The urban they wanted to plan was this one. They had ideas, Detectives, and hope too. That's why someone wanted to shut them up. Somebody didn't like their ideas."

"Did those ideas include anything about education?"

"Are you kidding?" Ms. Johnson chimed in. "Education was the foundation of their plan."

Karen's pen stopped scratching.

"You have children?" Ms. Johnson asked.

I nodded. "Two daughters."

"You want them in a class with fifty kids when they're six years old?"

I had a quick image of Lisa flipping out and tearing through a room overcrowded with restless first-graders, fists slashing the air like buzz saws.

"I wouldn't."

"We don't either. That's what Amber means by policy. Somebody in charge decided only a small amount of resources should go toward teaching our children. How do you learn in a room like that?"

"What was Jesse and Blair's plan?" Karen asked, the first thing she'd said in several minutes.

"They wanted to start right there with class size. Build it from the inside out. Which is what we never do."

I didn't know what that meant. Did she mean like a car? Construct a strong engine and then build the frame around it? Was Ms. Johnson saying all previous attempts to fix Detroit had been cosmetic paint jobs, the motor inside left to rot?

Amber Allen's tears had dried on her cheeks, like streaks of rain against a window.

"What Beverly means," she said, "is people always act like what we need is something we don't already have. Bring a casino in here. Bulldoze our neighborhoods and gentrify. Start an artist's colony so white people will come back and we'll be vital again. Jesse and Blair thought we should start by making things better for people who live here *now*. They wanted a cap of fifteen students per class. Kindergarten right up through high school. That way, the teacher could pay attention to everyone. They would need more classrooms, of course, more schools to make that happen, and that's what would rebuild the city. The neighborhoods would grow around the schools. Teachers could be offered discounted housing in the same area and then some really good people, smart young people, hopefully, would stay here and raise families and be part of building something fresh. The contractors could get even more work remodeling all these abandoned houses so teachers could live there. Then the contractors would have money to spend at local businesses, and the teachers would be living in the community and spending their money here too, and things could start to turn around."

She stopped talking for a minute and sipped at her coffee. Her eyes were lit and the dried tears on her face looked less to me like stains on a window than roads on a map. It was as if whatever spark had ignited the hope in her son still lived in her. I felt like going into the yard next door and spending the next few hours picking up trash. I felt like moving Lisa and Jenna into Detroit so they could grow up to become teachers. And start an inner-city field hockey program.

"I want to tell you something, Detectives. I know that plan sounds crazy, but I've been living in this city for almost fifty years. I'm as cynical as they come. I never believe anybody's plan will work, but this one starts with the children. It tries to fix things so they can have it better than we did. Their vision wasn't about emergency managers appointed from somewhere who come in and break all the union contracts. It was about innocence. Blair and Jesse called it The Innocent Child Project. Not legal innocence, but about giving our kids what white kids get, a chance to dream of possibility. I think that could work, I really do. I think whoever shot our boys thought it could work too. That's why my son bled to death on the street, Detective, and that's why whoever did it won't ever get caught."

After he zipped his pants up, Jarrold paid for, and drank, a milkshake.

It was cold and thick, but not as satisfying as he'd hoped it would be. So he bought more. Two quarter-pounders with cheese. Large fries. Then a filet-o-fish. Something he'd never had before. He found himself immensely enjoying the tartar sauce. He ordered another one. Some more fries. An apple pie rolled up like a chimichanga. It was all delicious. Every last bite. He hadn't been to McDonald's in at least a decade and he'd forgotten how good it was. He ordered a six-piece of chicken nuggets, then a nine-piece. A large Coke.

Now, parked in Detroit, the dregs of bags, boxes and ketchup packets decorated his car. The smell too. A wondrous smell. He still felt hungry, but also full, too full, yet he wanted more fries, just a few more, just another handful.

But there were no fries. Not even bits of fries. He clawed through the two cartons he'd already eaten, licked the salt and ketchup from his fingers. Dipped his thumb in the small container of tartar sauce and licked whatever was left there too, then looked for sesame seeds that might have fallen off a quarter-pounder bun, and found a smattering on the floor near the gas pedal. Ate them one at a time.

Had he been foolish to stop following the cops?

Apparently not. Here was their car.

Parked where he'd expected it would be. Outside the building where the fat moms with their fat mouths lived. That was bad news. It meant the cops had connected the nerd's death to the drive-by and that meant they knew something Jarrold didn't.

He dug into one of the French fry cartons and scraped off a nib of ketchup that had gotten stuck to the carton's sides, then sucked it from beneath his fingernail. The jabbering fools were at it again on the radio, talking now about whether they liked women who fought more than women who didn't fight. Idiots. Slobbering pigs who probably feasted on McDonald's like he was doing, but, unlike him, did it every day. That's why they were in radio instead of television.

The cops had been inside for too long. What could they be learning?

Damn the people who hired him.

Why did he get involved in such stupidity?

He had enough money. He could settle down in a small town somewhere, marry the cop's daughter and add an ice cream station to the teashop. Serve that fancy gelato for twelve dollars a scoop.

Jarrold clawed through the French fry carton, searching for more salt, more ketchup.

When Amber Allen said white kids get to dream about possibility, I knew that was one thing Molly and I always agreed on. We didn't think about it in terms of our kids are white so they can do whatever they want, but no matter what, we wanted Lisa and Jenna to grow up trusting they could do something great.

That's why we paid for every field hockey clinic, every travel team. Why we gave them music lessons and art classes and took them out to eat good food and to theater productions and museums. We never wanted them think there was a place they couldn't go.

And yet, kids in Ann Arbor still snuck into frat parties when they were thirteen and got blunted at midnight on the same swing sets they used to fly on when they were first-graders.

And some had gravitated to needles.

I thought about Kevin Trouma cleaning his house, tending his yard, and then heading to his huge basement to write in his journal and think about how Tammy Binder's addiction was his fault, how he should have loved her more. All the privilege in the world for that kid, yet he still had compassion, still believed it was his responsibility to try and hold other people together.

"I'll tell you something else," Ms. Allen said. "This city's not ready to die yet. It might not happen soon, but one day we will invest in our children. We have to. And that's when we'll come back. *We'll* be the ones who rebuild. Nobody's going to come in from outside who can help us, and that includes both of you. Again, I thank y'all for caring, but the only thing that's going to save us, is us."

I took that as our cue to leave and started to rise from my chair. I was inspired in a vague way, but despite the good coffee, my sluggish brain wasn't sharp enough to catch whoever barbecued Sanders Bolgim or put holes in the sons of these women. I needed sleep—more sleep than a catnap in a car could provide.

Karen had more questions though.

"What did Jesse and Blair think about charter schools?"

"Don't get me started," Beverly Johnson said. "You know I work for a charter school, right?"

We didn't.

"I used to be a para-professional—a teacher's aide—in the elementary school two blocks from here, down by where the old ballroom used to be. Did that for nine years. When the classes got big like they do, they would assign me to help the teacher. I could put children in small reading groups or work with the little ones who didn't know how to make their letters and numbers. I get second-graders, third-graders sometimes, who can't spell out their own names. Most children can do that in preschool. We get a lot who never went to preschool. You know what they went to? Television. They can't spell their names but they know every episode of *SpongeBob SquarePants*. What's the sense of that?"

"I don't like SpongeBob," I blurted.

"Two years ago, the Governor cut funding and I got pink-slipped." Ms. Johnson continued as if, thankfully, I hadn't said anything moronic. "All the paras did. Didn't matter if we were doing a good job. Didn't matter if we had a negotiated contract. The emergency manager said the schools couldn't afford us so we were gone."

Outside, another siren. I tried to make my brain work better. The light through the spotless window whispered a transition from early afternoon to later, the kind of moment you'd miss if you weren't paying attention. With the warm weather, the leaves in Ann Arbor had only recently turned, releasing their bounteous gold, red, orange. That too was an innocence my kids got to hold onto. Leaves in parts of Detroit like this, where trees had been gone for decades, were more legend than memory.

Amber Allen was right. If someone were going to save Detroit, it wasn't going to be Karen and me, and if we didn't head back soon, I'd be late for practice. Maybe Kevin Trouma was going to show up and I didn't want everyone bumbling around waiting for me, trying to get into a locked wrestling room, making it look like I was running a sloppy program. If I had a minute, I wanted to check in on Lisa too, see if I could discourage her from calling out douchewads on the public airwaves, at least until the attention from her slugging that girl died down.

"Most of us wound up working at charters," Ms. Johnson continued, "at about forty percent of the salary. A lot of teachers were the same teachers from public schools too, the younger ones who got let go because they didn't have enough seniority. They were also making less money, like fifty percent less. The others were Teach for America people with no experience and no training. Don't get me started on them either."

"But I thought charters were in demand," Karen said. "That parents want to send their kids there. If they're saving all that money on salary, what's the attraction? Are the class sizes smaller?"

"Not really. The school day is longer, but kids sit in front of computers almost the whole time. To me, everyone's just bored. Believe me, when students first come to our school, they think it's something new and different because their parents told them it was. They think they're special to go there and some of these young teachers stay enthusiastic even if they're overworked and so poor they can't afford to buy a house in Detroit—where houses are cheaper than water—and maybe the children have to wear uniforms or say a special cheer in the morning, so, yes, it feels exciting. After a while though, it's still big classes, still not enough books or bathroom tissue. Still just staring at a screen and children who read too far below grade level and have no heat in their houses or maybe only one meal a day. For all the hype, most of the charters aren't any better than the schools the children just left. A lot of them, to be honest, are worse.

"Jesse and Blair wanted more funding and more teachers for our own public schools, paid for with our own taxes. You know, just like how it happens in the suburbs. Whoever was getting rich off that not happening—that's the real gangsters, that's who killed our sons."

"Jim, are you all right?"

Karen was impatient. We were outside the apartment building but hadn't left. She knew we should be hustling back to the station, catching the chief up on what we learned, trying to convince her to give us more leeway. She had to, right? Two more dead kids researching education and making plans about rebuilding public schools? No way she could shut us down.

Actually, the longer we made her wait for us to report, the more likely she'd kill the case. I could envision her, playing with her phone, toying with the idea of texting us, just wanting to yell at somebody because she was tired of waiting.

I was picking up garbage.

I'd pulled on a pair of evidence gloves and now I was tying together a split-open bag and stuffing in the remnants of fast food, coffee cups and orange rinds. Something liquid spilled on my wrists. Dirty diapers were strewn by my feet. I picked one up and stuffed it in the bag. The bag ripped further and everything fell out.

"Jim," Karen said. "We don't have time for this."

My feet moved as if I were wrestling, shuffling through weeds and broken glass. I scooped up a dozen off-brand baby food jars—nothing like the locally canned organic kind with hand-painted labels Molly insisted we buy for Jenna and Lisa—yet the Ann Arborite in me instinctively felt guilty about these generic jars being recyclable. I hesitated about whether to re-bag them or take them home in the squad car and recycle them later. Bad move. Applesauce oozed onto my shirt.

I squared my shoulders and faced the mess.

I tell my athletes you can't hesitate on the mat. There's a split second of time between push and pull. This is where the best wrestlers live. We shoot into that moment and use our opponent's momentum against him, push into him just prior to his retreat, pull him forward as he surges to attack. If we can control his balance, we win.

I saw the picture in my head of the two boys in their

graduation gowns, their smiles as bright as the neon lights on the outside of the Motor City Casino, and I wanted to take on all the refuse in Detroit. I feinted, moved left, shot right toward the protruding leg of a demon made of trash. Dug in deep and sucked his five hundred tons of fumes toward my face. I was quick with my hands, bagged the baby food jars, grabbed a coffee cup, some rotting potato shards, a diaper by its edge. I squeezed the bag like it was somebody's neck, pinning its sides together. Tied it so it stayed. There was more to do. There was always more. I settled back into my stance.

"The chief," Karen said, her voice a sparkplug itching to ignite.

I thought about Kevin Trouma showing up for practice and my not being there to welcome him. My head was hammered with tired. The dead boys smiled as wide as Woodward Avenue. My feet circled the carcass of a half-eaten turkey. I shot and tried to stuff it back into its own broken bag and it fell out along with a slush of canned beans. Something brown spilled across my arm. I howled, my voice a roar against the hulking burned-out train station blocks away that no one could figure out how to tear down or rebuild. I tried to stuff all the trash, everything, all the white people who left the city—including both my parents—back into the bag.

There was so much loss.

So much garbage.

I looked back at the building where Amber Allen lived in her spotless apartment. The air smelled like sludge.

My shoulders ached.

My knees throbbed.

I saw an opening, shot in, wrapped my arms around the demon's gaseous thigh.

"Here," Karen said, gloving up, "let me help."

The cops finally trudged out of the apartment building. Even the hottie—the smoking hottie with the tight cooze! The sizzling snatch! Even she looked worn out, her shoulders defeated. Jarrold was no longer interested in her. Old bitch. The cooze was probably wrinkled. His car was filthy, fast food garbage everywhere, soiled napkins a pile of gunk on his passenger seat. He regretted shooting the black kids. Not just the lack of subterfuge, but that he'd killed them at all. He didn't regret it as much as he regretted throwing Monique into the nighttime, still, it was one thing to kill rich white kids on their vacations, even to roast a nerd in his room. But the black kids, that was messed up.

Make sure his laptop fries. Make sure all his files fry, he'd been told about the nerd. The challenge of the task had intrigued him. He'd felt like the financial manager he'd once wanted to become, fashioning an investment strategy, then watching it unfold. The fake party operation. The promotional boxes around town. He still remembered the glee he'd felt, dumping out the boxes onto his beer pong table, scanning through names and addresses until there it was, glowing, like a Willy Wonka golden ticket, the target's name and address.

Finally.

From there, it had been simple, bring Monique in and tell her what she needed to do, hang out and beer pong at the party, enjoy blowjobs. Get the rented Tailgate minions to clear the equipment out of the house but leave the couch. Creep back upstairs and have Monique let him into the target's room. Send her home. Open the beer and pour it all over the comatose target, over his computer and anything else that looked like part of his research. Light it and then sneak back downstairs and drop a lit cigarette onto the couch on the front porch.

Go to the sandwich shop around the block and order something spicy. Drink iced tea. Wait for the sirens.

And it had all worked.

Stunningly well.

The kid crisped.

Everything in his room, ash.

His computer a smoking husk.

What did the cops know? And how did they know it? What had led them here, to this God-forsaken shithole neighborhood?

And what on earth was the midget cop doing now? Cleaning up garbage? Fucking moron.

Jarrold wanted another milkshake. Wanted another filet-o-fish. It seemed like the hottie cop was the midget's mom, exasperated, waiting for her excitable son to finish playing in the sandbox.

He thought of something he'd witnessed in high school, a girl in jewelry class—he'd taken jewelry class! What a geek!—and how one day she hadn't been paying attention and fed her hand into a precision saw and sheared the skin off half her pinky. Blood spurted as if shooting from a broken water pipe. People ran from the room screaming. Not Jarrold. Not the girl either. She stayed, unmoving, peering calmly at her gushing finger as if fascinated it could contain so much fluid. Jarrold, watching her, had been equally fascinated, couldn't look away even if he'd wanted to. He had the same feeling now watching the miniature detective. He couldn't look away. Thought about opening his daughter's golden thighs—*that* cooze would be fresh! Thought about the cop attacking the garbage like he was in a fight. Watched the hottie break down and help him.

Wanted to know what they knew.

Where they'd go next.

CHAPTER FIFTEEN

"DO ME A FAVOR," I said to Karen in the car. "Humor me."

"What do you think I've been doing?" she said.

"Yeah, sorry about that back there."

She smiled. By far the best thing that had happened all day. "I'm not talking about the lot," she said. "I'm talking about our whole career. How do you think we stayed partners? Humoring you is my life's work."

Out the window, the landscape was industrial. Plants that looked half abandoned. Boarded-up gas stations. In a couple miles, we'd pass the turn-off for I-275, that squiggly line that takes you north to Mackinaw, south to Toledo. I always thought if you had a giant knife, you could carve along that road and fold the lower peninsula of our state, one half on top of the other, like a sandwich.

We'd been silent so far, no radio.

"I don't want to come with you to report to the chief," I said.

"What are you proposing?"

"That you stall her. Ask for more time, by yourself."

"*I* stall her?"

"She's already fed up with me. You have more credibility."

"Which you'd like to see diminished?"

"There's nothing about you I'd like to see diminished," I said. "Not one single thing." We passed an electronic billboard that urged us to Vote YES! for Education Fairness. *It's the New Civil Rights Issue of Our Times,* a tagline on the billboard flashed.

"I need more room to put everything together before opening my mouth up to Chief Taylor," I said, not telling Karen what I really wanted was to get to wrestling practice on time in case Kevin Trouma showed up.

She lifted her foot from the accelerator and the car slowed to the speed limit.

"You see that guy following us?" she asked.

"Grey sedan?"

"I think he started tailing us from Ann Arbor, then quit partway, but he must've known where we were going in Detroit because he was back ready to follow us again when we left."

"You sure it's the same guy? How could he have known where we were going if he'd stopped following us?"

"Maybe he knew where we were going. Maybe he's the killer. You know, Jarrold?"

"The killer, Jarrold or whoever, wouldn't follow us. The killer would try to get away from us."

"Maybe he wants to know what we know."

"That's what I want to know too. Because I'm unclear what exactly that is. Most of what we think we know is public knowledge, and nobody knows we're still digging. It can't be the same car."

Karen was quiet, her eyes squinting at the road in front of us. I was not uncomfortable with her silence. I imagined the two of us as old people, sitting in a canoe on a small lake up near the top of I-275, listening for the call of loons.

"I think he saw us when we made our initial foray to Minty's," she said. "That's why he killed her."

I nodded. Though the thought made me sick, it sounded plausible. We'd been sloppy. We weren't thinking about how murderers act because we don't encounter murderers. As a result, a pretty girl wound up with her face painted on the pavement. "You think he'll target Ms. Johnson and Ms. Allen?"

"Monique could identify him. They can't."

"Still."

"No chance. There's a possible explanation that Monique jumped because she was devastated by Sanders' death. Witnesses can testify how friendly they were. If something happens to two mothers of two dead sons, everything's called into question and DPD goes all-in on the investigation. Every case we suggest might be connected would be reopened. The killer can't risk that."

"What'll he do then?"

Karen banged the steering wheel with her palm. "If I'm him, I head out of town. Cut my losses and get as far gone as I can."

I knew where this was going and didn't like it. "So we should radio in and slow down? Pull this guy over before he departs to points unknown?"

"How's Chief Taylor going to approve a pullover? We've got zero evidence Monique and Bolgim were murdered, nothing except a hunch to connect their deaths to Jesse and Blair, and even less reason to believe the grey car behind us contains a killer named Jarrold."

"We do believe it."

"But we're the only ones who do."

"We can't do this ourselves, Karen. We can't just cowboy off the highway and see if he passes us so we can zoom up and take him out. We have no idea what kind of arsenal he might have with him. We have no idea of anything, really."

"Yeah, but what if it *is* him?" The lines in her face got hard and her hands on the steering wheel tightened. I could see the fierceness in her that I loved more than anything, the same fierceness Lisa had learned, watching her stay after practice and bang ball after ball into the field hockey goal, swinging her stick so hard it looked like she'd break something in her body if she ever swung and missed. "What if everything we've been thinking is exactly right and we've got a nutcase out there murdering students and we have a chance to bust him and we don't even try? We bully fratboys because we've come to believe they're the worst we have to deal with, but what if that's not true? I don't know about you, but I never want to feel the way I felt when we saw half that girl's brain on the street. I can't live with letting this guy kill anyone else. Can you?"

I looked in the rearview mirror.

"Doesn't matter," I said. "It's too late."

The grey sedan was gone.

Why was he still following these psychotic detectives?

Jarrold was so hungry, it was hard to concentrate. What if he stopped at Taco Bell? He'd seen a billboard a couple miles ago. What was that new product they had? A burrito made out of a potato chip? Wrapped inside a quesadilla made of a Frito? That was genius! He could eat ten of them. Twenty!

His stomach felt like he'd already devoured an entire cafeteria. As if somebody who didn't know how to play tuba were practicing beneath his ribs, blowing serial burps and gas. Yet, he was still famished. He hated these cops. Picking up garbage as if they'd been sentenced to community service. What idiots. Why should he keep following them? What could he learn from going back to the police station? It would be fun to see if that bum was still stuck in the recycling bin, but he didn't have time for fun. Were the cops fucking? Were the midget and his porn-star partner fucking? Now that was an intriguing prospect. That was worth watching. Even if they were geezers.

He was so hungry, though.

What about some pizza? A whole pizza! The kind with gooey cheese threaded inside the crust. How did they do that anyway? Drill a hole in the crust and shoot pressurized cheese into it?

He could do some drilling and pressurized shooting too. To the cop's daughter. He could do some fracking. Some freaking fracking! Release his own natural gas!

Oh!

He took his foot off the accelerator.

He was being stupid. He had to forget about the girl. Forget about Monique. But he was so hungry. His mouth felt like a graveyard for old boats of gravy. His stomach felt like an inferno of sautéed onions.

He burped an enormous burp that stank of fries and ketchup. He breathed in the smell and turned up the radio. No more sports idiots. Hard rock that made him smack the dashboard. *Inagodavida, honey!* He rolled down the window and sucked in the air. Let the cloud of hamburger and nugget escape.

If he followed the cops, he'd be behind the cops. Why should he be behind cops? He should be ahead of cops. He should be *two steps* ahead of cops. The question wasn't where they were headed now, but where they would be headed after that.

They knew about the Detroit kids, so who else did they know about? Who else *could* they know about?

He chewed his tongue, tried to think.

He knew.

He slowed, thought about flicking on his turn signal,

then thought better. Why give anybody any idea what he was about to do? He'd head south. Be there before the detectives had a clue.

But, what was that on the radio about a barbecued beef sandwich? A side of curly fries? Maybe he'd stop now, grab something quick, just a snack, and then—before going south—there was somebody in Ann Arbor he wanted to ask to dinner.

Oh!

He could go south on her!

Better yet, she could go south on him!

Get tropical, baby!

Oh! Oh!

CHAPTER SIXTEEN

WHEN I GOT HOME, my house was not my house.

The kitchen countertops and all the appliances sparkled. The floors, vacuumed and knees-on-the-ground scrubbed. Even the TV screen in the living room gleamed like it was straight from the store.

Lisa sat at the kitchen table next to a neatly organized pile of mail, her physics textbook open, one hand punching numbers into a calculator, a pen in her teeth.

"You feel bad, huh?' I said, gesturing around the house.

"What?"

"You feel bad about missing school, missing practice. The cleaning is penance."

Lisa waved away my theory with her calculating hand in the way teenagers wave away any accurate insight on behalf of their parents. Then she tapped the mail. "Your DTE is past due and so is the water. In less than a week, you'll be without utilities."

"You opened my mail?"

"Somebody has to."

"Perhaps this is a good time to suggest I keep an eye on

what needs to happen in my life, and you try to avoid agitating the masses through the public airwaves."

Lisa pulled the pen from her teeth, tried to see if I were teasing or serious.

"Are you saying I should let those dumb-asses keep talking without challenging them? Just let their misogyny drift unmolested into the ears of every 18-34 year-old male listener who thinks it's okay to talk about women as if we're horses?"

Of course, I wasn't saying that. I tried to imagine Chief Taylor's reaction as she listened to my daughter verbally assault people on the radio.

I decided she'd nod her head in approval.

"Want a sandwich for dinner?" I said. "I could pick up sandwiches on the way back from wrestling."

"I can make something here."

"Thanks." I headed out of the kitchen so I could change into my practice gear. If I hustled, I could still be only ten minutes late.

"You're not going to date my English teacher, are you?"

"Nope."

"Are you sure?"

"Pretty sure there are rules about that. And even if there weren't, she's probably too smart to say yes if I asked her."

All my laundry was folded on my bed. I grabbed a Pioneer t-shirt and some shorts, peeled off the jeans and striped button-down I was wearing—both soiled from my bout with the trash—and threw them in the hamper in the closet.

Back in the kitchen in my bare feet, I sat down across from Lisa and tugged on clean socks.

"Thanks for doing my laundry. Why are you worried about my dating your teacher?"

"Because her phone number was in the pocket of your shorts."

"Oh."

"Don't ask her. Because your track record isn't great."

This was not a conversation I had time or energy for. Most of me wanted to go back in the bedroom, sweep the clothes off my bed, and sleep until next week.

"Lisa, you know it's more complicated than that. Me and your mom—"

"She still loves you."

"And I love her." Which was sort of true. "Part of me always will. But we were making each other—and you guys too, if you remember—god-awful miserable."

"Yeah, I know, but—" Lisa stopped, her voice quivering.

My daughter's voice does not quiver. I fought the urge to get up and put my running shoes on. Stayed seated at the table.

Lisa picked up her calculator and tossed it from one hand to the other. Wouldn't make eye contact.

"Never mind."

"What? Tell me."

"I said never mind. You have practice. Go."

"Lisa, I do have practice, but I'm not leaving until you tell me what's on your mind. Think of those kids anxiously waiting to get into the wrestling room so I can make them run and do push-ups until their breath expires. You wouldn't want to delay that experience, would you?"

"Funny, Dad."

"Those poor kids. So excited to enter that lovely fragrant room and make it more lovely and fragrant. I can practically see them salivating. The drool is oozing down their chins. Their tongues are slobbering."

"Okay, okay." Lisa was laughing. "Stop grossing me out."

She got quiet again, and it was on my tongue to talk, to craft more descriptions of my gross wrestlers, but then, slowly, again without looking at me, she spoke.

"It's just that, the other night, after I got suspended, Mom had a couple glasses of wine, you know?"

I nodded. Molly having a couple glasses of wine, or more than that, had become something of a staple toward the end of our relationship. I thought I knew what was coming.

"What she said was, well, she said..." Lisa hung her head even lower, stared hard at the gleaming kitchen table. "She said you would never blame Karen—Coach, you would never blame Coach—for me being out of control because, well..." Her voice got even softer, so it was barely audible when she spoke directly to the tablecloth. "She said you were in love with her and always had been."

This, I knew, was not an appropriate thing for my ex-wife to tell our daughters. It had also been a frequent accusation Molly flung toward me while we were married. It's not that she hated Karen. In fact, she had a lot of admiration for her and considered her a good friend. Which was probably why it was even more painful for her to think what she thought.

Was it fair to say I'd always loved Karen?

I didn't know.

I did know I'd loved Molly with everything in me, that I hungered to be around her always, that sometimes when I saw her I still felt like my breath couldn't hit my throat fast enough. I did know that when I was married to Molly, Karen was my partner on the job and my best friend after Mikey, but nothing more. And I didn't believe she was the reason Molly was unhappy.

Or was unhappy now.

"Listen," I said. "Your mom and I had years where we loved each other deeply, years I never want to forget and would never want to give back. Our love is what made you and Jenna, and I know your mother and I both agree that's the best thing we ever did. It's also okay for you to love

Karen. I know what she's meant to you. It's not a betrayal of your mom for you to care about her. You don't have to choose."

"I know that, Dad."

"I'm not going to ask Ms. Waterman out."

"Then why do you have English stuff?"

"What English stuff?"

Lisa pulled out a plastic bag that had been hidden beneath her textbook. "I found this when I was doing laundry. It was also in one of your pockets. Some of these are talking about books we read in ninth and tenth grade."

I recognized the bag. Inside it were the scraps of paper I'd scooped up outside Sanders Bolgim's house. I hadn't logged them in at the station because I wasn't sure if they meant anything. I'd forgotten about them.

"You didn't open that, did you? Those pieces of paper might be evidence."

"In your pants?"

"Yeah, well, the point is, did you touch those scraps? Get your fingerprints on them?"

Lisa shook her head. "No, I can read them through the plastic. It's called being transparent. I can't see everything, but I recognize some of the references."

She angled the bag toward my face and pointed at one of the larger pieces of type-written text. "See what it says here?

I ain't got no people. I seen the guys that go around on the ranches alone. That ain't no good. They don't have no fun. After a long time they get mean. They get wantin' to fight all the time… 'Course Lennie's a God damn nuisance most of the time, but you get used to goin' around with a guy an' you can't get rid of him.

"That's George from *Of Mice and Men.* He's talking about his best friend Lennie who he has to shoot at the end."

"I remember that. Not the quote specifically, but when

George shot Lennie. Everybody remembers that. That's a traumatic ninth grade moment."

Lisa shook the bag again so another scrap became visible. "Then, there's this—a description of Roy Hobbs from the book *The Natural.* We read that in tenth grade when we had Mr. Knack, remember, that strange guy with the bad hair and awkward sense of humor?"

I nodded. The girls had hated their English class that year. Were only sure they were learning something about a third of the time. The guy wore purple Crocs to school, seriously. Seemed like a nice enough person at parent-teacher conferences, but dull as a plank. Missing that kind of with-it sharpness Olivia had. The piece of paper, what was still legible, said, "Malamud describes Roy as almost regal, saying, *He stood at the plate lean and loose… The bat he held in a curious position, lifted slightly above his head as if prepared to beat a rattlesnake to death, but it didn't harm his smooth stride into the pitch, nor the easy way he met the ball and slashed it out with a flick of the wrists."*

"There's more," Lisa said, shaking the bag another time.

"And I'd love to look at it," I said, taking the bag and putting it back on the table, "but I have to get moving, those kids waiting for me so they can start sweating, right? Am I bringing home food, or what? That's what I need to know."

"I'll cook."

"Don't burn down the kitchen."

Kevin Trouma looked nervous about being nervous.

"It's okay," I told him. "This is new for you. You're not going to get it perfectly the first time."

We were drilling single-legs and he was more awkward than I thought he would be, his weight on the wrong foot, his back stooped instead of straight when he shot. His arms were ropey though and, at least he'd followed directions and showed up in a t-shirt and a pair of athletic shorts.

"I don't know if this is for me," he said.

Out of the corner of my eye, I saw Hugo trip the 167-pounder and land on him. If I didn't get over and start beating on him soon, he was going to squash somebody like a rotten melon.

"No one ever does," I said. "The room smells horrible. It hurts to get slammed into the mat."

"Maybe I'm not tough enough."

"That's not what I see."

"I mean physically."

"You'll get there. The mental part is the most difficult and you have that already. Besides, you didn't miss a push-up or sit-up at the beginning, I noticed."

"I almost died."

"But you didn't. You're moving around, sweating all over my mat, breathing in the lovely funk. Enough talk. Pull your hips down, bend your knees and straighten your back. Weight on the balls of your feet. Now, when you shoot in on my leg, I want the side of your face to smash against my inner thigh. Then, imagine yourself pushing upward with all that soccer strength in your legs, with everything you've been carrying about Tammy and your mother in your shoulders. Lift me off my feet."

He did.

Jarrold ate a churro. It was awful. Too much sugar, the whole crispy over-fried mess a slab of gunky grossness in his mouth.

So good, though.

So good.

He watched the twin who wasn't gone. Someone—a

fatter, ugly girl—passed her the ball and she shot it. It was a terrible shot, fluttery and right at the goalie's chest. Jarrold was disappointed. Who wanted to plow a girl like that?

He only messed with the best.

Her next time down the field, she smoked it though, connected perfectly and rifled a shot low and hard into the corner. The goalie had no chance.

Jarrold looked at his watch.

Practice had to be almost over.

He felt his groin grow.

I put Kevin up against Hugo.

It wasn't pretty.

The big kid underhooked him, then pancaked him into the mat.

Four times.

"Try something different," I yelled, as they squared off against each other for time number five.

I wanted Hugo to challenge himself by leaving alone a move he knew Kevin didn't know how to defend, but I think Kevin thought I meant for him to stop getting pinned.

The kid looked hurt for a moment, hung his head and examined the pair of wrestling shoes I'd let him borrow. Then seemed to find something else on the ground.

His neck snapped up.

He pulled his hips low, bent his knees, centered his weight.

Hugo, being Hugo, and thrilled by the success he'd been having, tried again for the underhook.

Kevin shot quick, lunged beneath the huge kid's arms, slammed the side of his face against the tree trunk of Hugo's inner thigh. Tried to surge upward and lift him off the mat.

Failed.

But, come on, who can lift Hugo up? The only person in the room strong enough to do that was me.

Hugo laughed. Patted Kevin's head as if he were a puppy.

Kevin kept trying.

Hugo kept patting, laughing.

Then he stumbled backward, his heel off the mat. Steadied himself easily.

Nevertheless, his heel.

Off the mat.

Not much, maybe just an inch or so, but still.

His heel off the mat.

"You know what I really liked?" Jarrold said to the not-quite-as-pretty twin. "How after you had that shitty shot where you hit the goalie in the chest, you didn't give up on yourself. You came right back and ripped it the next time. That shows fortitude. Fortitude and guts."

The girl smiled. They were in the school's parking lot, next to her car, a light green crossover vehicle that looked a couple years old. Probably her mother's. He reached out to brush his hand across her upper arm. She let him. He gave her bicep a squeeze.

"You're strong, too. You go to the gym a lot?"

She blushed and her face, already red from sprints at the end of practice, took on a kind of rosy glow. Jarrold's groin felt enormous, ready to push through his pants like a battering ram. The detective's daughter! Oh!

He bit into another churro to calm himself down.

"Not really," she said. "Just playing a lot of hockey keeps me in shape. What'd you say you study at U-M? Engineering?"

"Yeah, but from a bio-mechanics, physiology perspective. The machinery of the human body. That's why I check out different sporting events, like your practice. What excites me watching incredible athletes like you, is how the body works in perfect synchronization, how all the parts seem to flow together with a kind of choreographed music." Amidst his bullshit, he tried to peer through the mesh of her reversible tank top. It'd take about a second for him to peel it off, start licking her sweat.

Her face got redder.

He shivered, mashed another churro into his mouth. She seemed fascinated by him. He flexed his neck muscles so she could see how strong he was.

"What I'd really like to do," he said while chewing, "is make a more concerted study of the way your body works, of its fluidity. Since you don't spend a lot of time lifting weights, I'd like to explore the natural nature of your musculature. It would probably take a fair amount of time. I don't rush through things the way the boys you know—your high school lab partners—do." He smiled. "Can I buy you dinner so we can talk about it?"

She backed away.

"Uhh, it looks like you've already eaten." She pointed to his bag of churros, the crumbs of sugar on his lips.

He'd gone too far.

Maybe he should just shove her inside her car right now, pin her down and steal her keys. Take her back to the apartment where he used to do Monique. Monique! Oh!

He looked around the parking lot to see if anyone else was watching. Spotted a couple of her teammates, the fat one and another loser, sitting on a bench by the curb staring at him, dumb fucks who hadn't even passed their driver's tests, probably waiting for rides from their loser fathers.

"No, no, I didn't mean tonight," he said. "I've got class. It's what, 5:30 now? I guess we could meet up after, around eleven or so, get coffee or something. I mean," he cocked an eyebrow, smirked, "if your parents will let you out."

"I don't know. I've got homework."

"High school stuff? You can handle that." He flexed his neck muscles again, could feel her riveted. Man, he was strong. Beautiful. A god.

"I need to think about this."

"Of course, just don't think too long. I mean, you're a special athlete, no question, a nearly perfect specimen for what I want to do. But if I have to, I can find someone else."

CHAPTER SEVENTEEN

LISA MADE SCALLOPS WITH SCALLIONS. Fresh garlic bread. A leafy salad with heirloom tomatoes.

"Where'd you get this stuff? You weren't supposed to leave the house."

"That's all you care about? Doesn't it look great?"

"It looks delicious. That's not the point."

"Why not?"

"You punched a girl in the face."

"She deserved it."

"Lisa."

"All right, I'm sorry. I shouldn't have gone out to get food without your permission. Does that mean you're not going to eat it?"

"Of course I'm going to eat it. What'd you do with those pieces of paper? I don't see the bag they were in on the table."

"I'll show you."

She walked into my bedroom where, I saw, there was a fresh sheet on the bed, but no blankets or pillows. On top of the sheet was a four-foot long rectangle of aluminum foil. On top of the foil, the pieces of paper were neatly organized into several small piles.

"Lisa, that stuff could be evidence."

"I know. That's why I stripped the bed and put them on a fresh sheet and the aluminum foil. I didn't touch the papers either. I used some of those gloves you have in the box under the sink in the kitchen. Let me show you what I found."

She ran back into the kitchen to get a new pair of gloves. When she returned, gloved, she picked up the pile on the left side of the foil.

"These are the pieces we talked about before. They're from *Of Mice and Men.* Then these next three piles are also ninth grade books. This pile is from *To Kill a Mockingbird,* this one's from *Romeo and Juliet,* and the last is from *Animal Farm."*

"That's a lot of stuff to read as a freshman."

"Don't interrupt. These next two piles are from sophomore year. *The Natural*, like we talked about, and *Lord of the Flies.* Then these three piles are from junior year, *Gatsby, Catcher in the Rye* and *MacBeth.* Don't ask me why we read Shakespeare in American Literature, but we did. The last four piles, I think, are all books that people do as seniors for World Lit, but I'm not sure because I've only read *In the Time of the Butterflies,* which is what we just finished. The quotes here actually gave me some ideas for my essay, which got me thinking."

I had no idea why any of this was important. Seemed like a waste of time. Bolgim was supposed to be studying charter schools, not a high school reading list. My stomach rumbled. The scallops were calling me. And my head hurt. I needed this stuff off my bed so I could sleep. I'd had about three hours in the last twenty-four.

"All right, what'd you come up with?"

"Well, I realized while I was reading, that the analysis is kind of average, you know? Like, not super sharp, but the grammar is solid and, in some cases, the vocabulary doesn't quite fit the grade level, like the words are too big for the ideas. And the writer's voice is the same for all the examples, and even sometimes, like, the sentences are exactly the same, like the writer cut and pasted them to use the same ideas to talk about different books. It's weird."

"Lisa, what's your point? I'm hungry."

"Jeez, Dad, chill out. You're like my lab partner at school, no patience. Just tries to fly through everything. Like he doesn't really want to understand the concepts, just wants to get it over w—"

"Lisa."

"All right, all right. If I had to guess, and I'm just guessing, but whoever this was, it's the dead dude, right? The guy who died in the fire? That sucks too. You go to a party and then—"

"Lisa!"

"Yeah, okay, chill, jeez. My guess is this guy was writing essays for other people. Like charging high school students money to write their papers."

"That doesn't make sense."

"Why not?"

"The guy was a grad student living like a monk. He had one friend he went to Blimpy's with to eat cheap burgers and his housing was paid for by his program. I don't see him reaching out to high school kids to write papers for fifty bucks a pop."

"Fifty? Try five hundred."

"Get out of here. High school kids don't have that kind of money to throw around."

"Are you kidding? You have no idea. People carry cash like that into school all the time and buy sneakers from each other."

I raised an eyebrow.

"They do. I've seen it."

"That's not right."

"I'm telling you, this guy was writing fake papers. I know it."

"All right, all right. Can we eat now? After dinner, I'll call Olivia, see what she thinks."

"Oh, you call her *Olivia*?"

"We're friends. We call each other by our first names."

"Huh. I knew you wanted to date her."

"That bothered me, what you said about kids selling sneakers to each other. That's a lot of money involved."

We were in the kitchen cleaning up after dinner, which had been terrific. I was washing dishes, Lisa working on making chocolate chip cookies. My eyes hurt. I needed sleep.

"Better than selling drugs."

"Speaking of which, have you heard anything else about opioids? Any other kids involved besides Tammy and Austin?"

"I'm suspended, remember? I haven't been in school. I doubt it though. I mean, there probably are a few more, but I really think it's mostly the same as it's always been. A lot of kids smoke weed. A lot of people drink."

She licked the spoon and nodded as if satisfied. Even though Molly drank more wine than she probably should have, I had to admit it seemed like we'd done a pretty good job keeping our kids away from any kind of substance abuse. Then again, maybe it was just how much they loved sports. I guess that was a kind of addiction too.

"Olivia—*Ms. Waterman*—said she thought it was harder

to connect to her students because classes are too big. You think that might drive harder drug use?"

"Dad, look at you. You're a wreck. Go to sleep."

"In a second. Just answer my question."

"I don't know, Dad. I don't know what it was like back in the day. I'm used to how it is now. Yeah, lots of people have anxiety and depression, and a lot of people self-medicate, but for me, since middle school, it's always seemed like that."

"What about charter schools?"

"What about them?"

Lisa didn't look very interested, her attention back on the batter. She got a clean spoon from the drawer and began to stir again.

"They drain money from public schools. Some people say they're why your classes are so big, why there's not more counseling, why the bathrooms aren't clean and the air conditioning doesn't work."

"The bathrooms aren't clean because people are gross. Somebody wiped her tampon on the wall of a stall last week. I don't think that has anything to do with charter schools. Honestly, some teachers are boring. They teach everything the same way all the time. If somebody can do better in an online class, or at a different kind of school, I don't see anything wrong with that."

"What if that school's for-profit and someone's spending less money so they can pocket more of what the state pays for every student? What if they're getting richer off the classes at your school getting bigger?"

"So, that's what happens? The profit thing?"

"If it's not happening already, it's where we're headed."

She licked the spoon again, then dropped it on the counter with a clang that felt like a gong ringing inside my head.

"Jesus, Lisa, can you take it easy?"

"You're grumpy. Take a nap."

"My bed is full of paper."

"Use the couch."

I disappeared for two hours, then bolted upright on the couch, disoriented. I fumbled for my phone and called Olivia. Explained about the papers from Bolgim's house.

"I can't really tell you for sure without seeing the scraps up close," Olivia said, "but I think I'd trust Lisa's insights. She's pretty intuitive, that girl, kind of like she has a sixth sense about things."

It's amazing what you can learn about your own kids from other people. On the field, sure, it sometimes seemed like Lisa knew where the ball was going before it got there, but I guess hadn't really thought about her intuitions elsewhere.

"I don't know. I might call her overconfident, sometimes reckless."

"That too, but maybe you can't separate those elements. Did you find out more about Kevin?"

"Pretty sure he's not involved in any drug use. I got him to join the wrestling team."

Silence.

"Is that a problem?"

"Sorry. I'm thinking about something I just found out. It's bothering me. Two kids were caught having sex at the top of a staircase the other day. Apparently, chaos is ensuing."

"Kids have always had sex."

"It was two boys. Gay sex makes the powers more fearful."

"Even now it does?"

"It's about appearances. More and more, that's all it is. If the test scores look good, if students are behaving themselves and not screwing in a stairwell, if the drug problem is kept quiet, everyone's happy."

"Let me ask you a question," I said. "How do you feel about charter schools?"

CHAPTER EIGHTEEN

JARROLD CHEWED HIS NAILS. Cooped up again in his nondescript car. In a wilted suburb in Ohio. He wished he had another bag of churros, a twelve-pack of chicken nuggets. Another milkshake. He ripped a nail off his thumb with his teeth. The salty French fry residue thrilled him.

The target's family was carving pumpkins. A boy and a girl, both under ten, both whiny brats. The target was listening patiently to the screams and screeches of his spoiled kids, attempting to translate their desires to have their pumpkin faces look friendlier or scarier. Monique had fucked this man, a snowflake who allowed himself to be bullied by his children.

Pathetic.

Two yellow leaves fluttered onto his windshield. A jogger flopped past, a busty woman wearing spandex too tight for her. He'd do her. Why not? Lay her out right now behind a driveway hedge. Make her shake so hard the remaining leaves fell.

Jarrold had never liked the business with the professor. Why the convoluted scheme to force him to relocate to a small college no one cared about? Why not just take him out? The whole blackmail thing with Monique setting him up, the video they'd filmed—Jarrold had kept a copy and still enjoyed watching it on occasion, Monique's ass bouncing like a basketball—Oh! Oh! It had been a good plan, but why not just eliminate the professor? Why not hang him from his bedroom ceiling fan and leave the video on his computer along with a note about how ashamed he was?

It was a pain to have to deal with the hassle now, a year later, but at least he'd gotten here before Detectives Midget and Formerly-Gorgeous-But-Currently-Wrinkled. Sooner or later they'd figure out it was worth talking to this guy and then who knew what he'd say with his guilty conscience?

The brats finally seemed satisfied with their pumpkins. The boy held his up and danced around with it. The girl hugged hers, then kissed its top, next to the stem. The mother shimmied onto the porch and both children showed off what their father had done, the rudimentary faces he'd carved. She was a pretty mother. Didn't have that sexy fire Monique had, so it made sense for the dad to get sucked in, but her small breasts looked pert beneath her sweater, her face bright and cherry-cheeked. The children leapt into her arms and the family looked as happy as a family can look considering they were probably still adjusting to their new neighborhood and the shadow of regret and secrecy their father must be living in.

The mother explained something to the daughter, Jarrold heard *tap class* and *get changed,* and then the boy jumped on his toes and spun clumsily around and said he wanted to go too. The mother nodded and told him to go to the bathroom and to hurry up.

Jarrold liked the timbre of her voice in the autumn air.

She didn't deserve such a weak-willed, treacherous spouse.

Five minutes after the mom packed her kids into a silver station wagon, Jarrold rang the doorbell. The target, clearly pissed off at having his precious solitary moments in the house interrupted—probably whacking off to memories of Monique—took his sweet time answering. When he saw who it was, he made a lunge to grab the carving knife from the porch. Jarrold slammed the door on his wrist and pushed into the house, shoving his knee into the dude's groin so he fell backward.

Jarrold did not like the color the walls were painted in the living room, a yellowish-green that reminded him of an infected wound. Also, the room held only a small television, one that looked like it came from the 80s and was attached to a VCR. Probably didn't get any reception. Probably was only used to play old children's movies like *Mary Poppins* or *Chitty-Chitty-Bang-Bang*. Jarrold hated families who made political statements like that.

When he could talk again, the professor sputtered, "What are you doing here? I've done everything you said. I resigned from my job. I burned the research. I'm just teaching at this little school now, not talking to the press or anything. I'm not even on any committees. I have no friends. I've done everything you said."

"We're past that now," Jarrold said, looking beyond the sad man on the floor and his stupid sweatshirt that said *Music is the soul's language* and up the stairs toward where he assumed the children's bedrooms were. "You need to make a choice."

"I don't understand."

"You're boring me with that. We should do what we need to do quickly before your family returns. You don't want them to see it."

The man fake-groaned and feigned his groin was experiencing a rush of pain, then tried to spring up and slash past Jarrold to the doorway. Jarrold made his hand a metal plate and chopped him in the throat. The professor crumpled to his knees and whimpered. Jarrold grabbed him by his hair and yanked him to his feet.

"Your choice is the following," he said, pulling a length of rope from the inside pocket of his jacket. "You can be reasonable and do what I tell you, or I can tie you up and gag you, then make you watch while I slit the throats of your wife and children. After which, I will carve you up as slowly and painfully as possible. Matter of fact, I won't kill your wife right away. First, I'll show her the tape of you and Monique. Then, I'll undress her and enjoy those teacup tits she has. Then, I'll bang her until she comes like a porn star. I won't let you watch either because I know you'd get off on it. I'll let your kids watch though. They'll be tied up and gagged too, but at least they'll get to see. Then I'll use that pumpkin knife and make jack-o-lanterns out of their necks. Afterward, I'll bring you over to see what happened because you made the poor choice of refusing to be reasonable. Your dead wife and children carved into small pieces will be the last thing you see before I turn the knife on you."

The man lashed out, a wild sloppy lashing, and Jarrold caught his fist in the air and twisted his arm so it was on the verge of breaking. The man could have endured the break and kept fighting but he didn't, which disgusted Jarrold even more. Guy had no survival instincts. None.

When the man bent to his knees again and started to cry, Jarrold patted him on the head.

"It's okay, Professor," he said. "Do what I tell you and I promise it'll be over soon. You have pen and paper somewhere? It's time for you to write a few things down."

It would be hard on the kids, Jarrold knew, but they were young. They'd get over it. Hopefully, their father was the driving force behind their farce of a television and soon they'd have a big screen.

"What's your wife's first name?" he said. "Let's start there."

"That's a long story, Jim," Olivia said.

"What do you mean?"

"You really want to hear this?"

"I do."

"Look, I'm not a traditional teacher. The reason I got into education was because I didn't like how most teachers did things. The original idea of charters, I was totally for them. The whole point was to offer opportunities for teachers to innovate. There was never the market mentality that charters were going to compete with traditional schools. More like charters were going to be a laboratory where teachers could experiment and share results with the rest of us."

"It hasn't worked like that."

"Not even close. When the voucher movement failed, the same crowd that wanted to convert tax dollars into private school tuition for their children shifted to charters and sold them as an opportunity for poor kids to equalize the playing field so students wouldn't have to go to neighborhood schools if those schools were lousy."

"Like in Detroit."

"Exactly. That's why you hear these ads about *The New Civil Rights Movement*. It's all bullshit. Real civil rights would mean more funding for all schools, not less. These people only care about profit."

Olivia was silent again.

I waited.

"You know what happened today? I got an email about a kid who told me three weeks ago she had cancer and was just starting chemo, a sweet quiet kid who'd been missing a bunch of classes because she said she was too sick from radiation. She still had a full head of hair though, this lovely muddle of strawberry curls, and I asked her once, tentatively, you know, because I didn't want to hurt her feelings, if she were going to lose it. Eventually, she told me, eventually she would, she'd already lost some from her arms.

"You know what, Jim? I never checked. I never looked at her arms, she had long sleeves, and today her mom sent me an email saying she made the whole thing up. She had a lump on the back of her thigh she was anxious about and she told her friends she had cancer, maybe to get attention, maybe because she was legitimately worried, who knows? When she went to the doctor, it turned out to be just an infection, which is the best news, of course, but she didn't know how to tell people the truth so the lie got bigger. This is what happens when you have huge classes. A kid can pretend to be deathly ill and you believe it because you just don't have time to check her story.

"This is a disturbed kid, obviously, and engaged in some extensive magical thinking to believe it wouldn't eventually all come out, but still smart enough to understand her relationships with her teachers are so distant now, she could get away with it for a fair amount of time. This is how it happens, Jim. When funding disappears, you can only patch so much. The slow deterioration kills us. You look up and your school is no longer the vibrant place it was ten years ago. Incrementally, we all become the teachers we never wanted to be."

I let the narrative sink in, thought of the old Marvel Comics character Galactus using his Power Cosmic to suck the life force out of planets, hording all the energy for himself. I pictured a giant vacuum cleaner hovering over Pioneer High School, siphoning dollar bills through the ceiling.

"That story's pretty disturbing."

"That's just one example. There's Tammy Binder and other kids too. So many children I'm not reaching the same way I used to. I had to send a student to the office this week because he was being so disrespectful when I insisted he put his phone away. It's been fifteen years since I've done that."

"You're still my daughters' favorite teacher. They tell me they love your class, and philosophy, and humanities, and other than that—well, and field hockey—there's no real reason for them to be in school."

"You're talking about three classes administrators dislike because there's no measurable test score and they don't know what to make of us. None of our courses are so-called core academic classes, so we're all on the chopping block. Probably humanities will hold out the longest, but the runes are on the wall, Jim. Barring the miracle of a complete policy turnaround, in less than a decade, we'll all be gone."

"How can that be?"

"Intentional strategy. These classes are reasons parents choose our school for their children. Policymakers bleed electives out of public schools so parents will run to private schools and charters and take their tax money with them. Trust me, the day creative writing is cut from Pioneer is the day a for-profit creative writing academy will spring up for students frustrated with the public schools' lack of imagination."

"Why doesn't anybody speak up about it?"

"People have been speaking up. For *years*. This kind of thing used to make headlines. There was a professor at Western, pretty well-known—at least among educator circles—guy named Benjamin Benson Jr., for about two years he was—"

"Hold on, Ben Benson Jr.? As in, Ben, son of Ben Benson?"

"Yeah, people tend to have a lot of fun with that. And a lot of people didn't take him seriously because of it. But he's a smart guy, did all this research about charters, about who's making money from them, about their lackluster results and how the new laws don't hold them accountable for whether students actually learn anything. He was the one guy who spoke up with any impact, but just when he was starting to gain traction and the media was finally paying attention, he stopped."

A professor. It seemed so obvious. Karen and I been concentrating on students and hadn't even thought about their instructors. Talk about stupid.

"What do you mean, stopped?"

"I mean, totally vanished. No more talk-show appearances. No more blogs. No more articles. Left Western like a canceled sitcom. Rumor was some kind of scandal, but nobody really knows."

"Ben Benson Jr., you're sure?"

"Come on, Jim, nobody forgets a name like that."

Ben Benson Jr.

A slew of articles and commentaries in print and online, several appearances on National Public Radio, CNN and MSNBC. Even a handful on Fox News. An interview on *Good Morning America.* A sit-down with Oprah. Kind of soft-looking, this dude, with John Lennon glasses and thinning hair.

I read articles and watched clips on my laptop for an hour. Everything seemed urgent, but nothing pointed to what to do next. Benson talked a lot about charters and how many of them, especially in inner cities, did little beyond drop kids in front of computers while inexperienced, uncertified teachers walked around the room and made sure students were on task. Exactly what Beverly Johnson had told us.

Then—like Olivia said—all the articles, all the TV and radio appearances, just halted. Dead. There were a ton, then, abruptly, a little more than a year ago, nothing. No pieces about the man's decline in influence or a scandal discrediting him either. Just all his efforts to get the word out about his research, and then it was suddenly like he didn't care anymore. And it didn't seem like the news outlets cared either. If he didn't want to debunk the myth of charters being so much better than public schools, neither did anyone else. It was like, oh, dude found something else to focus on, we will too.

There was no social media anywhere either, no Facebook or Instagram. No Twitter. I couldn't even track down an email account. Maybe True North would have been able to, but for me, this professor—beyond the articles and videos posted by other people—was as much a cyber-cypher as Sanders Bolgim.

I decided to read the last thing he'd written, an op-ed for the *Detroit Free Press* headlined—*Hell no for Education YES!!!* It started with a description of the beginning of the project, how Dot Warren had bankrolled a Super PAC to pay for TV, radio and billboards, and to contribute millions to the campaigns—in both parties—of legislators all over Michigan.

Including over $500,000 to Governor Lambright.

One thing made sense. Whoever wanted this referendum to pass—Warren or Lambright, or whoever—definitely would benefit from shutting this professor up. But, how'd they do it? There was no way this guy just stopped caring.

I dove back into the articles. Somebody had to know

why Benson stopped talking. After another twenty minutes, my eyes barely able to focus, I saw something. A lead. Finally. Maybe. A note at the end of a piece about how much money was at stake mentioned that someone named Max Leneroff had aided in the research.

A student?

Another professor at Western?

I pulled up an online phonebook for Kalamazoo and crossed my fingers.

A woman answered the phone.

"Um, Ms. Leneroff?"

"Yes."

"Is Max available?"

"And you are?"

"Detective James Harrow from the Ann Arbor Police. Please, Ma'am, I need to talk to your husband right away if possible."

"I'm sorry, my husband doesn't exist."

Doesn't exist?

Damn.

Divorced?

Is he dead? Did the killer—Jarrold—get to him already?

"I don't understand."

"I'm sure you don't, Detective," she said with a chuckle. "I'm just messing with you and your assumptions. I'm Maxine Leneroff. How can I help you?"

Jesus.

One day I'd learn.

"Uh, Ms. Leneroff?"

"It's Dr."

Today wouldn't be that day.

"Sorry, uh, can you tell me what happened to Ben Benson?"

"What do you mean? *Did* something happen to him? Is he in trouble?"

"Honestly, that's what I'm trying to find out. Do you know why he stopped publishing articles and appearing on television? Like he seemed to just stop caring?"

"He left."

"Left Western, is that what you mean? Do you know why?"

"I'm sorry, Detective. I don't feel at liberty to talk about this."

My head still felt like a soggy bog. The nap had taken the edge off, I guess, but that was pretty much it. Lisa bustled into the room carting a tray of cookies. Gestured to see if I wanted one. I shook my head and waved her away.

Why hadn't I asked Karen to call this woman? She probably would have had more success. Then again, she was probably rolling around with Roland right now. Also, how was I supposed to know Max was a woman?

"Listen, Dr. Leneroff, I apologize for my frankness. I've been awake for most of the last two days. My head can't operate with courtesy. It's possible your colleague might be in danger. I know it sounds crazy, but we believe a student here might have been murdered in connection to Benson's research. If you know anything, anything at all about the circumstances under which he left Western and stopped being the public face of the anti-charter movement, I need to know. And I need to know now."

Silence.

I waited.

"Actually, what you're saying doesn't sound crazy."

"Why not?"

"Well, this vote coming up, there's billions—"

"Yes, I know billions of dollars at stake. I read the article you helped with. That's why I called. I'm sorry, I just—can you tell me why he left?"

"Well, the truth is, I don't really know. There's a rumor, but, who knows if it's true?"

"A rumor?"

"You really think he might be in danger?"

Good lord.

"Yes, I do."

"Well, what I heard, and I can't confirm this, it's just hearsay, but I heard he was cheating on his wife."

"Okay."

"With a student."

"Okay."

"Apparently somebody anonymous tipped off the campus police and they found the couple in the stacks of the Rare Books Library."

"They were a couple?"

"I heard the young woman was quite the looker. Dark hair, I think. Extremely sexy, was how she was described."

Monique Harvey. Had to be.

"So, yes, he packed up and left after that. Shut down his research and disappeared."

"Any idea where he went? Any idea what his wife's name is?"

"Well, sure, Holly Benson. Not sure where he is now, but last I heard, this was a year ago, he was teaching night school at some community college. Terra State, I think, in Ohio."

After hanging up, I Googled.

Found the place in Fremont, Ohio, about a half-hour east of Toledo. No Ben Benson listed on the faculty page.

Combed through Fremont in the online phonebook.

Found a number for a H. Benson.

Called.

No answer.

Called the station, had Standish run the number through the reverse directory. Got an address.

Closed my laptop.

Called Karen.

CHAPTER NINETEEN

"WHAT THE HELL, JIM?"

"I'm sorry if I'm interrupting, I really am." And I was, I think. "But we've got a problem."

I described what I'd found out about Ben Benson Jr. and told her I thought the maiden who seduced him was Monique Harvey.

"That's what I'm thinking too. Along with the fact that most of the male species is a bunch of horny, useless rhinoceri."

"I'm pretty sure it's rhinoceroses."

"Whatever. If it was Monique, that would bolster our theory. Jarrold uses her as bait. Sanders Bolgim was set up. We can establish a pattern."

"Yeah, but the whole thing happened more than a year ago. Benson resigned and took his research with him, every scrap, just like the B-School kids who started the brothel, and he uprooted his family and moved out of town. Took a job at Podunk College in Ohio, hasn't published or spoken at any conferences since."

"So?"

"So the car that was following us—"

"The grey sedan."

"Yeah, think about where we lost track of it. It was right after we passed 275, remember? What if he headed south?"

"Holy shit," she said. "You get Benson's new address?"

"Yes."

"Meet you at the station in ten minutes."

It was after midnight by the time we rolled into Benson's neighborhood.

"I have a bad feeling," Karen said.

I knew what she meant. The rhythm wasn't right. Not enough lights on in the houses, or too many. Nobody walking a dog, or just one guy, but he was doing it too quickly. The wind blowing the wrong things.

A minute later, we passed a blue sedan, an older woman driving. She sat straight and tall, as if she were making a conscious effort not to collapse into herself. Her eyes, focused straight ahead, didn't seem to register us when she drove by.

A child in the back seat—it looked like there were two of them, but one, a small boy—stared at me, looking as forlorn as I'd ever seen anyone look, both palms pressed against the window as if he were wishing he could escape.

"This is going to be horrible, Jim," Karen said.

I wanted to say something in response, but my throat was stuck. I felt like the boy's palms were pushing through my ribs, forcing themselves against my lungs.

Crime scene tape extended across the front lawn and driveway when we pulled around the corner in view of the professor's house. There were two police units parked by the curb and an unmarked vehicle. No lights flashed.

Whatever happened had been too long ago to do anything about it.

An obese pine tree sat in the front yard, keeping guard. The garage door was wide open. A shape moved behind the plate-glass window that fronted the house. We headed toward a porch decorated for Halloween with fake spiderwebs made of cotton, and a huge cardboard spider with orange eyes affixed to the front door.

"Guy's dead, you think?" Karen said

The shape we'd seen moving behind the window was a uniform named Randall. He didn't say whether that was his first or last name. He was round and young and skeptical when we showed him our badges and said we were detectives from Ann Arbor.

"What are Michigan folks doing down here?" he said, nervous as if he shouldn't be talking to us. A tad disdainful too, as if people from Michigan generally had no business in Ohio, or even interacting in any kind of civil fashion with other members of the human race.

"We think what happened in this house might be connected to a case in our jurisdiction," Karen said.

"I doubt that." He cast a glance behind him toward a room with a closed swinging door I was guessing had to be the kitchen.

"Why?" Karen said. She was being much more polite than I felt like being. "Because the guy killed himself. Turned on his car in the garage and inhaled the carbon monoxide. Left a note explaining why and it didn't mention anything about Michigan."

He said it like the state in general shouldn't exist. Or maybe I was just imagining his dismissive tone because I assumed he was a Buckeyes fan. I tried to conjure a scene of the two of us sitting down and having a beer, toasting each other and talking about our collective misspent youth. It didn't work. The kitchen door swung open and a slim pissed-off woman barreled through it like a gunfighter bursting from a saloon. Her hair was the color of peanut shells and she was wearing a grey-blue sweater with the sleeves rolled up. She reminded me of Molly, except maybe half a dozen years younger. "No," she spat, turning around and shouting back toward the kitchen. "I won't accept what you're saying. I can't."

A man and a woman hurried through the door behind her. Karen and I nearly fell over. We were looking at ourselves, a couple of forty-something detectives, the female one taller and more attractive.

"Ms. Benson," she said, "we know you're upset—"

"I'm not upset," the woman said, her face twisted like the bashed-in side of a totaled car. "I'm furious. My husband's dead. Everyone's telling me he did it himself. He didn't. That's a pile of bullshit."

Her cheeks looked hot and red and she rubbed at them with the crook of one of her elbows.

"I believe you," Karen said. "My partner does too. Right, Jim?"

The woman looked at us for the first time. I nodded.

"Who the fuck are you?" she said. "And what the fuck are you doing in my house?"

Karen and I introduced ourselves and explained our theory that Professor Benson's death was connected to at least two deaths in Ann Arbor. The weather inside the house changed. The grapefruit-shaped cop slinked outside and I imagined he was remorseful at the way he'd treated us. My imagination was likely wrong. He was probably beneath the pine tree trolling for Buckeye porn on his phone.

Surprisingly, the two detectives who looked like us did

not behave in hostile fashion toward us. They seemed unconcerned with the idea of protecting their turf, or with the notion they might have drawn wrong conclusions about the crime scene. In fact, they ushered us back into the kitchen and offered us coffee.

"You're saying Professor Benson was killed because he was researching something connected to your victims?" the male detective said. His name was Paul Burg and he was taller than me by an inch or two, and burly, but I was almost definitely sure, if it came down to it, I could take him.

"That's our theory," I said. We hadn't gone into specific details yet. Karen was rubbing Ms. Benson's shoulder, trying to calm her so we could ask additional questions. The woman was still smoldering, but Karen's efforts seemed to be helping. I turned toward her and spoke slowly. "Ms. Benson, we think whatever your husband was working on at Western caught the attention of some nasty people. They have some kind of hired gun working for them who makes murders look like accidental deaths, or suicides. Whatever your husband was working on, they wanted to suppress, keep it out of the public eye."

Karen said she believed whoever was behind the killings had initially deemed it sufficient to compel Professor Benson to resign his position, scuttle his research and exile himself. However, they must have recently reconsidered, possibly because our investigation led them to believe they needed to eliminate potential loose ends.

"That doesn't make sense," Ms. Benson said. "Ben left Western because he had an affair. He had to leave or they would have destroyed his reputation. He wouldn't have been able to get a job anywhere."

"He told you about the affair?"

"Of course he told me." She raised her shoulders as if she were proud her husband had trusted her with his betrayal. "I wasn't going to believe he was giving up the passions he was so obsessed with because all of a sudden he wanted a quieter life. The truth is—" Her voice broke and she paused, gazing toward the living room and the ensuing picture window through which, if it were light out, she could have seen the pine tree and the unfortunate Randall fiddling with his phone. After a moment, she continued. "What I'm trying to say is that for Ben, and for our family, everything has been better since we moved here. We don't have as much income, and Ben wasn't on TV, but he was around a lot more and he was really trying with the kids. That's why I know the note isn't true. His guilt wasn't something he was hiding, letting it eat at him. He'd told me everything. We were in therapy together. He was happier here than he was in Kalamazoo."

I believed her. So did Karen. I could tell by the way she squeezed her upper arm.

"We think the affair was integral to the plan," I said. It seemed safe to phrase it like that, clinically. "The woman involved was tied to the people who wanted to suppress your husband's research. We'd know for sure if there were any pictures of her, but we suspect the whole thing was a setup."

The female detective looked pained. She'd introduced herself as Annalisa Martello—which was a name I loved, the trilling music of it, *Annalisa.* I'd always wanted to name a daughter that, but then we had two of them instead of one, and Molly liked J names better than A names so we settled on Jenna and Lisa. Sometimes I still liked to call the two of them as if I were saying one name: *Jennalisa, we're leaving in five minutes. Jennalisa, come on.*

At second glance, I could see the detective was more weathered than I'd thought. A couple of lines cut across her forehead like dry streambeds. I wondered if there were more murders in small-town Ohio than in Ann Arbor.

"There's video," she said, the cuts in her forehead deepening as she looked at the floor instead of Ms. Benson. "We found it on Professor Benson's computer."

"Look," Ms. Benson said, "don't spare my feelings. You need to look at the video, look at the video. I'm not embarrassed. Ben made his choices. Set up or not, nobody forced him to sleep with that woman. We've spent the last year talking about how stupid he was and he was holding himself accountable. He wanted us to move forward as a family. He didn't kill himself. I know he didn't."

Something wasn't adding up. This guy Jarrold killed Monique Harvey because he didn't want her talking to us. He made it look like she jumped, but he had to know if we tracked down Professor Benson—and he wouldn't have killed Benson unless he were worried we would—it made no sense to leave evidence of Monique's relationship to him. Nobody was going to believe in accidents when there were three deaths connected like a perfect triangle, all taking place in less than a week. It also would have taken True North about twelve seconds to figure out if the video had been on the computer for a while or if it'd just been uploaded today in order to further implicate Benson. A ruse like that was too flimsy for a killer who'd concocted something as elaborate as the Take-Home Tailgate scheme.

That left two possibilities, either Jarrold had made his first serious mistake due to carelessness, or he'd passed the point of caring whether we knew the deaths were homicides. Either way, the implications weren't good. Our odds of catching him might have gotten better, but so had the chances he'd explode in a messianic grand gesture, killing a horde of innocent people as he went down in a flaming roar.

I didn't want to look at the video. Primarily because I didn't want to be accused of *wanting* to look at the video. With a chin-nod, I signaled to Karen she should be the one to make the visual and verify Monique Harvey's identity. Detective Martello seemed to understand my chin-speak and sent her own telepathic message to Detective Burg, advising him he should help get Karen set up the laptop. Had she helped Karen, the grieving widow would have been alone with a duo of stupefied males while the two people who might have had a chance to keep her calm were watching her dead husband copulate. Instead, the result was a weird wife-swapping experience where I momentarily found myself partnering with Annalisa Martello.

"Not to be crude, Detective Harrow," she said, "but we still don't have any evidence anyone else was involved in Professor Benson's death. The handwriting on the note matches other writing samples in the house. He wrote it, didn't he, Ms. Benson?"

She shook her head. "Couldn't this person have forced him to write it?"

I don't know if it was the plaintive tone of Ms. Benson's voice, or the violence of her headshake, but suddenly I felt as if I were in the middle of a match and could see my opponent's intentions before he could. I knew what had happened in that house as clearly as if I'd witnessed it.

"You mentioned you have kids, Ms. Benson?"

She nodded.

"Where are they now?"

"I called my mom to come get them." Her voice quivered again as she fought to stay in control. "That's the reason we moved here instead of somewhere else. That was the deal when we left Kalamazoo. We had to go someplace small so we could start over. I got to choose where that would be."

The boy in the blue sedan pushing against the window was her son. I'd suspected that already, but it hurt again, harder, like a fist to the chest, to hear the truth from her trembling mouth.

"Were the children here with you before you left Ben in the house?"

"Yes, we left because Rachel had dance class. Charley wanted to come. He loves dancing." She broke, couldn't keep talking and covered her face with both hands, shoulders shaking as she wept. Annalisa picked up where Karen had left off and rubbed her arms. I waited.

"I'm sorry," she choked between sobs, "It's just Ben loved dancing too. He was light on his feet, so joyful. I can't, I'm sorry, I—"

"It's okay, Ms. Benson, take your time."

Karen and Detective Burg pushed through the kitchen door, quietly. They must have heard sobs from the other room. Karen nodded at me with her eyes. It was Monique in the video.

I waited a couple more minutes and then asked Ms. Benson if she remembered what she and the kids were doing before they left.

"They were outside carving pumpkins," she said. "The kids were so excited. Ben was smiling when they showed me."

"On your front porch? Your whole family was out there?"

She nodded again, wiped the tears streaming down her face.

The bastard had been watching them. Biding his time.

I leaned in and took her hands with my mine, did what I could to anchor her eyes with my own, to stop everything else in the world from mattering. I could feel Karen behind me, worried.

"The killer threatened your husband, Ms. Benson. Said he'd harm you and the children unless Ben did what he wanted. That's why he wrote the note. You were right. He cared about being your husband, about being a father, more than he cared about anything else."

I stopped and held her eyes.

"Your husband gave up his life," I said, "so his family could live."

An hour later, Holly Benson was ready to talk again. We'd spent the intervening time investigating the house and its surroundings. We found some minor scuff marks on the vestibule floor near the front door, as if there might have been a struggle there, but Ms. Benson wasn't sure if she'd noticed them before so we couldn't draw definite conclusions. Near a tree across the street, the wash of our flashlights revealed a cluster of crumbs that might have recently been French fries or chicken nuggets, and a smattering of sesame seeds. If the killer had been parked there in the early evening, he would have had a clear view of the porch.

Annalisa was in the living room messing around with the laptop. I'd called True North. He'd been pretty pissed to be awakened at 3:30 in the morning and had hurled a number of colorful words at me, but he'd grudgingly agreed to assist her over the phone and I could hear her consulting with him as Ms. Benson tugged at her sweater sleeves and tried to think.

"Can you tell me about any new research your husband was doing?"

"None that I know about."

That was the crux of it. Professor Benson had published research on charters for years. He'd written dozens of articles and pontificated on television about public money funneling to CEO pockets and there'd been no communal outcry. And nothing to connect him with the other victims. No co-authored papers or joint TV appearances.

"Did he ever mention a graduate student at U-M? Someone named Sanders Bolgim?"

"Yes, yes, he did." Ms. Benson was nodding now, feverishly. "I remember that name because it sounded so odd. He was very excited about Sanders. He said Sanders was a genius. He said if Sanders could pull off what he was working on, he'd tear it all down."

I was about to ask Holly Benson what she meant, if she knew *what* Sanders was trying to pull off, when Detective Martello burst into the kitchen.

"We've got something," she said. "The professor took a screenshot."

"A screenshot?" I asked.

"Yeah, your guy Truevayne told me to open Photoshop. Professor Benson had to load the video file exactly the way the killer wanted, wiping out the record of when it was put on his computer because the guy was looking over his shoulder the whole time, watching everything he did. Except the professor took a snapshot from his laptop's camera. It would have only taken a second, and the guy behind him wouldn't know."

She turned the laptop toward us so we could all see. Holly Benson gasped. Her husband was on the screen, looking frantic, his eyes behind his glasses blurry and panicked. Sweat swam across his forehead. Directly behind him stood a man with sharp cheekbones, wearing a maize and blue U-M t-shirt, his sandy hair cutting diagonally across his forehead. Handsome enough to be a model. Had one gloved hand gripped around Benson's shoulder and a sharp knife against his throat. A smug look on his face assumed everything would happen exactly the way he wanted it.

Jarrold.

"My God," Karen said. She looked more scared than I'd ever seen her. Angrier too. Her hands shook. "I've seen that guy in Ann Arbor."

"Where, Karen? Where have you seen him?"

"Earlier today, well, now it's yesterday, actually, at field hockey practice."

"What do you mean?" I said. "I thought you couldn't go to practice."

"I was watching from behind the fence. After I dropped you off and talked to Chief Taylor. I wanted to see the last five minutes. Get a feel for the intensity level of the girls without me there."

"And you saw this guy? Jarrold?"

"His name is Jarrold?" Detective Burg asked. "Jarrold what?"

"We think so," I said. "We don't know his last name yet. Not sure he has one."

"Jim, the thing is," Karen said. "I didn't actually see him at practice. I saw him after practice when the girls were walking to their cars."

I froze as I watched the words begin to form in Karen's mouth, knowing what she was going to say before she said it.

"Jim, he was talking to Jenna."

CHAPTER TWENTY

I BOLTED FROM THE HOUSE.

Karen followed, our footsteps hammers on the floor as we ran. I don't remember seeing the pine tree or the uniform cop or the crumb-ridden spot where Jarrold had parked his car, the place where he watched a father carve pumpkins with his two children before murdering him.

Karen drove but she could feel me itching. I barked into my phone at Annalisa Martello, saying words I'd never said before, and never thought I would say. "Send the screenshot out nationally. We need an immediate BOLO. I want every State Trooper in Michigan, Ohio, Indiana and Illinois looking for this guy, plus every local cop who can be spared. He should be considered armed and dangerous."

"We don't know he's armed," Detective Martello said.

"You notice that pumpkin knife anywhere in the kitchen?"

She didn't respond right away and I assumed she was casting her eyes around the room, looking for a knife that wasn't there.

"All right," she said. "Armed and dangerous. Anything else?"

I looked at Karen and she nodded.

"He's driving a grey vehicle. Probably a rental."

I looked at Karen again, another nod. "Mid-sized four-door, not sure what make."

"Got it," Detective Martello said.

I hung up.

"You thinking," I said to Karen, "he didn't head south to Ohio right away like we thought? Went to the field hockey practice first, Ohio after that?"

Karen waved her hand as if the sequential details weren't as important as something else.

"Jim, I was kind of far away," she said, her eyes anxious, "so I can't be sure, but the way Jenna was standing, holding her body, I'm guessing she's interested in this guy. I thought it was just some dude flirting. Jim, I'm sorry, I can't believe I didn't realize. I'm so sorry. I just didn't put it together. I don't know, maybe my head was on coaching, the guy was wearing a Michigan shirt, he looked like a student. In my mind, I still had the context of Jarrold in his car somewhere, I don't know how I missed it. I'm just so sorry."

I didn't want to think about that. Called Molly. It was 5:42 a.m. It took her six rings to answer and she was not happy when she did.

"Where's Jenna?" I said.

"Upstairs sleeping, what do you think?"

"Molly, this is serious. I need you to check on her right now. I promise you this is not about who's a better parent, please just check."

My brain felt on fire, as if Jarrold had dipped the pumpkin knife into a furnace until its sharp point glowed orange and was now twisting it into my skull. "Molly, please," I said again, "I wouldn't be calling like this if I weren't worried. Please, just check."

She did. Saw Jenna safely asleep, curled up like she was still an infant, her mouth open, lips suckling slightly as if, sixteen years after Molly had cut her off, she was still searching for a nipple, trying to get to it before Lisa did.

"What's this about, Jim?" Molly said.

"Listen, I can't talk long because I have more calls to make. Have you seen any kind of grey or silver car parked in the neighborhood? One you didn't recognize? Or a guy, real handsome, sharp cheekbones, sandy hair, Michigan t-shirt hanging around?"

"Jim, what's this *about?"*

"Molly, you need to answer my questions. A man we believe is very dangerous may be targeting Jenna. We can't waste any time. Have you seen a car or man like I described?"

"What do you mean, *targeting* Jenna?"

"Molly!" I was shouting into the phone. "Have you seen a silver or grey car or a man who looks like a model, kind of a half-fratboy-half-model? Have you seen somebody like that hanging around the neighborhood? Please, let me do my job!"

"No, I haven't fucking seen anyone like that," Molly shouted back, "but I don't spend all day looking out the fucking window! Cars drive past here all the time. People walk past here all the time. How the fuck am I supposed to know which ones are important?"

"Molly, I get it. I know this is crazy. I'm going to have Chief Taylor send a squad car to the house and have it sit on the street until Jenna goes to school. Then it'll follow her and watch Pioneer all day. If you see anything suspicious, anything that makes you uneasy, you need to call me right away."

"Jim, *everything's* going to make me uneasy now!"

"Just call me if you see or hear anything, even if you

smell something that makes you worried. Let me decide if it's important."

Molly agreed, finally, and I hung up. Karen hadn't said a word and didn't when I looked at her. I called Lisa. Molly picked up. "I took her phone from her, Jim, remember?"

Fuck.

"You need to bring it back. I'm going to call my house phone right now. Hopefully, she'll answer. When the patrol car gets to your house, I want you to leave and bring Lisa her phone." I thought for a second, the hot knife pushing against every nerve in my skull. "No, forget that. I'll have another car pick Lisa up and bring her back to your house. Better for all of you to be together so we can keep an eye on you at the same time. I'm calling Lisa now. As soon as I talk to her, I'll call you back and let you know she's okay."

"Jim, what's this *about?*"

I hung up without answering.

Lisa did not pick up my phone. I heard my own voice telling me I wasn't home and I shouted my daughter's name into the machine, urging her to pick up, pick up, if you're there, pick up.

She didn't.

Karen was flying at over 90 mph, but we were still an hour from Ann Arbor. She was on the phone too, updating Chief Taylor and asking her to order the two patrol cars, one to Molly's house, the other to get Lisa.

I called again.

No answer.

Shouted into the answering machine.

Nothing.

I hung up and punched the dashboard, almost broke my hand.

Karen glared at me while she was gunning the gas and answering the chief's questions.

My phone rang. Thank God.

Roland Roethke.

No, oh no.

"Jim, sorry to be calling so early. But the DNA just came in and I thought you'd want to know."

"DNA? What the hell are you talking about? I can't talk now."

"The condom you found in the alley? We've got results."

"The condom, okay, yeah." My brain wasn't functioning. Who cared about a damn condom? My voice rose. "Roland, I cannot fucking talk now, understand? Call me later. Period."

"Sure, I guess. You don't want to know—"

I hung up on him too.

Karen stared at me. I'd just cursed out and hung up on her boyfriend. A guy who'd never done anything but worked his tail off for us. I owed both of them an apology, but fuck it, I tried my house again, hoping, praying Lisa would pick up.

On the third ring, she did.

"Why are you such a nut, Dad?" my daughter said. "It's barely six o'clock. If I can't go anywhere, can I at least get some sleep?"

"Lisa, you need to listen to me carefully. A patrol car should be at the house in a few minutes. Pack your stuff and go with the officer. He's going to take you back to Mom's and he'll stay outside all day. You need to keep your eyes and ears open for a silver or grey car you don't recognize. Also, if you see a really good-looking dude with sandy hair, looks like a college student but he's probably thirty, might be wearing a Michigan t-shirt, guy named Jarrold, you need—"

"Did you say Jarrold?"

"You know him?"

"No, but he asked Jenna out to dinner yesterday."

"What? What'd she say?"

"She was creeped out. He came up to her after practice, started telling her how incredible a physical specimen she was. He was cute, she said, and seemed nice, but she thought it was weird, a stranger talking to her like that. He told her he went to U-M."

"He doesn't. He's very dangerous. If you or Jenna see him again, you need to call me right away. Do not hesitate. You understand?"

"Yes. What's going on, Dad?'

"Hopefully nothing, but if you see this guy, call me immediately. Right now, I want you to call Mom, tell her you're okay, then get ready to go with the officer. Text me as soon as you get to Mom's house so I know you're there. I'll be home in half an hour. We'll let you know what's next."

"Half an hour?" Karen said, after I hung up. "I don't think so. We're already going ninety-five."

"Go faster," I said, my head a volcano, lava boiling. "Go as fast as you can."

"I'm not going to get us killed. That won't help anybody."

I told her how Jarrold had asked Jenna to dinner.

"Your girls aren't stupid," Karen said. "I know I said Jenna looked interested, but she's still not going to fall for some stranger just because he's good-looking. Give her credit."

"I don't think consent is part of this guy's vocabulary."

The sun was beginning to rise. Northeastern Ohio was everything you wanted if you were trying to cover ground as quickly as possible, scenery unimpressive, roads flat and empty. I could not understand how Karen didn't put it together. Older guy talking to Jenna? How did she *not* think it might be the dude we were looking for?

I tried to put myself in her shoes. If I'd just been thinking about busting some guy and fired up and adrenaline-crazed and then he disappeared and I thought maybe he didn't exist after all, was doubting myself and all my instincts, and then saw somebody who fit the description in a totally different context—when I was out of my role of cop and into my role as coach, or suspended coach, actually—would I have reacted the same way Karen did?

Maybe.

Maybe not.

"I'm sorry I hung up on Roland."

"Don't worry about that. I'm the one who fucked up, not you."

I gritted my teeth.

"There's no one around. Drive faster."

"Jim, we need to slow down."

"We do *not* need to slow down."

"Not the car, our thinking. Listen, I messed up, I know it, but I don't want to make another mistake. Something's not right."

"*Everything's* not right. The guy's a psychotic killer and he knows who my daughters are. He's contacted one of them, *flirted* with one of them. We need to take him out."

"But he had to know Jenna wasn't going to wilt under his charms. He had to know it'd get back to you. He talked to Jenna for a reason. Just like he killed Benson when he knew we'd never buy suicide. He's telling us something."

We passed a cell phone tower. Every few miles we did that. Everybody was telling somebody something. This was America now. One mammoth signal tower, then another.

I tried to calm down, let the fires recede from my head. Thought about Olivia telling me teaching had grown harder, how kids tucked themselves into their smartphone worlds and didn't want to leave. How just at the national moment when teachers needed to make deeper connections to kids, classes were growing larger, curriculums were growing more impersonal, school psychologists saw the hatchet.

She said she had more kids checking into the U-M psych ward than she'd ever had, probably a dozen a year. A dozen out of a hundred and fifty. How could that be happening?

"Maybe Jarrold's had a psychotic break," I said to Karen. "Both the professor and Sanders slept with Monique, right? Maybe he was in love with her and now he's emotionally messed up because he killed her and doesn't care about hiding what he's doing."

"Maybe," Karen said.

"You don't think so?"

"I do think so, but it's also deeper. Jarrold is working for someone, right? He's not doing all this killing just because he wants to. Ben Benson had gone underground. He was trying to make his new life work. But his death puts him back in the news, makes people talk about his research, maybe somebody else decides to pick up the torch. Shutting him up, exiling him to the small town made him irrelevant, as if he weren't interested enough in his own cause to continue pursuing it. Dead, he's relevant again. It makes no sense to kill him."

"So you're saying Jarrold's even more dangerous. He's not following anyone else's rules anymore. He's killing whoever he wants."

"True, but why go after Benson? Maybe it has something to do with Monique in his twisted head, but it also has to be because he knew we'd figured something out. Assume he followed us to Detroit, and because he saw us there, he went after Benson. He did it because he knew we'd go there next. But killing Benson wouldn't throw us off the trail. If anything, it makes the trail hotter. I think he just wanted to beat us there to show us he *could* beat us there. Just like he flirted with Jenna at practice to show us he *could* flirt with Jenna."

"You're saying this is personal? He wants to force a confrontation?"

"Yeah."

"Why?"

"Maybe it's a macho thing and he wants to best you, bait you by showing you how easy it is for him to get close to your daughters, or maybe he blames us for his having to kill Monique."

The day was dawning moist, the landscape still too green for late October. More cell towers and several dilapidated barns burned past us, the world warming more than anybody wanted it to, my kids in danger, Karen intense and glowing next to me.

We crossed the border into Michigan and immediately saw a billboard urging us to *Vote YES for Education Fairness!*

Best me?

Bait me?

I envisioned cheekbones, sharp and angled, splintering against my elbow. The handsome face bloodied against the ground. My knee thundering into his back, his bones fracturing.

"What's his next move then?" I said.

"I don't know, but I suspect he wants us reacting with emotion right now, racing to do something, anything, when we don't know what to do. That's why we need to slow down, think, avoid making another mistake that leads to another death."

"Pull over," I said.

"Why?"

"You think. I'll drive."

"You sure you trust me after I blew it like that?"

Karen's eyes were set on the road ahead of us, but moisture leaked from the sides. I was mad at her, sure, but she'd been right too. The guy had been in the car behind us. She'd felt him out there. I was the one who'd wanted to call it quits for the day, who'd turned off her senses.

"You know how many times I've screwed up?"

She didn't say anything, kept peering ahead. I put my hand gently on her wrist.

"Pull over," I told her again. "You think, I'll drive."

Jarrold sat in his apartment, tossing a ping-pong ball against the wall, watching it bounce onto the table and sometimes land in the red cup in front of him, sometimes not.

Sadly, he didn't care if it made it in the cup or not. Either way, he would retrieve the ball and bounce it against the wall. It would land in the cup or it wouldn't. Monique would still be dead.

Ugliness was an unfortunate fact of the world. And mostly the fault of rich people and their greed. So much was still pretty though. The Grand Canyon. The cop's twins. Jarrold himself. The way the ball bounced when he was in control. Pretty and pretty should be matched up. Ugly should be eliminated.

He should never have killed Monique.

She would have forgiven him. She shouldn't have said that thing about the nerd being a better lay than he was. She couldn't have meant that. She was just trying to get him mad. Or aroused. Still, he should have controlled himself. Kimmie was different, immature, a bitch. Maybe she didn't deserve to die, but it had been an accident. With Monique, he'd looked in her eyes and seen her contempt for him, her lack of fear. *Then* he'd thrown her off the garage.

He got up from the chair and snaked his arm under the couch. When he pulled the ball out, it was covered with dust. He was hungry and licked the dust, then put the ball in his mouth. What if he deep fried it? Could he eat the whole thing?

That was ridiculous. He didn't know how to deep fry anything. Couldn't make a churro if he wanted to. He'd probably burn the apartment down. He spit the ball back onto the carpet like a slobbering dog. You know what he wanted right now? Some Blimpy Burgers. A quartet of quads. Slathered in onions and mayo.

Could he risk it? Cops were probably out there now. Spread everywhere like insects. Not just them either. The people who paid him had to be furious he'd killed the professor. Or they would be, as soon as they found out. Then they'd be looking for him too. Why had he allowed himself to get so ugly? He should have left the pussy professor alone.

It'd been the cop's daughter. Her voice on the radio. Oh! The other one at field hockey with her bullshit lies about homework. He felt himself getting hard again. His erection sprouting like a beanstalk. Jack's beanstalk! All the way to the sky!

He needed some gash.

Now.

He wished there were a party going on. He could be face-deep in some mostly attractive drunk girl in less than half an hour. Panties in the pantry. Oh!

It wouldn't be Monique though.

Wouldn't be the cop's tight-twat twins.

Some food then. Some Blimpy's. A bun with sesame seeds. Was the lovely establishment open this early in the morning? Breakfast burgers?

Probably not.

He'd have to wait. For food. For hot college poon. Maybe the midget cop's partner wasn't too old after all.

Maybe he could get her alone and give her a giant beanstalk.

He thought about the Bushmaster 223 rifle leaning against the wall in his closet, of his Glock and Sig Sauer pistols.

He put the ball back on his tongue. Sucked the hair and dust clean. Spit the ball into his hands, then dried it on the bare skin of his stone-slab chest.

Sat at the table again. Stared at his hands until he felt his focus returning, his mind sharpening. Bounced the ball off the wall. Swish. Dead into the center of the cup. Bounced it again. Swish. Again. Swish. Again. Caught it in his hand before it got to the cup and popped it back in his mouth. Bit down hard with his teeth and cracked the ball in two.

Swallowed.

Twenty miles later, Karen spoke for the first time since we'd switched driving. It wasn't the first sound she'd made. She'd chuckled when I'd had to move the seat forward. Now she said, "The big question is what Jarrold's going to do next, right?"

"That's what you came up with? *Of course,* that's the big question," I snapped. "Have you been thinking *at all?* Or was your mind on Roland? I'm sorry I hung up on him. I told you that already."

"Jesus, Jim." Her eyes were cloudy. "Do you have to be such an asshole? I'm trying here."

"Sorry." And I was, sort of.

"The big question," Karen tried again, her voice thin, "is whether Jarrold headed to parts unknown, or if he's back in Ann Arbor."

"If he's smart, he's as far away from Ann Arbor as possible. Killed Benson and could be in North Carolina by now, or Minnesota, or upstate New York. If I'm him, I ditch the car, snag another one, and disappear."

"Well, we know he's smart, but he's also making mistakes. If he cares about disappearing, he will. In a way, that's what I hope he does. Leaves the girls alone, even if we don't catch him. But if he's obsessed with them, or with you, if he can't get over what he did to Monique, then he's probably still in town. Plotting."

I hit the gas, harder.

CHAPTER TWENTY-ONE

THREE HOURS LATER, Karen and I were outside Chief Taylor's office watching through her window as she read our reports. I'd checked in with the girls, escorted Jenna to school and left Molly and Lisa in the hands of two uniforms parked outside the house and one more stationed inside the living room—Chief Taylor had not, for an instant, hesitated to allocate whatever resources she could—and then I'd showered, grabbed a bowl of raisin bran mixed with dried pineapple, and hustled in to type.

Karen looked like she hadn't been home. Her hair was tied back in a tight ponytail, but strands of it were breaking free and she kept sticking her lower lip out so she could blow them upward and away from her nose.

"I did some following up about the impact of the Education Fairness vote next week," she said. "If the vote goes through, new laws will eliminate all caps on charter schools in the state, both brick-and-mortar and cyber. Not only that, public schools the state closes down will be forced to offer their buildings for sale to for-profit charter companies for a dollar."

"You're serious?"

"As a bank when you miss a mortgage payment."

I wondered if that had ever happened to her.

Pay cuts hadn't hit us yet the way they'd hit teachers. Maybe they'd come after us last, we vaunted First Responders, but I had no doubt, like the long inevitable winter, they were coming.

"That's not the worst though," Karen said.

"What could be worse?"

"Stuck in the fine print, they're barring funding for any research on the effectiveness of charter schools for the next two decades."

"What?"

"Yeah, I guess they got tired of making the effort to kill people."

"Can they do that? Just stop people from studying whatever they want?"

"They claim they don't want to abort—they actually used that language, *abort*—the project during its gestational period. The NRA did it with guns. That's the precedent. We're talking about public universities. They can defund any studies they want, stop paying professors, make sure nothing gets published in university journals or presses."

I was about to say *wow* when Chief Taylor opened her door and ushered us into her office.

"You two should go home and sleep," she said without preliminaries. "There's nothing you can do until this guy Jarrold shows himself. When he does, I want you sharp."

The idea held some intellectual appeal but my body told me *no chance*. The shower had cleared my head. The cereal had fueled me. What Karen just told me turned that fuel into rage. I had at least another four hours before I crashed.

"I feel sharp now," I said. "Didn't he rent that car? Does he have an address? Is there no paper on this guy?"

"No record of his renting anything—car, house,

apartment. We haven't yet matched his face to a name. I've got Truevayne on it and everybody else, and we circulated the picture everywhere, but the guy's underground. We won't find him until he decides to surface."

"What about the other end? We've got investigating to do if we want to tie these murders to the governor. There's got to be a trail that leads to his office. Now that we know to look, we'll find it."

Chief Taylor shook her head. "You're talking about the highest elected official in our state. You can't investigate him based on a campaign contribution from a Super PAC that funded pretty much every other office holder in the state too. No way."

She pushed her expensively framed glasses farther down the bridge of her nose so she could peer at both of us. "We can't start interviewing people, or subpoenaing emails or phone records or whatever you have in mind, based on so little."

"But it's like Jim said before," Karen insisted, "it's got to be somebody like a university regent who's got an eye on all these students, red-flagging research. And who are regents beholden to? The governor."

"They're elected officials, Detective. He doesn't appoint them."

"But he's the one who decides funding. If they don't cozy up to him, he cuts the allocation, tuition goes up, and they get voted out of office. Maybe not all of them are that craven, but he just needs one or two who can pressure deans of Schools of Education and Business to keep an eye on what kind of research is happening around charters. Then if someone gets close, whoever's paying our killer gets notified and, bam, some kind of accident happens, problem solved."

"Close to *what*, Karen? You're conjuring an evil cabal that manipulates the governor and plots to kill students.

This isn't a comic book. We need something more specific than a fuzzy cloud of shadowy forces."

"Are billions of dollars specific enough? Can't we at least start drawing lines between the governor and Dot Warren?"

Chief Taylor shook her head again. "It's too big a leap to murder. You still don't know what Bolgim was working on —Jim thinks he was writing papers for high school kids, for crissakes—or how it ties to anything at the state level, and until you do, we can't proceed with an intrusive investigation."

"Look," Karen broke in. "We know Sanders was on the verge of something threatening. That's why Jarrold set the fire. If we start pushing the right buttons, maybe what Sanders was doing will become clear."

Chief Taylor settled her gaze on both of us and spoke slowly. "It's not going to happen, Detectives. I want you to sleep. Come back in a few hours with better reasoning. Find out what Bolgim was working on. Bottom line, until we know what the kid was doing to provoke whomever he provoked, we're not storming the governor's office. Period."

Karen pursed her lips and didn't respond. Her back and thighs tightened as if she were preparing for a fight and then she loosened and calmed herself. I could see her brain trying to work out ways to get around the chief's directive.

"Don't even think it, Detective Evans," Chief Taylor said. "The two of you have done outstanding work on this case. I apologize for doubting you earlier and I commend you for what you've uncovered, but don't blow it all to pieces now. Go home and rest. That's an order."

Despite the warning in her eyes, I endeavored to blow it all to pieces.

"You're forgetting the political angle," I said. "What would've happened if Bolgim's research came to light before the big vote? All we see are these damn billboards. All we hear are the TV and radio commercials. A student is dead because the governor wanted him dead. Obliterating public education is his pet project."

"I'm not forgetting anything, Detective. Perhaps, *you're* forgetting you've already got one allegation leveled against you for smacking around a college kid. In addition, your daughter was involved in a violent incident against another student. We have no leeway to go off half-cocked in any direction, let alone in one pointed toward Lansing. If we have reason to believe the governor's involved in a crime, we will pursue it with all the resources we can muster. At the moment, we *don't* have sufficient reason to believe that. Show me proof and you do what you want. Until then, I am ordering you to leave these premises and get some sleep. Now."

Karen shrugged and headed toward the door. She was telling me to shut up and live to fight another day. I turned to follow.

"And, Detective?" Taylor said.

"Yeah?" I prepared to be bitched out some more.

"Detective Evans mentioned in her report that you developed a strong rapport with the victim's wife. Nice work. That's what I want to see more of. I can't emphasize enough the power of empathy."

I wasn't sure what shocked me more, praise from Chief Taylor, or the fact that Karen mentioned it in her report. I didn't know how to respond, or even if I should respond at all. I just stood there in the doorway, half in the office, half out, grinning like a moron. Fortunately, my phone buzzed.

Roland Roethke.

I stepped into the squad room and answered it. I almost asked the medical examiner if he meant to call Karen and dialed me by mistake, but I resisted.

"You have time to talk now, Detective?" he said, his voice lacking its usual perk.

"Roland, I'm sorry. I shouldn't have cursed at you or hung up like I did. We were in the middle of a stressful moment."

"It's all right, I can understand that," he said. "You want to know about your DNA?"

"My DNA?"

"The results, I mean, from the condom you asked me to test, the one you found in the alley? We got a hit. Actually, we lucked out. We got two hits."

"Two hits? Two guys wore the same condom?"

"Don't be stupid. Semen on the inside, other genetic material on the outside. Secretions from the female partner. Blood, actually."

"You get identifications?"

"Sort of. The semen comes from a man named Barton Bindwell. Thirty-six years old. Priors for possession with intent to distribute and burglary / home invasion. Current address on North Fourth, about five blocks from the station. White male. Detroit native. File's pretty thin, but says at one time he enjoyed success as a street dancer. I'm sending his address and mug shot to your phone right now."

The image that came up on my screen was a few years old, but the guy's face looked like it was made of clay, like it could be molded and stretched to fit around his skull a dozen different ways.

Gumby. Had to be.

"And the female?"

"We can't identify her specifically because the info comes through medical records and she's a minor. Center for Disease Control tracks data when people check into the ER for drug-related incidents—overdoses, manic episodes, automobile accidents, etc. The genetic material on the condom comes from a fifteen-year-old female who was treated recently in the U-M trauma center after a heroin-related blackout. She tested negatively for HIV, fortunately, but we don't know who she is."

"I think I do," I said. An image of Tammy Binder sulking on the field hockey bench thudded my chest.

"Whether you do or don't matters less than you think. We already know for certain she was under the age of consent."

And Gumby was over it.

After thanking Roland, I hustled Karen back into the chief's office.

"Why aren't you sleeping?" she snapped, without looking up from her paperwork.

I told her what Roland had told me.

"Great," she said, eyes still on her desk. "Go home and sleep. I'll have Standish and Gumpert pick him up."

"But this is our case," I protested.

"You already have a case, in case you forgot. And this suspect has a prior for home invasion, maybe he's involved in the break-ins on the West Side."

I looked through the office window at Standish, who was reading the sports section while sipping from a latté the size of an oil drum. Gumpert was on his phone playing Angry Birds. It's not that they were bad cops. They were fine. No way I was going to let them deal with Gumby though.

"We get it, Aricka, you're chief. We do what you say. But we did all the work on this, the interview with the kid, the follow-up to find the condom. We're talking about a scumbag who traded heroin for sex with a fifteen-year-old girl who was friends with my daughters. We know—"

She looked up this time when she interrupted me.

"That's another reason I don't want you handling this. It's too personal. I don't want to lose the arrest because you rough this guy up."

"Nobody's roughing anyone up," Karen said. "I give you my absolute word we'll do everything by the book."

Aricka turned her eyes back to her paperwork and made a shooing motion for us to leave the office. "No."

"Nobody in this department knew squat about this heroin thing with high school kids until we uncovered it, just like everybody was ready to believe Bolgim's death was an accident except Detective Harrow and me."

The chief took her glasses off and pursed her lips. Karen softened her tone.

"Chief, we know this city. It's in us the same way Detroit is in you. It *is* personal when some piece of shit sells narcotics to our children. Look at the teenagers dying in Vermont. Look at Staten Island. West Virginia. You think we want Ann Arbor to be next? How do you think Jim found that condom? What do you think he was doing out there at four in the morning? We bleed this city. We live it. We should be the ones to grab this guy."

"You don't trust your colleagues?" Aricka said.

Just then we heard Gumpert whoop and turned to watch him thrust his fist in the air, jump up from his desk and show his phone to Standish.

"I beat the toughest level!" he shouted loud enough for us to hear through the glass. "Crushed it!"

Then he clutched the phone to his chest, outstretched his other hand, lifted one knee and assumed a Desmond Howardesque Heisman Trophy pose.

"No," Karen said, her face as deadpan serious as I'd ever seen it. "I trust them completely."

Aricka burst out laughing.

"You two are relentless," she said. "Go bring in Bindwell. Do not fuck it up."

CHAPTER TWENTY-TWO

THE HOUSE where Gumby lived reminded me of the one Sanders Bolgim had died in, an old beater with a lawn littered with weeds and cigarette butts and subdivided into a dozen closet-sized bedrooms.

Though it was only a ten-minute walk from campus, a lot of kids who lived in the area didn't go to U-M, but to Eastern or Washtenaw. Some weren't even students, but older still-hanging-around-Ann-Arbor types trying to boost their alternative-ska bands past gigs at The Blind Pig, or Frisbee-golf enthusiasts in their twenties and thirties who worked as waiters and baristas or valet-parked for university fundraisers. Good people for the most part. Drank and smoked too much, but generally stayed out of trouble and kept the Co-op supermarket thriving with bulk purchases of quinoa, kale and kiwi. Gumby figured to be a little old for that crowd, but if he dealt buds as well as skag, he was likely tolerated.

"You sure we should be doing this?" Karen asked as we headed toward the front door of Gumby's house. "Maybe Aricka's right."

"We're not sharp enough? Need more sleep?"

"I was thinking more what if Jarrold shows himself while we're in the midst of this exploit? What if he kills somebody while we're stuck trying to arrest a junkie street dancer?"

I considered what she was saying, but not too deeply. After the manic drive home, walking to Gumby's felt calming. I'd lost track of how long I'd been awake, but for now, I wanted to be moving, not at home asleep. Something was more likely to kick in my brain if I stayed active. In fact, I could almost feel it kicking in already.

A professor biked toward us, upright on one of those fifty-year-old Almira Gulch bicycles, his tattered bookbag trapped in the basket in front as if it were Toto. The guy wore rimless glasses and a maize and blue scarf and reminded me of my dad, who used to bike to campus even on days when a foot of snow and frozen slush covered the streets and sidewalks. I offered the dude a chin nod as he passed, but it turned out he wasn't like my dad because he ignored it.

"You know something, Karen? I'm thinking these cases might be related."

"How so?"

"Olivia said she's never had more students suffering from anxiety and depression. If schools only care about test scores, maybe more kids self-medicate, indulge in risky behaviors as a cry for attention."

"That's a stretch, Jim. Kids have always done drugs. You can't blame charter schools for somebody's habit."

"Yeah, but think about this, did you ever once in your life take a test and imagine your teacher's job depended on how well you did on it? I sure as hell didn't. I mean, was it my teacher's fault I spent half my time daydreaming about throwing a forearm across another kid's face and the other half wondering if you were ever going to make out with me?"

Karen stopped walking. Her face twisted like I'd either just kissed her or we'd had the biggest fight in the history of modern relationships. Hard to tell.

"How am I supposed to take you seriously when you say shit like that?" she said.

The entry to Gumby's house was a door with a cracked glass pane instead of a screen. Taped to it was a Magic-markered sign that said, "Welcome to the Pleasure Palace of Sensory Delights." The phrase struck me as overly wordy.

The guy who let us in appeared only slightly more stoned than I expected he would. Short and plump and with pale doughy forearms that looked like they'd never in their existence helped to maneuver a shovel or push a lawnmower, he had a mammoth unkempt beard and a t-shirt that said *Buck the Fuckeyes,* which I appreciated.

"This only cost me twenty-five cents," he said handing me the faded case to an ancient videotape. "At the thrift shop. You believe that?"

A pall of smoke hovered below the ceiling. Two other men and one woman sat on a couch that looked held together by luck. Both the men were short, bearded and pale, from the same tribe as the gnome standing before us. Neither was Bindwell. The woman was awake, but seemed like she could have been asleep with her eyes open. Her hair was dyed jet black and her face was lined with a hard thirty years, but she was so thin she looked pre-adolescent. There were track marks all over her left arm.

"Where's Gumby?" I said.

No one answered. A six-foot tall crimson-colored bong sat

on a plastic coffee table in front of the couch. A third of the way up its giraffe-like neck, someone had affixed a swath of white athletic tape and written "Millennium Falcon" in black ink. The guy who'd handed me the video case, said, "Check it out. It's called *Animal Adventures.* This shit is so *real.*"

I followed his pointing finger to the pre-Woodstock-era television where a squirrel was watching a bird peck at a birdfeeder. The squirrel was doing play-by-play in a British accent—*Look at Harriet. Goodness, she must be hungry today. Perhaps she missed her supper yesterday.* The color tube on the ancient television was broken and everything had a salmon-colored tinge.

"This is Episode 4," the Gnome said. "The best one. Watch what happens to the seeds in the feeder. It's hilarious."

The camera moved to a close-up of the squirrel's twitching snout, then panned back to Harriet nibbling. At least three inches worth of seeds had disappeared in half a second. The two men on the couch collapsed in laughter. The woman didn't move, her eyes fixed on the screen.

It occurred to me that though neither Jonas Warren and his fraternity brothers nor the Gnome Patrol would care to admit it, both groups essentially lived parallel lives. The fratboys had more expensive furniture and focused on sports instead of British animals, but neither crew seemed to harbor much ambition beyond getting high and watching TV.

Karen shut off the fossilized set, which she had to do by hand, turning a knob to the left.

"Where's Gumby?" she asked.

"In the kitchen like he always is," said the original gnome in the Fuckeyes shirt. "He's a particular kind of person who's always eating. He's probably making a grilled cheese sandwich right now."

Without removing her eyes from the now-blackened

screen, the woman on the couch said in pitch-perfect imitation of the squirrel, "Perhaps he missed his supper yesterday."

The men on the couch again fell out laughing and Karen and I stepped over a pile of maybe fifty vinyl records mixed in with a mess of dirty laundry and headed down the hallway toward the kitchen.

Gumby was seated at a table, lifting—as was foretold—a behemoth, triple-decker sandwich to his mouth. Melted cheese dripped off the sides and onto his chin.

"Barton Bindwell?" Karen said. "I'm Detective Evans and this is Detective Harrow from the AAPD."

With his sandwich still in his teeth, Gumby bolted from his chair, leapt over another pile of laundry and records and spun through what looked like a door headed to the basement. He was quick and lithe, still moved like the dancer he'd once been, and by the time we got to the door he was already down the stairs and had disappeared into blackness.

"Look for a light switch," I shouted to Karen and headed through the door.

I heard the slap of feet against cement and some rustling, but unless there were some kind of secret tunnel—which was vaguely possible, rumor had long suggested old houses in the area had been Underground Railroad way stations for slaves headed across the Detroit River to Canada—there really wasn't anywhere for him to go.

A glint of green light illuminated a bulky piece of electronic equipment tucked against the far wall, I was guessing some kind of mixing board or synthesizer, and my eyes adjusted well enough to see side walls of dirt and rock. Next to the mixing board or synthesizer was a pile of large wooden crates. Gumby had to be hiding behind them.

"There's nowhere for you to go, Bindwell," I said, after a few moments during which I heard additional rustling.

"Come out and we'll walk you to the station. The weather's pleasant. Professors are biking around with only scarves and light sports jackets. We'll even let you finish your sandwich."

"You made me drop my fuckin' sandwich on the floor, asshole. Check it out, it's right by your feet."

His voice reverberated around the basement and a bank of lights on the synthesizer/mixing board lit up. He was speaking through a microphone and his words were tinny and robotic. I couldn't tell where he was.

I took a step toward the crates and stepped on something squishy. It could have been the sandwich and I experienced a moment of regret. I really would have let him eat it. I glanced downward and then he was on me, having leapt onto my head from the ceiling where he must have been hanging from a cluster of exposed pipes. He smacked me in the jaw with the microphone and the synthesizer squealed with high-pitched feedback. I felt something slash into my shoulder and realized he must have been holding some kind of sword in the hand that wasn't holding the microphone. Fortunately, the blade was dull and it didn't penetrate my sweatshirt. I grabbed one of his elbows and flung him off me just as he again swung the mic toward my face, catching my nose and drawing an eruption of blood and another scream of feedback. I was hoping he'd fall to the floor so I could pin a knee to his chest and cuff him, but he landed on his feet.

Still, I was comfortable squared off against him in the dark. He had a microphone and a dull sword as weapons, but I'd taken down a thousand people in a thousand matches. I sensed him trying to move to his right and I shot in toward where I imagined his left leg would be. The side of my face jammed into his thigh and I picked his leg up and put his heel on my shoulder so he could only hop on his right foot. He dropped the sword with a clatter against the cement but still tried to smash my face with the microphone, barely missing. Just as Karen flicked on the lights, he hopped onto the sandwich and lost his balance, falling backward with a thud.

He was wearing a mask, furry and brown, that looked like the face of a buffalo, with two horns protruding from its head. "You're under arrest," I said through the blood in my mouth, "for violating Statute 3414 of the Lower Michigan Stupid Behavior Code—assaulting an officer of the law with sound amplification equipment while simultaneously impersonating the facial features of a large bovine. Don't move, please, or my partner, whom you might have noticed has her gun drawn, will shoot you."

Whether my nose was broken was a question that would have to wait. Whether Barton Bindwell would appear in his buffalo mask for his interview was a question that would be answered quickly.

He wouldn't.

I washed the blood off my face and bandaged my nose in the bathroom, then entered the squad room to a level of comedy I hadn't experienced since Lisa decked the field hockey player.

"You got hit by a microphone?" Standish said. "That *sounds* awful."

Gumpert had already drawn a cartoon of a wooly microphone with horns and boxing gloves that he labeled *Mic Bison*. "Want us to watch your interview?" he said, giggling. "Offer some *feedback?*"

"You guys ever think about applying for sense of humor school?" I said. "You might not get accepted, but it's worth a shot."

I grabbed a few folders from my desk to bring to the

interrogation room. I wanted Gumby to think we'd been working on his case for a long time and had built up a ream of evidence.

Karen was sitting across from Gumby when I walked in. The dude's face looked more haggard than in the photo from a few years ago. He was nervous, clasping and unclasping his wiry hands on the table in front of him.

"Mr. Bindwell has something he wants to say to you," Karen said. She nodded in his direction to signal it was okay for him to speak.

"I'm sorry I hit you," he said, sounding like a middle school kid. "I didn't mean to. I was scared."

I could see Karen wanted me to stay calm, but my nose still stung. Gumby didn't *mean* to hit me? He'd jumped on my head with a sword and a buffalo mask. "Look, Gumby," I said, slamming my folders on the table, the papers inside flying out like warnings. "We've got you for statutory rape of a minor who checked into a rehab clinic. Scared or not, you assaulted a police officer. You're going to be locked up for a significant interval of time. The only question is whether you're going to help yourself by letting us know where you're getting your product. You give us good information that leads to an arrest of someone higher up the food chain, maybe the DA takes that into account when she proffers charges."

Karen gave me a pissed-off look that said I was rushing things, failing to demonstrate empathy, but I didn't care. Gumby was talking but I wasn't listening. Something *was* kicking in my head. Something about the broken education system, the products it produces.

"Did you hear me?" Gumby shouted, chasing away whatever my brain was close to clutching, making me want to punch him even more in his claymation face. "Did you hear what I said? I think I know something you might be interested in."

"You're willing to give up your supplier?"

"Nah, man, that dude right there? The one who died in the fire?"

He was pointing to the blown-up yearbook picture of Bolgim that had fallen from one of the folders. "I know where he used to hang out."

That was bullshit, and I didn't want to hear it.

"Not relevant," I said. "And sit up straight in your chair. Stop slouching."

Gumby sat up. Crossed his arms against his chest. "Dude, I'm serious. I read the news online. I know everyone said it was an accident, but somebody killed that kid on purpose. I bet you think that too, or you wouldn't still have his picture. I saw him all the time. One, two in the morning. He was always looking over his shoulder. It was some sort of secret shit, trust me."

"Trust *you?*"

"I know a sketchy situation when I see it."

"He has a point," Karen said.

I didn't want Gumby to have a point. I didn't want him to have anything except the next decade in a cell. "All right, tell us what you know."

He leaned back in his chair again, smiled. Then looped a long finger around a strand of his ratty hair.

"Nah, man. Not until I have a deal in writing. You want what I know, get me some immunity."

"This isn't television. You're not testifying against the mob, Bindwell. You deal heroin to high school kids. Exchange drugs for sex. Immunity's not an option."

"You can help me some way, you said that before."

I looked at Karen.

"We can talk to the DA and recommend lighter charges. That's all we can do," she said.

"Do that, then." He stabbed his finger against the table

twice to emphasize his insistence. "Get me something in writing that says you'll do that."

Karen shrugged. Told him to sit tight and we'd run it by the chief.

"Go ahead," he said. "You want to know about that burned-up kid, you need to hook me up with some recognition of my positive attitude, you feel me?"

"Gumby," I said. "The day I feel you is the day I shove your sword down my throat and turn my intestines to sushi. That positive enough for you?"

"What do you think?" Karen asked.

We were in the squad room and I was playing with the Michigan football, trying not to burst back into the interview room and break Gumby's head.

"I think the guy's a scumbag and doesn't know anything that can help us."

"I think you're tired and embarrassed and your nose hurts and, as a result, you're forgetting the description he gave us matches almost exactly what Danny Root told you."

It was true. I was embarrassed. How had a derelict like Gumby gotten the jump on me?

"Actually, I've been thinking," I said. Maybe it was Gumby smacking my face with a microphone, but just then, right there in the squad room with our antediluvian computers and walls stained by two decades of stale air and Gumpert's dumb cartoons, I felt my sluggish brain un-slug itself.

To Karen's credit, she didn't make a caustic comment and tell me it was about time. She seemed to perk up too, as if my claiming to think meant we were getting somewhere. And because she perked up, because she instinctively trusted my unique sleuthing abilities, was exactly why—despite Roland—we were forever partners.

"Tell me," she said.

"I'm thinking the reason people deride public schools isn't because of low test scores. It's because they look around and see morons like Gumby and his housemates, or J-Dubs and the Psychos, and they think, who's teaching these clowns? What kind of school produces idiots who suck on six-foot bongs or dedicate their lives to acquiring beer pong trophies?"

"I doubt very much Jonas Warren went to public school," Karen said.

"Doesn't matter. There's a general dissatisfaction with all the dumb-assedness in our culture. We watch Reality TV and see people hoarding a thousand flowerpots in their living rooms, or arguing self-righteously because somebody in the house is infringing on their God-given right to drink until they pass out and sleep with someone else's boyfriend. Or we see talking heads on news shows proposing the way to stop school shootings is to arm teachers with assault weapons, and then someone calls in and agrees, or maybe somebody just drives too slowly in front of us, or takes too long at the ATM or the post office, or some teenager ignores us because she's too busy playing a slice-the-fruit-in-half game on her phone, and the result is a daily undercurrent of too many stupid people in our country. And who's to blame? Schools. Teachers. The government employees clearly too lazy to teach these fuckups how to avoid turning our once-beautiful country into a sewer."

"What does that have to do with Sanders Bolgim?"

"The abstract concepts don't mean anything. Mediocre test scores. Shady financial setups. Those facts don't register. Until people see something tangible that shows charter schools suck more than public schools do, there's not going to be the groundswell of outrage Professor Benson wanted. Bolgim knew that."

"So?"

"So whatever he was working on has to be simpler than what we've been thinking. It's not going to be some grand statistical analysis or sophisticated research. It's got to be something the average idiot who'd rather be leering at Miley Cyrus doing her culturally exploitative twerkfest can see and be like, damn, those charter schools are a disaster. That's why they torched his whole room and tried to get rid of everything. He had to be on the verge of something painfully obvious, something easy for the public to digest. It's got to be right in front of our eyes and—speaking of dumb-asses—we're missing it."

"Except they didn't get rid of everything," Karen said. "Because Sanders had a hideaway where he did most of his work and they didn't know that. And maybe Gumby *does* know. Or at least knows where the hideaway is."

My nose hurt again. "Gumby doesn't know shit."

"You don't know that, Jim. Just because you can critique Miley Cyrus in a somewhat enlightened way doesn't mean you know everything."

"I know he sold heroin to one of your athletes," I said, "then made her screw him to get more. The guy's a lowlife."

"You need to keep your ego out of this. He jumped on your head, so what? Gumpert and Standish are laughing because they weren't there. And believe me, they're overjoyed they weren't. Everyone in this department knows you're the only one who could have handled him in the dark the way you did. Stop feeling sorry for yourself. Jarrold's a way bigger menace than Gumby will ever be. If there's any chance this d-bag can help us, we take it."

I threw the football in the air and caught it. Hated the

idea of giving into Gumby. A punk like that needed his face pounded into the ground.

I looked at Karen.

Her eyes told me my anger was contributing to the country's general dumb-assedness.

Jarrold polished his rifle.

He wanted to masturbate, take the edge off. He thought of the midget's daughter. Not the one he'd flirted with. The one who'd torn into the clowns on the radio. What a firecracker!

He felt himself growing as hard as the rifle-barrel. Harder!

He polished the gun until it gleamed. Went to the window and looked through the telescopic sight, saw two women walking a large dog down the hill a hundred yards away. He imagined shooting one, then the other, then the dog, pop-pop-pop, three skulls blown to oblivion.

It wasn't fair he couldn't go to the gourmet deli and order an artistically crafted sandwich and wait to see if the midget's daughter would show up. He needed a next step, something, anything to end this claustrophobic boredom.

He never should have killed Monique.

He hadn't thought it through enough and, now, everything had fallen apart.

Things Fall Apart. He remembered that from college, the one literature class he took. Something about a dude with anger issues wrestling people and then killing his adopted son with a machete. Why didn't he just slice up the other wrestler? Pick on someone his own size? That's where Jarrold went wrong too. He should never have picked on Monique. Her size was perfect, how she curled against him. How she rode on top of him.

Her breath panting.

Skin warm.

Hair heavy with sweat.

It was all the detectives' fault, the midget and his pretty partner. Why hadn't they just believed the nerd's death was an accident? Who cares about a loser like that?

They killed Monique.

He pulled his shirt over his head. He'd been eating all those horrible and delicious fries, those onion rings and greasy sandwiches. No more. It hadn't affected his weight, but still. Look at him. He was lean, his stomach muscles as hard as his rifle. He felt himself swelling with anger. He peeled off his shorts and boxers. Every part of him was hard. His thighs! His calves!

Naked, he bent to the floor and pressed his hands against the carpet. Twenty-five push-ups. Fifty. His arms like cords. Down, up. Down, up. A hundred push-ups, his eyes swimming in the rust-colored murk of the carpet. The cheap apartment. A hundred and thirty-three.

At a hundred-and-forty, his arms trembled. He kept going. Down, up. Down, up. Sweat plastered his face, dripped onto the rug. Down, up. At a hundred and fifty-two, his body spasmed and his arms turned into squid arms. Down, up. He got to one-fifty-nine, then collapsed, his face falling to the carpet, splashing in the puddle of his sweat.

He licked the salt off his lips. Intoxicating! As if he were his own martini! Rolled onto his back, extended his legs in front of him. Held them six inches off the ground. For thirty seconds. A minute. Three minutes. His smooth ass bare and sleek against the wet rug. The pole between his legs a pulsing throb. He scissored his thighs, spreading them out and in, out and in, keeping his heels off the ground. The ceiling above him opened into a galaxy. Monique's bright eyes the new stars.

A plan formed in the stucco. A trial by fire. The rifle. Pop-pop. Two dead cops.

He'd be sorry to end the life of the hottie, but, face it, she was ten years past her prime.

At seven minutes, his sweat was a river flowing off his stomach.

At nine minutes, he could feel his teeth falling apart.

At eleven minutes, his legs hurt so much he put his fingers into his mouth and bit them. Drew blood. Let it swish on his tongue.

He held his legs in the air for fourteen minutes before he let them fall, his body shaking in agony.

The cops would die for this pain.

Both of them.

Pop-pop.

CHAPTER TWENTY-THREE

WITH ME TRAILING BEHIND, Karen walked Gumby toward campus. We couldn't do anything about the rape charge. Gumpert and Standish were searching his room at the Pleasure Palace of Sensory Delights as we walked. If we could prove he was dealing heroin, then we wouldn't be doing anything about that either. Best we could do was drop the charges for resisting arrest and assaulting an officer. "Take it or leave it," Karen had said in her sweetest good-cop voice, her eyes tombstones.

Gumby took it.

"He says he'd see Bolgim in the tunnels," Karen said, her mouth turned down in a line as thin as sewing thread.

"Tunnels, huh? I told you he was full of shit. Let's go, Gumby. Back to the station."

"You don't know about the tunnels?" Gumby asked. "You're cops in the city for what, fifty years, and you don't know about the tunnels?"

"There aren't any tunnels, Gumby. It's an urban legend. Stop wasting our time."

He made a whistling sound and grabbed his crotch. The bridge of my nose throbbed.

"Maybe there really are tunnels," Karen said. "It's come up a bunch of times in this case. Think about it, Jim. We're never really on campus. The Public Safety Officers handle that. Maybe there's a network underneath all the buildings like people say."

"I don't know about a network," Gumby said, smiling, and I noticed how straight his teeth were, "but there's tunnels, trust me."

"That's where you saw Bolgim?" I highly doubted it.

"Bro, he's got a whole lair down there."

"Show us," Karen said.

We went up the crumbling steps to Angell Hall and through the front door. I always thought the lobby was less impressive than it should have been. All the marketing brochures featured photos of the Union with its tall tower and the steps where JFK kicked off the Peace Corps, and Angell, the stately dame across the street with thick Doric columns. Except, inside of Angell, it was shabby floors and uninviting foyer. Staircases and elevators that failed to inspire. Maybe it was because the English Department was housed there instead of something impressive like medicine or business, but it seemed like for decades, nobody had put any resources into the building.

They did have the worst of the crumbling stairs leading to the entrance blocked off with fake crime-scene tape and a series of rusting chains, which perhaps indicated they'd repair them soon, but the tape, now drooping, had been up for months and the fixing-the-steps part of the plan had yet to materialize.

Inside, Gumby led us down a stairwell to the floor that connected Angell to Mason-Haven, where the Fishbowl was. I was still skeptical, wondering whether his plan was to try some kind of breakdancing spin move and run. I figured I'd stay focused on his hips. Where they moved, the rest of him would follow.

We walked down a side hallway with dim lighting and walls the color of cold coffee. We seemed to be in a warren of offices for adjunct professors, each door boasting a laminated schedule for office hours and a plastic bin for students to hand in late papers. Past a set of dingy-looking bathrooms and an inoperable drinking fountain, we stopped at a door marked *Maintenance.*

"When you first turn the knob, it feels like it's locked," Gumby said, "but if you push downward on the handle, the door opens."

He seemed to be proud he knew something we didn't, as if we were supposed to be impressed and therefore forget he'd raped a teenager.

"How'd you find out?" Karen asked.

Gumby didn't answer, opened the door and switched on the lights to what looked like a break room. There were a dozen rusted lockers in a shade of pale green, two mop buckets with dried-out mops, a portable radio circa 1979 with a hanger for an antenna, and a beat-up refrigerator. Four chairs that looked like they'd been borrowed from a high school classroom sat around a table with a scratched Formica surface. Two pinkish folders sat on the table, and an advertisement for a Columbus Day sale at Art Van Furniture. Gumby walked toward another door at the far end of the room.

"How do you know about this place?" Karen asked again.

"I plead the fifth," Gumby said, then pulled open the door and flipped on another light, a faint one that couldn't have been more than a forty-watt bulb.

A metal stairwell, the kind that looked like it was composed of sewer grates, led down into a large storage room that seemed to have no rear wall, ending in darkness.

I hated those kinds of stairs, narrow and steep where hobbling down them felt like somebody whacking my knees with a sledgehammer dipped in fire. I inhaled through my busted nose when we reached the bottom, which made it sting like it'd gotten smashed all over again, but at least it transferred most of the pain away from my legs.

Several metal shelves surrounding the bottom of the stairs were stacked with boxes covered in mold. "Old files," Gumby said, but didn't elaborate. Against one of the room's visible walls, numerous rolls of musty-looking carpet sat in a pile. The whole place smelled like rotting fruit.

Gumby beckoned toward the darker shadows where hundreds of bins and crates were stuffed with discarded lamps, chairs, bolts of fabric and items of clothing. "You can find anything down here," he said. "That's where I got the sword and the buffalo mask."

"You put something from down here on your *face?*" Karen asked.

"I am not afraid!" Gumby shouted, as if he wanted to hear an echo and I began to get the feeling that whenever he ventured underground, things got a little crazy for him.

"I will put my face anywhere!" he shouted even more loudly. "My face goes here! My face goes there! My face goes everywhere!"

"Bindwell, calm down," Karen said. "Stop warning whoever you're warning to go hide. We're not trying to bust anyone. We want to see where you saw Bolgim."

"They just want to see the nerd's lair!" he shouted. "No fear!"

We heard a clattering of footsteps in the distance.

"Listen, Gumby," I said. "You are not an entertaining person. You coerced a fifteen-year-old girl into having sex with you for drugs. Show us what you're going to show us and resist the urge to pretend your life's a movie."

He looked at me with contempt, as if I were too old to appreciate his comic genius. I felt like tearing his arm out of its socket.

"Damn, Officer," he said. "Talk about uptight. You need some ass or something? Doesn't your partner hook you up?"

Before I could stop her, Karen punched him in the ear. A right jab that flicked through the dim light like a darting bat. He crumpled and grabbed his head with both hands.

"Why'd you do that?" he whined.

"We've been up all night and we are not patient," she said. "Where'd you see Bolgim?"

"Over here, all right?"

He walked toward the darkness and Karen pulled a flashlight from the pocket of her sweatshirt, because she was smart enough to bring a flashlight in the pocket of her sweatshirt. Shelves of file boxes surrounded us. Probably fifty years of exams read by graduate assistants that students hadn't cared to retrieve. Above us, pipes and cobwebs painted a mosaic across the ceiling. Something electric coursed through my shoulders.

I don't know if I'd classify where we were as a tunnel. It was basically an unused sub-basement. But Sanders had spent a lot of time down here, I could feel it.

Past the rows of shelves, a far wall finally became visible. Dozens of McDonald's bags lay against it, as did several mismatched couch cushions and a couple of soiled mattresses. Cigarette butts, the remnants of blunt tips, beer cans and liquor bottles were strewn about like toys in a messy kid's bedroom. Needles and rubber tubing on the floor too. If I poked around under the cushions, I was betting I'd find more used condoms. Kevin Trouma's poem had been right. Nodding out underground. It was a treasure trove of potential evidence that could lock Gumby up for decades. Which he seemed to suddenly realize, and tried to rush us past it.

"The nerd used to hang out over there." He pointed toward another row of shelves about fifty feet away. "I'll show you."

"Hold on, Bindwell," Karen said as she handed me the flashlight. "I'm about to take numerous pictures with my phone. Evidence technicians will come by later to process this area. If the scene looks any different when they get here than it does in these photos, you will be charged with evidence tampering and obstructing justice. Do you understand what I'm telling you?"

"I thought you weren't trying to bust anybody right now," Gumby said.

"The thing is, Gumby, you're already busted."

"I'm just trying to help. Why y'all have to be such lying motherfuckers?"

I shined the flashlight directly in his yellowish eyes. He flinched. "Does Detective Evans need to remind you ear cartilage is full of nerve endings?" I asked. "Which makes a strike there exceedingly painful. At the same time, the ear is unlikely to shatter in the manner of, say, the nose, causing it to spurt blood. Nor does it purple easily with bruises. Thus, it should be clear even to someone blessed with gnat-like intelligence such as yourself, that the ear is the ideal place to administer repeated blows."

Gumby scrunched his face so he looked like a disappointed goblin—a goblin toddler who got nothing under his tree for goblin Christmas.

"I'm just trying to help y'all," he said again.

"Then do it," Karen said, pocketing her phone. "I've got what I need."

With a defeated slouch and a rub of his ear, Gumby led us toward the series of shelves he'd pointed to a moment ago. These seemed to house old textbooks. We wound through several rows, Gumby hesitating two or three times at various intersections before deciding which direction to go. It appeared he might be trying to create a confusing route for us in case he decided to bolt. I glued my eyes to his hips.

At last, we turned a corner and encountered a cobbled-together version of the bridge on the Starship Enterprise. Six different laptop computers sat on three standard-sized doors held up by a quartet of file cabinets and arranged in a rectangular C-shape around a wheeled office chair. The computers were locked inside what looked like a large and sturdy hamster cage—probably so the junkies wouldn't steal them—and plugged into a surge protector attached to an orange extension cord that led off into the darkness. There must have been a working outlet for the cord somewhere because the computers, though shut and secured, all had glowing power lights.

"Nerd headquarters," Gumby said.

"How often did you see him?" Karen said.

"You kidding? He was *always* here. Sometimes he would give us money, or buy us food. A lot of nights, he slept in that chair."

My body was glowing too. Sanders Bolgim had been here for uncountable hours, hunched over this makeshift conglomeration of desks and computers, sharing this squalid space with kids shooting up, staring at these screens for months, maybe years. Why? What attracted enough attention to get him killed?

Karen tried to open the first file cabinet on the left, but it was locked. Fortunately, in her Batman-like utility-sweatshirt, she carried a tool modeled after the one car thieves use, which resembled a screwdriver with its head sharpened to a fine point. It took her less than thirty seconds to jiggle the lock and spring open the cabinet. The files inside were neatly organized in alphabetical order. Karen pulled out one labeled *Hashem Abu Tabech.*

He turned out to be sixteen-year-old kid taking algebra, biology, tenth grade English, and a course called Theory of String Music at a school called Supernova Cyber Academy. Inside the file were hard copies of papers and tests that must have been print-outs of what he'd submitted online.

"There's a record of all the grades this Hashem person got," Karen said. "Looks like a solid B student."

"Why would Bolgim have this kid's records? How'd he get them?"

"Holy shit," Karen said. "Look at this."

She handed me a sheet entitled Personal Information. Only one of Hashem's parents was listed. His father. Sanders Abu Tebech.

Karen grabbed another file. Lawrence Albert. He, too, was sixteen. He, too, was taking online classes and being raised by a single father. Sanders Albert.

The next file was Meghan Allen. She only had a mother. Sandy Allen.

"Wait," Karen said, "these kids all submitted the same papers. The same exact assignments. Maybe that's who Sanders was selling essays—oh my God."

She flipped through a couple more files, then gestured at the remaining cabinets. "Jim, don't you see? Our nerd fathered, and/or mothered, hundreds of children. Maybe a thousand."

"I still don't ge—"

Then I did.

It was a little different this time. No couch on the porch. No crazy idiot football fans to make the whole city a giant frat party. He couldn't just pour alcohol all over everything and light a match.

That was all right though. Jarrold didn't need to burn the whole house down. He just needed to make enough smoke to rouse the authorities. He could even start a kitchen fire, make it seem like somebody left the oven on after baking cookies. If the whole house went up in flames, awesome, but not necessary.

Dumb-ass police officer in his faggot city.

Thought he was so safe he had a home phone with a listed number.

Address too.

At least his withered fuck buddy was smart enough to be unlisted.

Didn't matter though, she'd show up with him anyway. Partners to the end.

Pop-pop.

Then he'd get out of here. For good. Get on his motorcycle and high-tail it out of town. He could go anywhere. He had nothing to tie him down. No Monique, no nothing.

Maybe he'd visit the burial site for Kimmie. Hold a mock funeral there for Monique. Yeah, that's what he needed. Closure.

He'd come back here though, in a year or so, comfort the twins in their grief.

Tell them he knew what it's like to lose a father. That'd pretty much wrap it up.

One at a time though, first the little bitch who wouldn't have dinner with him. Then the feisty one. Plow-plow. Pop-pop.

God, he loved Walmart.

He could get everything here.

Canola oil to spray all over the kitchen. Matches.

Ping-pong balls to play with.

Bullets.

It was so obvious. I don't know how we missed it.

Gumby and his hophead crew nodded out down here in the dark, scarfing fast food and sticking needles in each other, surrounded by old papers stuffed in boxes students had no use for.

The shiny campus above sparkled pretty for the public.

Beneath it, the underbelly, the truth.

The fraud.

Hundreds of students who didn't exist, digital Frankensteins created by the mad genius Dr. Von Bolgim.

I looked at Karen, her eyes on fire in the gloom.

"It's like ACORN," she said. "Remember those Young Republicans who posed as prostitutes? Who made everyone believe the whole organization was a sham?"

I nodded.

"It's simple, like you were saying," she said. "But it's also brilliant. Bolgim wasn't selling papers to other kids, he was writing them for students he was pretending to be. Hundreds of fictional students at charters, cyber-charters actually. That's the question people really have, right? How can a cyber-school prove it's the actual kid signed up for the class who's doing the work? Or not cheating?"

"They can't, that's the whole point," I said. "Sanders was trying to show online schools are as flawed as the skeptics say they are. He was going to bring the entire mock-institution down in the most obvious way possible, by getting credit at, maybe even graduating from, multiple programs at the same time."

"Look at all these files," Karen said. "The kid was a mole, sitting at his Captain Kirk bridge, plotting how to take over the cyber-school universe. Can you imagine trying to be hundreds of fake students at the same time? How many assignments he must have submitted? No wonder he had no social life."

I could feel Gumby itching to run. Waiting for a chance to slip away and lose himself in the maze of bookshelves.

There's push and there's pull.

And there's the space in between.

With Karen in a catcher's crouch peering at the next file, I turned my back on Bindwell and made as if I were about to try and jimmy the cage lock and boot up one of the laptops, saying as if I were super excited to find out, "I wonder if we can see what's on the computers."

Something in the air changed. When Gumby spun his kick at the back of my head, I reached out and caught his heel before he could connect, then—just like in the basement of his pleasure palace—pulled his ankle high over my shoulder. With a quick twist, and using all the energy he'd mustered for the kick, I smashed his face into the floor and for good measure landed on top of him with the point of my elbow crashing into the same ear Karen had punched.

He yelped, then groaned, and I jammed my knee into his back and cuffed his hands behind him with plastic ties.

"That wasn't exactly a fair fight," Karen said.

"It almost never is."

As we emerged from Angell Hall, Gumby walked gingerly in front of me with my right hand exerting downward pressure against his cuffed wrists. A blast of sunlight pierced my eyes and my still-tender nose throbbed.

The exhilaration of finding Bolgim's research and the comedown off the adrenaline spike of smashing Gumby's face into the ground left my body feeling like I'd just finished battling Mikey for two hours.

And lost.

I wanted a bed.

We deposited Gumby in the cruiser we'd radioed to meet us and briefed Gumpert and Standish on the massive storage room so they could go gather evidence. My eyes hurt, my knees howled, and my head was ringing. I was unprepared for Chief Taylor to be so disappointed.

"That's all you found?" she said, her face flat with boredom as she sat behind her desk. "The kid was writing fake papers?"

"What do you mean?" I said, wanting to shout, actually, but my throat throbbed too. The air down there had been rank. I hated to think about how much mold we'd breathed in. "That's *everything*. The whole cyber-charter system is a joke. Sanders proved it."

"Yes, but where's the evidence of a *crime?* What ties him to your killer, or to anyone else for that matter? You've got fake papers, but no actual paper trail to anyone responsible for his death. The only criminal act here is the fraud Bolgim committed, these stolen social security numbers he used to register for classes."

Karen and I looked at each other. I could see the cogs turning in her head, then, they stopped. Her mouth turned down in defeat. She was exhausted too, probably also longing for her bed. Preferably with Roland in it.

"It's true, Jim. We've got nothing. We know why they killed him, and we can guess at how, even at who lit the match, but the people behind that, we're nowhere."

"Wait a second, what about Dot Warren, the money he gave Governor Lambright?"

"Speculation," the chief said. "You can't prove any connection to Bolgim."

"Unless we catch Jarrold."

"Any idea where he is?"

It was so perfect. All the ingredients were already there. Eggs, flour, butter, sugar, milk. Even chocolate chips.

The cookies weren't half-bad either. He'd done a pretty good job making them, if he did say so himself.

He'd wolfed down about a dozen in what, maybe, two minutes?

Slow down, Jarrold told himself. No need to rush.

Enjoy these moments in the midget's kitchen. In his house he was too stupid to buy an alarm for. Spray the canola all over everything. Burn up the fool's mail, his unpaid bills. It's not like he'd ever be able to pay them anyway.

No rush. No rush. Take your time. No need to light the match yet.

He walked into the living room. At least the cop had a decent TV. Probably watched football like the rest of the idiots in his city.

In his bedroom, his laundry was all folded, everything neat. Faggot.

Probably where he does the dried-up bitch too. Gross.

Another room had twin beds. Twin beds for the twins!

Jarrold looked in the dresser. Closed his eyes, felt around with his fingers. Yes! Underwear. Satin. Navy blue. So soft. Oh, it even smelled like her! Which her? Which twin? Did it matter?

No!

Jarrold laid down on the bottom bunkbed. Which twin bed? Which twin? Did it matter?

No!

He rubbed the underwear across his face. Licked the chocolate off his teeth. Fingered the ping pong balls in his pocket. Two of them! Felt himself growing. So beautiful. So huge. Inhaled the blue satin.

Crushed the ping pong balls in his hand.
Oh! Oh!

"Look," Chief Taylor said. "At least you got the drug dealer, what's his name, Chewing Gum? We can still go at him, see if he'll give up anybody else. That's important work. We can do some good, try to slow this opioid thing before it grows any bigger. But the conspiracy you're talking about? No, there's nowhere to go."

I felt a stench growing around me in the office. I'd heard rumors Governor Lambright was planning to pursue right-to-work legislation, but he was negotiating behind the scenes to exempt police and fire unions. Then he could go directly after teachers and nurses without the cops joining a massive protest on the capitol steps.

I hadn't believed it until now. That kind of cynicism seemed beyond even his well-coifed and calculating braincase, but something in Aricka's tone suggested it might be true.

"This is about money, isn't it, Chief? If there's some kind of deal you don't want our investigation to get in the middle of, why don't you just say it? Why don't you just admit you're afraid to have this aggressively regressive legislature turn its sights on us? Because if you want my opinion, if we don't stand with these other unions—with teachers and nurses and everyone else—we're cooked anyway. Rich people can afford their own private security, don't forget."

I thought she might fly out of her chair and pistol-whip me with the butt of her revolver, but she just stared, her eyes narrow and unflinching.

"What I'm worried about, Detective Harrow, as I've now told you several times, is you've already got IAD looking at you for whomping a frat guy. We've still got unsolved break-ins. Maybe these hopheads are the ones doing it. That's our job, to protect and serve this community right here, not to chase phantoms in Lansing."

"Oh, come on, Aricka, that's garbage and you know it. You've been holding us back on this case from day one. What are they offering you? The top job in Detroit with a big new budget? It's a lie, Chief, whatever they're promising. It's a lie."

She stood up, towering over me a good half-foot. Leaned across her desk, her chin quivering with anger.

"You are overworked and not thinking clearly, Detective Harrow, so I'm going to ignore what you just said. Do not believe I will do so again. What I need you to do—right now—is to go home and sleep. For several hours. Come in tomorrow and re-interview Chewing Gum. Find his supplier. See if he knows anything about the home invasions. Please be clear about what I'm saying because I will not repeat it. Forget about charter schools. Forget about Jarrold. He's long gone."

Karen put her hand on my wrist. I wanted to fight more, but I could feel energy seeping from my legs, my shoulders.

"Aricka's right, Jim," she said, her voice like water. "It's over."

That was bullshit, and all three of us knew it, but, damn it, what could we do? Money talks. Always.

Karen turned to leave the office. I followed her.

"Oh, and, Detective?" Aricka said.

"Yeah?"

"If you ever again question my integrity, wrestling hero or whatever you think you were, I will beat you within an inch of your life."

Outside, the sun felt like a blowtorch on my forehead. Karen and I lumbered toward our respective personal vehicles.

"You really think he's gone?" I asked, as she went to sit in her car.

"I do," Karen said. "We were wrong. He's not obsessed with you, or the girls. He's smarter than that. He didn't cover his tracks at the professor's because he knew if we ever found what Bolgim was working on, it wouldn't connect to him. Same with Jenna. He was taunting us, sure, but, ultimately, he doesn't want to get caught. Chief's right. He's not coming back here."

I'm not sure I believed that. My bones didn't, but what did they know? With my remaining stores of adrenaline drained, they were like the rest of me, worn to the nub. Even if I were fresh-faced and wide awake—and I was the exact opposite of that—what choice did we have?

I was pretty sure Chief Taylor wasn't really going to fight me, but I can't say I wanted to push her any more either. If I were her, I'd have fired me five times already, or at least smacked me with her clipboard and bloodied my nose again. Given Gumpert and Standish another reason to crack up in the squad room. And if Karen was ready to cash in, if she wanted to head home and cuddle with the coroner, what did I have left?

Nothing.

I mean, big picture, what did we really find?

A social recluse wrote fake papers and tried to scam some bullshit corporations. We couldn't prove they killed him, couldn't prove Jarrold was anything more than a psycho who aced a professor who slept with his girlfriend, couldn't prove anyone else was involved at all.

We knew it though. Lambright with his yellow marshmallow hair, wanting to dump garbage in the Great Lakes, also wanted to sell children to the lowest bidder. But we couldn't get him, never would. People with money like that never paid any real price. Or if they got sentenced, like Dot Warren did, they served what, less than two years? Just enough time to sit back and let their stock portfolios bloom.

I was done.

At the edge of the parking lot, propped up against a mailbox, was a homeless guy I'd seen before. One of those perpetual drunks whose muscles have the consistency of a wet napkin. He looked even worse than usual though, his head wrapped in a bloodstained bandage, one of his pant legs ripped. He looked, in fact, almost exactly the way I felt. Maybe Aricka actually could have beaten me within an inch of my life. I was probably only two inches from there already.

The homeless guy gestured, as if he wanted me to walk over so he could tell me something. No way I was going to do that. How I was feeling, it would take me ten hours to slog over there. Didn't matter anyway because I turned away when, across the street, the fire station doors lurched open and two trucks barreled out, sirens blaring. They felt like pneumatic drills in my head. The trucks headed south across Fourth, toward Packard.

I got a bad feeling.

Karen did too. She looked up at the sky, then slammed her car door and stood next to me. My bad feeling got worse.

When my phone buzzed, I already knew what Chief Myers would tell me.

My house was on fire.

For some reason, the thing I was most concerned about was a notebook of Hall of Fame baseball cards I kept in my bedroom closet. There was an Al Kaline rookie card in there from 1954. A couple mint Hank Aarons too.

If we drove fast, we could get there in under four minutes.

"Come on," I said to Karen. "Let's go!"

"Hold on, Jim, don't you want to think about *why* someone set fire to your house?" She grabbed my arm.

"Actually, no. Someone set fire to my house. Shouldn't I check that out?"

"Think it was the frat kids?"

"They made their point last time and we haven't messed with them since. Why would they want to escalate?"

"Who then?"

It hit me. Like a Kaline line-drive to the shins.

"Jarrold."

"That's what I'm thinking too. Why, though?"

"Because he's psychotic. Because we were right. He hates us."

"True, but everything he's done, he's had a plan for, and been a step ahead of us. Before we react blindly, and maybe get out noses bloodied again, maybe we should try to figure out what he's up to."

I closed my eyes. Inside my head was its own crime scene, a warzone. Bombs were going off, sending shrapnel all over campus.

"I know what Jarrold's doing," I said. "The fire is a huge flaming billboard. We're the targets now. If he burns my house, he knows we'll show up to investigate."

"So, Jarrold's going to, what? Stake out a line of sight and shoot at us when we arrive?"

"He did the drive-by in Detroit. He can shoot."

"So maybe—"

"Karen, my *house is on fire*. No maybes. Let's go."

CHAPTER TWENTY-FOUR

FLAMES UNDULATED on the roof of the midget cop's house, swaying like a stripper, like the funeral pyre for a sexy Viking. A tribute for a woman who knew how to move.

For Monique.

He owed her. The cops would pay.

Jarrold watched through his rifle scope.

After showering and shaving in Harrow's bathroom, he felt great. His arms were coiled springs, his fingers the fangs of a deadly snake. Soon enough, the midget and his used-to-be-hot sidekick would show up and he would make sidewalk art out of their skulls. He could feel the excitement rippling his thighs, his groin aflame with pride. He was finally initiating instead of waiting. If he spotted any of his so-called handlers at the scene, he'd shoot them too. He'd found the best spot. A kid's treehouse in the yard across the street and two houses down. Maybe seventy-five yards from the fire.

Then he'd eschewed it, too obvious.

Instead, slightly farther from the burning house and still

an easy shot, he'd found a hedge surrounding one of those large electrical phone link boxes so ubiquitous no one paid attention to them. The hedge was thick, and in this strangely warm autumn, still leafy. Inserted within it, Jarrold was invisible to anybody who wasn't paying attention. And nobody was paying attention because nobody looked at those boxes, maybe because nobody wanted to be reminded of the aesthetic cost of broadband internet, and besides, there was a real live burning house to document and post on Snapchat.

Jarrold could actually prop his gun on a thick branch as if it were a tripod while he was still hidden, almost as if he were standing in a duck blind. It was unfair, really. With the silencer around the barrel of his rifle, he could've shot a dozen firemen and nobody would have known why they'd dropped. The biggest challenge was to avoid chuckling at how easy it was going to be. He'd sight the detectives and he'd pull the trigger twice.

Pop-pop.

Before anyone realized what happened, they'd be dead and he'd be calmly walking toward campus. Maybe he'd find a place he could stash the gun for an hour so he could get something to eat. He hadn't spent much time in this neighborhood by South University so nobody would recognize him. Maybe he could find a place that sold chicken shawarma. That's what he was looking forward to, chowing down on some chicken shawarma.

The only problem was, the detectives hadn't shown up yet. The fire had been burning for nearly forty minutes. What else could the stupid dwarf be doing on a sunny day like this? Was it possible Jarrold's case *wasn't* top priority? What if the two cops weren't even thinking about him and were screwing somewhere? The thought of the elderly, rotting, rutting babe opening up her legs for the midget made Jarrold furious. He'd shoot her first just because she made him think that. Shoot her whole face off.

His stomach roiled. "Calm down," he whispered to his beautiful ears. This was not good. His phenomenal fingers were trembling. He couldn't tolerate shooting and missing.

He looked to see if any cars were coming. None were. He let go of his gun and backed out of the hedge. Patted his rock-hard abdominal muscles. No one was watching. Everybody was still looking at the fire. He bent down and touched his toes. Stood back up slowly and swiveled his neck to the left, then to the right.

That's when he saw the used-up hottie.

Gun drawn.

Approaching the treehouse.

Why was she doing that?

She was looking for him.

Had to be.

Which meant she'd already figured out the fire was a ruse. Which meant he'd have to shoot her right now, out here in the open, because he'd have no shot in that direction from the hedge. Could he do it without being discovered? Maybe not. But if she started to climb the ladder up the crotch of the tree, she'd be totally exposed. He'd never have a better chance.

He reached through the hedge for the rifle. The nervousness was gone. Now that it was finally happening, he felt calm again. Sixty yards to the target. What a joke. Too bad, bitch, shouldn't have split your legs for the midget. He shouldered the rifle. Sighted her through the scope.

Narrowed his brain to one sleek arrow. Shut down all his other senses and only saw her.

The beautiful cop about to die.

She reached for the ladder, stepped one foot onto the bottom rung.

She looked so elegant, her leg bent, all the muscle in it flexed. He focused on her face. Just as the point of the X centered on the crow's feet below her left eye, the thought intruded to wonder why she was alone.

Smashing into Jarrold felt like tackling a telephone pole.

The guy was all muscle and my shoulder exploded when I hit him, the kind of pain that sends a hurricane of nails directly through your skull. It happened quick, but I saw it slow. He'd twitched when he heard me, but moved too late to avoid my driving into the lower part of his cement block back. I heard the *pffft!* of his shot through the silencer and the ladder Karen was on burst into woodchips. She dropped her pistol and fell hard.

We crashed to the ground, my knee crunching against the sidewalk and I howled like a dying animal as Jarrold slid away from me, his gun skittering into the grass.

He sprang to his feet and I staggered to mine. No way I could put any weight on my right leg, my ligaments torn all over again. Jarrold stared at me with hatred so visceral it seemed like it had teeth.

"You bastard," he growled. "You killed her."

I knew he meant Monique Harvey.

"Wrong, Asshole. You're the one who threw her off the roof."

"Your leg's fucked," he said. "You can't stand against me."

There's push and there's pull.

"What did her eyes look like when she went over the railing?" I said. "She knew, didn't she? She knew what a piece of shit you are."

I thought he'd lunge at me, but he didn't. He spun and kicked my right knee with his pickaxe foot and I heard another crack and it felt like the lower part of my leg tore straight from my body. I could not see because of the flash of hot white sky that swallowed my face, but I did not fall because my weight was already on my other leg and, stunned, he tried to punch my torso and break my ribs and I did not think but my arms did what wrestlers do and I grabbed his wrist in a Russian two-on-one and used his momentum to yank him forward, and then I was behind him, my hands locked around his waist.

Because I could only stand on one leg, I couldn't lift him and slam him to the sidewalk the way I'd slammed Gumby. But I could still hold him. And holding people is what I always did best. I don't mean with affection. In all my years of wrestling, if I managed to fully clasp my hands together around someone's waist, never once did anyone break my grip. Not one single time. Not Mikey. Not Eric Lockhard. Ironic, right? I was the one who locked hardest.

Jarrold slammed his elbow into my sternum.

I did not let go.

He stomped as hard as he could with his boot heel on my left foot.

Another white sky swallowed my face and my teeth rattled as if I'd been in a head-on collision.

I did not let go.

He butted my face with the back of his head and ground it into my broken nose and my eyes watered and blurred but I did not let go and I could barely see Karen behind him scrambling to her feet and collapsing again and reaching for her gun, but I knew she wouldn't shoot from that far away. She couldn't be sure if she would hit Jarrold or me and she'd never take that chance. It didn't matter. All I had to do was hold on. Karen was on her radio and in ten seconds the officers across the street would be on us and Jarrold would be in custody.

All I had to do was hold on.

He pushed as hard as he could against my hands and stomped on my foot again and slammed his head back into my nose and I was nothing but searing, blinding pain and iron-vise grip. Pain and grip. I saw Sanders Bolgim's body shoot through the dark. I saw Monique Harvey's head smash against the sidewalk. I saw Eric Lockhard's hand raised in victory and Lisa running toward me with her field hockey stick.

Lisa?

"Dad!" she cried.

"Lisa! Get the hell out of—"

Jarrold broke my grip.

He broke my grip.

I could not hold him and he shot forward like a snapped rubber band and landed in the grass.

He broke my grip.

Before I could react, he'd grabbed his rifle, bounded to his feet, and pointed it at my chest.

There was nothing I could do.

But Lisa could.

In field hockey, it's called a reverse-sweep.

It is not for beginners.

The player lowers her center of gravity then extends her arms outward, almost like a wrestler shooting for a single-leg takedown, except she's twisting her torso to her backhand side, instead of lunging straight forward like a wrestler would. She holds the stick in both hands with what's known as a "frying pan" grip. The head of the stick stays on the ground throughout the backswing and follow-through and functions, essentially, as a giant, lead-pipe fish hook. If the ball is struck correctly, it stays hard and low and can travel a hundred yards down the field.

When Lisa hooked Jarrold's ankle, he toppled like that huge statue of Saddam Hussein after we liberated Baghdad. The tip of his rifle clanged to the ground.

But he didn't stay down.

Spinning his rifle around, he bounced up and aimed at Lisa.

I roared, lunged off my battered left foot and crashed into him from behind.

I don't know what happened next.

Later, Karen said it looked exactly like my match in the NCAA finals. Somehow, I elevated Jarrold off the ground and swished him around like a rag doll, bouncing his head several times against the sidewalk. Then—she thought he was already unconscious—I lifted him higher, held him above my own head the way I'd held Lockhard, paused momentarily, my eyes to the sky, my back straight. Then arched my chest, pulled my left shoulder down, thrust my right shoulder up, and slammed his skull directly into the pavement.

I remembered the crack of his head on concrete. It sounded like Hank Greenberg crushing one out of the old Tigers Stadium, hitting it so far it landed across the river, past Windsor, somewhere in rural Canada.

His body crumpled, spasmed once, and stopped moving.

I didn't even bother checking his pulse.

Instead, with Karen crawling toward us through the grass and a ring of officers and firemen running to surround us, I sank to the sidewalk. My ruined knee wept in agony. My chest ached from the repeated battering of Jarrold's elbow and my shoulder was, if I were lucky, only dislocated. My stomped-on foot was definitely broken. I reached to check my nose and couldn't feel my fingers or my face.

The last thing I saw before I passed out was my beautiful daughter examining the head of her field hockey stick, checking to see if it was scratched.

CHAPTER TWENTY-FIVE

NOVEMBER: ANN ARBOR, MICHIGAN

THREE WEEKS LATER, I sat in the stands at River Rat Stadium to watch Pioneer play Huron for the state championship. The weather had finally turned and the sky was the undercarriage of a bus.

Olivia, dressed in purple boots, loose purple sweatpants that said Pioneer Field Hockey in white letters, a bulky purple coat and a purple tuque, looked like grape-flavored Kool-Aid. She wandered over to me during halftime, the game scoreless. Waves of students washed up to her and made jokes. She shooed them away, careful not to step on my crutches, and leaned in close to me.

"Kevin Trouma turned in something great yesterday," she said. "It's called, *When the Cops Come to Your House and Your Mother's Drunk.*"

"Seriously?"

"It's heartbreaking, Detective, but funny too. Have time to hear a few lines?"

I have to say I had not expected Olivia to read verse crafted by my newest wrestler in the middle of a field hockey game. Or to call me Detective in what sounded like an endearing way.

"Sure," I said.

Olivia read, not with the same urgent tone she'd used for the heroin piece, but with a voice that suggested a more mournful-sounding music. The words filled my ear and journeyed in a wire around my head, encasing my face and neck, like an astronaut's helmet made of language.

Some days my mother's not like this.
The police didn't see her digging weeds
from our garden, didn't see her growing
peppers and tomatoes and spending whole
afternoons making sauce. The police didn't
see her in the laundry room folding socks,
or when she used to take me to the Hands-on
Museum. We'd stand at opposite ends of two
giant metal discs across the room and what
you whispered into one disc, you could hear
like a prayer through the other. The sound
would travel and make me warm. "I love you,
good boy," she'd say, "I love you, my perfect
good boy

"Keep reading," I said. "Read to the end."

She wasn't always this stumble-around person
She used to only drink cough medicine when she
was sick. Used to clean her own kitchen
and know before I told her if my day at school
was bad. Some days, still, she's not like this. Some
days she dresses up to see her lawyer. Her eyes
are alive then. Her hair is brushed. Some days

she asks me about my homework. One of the cops told me to join wrestling. He doesn't know I've been wrestling for years. He doesn't know all I do, every day, is wrestle.

My eyes were blurry.

"Right?" Olivia said. "Right?"

All I could do was nod.

Jarrold's secrets had died with him. The official cause of death was blunt force trauma to his skull. Roland described the injuries that killed him as almost precisely the same as the ones suffered by Monique Harvey falling from the parking structure ninety feet high. So, other than Professor Benson, we couldn't prove he'd killed anybody. Not Sanders Bolgim, not Monique, not even Jesse and Blair from Detroit because ballistics didn't match his rifle to the bullets that had torn them apart. We had no idea how many people he'd actually murdered and no evidence to implicate anybody who'd hired him. We could speculate all we wanted, but—as Chief Taylor emphatically reminded Karen and me—guesses weren't enough to bust anyone.

Fortunately, speculation is exactly what click-bait newspapers are for, especially one that measures its success on frequency of front-page web-clicks and how many nut-jobs post comments. To be fair, once I pointed Bill Burkett in a fruitful direction, he dove headfirst into the story. We'd photocopied Sanders' files and True North made digital copies of everything on the laptops. Burkett told me it took him ten days to sift through it all. The story came out in a four-page double-spread in Treetown's Sunday print edition—the one people in the city actually read—and the comments online numbered in the thousands. Dozens of newspapers around the country glommed onto the story and ran follow-ups, including *The New York Times, The Washington Post, The Los Angeles Times* and *The San Francisco Chronicle.*

It turned out Bolgim had created 714 fake student identities and enrolled them in four of the biggest cyber-charters in Michigan, all of which were for-profit enterprises that also operated in other states. He used the same essays over and over in class after class, often for numerous students in the same class. In many of the courses he was enrolled in, a single non-unionized and underpaid teacher was responsible for 150-plus students on one class roster and was clearly incapable of actually reading, let alone keeping track of, everybody's work. Sanders pushed the envelope as far as he could, plagiarizing like mad. In chat-room discussions that were supposed to be holding him accountable for class participation, he'd post passages he'd cribbed directly from speeches made by Martin Luther King Jr., John F. Kennedy, Bob Dylan, Kanye West, and Rodney Dangerfield.

When it came to academic dishonesty, you had to admire the guy's creativity.

For a solid week, Twitter, the talk radio airwaves and cable shoutfests vibrated with little more than the scandal that became known as Chartergate. So many photographers and cameramen flocked to the underground nerd lair, Karen and I wondered if Angelina Jolie hadn't been spotted down there hooking up with brother J-Dubs.

The Education Fairness Act went down in flames, rejected by a mammoth 82% of the voting public.

In a press conference held on the quickly repaired front steps of Angell Hall, Governor Lambright vowed to veto any future bill seeking to eliminate the cap on charters and to sign one written by Ann Arbor's State Senator Rhonda

Janssen requiring all charter schools in Michigan be run on a not-for-profit basis and that rigorous studies be undertaken to determine what kind of education kids were actually getting.

"Fine," Olivia said. "Let's see him restore full funding to public schools before he takes any bows. And if he thinks every teacher in this state won't be spending every free moment over the next two years trying to get him voted out of office, he needs to stop plastering his hairdo and to sit up straight and pay attention."

While we couldn't directly tie the governor to any murders, Burkett dug out all his connections to campaign contributors associated with for-profit charters, especially the notorious Dot Warren. Then he did the same for state representatives and senators, and elected members of the board of regents at Michigan, Michigan State, Western, Eastern, Central, Northern and Wayne State. Threw in elected judges across the state too.

My Hall of Fame baseball cards did not survive the fire. Nor did my collection of Pioneer Wrestling t-shirts.

On the other hand, while my left foot was broken, it would not, according to both Danny Root and the expert surgeon he got me an appointment with, require surgery. My right knee, of course, would. Two surgeries. I'd be on crutches until at least the beginning of summer. Mikey would have to find someone else to tussle with for the next seven months, but I could still train my upper body and I promised I'd be ready to whip him when I came back.

Karen's ankle was also broken, but healing nicely. She'd be off her crutches in three more weeks. Tammy Binder, out of rehab but not yet back in uniform, stood next to Karen on the sideline in a Pioneer sweatshirt and blue jeans, holding her clipboard.

Molly sat about thirty feet away, also wearing a Pioneer

sweatshirt and a pair of tight jeans. She'd visited me in the hospital several times, but was now ignoring me, sitting with other mothers focused intently on their daughters.

Lisa was playing with the same stick she'd used to topple Jarrold. The sidewalk had definitely scraped some paint off the head, even splintered part of the wood, but she refused to replace it until after the season was over. "It's my lucky stick," she'd told me, her eyes as serious as I'd ever seen them.

She'd heard about the fire when the news had come over the hand-held radio belonging to the officer stationed in the living room at Molly's house. Immediately, she'd wanted to come over and see what was going on, but the officer told her no chance, she wasn't going anywhere. Enraged, she'd fled upstairs to her room and slammed the door, then snuck out her window and jumped off the porch roof. She couldn't say why she'd felt compelled to bring her stick, she just knew she *had* to.

It took her fifteen minutes to run across town and the first thing she saw when she rounded the corner to my street was my tackling Jarrold and Karen falling off the shattered ladder. She had no recollection of what happened after that. "I didn't think," she said, "my body just did what it needed to do."

I had no doubt she was telling the truth.

With less than thirty seconds to go in regulation, the game was still scoreless, as it almost always was when Pioneer and Huron played. It didn't look like Lisa was thinking now either. Her body was a poem, her stick and the ball a natural extension of her arm as she juked past one defender, then another, her legs pumping more efficiently than any pistons Detroit had ever designed. She spun toward one more defender—an All-State kid who'd earned a full ride to Northwestern—and deftly looped the ball over the girl's outstretched stick.

As the goalie pulled from the crease to cut off the angle of her shot, she push-passed the ball across the field and found Jenna mid-stride.

Ready to strike.

ACKNOWLEDGMENTS

Special thanks to Alex Kourvo and everyone at Fifth Avenue Press, without whom this book would be just a pile of unread(able) pages.

Thanks as well to Aimée Le, Gahl Liberzon, Rachel Kerby, Bruce DeSilva, Adam Mansbach and D.E. Johnson for early reads and advice.

Much of the insight about charter schools comes from work done by Steve Norton of Michigan Parents for Schools and David Arsen, Professor in the School of Education at Michigan State University.

Thanks to Coaches Bill Petoskey and Jane Nixon of Pioneer wrestling and field hockey for letting me into some practices and to the Pioneer English department for general tolerance of my foolishness.

And especially, thanks to Karen, Sam and Julius for constant encouragement and forbearance, and for not waking up in the middle of the night when I'm typing.

All mistakes are mine and I'm sorry I made them.

ABOUT THE AUTHOR

Jeff Kass is the author of the award-winning short story collection *Knuckleheads* and the poetry collection *My Beautiful Hook-Nosed Beauty Queen Strutwave.* His stories, poems, and essays have appeared in multiple literary journals. He founded the Literary Arts Program at The Neutral Zone, Ann Arbor's Teen Center, and is currently an English teacher at Pioneer High School and the Assignment Editor at *Current* Magazine.